THE TALK SHOW

THE TALK SHOW

a novel

JOE WENKE

Stamford, Connecticut

2014

Trans Über LLC
www.transuber.com

To reach the author or Trans Über email: joewenke@joewenke.org

ISBN: 978-0-9859002-9-8

Digital editions available.

Manufactured in the United States of America
First Edition

FRONT COVER PHOTO AND ART DIRECTION: GISELE XTRAVAGANZA
BOOK AND COVER DESIGN: JOHN LOTTE FOR BLUE MOUNTAIN MARKETING

www.joewenke.org

Follow Joe Wenke on Twitter @joewenke.

For Mark, Ryan, Olivia and Gisele

1

THE CALL FROM ABRAHAM LINCOLN JONES came just after 2:00 a.m. On one side of the flat screen TV, Chris Matthews was interviewing Bill Maher. On the other side, one of the contestants on *Worst Cooks in America* was barbecuing hot dogs and hamburgers. Winthrop hit mute and answered the phone in one ring.

"Yeah."

"Fuckin' A!"

"Yeah?"

"Fuckin' A!"

"Fuckin' A?"

"Yeah. F-U-C-K-K-K . . . N . . . A! Goddamn it!"

Silence.

"Hey, don't get cute with me, Winthrop. You know who the fuck this is."

Winthrop waited one more beat. Then he said, "Fuckin' A . . . LJ?"

Jones exploded. The Big Bang laugh. Just like on the show. "BING-O!" he screamed, "BING-O! THAT'S MY NAME-O . . . MOTHERFUCK-O!"

The two men had never previously spoken, but Jones was right. Winthrop had known. Instantly. Yes, it was ALJ, the one and only. The man who had dominated talk TV for the last two decades. The anti-Oprah. Raw. Rough. Never predictable, he was the ultimate survivor—hated by some but always loved—crazily, unaccountably, loved nonetheless by millions of people who, if they thought about it for a single second, would realize to their utter confusion that they agreed with Abraham Lincoln Jones on practically nothing.

"What are you drinking, Mr. Abraham Lincoln?"

"The usual. Blue on the rocks. You?"

"Patron. A few Dos Equis."

"Maybe then it's time for some real conversation. Some crazy E! Hollywood true revelations."

"Celebrity upskirt?"

"You got it, Jack. You ready?"

Winthrop was feeling weird. The call had come as a total surprise, but right away it had begun to feel as if it were somehow inevitable or, more precisely, something that he had already experienced, maybe in dream. "I'm always ready, Abe, ready for anything," he replied. "I guess it's the gift of paranoia."

"I know you're ready, Jack. That's why I called. I know you. I know your ass inside out. I bet you know my fuckin' ass too."

"How's that, Abe?"

"I know you—the best way to know a complicated white guy like you—through your work."

"What work?"

"What work?" Jones laughed. "What work? Don't be coy, Jack. Why, all your fuckin' work. Not just the fancy Pulitzer shit—the homeless pieces and the power and race book—but all your goddamn work. All the *New York Times* Gray Lady columns you write in twenty minutes and the *New York* magazine articles, too."

Winthrop fell momentarily silent. The bit about the work was flattery, but then again not. There was too much urgency in Jones's voice.

"You still there, Jack?" Jones asked, sounding for the first time just a touch subdued.

"Totally, Abe. Totally."

"Then let me get right to the fuckin' point. Winthrop—I am the Man. I been the fuckin' man forever. I know it, and you know it, too. But I must admit. Ever since I started, I've had not one, not two, but three motherfuckin' problems. That's three—as in one, two, three strikes you're out."

"Number one?"

"Number one, Jack? Number one, when all is said and motherfuckin' done, I'm just a goddamn good for nothing motherfuckin' TV slug."

"Abe, you're a huge star. Come on. Aren't you being just a little bit hard on yourself?"

"You watch much TV, Winthrop?"

Winthrop glanced at the muted screen. Chris Matthews had moved on to his Sideshow. Rush Limbaugh was referring to a transgender woman as an "Add-a-dick-to-me babe." Meanwhile, the *Worst Cooks* contestant had somehow set himself on fire.

"What's problem number two?"

"Problem number two? Problem number two?" Jones paused, out of breath. Winthrop could hear him gasping into the phone like an emphysema patient. Finally he spoke. "Maybe you haven't noticed, Winthrop, but I got a serious dermatological condition."

"You mean you're black."

"BING-O! And you know what that means, Jack, my man, right up to this motherfuckin' day when Barack Hussein Obama—black man, white man, Christian man with an infamous Muslim name is the one and only President of these United States of America."

"But that is truly remarkable, Abe. I mean undeniably, despite the birthers and all of the tea party madness."

"Yes, remarkable," replied Abraham Lincoln Jones, his voice dropping to a whisper.

This was very interesting, thought Winthrop. No one had more presence, more energy, more panache, more sheer, outrageous chutzpah than Abraham Lincoln Jones. And yet here he was with a phone call out of nowhere, revealing vulnerabilities one would never have guessed at. Once again, Winthrop could hear Jones breathing heavily into the phone.

"So here's my point, Jack."

"Your point . . ."

"My point, man, the goddamn reason I called you in the middle of the fuckin' night . . . my point . . . is change."

"Change you can believe in?"

"No joke, Jack. Change you can believe in. Ain't nothing harder, nothing more motherfuckin' rare than change, cos, you and I both know almost nobody ever fuckin' changes, not one little bit. Not even if it's easy, which it never is. Not even if we're talking about having a goddamn Henny Youngman Corn Beef on Rye once in a blue fuckin' moon at the old Stage Deli instead of your usual Jerry Lewis Muscular Dystrophy Telethon That Ain't Never Found And Ain't Never Gonna Find No Cure Turkey Club—go crispy with the bacon and fries!"

Winthrop just laughed. Couldn't help it. Jones laughed, too. He was on a roll.

"Take it easy on Jerry, Abe. He got canned after all those years. The Stage is gone too—but you were saying—"

"Right, Jack. I was saying. It's all about change. But let's put the issue another way. In fact, let's put it your way, Jack. If you're a fuckin' nobody, you don't fuckin' change."

"Did I say that?"

"Fuck you, Jack, you know you remember every goddamn precious word you ever wrote. So you tell me. What's the sure as shit sign of a motherfuckin' nobody? Come on, now, Jack. I'm practically quoting you."

"He thinks he's somebody."

"Exactly. A fuckin' nobody thinks he's fuckin' somebody. But in reality he's no fuckin' body. And as a fuckin' nobody, he's got nothing to change from or to."

"But you're about to tell me we're different, right?"

"Ain't you the cynical motherfucker? But give me a goddamn chance here, Jack. Let me talk. I'm fuckin' serious. We are different because as you yourself have written, we know we're nobody."

"And that what sets us free—lets us throw the switch, change, jump the tracks and go off the cliff like Butch Cassidy and the Sundance Kid—God rest Paul Newman's blessed soul."

"You got it, Jack. And I'm calling you well past the goddamn motherfuckin' witching hour to tell you your fuckin' switch man is here."

Winthrop paused for a second. "OK, Abe," he said, after taking a deep breath. "What's the proposition?"

"It's this: We all know TV is a swamp."

"Well, you did say you're a slug."

"Fuck you, Winthrop. My mama always said, no lie, you are judged by the company you keep. So who exactly is the mother-fuckin' company I keep on TV? Let's go up the list, starting at the bottom, with that fuckin' witch, Nancy Grace, scoring ratings points off of dead babies and missing girls, suckin' the lifeblood out of every tragedy that has legs. Then, even though he's gone, I still got to call out that fuckin' nut job, buzz-headed bigot, Glenn Beck—"

"He's gone, sort of. You can still watch him on the Web."

"That man actually made a big show out of baiting the one and only Muslim Congressman, ever, Keith Ellison from Minnesota, challenging him to prove he's not working with the enemies of the United States."

"He also said that Barack Obama hates white people. Actually that he has 'a deep-seated hatred for white people.'"

"And for a while he was everywhere—CNN Headline News, Larry King Live, Good Morning America, Fox News."

"Maybe he and guys like him are the new Establishment."

"You mean the swamp establishment—and it's not just the right wing nuts on Fox News like Bill O'Reilly and Shawn Hannity minus

Alan Albatross Colmes and all their Great American guests like Ann Coulter and Laura Ingraham."

"And the architect, Karl Rove . . ."

"Right. And that motherfuckin', toe-sucking, Clinton-bashing bastard, Dick Morris. Even Fox fired his ass. But it's not really an ideological thing with me. It's fuckin' personal. Personal to me, that is. This was my motherfuckin' medium. This was my way to communicate."

"I understand, Abe."

"I could go on all night, Winthrop, but I won't. It's a goddamn pandemic of pathology masquerading as news and entertainment. From that fat fuck, Lou Dobbs, demagoguing the illegal immigrants to those ex-wife-scary bitches on *The View*, with their cat fights every fuckin' morning. No way around it. TV is a polluted, reptile-infested swamp. And the other media—they're toxic too or they're dying. Like that dinosaur you work for, the great Gray Lady! And the magazines nobody reads—*The Nation*, *The Atlantic*, *Harpers*, *The New Yorker*. Then we have Talk Radio—a fuckin' cesspool filled with megalomaniacs and clowns—Rush Limbaugh, Mark Levin, Savage Nation. And the Internet, the goddamn Internet, totally full of shit with the YouTube racists and the Twitter haters and the hard core bloggers spreading horseshit that wouldn't pass a fuckin' smell test at the *National Enquirer*. Nobody gives a fuck. It's all just one big mind scam after another. It's all the same old shit."

"So what are you proposing, Abe?"

"What I'm proposing is something new, Winthrop. Something real. What I'm talking about is communicating with America—straight to the heart, straight to the soul, true and direct—that's the thing."

"How are you going to do that?"

"We're going to do that, Jack—through the grand and glorious vehicle of the Abraham Lincoln Jones Eeeh-mancipation Tour!"

Yes, thought Winthrop, the ALJ energy was definitely back. "OK, Abe," he said, "You say you're going to communicate with America, whatever that means. You do that and you're not a TV slug any-more. What about the other problem you mentioned? What about race? What about the serious dermatological condition? And, oh yeah, in case you've forgotten, what about strike three?"

There was silence again. Jones had gotten so excited, he had actually almost forgotten for a moment about number 3—the real serial killer of political careers—maybe even more deadly than dermatology. The silence continued. Finally, Winthrop broke in.

"Abe, you're gay."

"Right, Jack. I'm gay. Strike three. But here's the thing. That's what's changed. That's the new fuckin' news. Strike three might just be my motherfuckin' ace in the hole."

"Ace in the butthole."

Jones exploded again. This time it was scary—a combination of nuclear fusion and some weird strain of super mutated pertussis nasties. Winthrop found himself staring at his watch. After about a minute, he broke in."

"Abe. Hey, Abe. What up, man! Don't go all esophageal on me! We need you, man."

After a further pause, Jones finally spoke—stage whisper style and raspy—"No, Winthrop, No tobacco, man. Combination of Johnnie Walker and weed. And you set me off."

"Well, I think I know what you're going to say, Abe, and I agree—to a point."

"Tell me, Jack."

"Nothing's changing faster than attitudes toward gay people and marriage equality. It's amazing. Unprecedented."

"It is."

"My own position's a little different. You see, I'm pro gay and anti-marriage, so I've come out in favor of same-sex divorce."

Jones exploded again. "Hey, ain't you the fuckin' comedian, Winthrop! But that's why I like you, man. You don't give a fuck about anything. You just tell the fuckin' truth."

"That's it, Abe. Tell the truth no matter what. And the truth is, yes, attitudes are changing, but look out for the backlash."

"I feel you."

"It's coming. Like the birthers came after Obama, and it will be ugly. That's why people like Peggy Noonan say, 'Go slow.' They want to put a speed limit on change. They're afraid that freedom and equality might just be too upsetting to all of the Red State bigots."

"Which brings us back, Winthrop, to why the fuck I called you."

"The Emancipation Tour."

Several beats of silence went by. "Exactly, Winthrop, exactly. My Emancipation Tour." ALJ was quiet again. Practically whispering. "What I'm imagining, Winthrop, what I wanna do—it's beyond fuckin' talk shows, beyond all the politics, beyond all the mother-fuckin' bullshit and lies. What I'm gonna do, I'm just gonna go out there, tell the fuckin' truth and see what happens."

Winthrop was impressed—and not a little bit scared. He knew where the truth led. For a few precious moments, he just stopped and listened to ALJ breathe into the phone."

"You there, Winthrop?"

"I'm here, Abe. I'm with you, and I get the picture. Except for one minor point—why are you coming to me?"

"Jack, that's simple. I need your help."

The unabashed honesty of the statement amazed Winthrop. "So you're not looking for a handler," he said.

"Jack, you know nobody can handle me. This is on a much higher level. I'm offering you a fuckin' partnership, man. A partnership in a unique enterprise."

"But where's this going to lead, Abe?"

"Who knows, Jack? This is about fuckin' change. Getting out of the motherfuckin' box for real. Breaking away. Changing the system. I'm talking about some serious motherfuckin' shit."

"Sounds like town halls, Abe. Been there. Done that."

"Fuck you, Winthrop, don't try to categorize or minimize me. I say, bull fuckin' shit. I say my Emancipation Tour is a motherfuckin' heavy metal, foot to the pedal, totally digitized, mesmerizing, interactive referendum on freedom and equality in America. No speed limit but the speed of light."

"OK, Abe. OK. I said I was with you, but let me just ask you one more question. I hate to sound crassly commercial, but what's the money?"

"Double what the *Times* gives you for your phony-ass columns. And you can keep on mailing in those little gems three times a week. I don't fuckin' care."

"Double's a million."

"You got it."

"When do I start?"

"You already did, Jack. I got our illustrious senator, Jason Bradley, coming on the show this Friday along with his wife, Sheena."

"The super model—or whatever."

"Yeah, whatever. Do us a favor and stage a little show biz finale. Then get on over to the Grand Army Plaza off Central Park."

"That's right. You're the Grand Marshal of the African-American Day Parade."

"Just be there at the plaza on Friday. We'll be talking."

"Sounds good, Abe.

"So we got a fuckin' deal, partner?"

"Yes, Abe, you got a deal."

*　*　*　*

AFTER POKING AROUND A BIT, Winthrop found it—shoved between *Shemale Fuck Hotel* and a rare DVD of Bishop Fulton J. Sheen's *Life Is Worth Living*. *ALJ: Interviewing the Interviewers*. The shows were from maybe ten years ago. David Frost, Dick Cavett, Geraldo, Oprah, Barbara Walters.

Winthrop switched his system from V1 to DVD. Chris Matthews

and *Worst Chefs* disappeared and up came ALJ. The studio band cranked out "Soul Man," the ALJ Show theme, as Jones's announcer, Barry Bream, intoned the intro. "Hello, America," he announced, "from our home at beautiful Radio City, the Showplace of the Nation, it's *The ALJ Show* starring Abraham Lincoln Jones. Today, it's another special "Interviewing the Interviewers" show with ALJ's very special guest, David Frost. And now here's the Emancipated Mouth, the Black Hole that swallowed America, the Master Blaster of Talk Show Disaster—Abraham Lincoln Jones!"

As always, the curtains opened to reveal a huge elliptical plexiglass desk. It stood on a slowly turning platform that was rotating the seated Abraham Lincoln Jones into full frontal view at center stage. Ceremoniously, Jones rose and bowed to crescendos of applause. Dressed entirely in white, he was wearing a tux with outrageous tails like the Beatles in *Magical Mystery Tour*.

Fast forward. David Frost was still talking about his Nixon interview. Winthrop was reminded of a recent survey of high school students. Fifty percent had never heard of Richard Nixon. Twenty percent didn't know what came first, Vietnam or the Civil War. Ten percent couldn't find the United States on a map of the world.

FF again. Jones discussing some truly ancient history—*That Was the Week That Was*. A minor television moment: Frost transfigured from talk show has-been to neglected social satirist, a British Mort Sahl (also neglected), clutching his clipboard à la William Buckley.

Again, fast forward.

Abraham Lincoln Jones coasting along the gossip route. A segment on the once celebrated romance with Diahann Carroll (who again?) sparks an ALJ segue into interracial sex in America. Spotlight now on Jones. It's the sixties, and he's a teenage prodigy and interracial trailblazer, spinning STAX and Motown, running around town with hot blonde hippies in micro minis and pretty boys in bell-bottom jeans.

Then the slashed tires. A rock through his bedroom window. The bomb scare at the station. A melodramatic cross burning on his front lawn. The famous attack in the WSOL parking lot. A concussion, broken nose and three cracked ribs.

The outcome: national coverage and his legendary meeting with Dr. Martin Luther King Jr. just a few months before he was assassinated.

With unfortunate timing, Frost tries to put in his recollective two cents about Dr. King. The ALJ train rolls on as Jones proclaims King the greatest human being in American history. Loud, insistent applause, swelling to a standing O. King, greater than Thomas Jefferson, who owned slaves. Greater than honest Abe Lincoln, the PR man who supposedly freed them so he could ship them to Liberia. Greater, too, than FDR, who put Japanese-Americans in relocation camps.

*   *   *   *

AS HE WATCHED THE DAVID FROST PIECE, Winthrop had little difficulty imagining how *The ALJ Show* with New York Democratic Senator Jason Bradley would go. It was really very simple. It would be vintage Jones. Vintage Bradley. The show would cook up a tasty stew of social and political issues: abortion, race, gay rights, Tea Party craziness, terrorism, and more—a surprise appearance by Sheena Bradley, wearing, no doubt, a stunning Gisele Boulud design.

Having had enough of Frost, Winthrop popped in the Oprah tape. Fat, skinny or in between, Winthrop wondered. Well, it was the fat Oprah this time, and Jones was asking her about her listing in *Forbes* as the top-grossing entertainer in America, earning more than two hundred million dollars. Two hundred million! That put her ahead of Steven Spielberg. Ahead of Bill Cosby. Ahead of everybody. Jones himself was number eight on the list, sandwiched between Madonna and Spunk Gism, a heavy metal band.

On his MacBook Pro, Winthrop was cueing Sheena's surprise

appearance: Bradley plugs Sheena's Sotheby's auction of art and designer fashions to benefit the Bradleys' anti-bullying foundation. Then enter Sheena, stage right. Everyone nonplussed, including ALJ. Everyone marveling at the synchronicity of the superstar. Life at the top—more magical than childhood, more dramatic than fiction. Camera pans from Sheena to Jason. Then close-up. Let TV tell the story. America's new king and queen enjoy a warm royal embrace. And Camelot is born again.

⁂   ⁂   ⁂   ⁂

THAT WAS HOW WINTHROP IMAGINED IT ALL, wrote it all. Now it was actually about to happen. On stage at Radio City, the show was winding to a close. Bradley was riding hard a favorite hobbyhorse—one that had won him some important points with conservative voters, namely, U.S. vulnerability to terrorism. "You know, Abe," Bradley said. "I want to say something now about America that might sound controversial, and I don't want to be misunderstood."

"Jay," Jones said, "We have the most intelligent, informed, politically aware audience in television. Not like the cockfightin' WWE crowds on Jerry Springer. My people are different. They know. They're real. They're hip. They're into the future. In fact, they are the future. Ain't that right? (Applause.) Ain't that right? (More applause.) Yeah, that's right. So say what you want, Jay. My audience knows."

"Well, Abe, I'm about to be critical," Bradley said, "So allow me to preface my criticism by saying that I love this country dearly. I am serving as the senior Democratic senator from the State of New York for one reason only—my deep love for this nation and its people. With all our problems, we are still blessed. We are still without a doubt the greatest country in the world . . . the greatest country in the history of the world."

The audience applauded, stood. Some people shouted. Some whistled. Some stamped their feet. Winthrop had surveyed the crowd hours earlier as it was filing into Radio City. Notwithstanding Jones's characterization of their transcendent hipness, the audience in fact included a healthy percentage of vacationing hicks, ALJ lovers from the heartland of America. During Bream's warm-up, Winthrop had heard such names as Biloxi, Boise, Tuscaloosa, Fort Wayne, Enid, Sioux City and Waco. From across America they had come to New York City for Broadway, Bloomingdale's, the Empire State Building, Trump Tower, the Statue of Liberty—and *The ALJ Show*.

The reason was simple. They loved America. They loved television. They loved Abraham Lincoln Jones. And, at this moment, they also loved Jason Bradley. He was young, attractive, charismatic. And he enjoyed a powerful X-factor. He was married to Sheena Bradley, the world's reigning supermodel.

Yes, over the years there had been any number of Hollywood power couples, from the ancient wars of Elizabeth Taylor and Richard Burton right up to the magical coupling of Brad Pitt and Angelina Jolie. There had also been a number of interesting mixed couplings, that is, the mixing of supermodels with Hollywood or rock royalty—Christie Brinkley and Billy Joel, Iman and David Bowie, Cindy Crawford and Richard Gere. But Jason and Sheena had something extra. Combine rock and roll or Hollywood with high fashion and you got what? Glamour and sex, with a capital S-E-X, which was fine. But blend political ambition and charisma with the world's all-time perfect ten, the ultimate naughty and nice nymphet, and you had discovered the $E=MC^2$ of power and sex. Put that equation to work; feed it intravenously into the lifeblood of every single man and woman yearning for a piece of that indefinable something, that tantalizing promise of some personal relationship to the great American Dream, and you had the potential to make the country your lapdog.

That equation was operating now in the applause, which seemed to want to go on forever. When it finally did subside, Senator Bradley continued as earnestly as before. "My fellow citizens, I believe in the Constitution of the United States of America, and I strongly support our president. Every morning that I wake up, my first thought is of how truly privileged I am to be an American. But because I cherish that privilege, I feel obligated to criticize our president and my colleagues in Congress when they fail in their responsibility to do everything they can to protect Americans. And I do this on a bi-partisan basis. The sad fact is that now more than a decade since 9/11, we remain extremely vulnerable to terrorist attacks.

As the applause swelled once again, Winthrop began tuning out Bradley's voice. He knew all the rest anyway since he had lived it and written it—not real writing, actually just talking points to orchestrate the ending of the show. They were Bradley's ideas, but Winthrop could see where he had a point: America and Americans, to this very day, despite all the history and despite all the rhetoric, still, in many ways sitting-duck terrorist targets. It was admittedly a long history, seriously straining the attention span of the ALJ audience: Over the last thirty or more years, planes hijacked, marines blown up, Americans held hostage. The Reagan PR diversions of Granada, Libya, Nicaragua and Panama. The smart-bomb farce of Desert Storm. The paralysis over Bosnia. The Olympics bombing. The USS Cole embarrassment. The multifarious implications of the first World Trade Center and Oklahoma City truck bombings. The specter of enemies without and within. Then, of course, 9/11, followed by the monumental disasters and distractions of the Wars in Iraq and Afghanistan, not to mention the seemingly endless travesty of Osama Bin Laden evading justice until he was finally nailed by President Obama and a band of courageous Navy Seals.

In recent years when it came to the so-called War on Terrorism, Bradley had been viewed increasingly by his fellow progressives as a neocon-pandering crank, a not-so-closeted proponent of Big

Brother video and cyber-based surveillance tactics. After all, where were the attacks? Then came the Boston Marathon bombing, and Bradley's critics went silent.

All of this Winthrop knew—Bradley's fears about the country's vulnerable borders, harbors and power grid as well as the controversial need for surveillance everywhere. They were Winthrop's fears as well. It was all so disturbing. It was all so depressing, but it was reality. A new normal that would never feel normal and would never go away. For the moment he turned down the sound on Bradley as he often did at home watching Benny Hinn or Pat Robertson or classic video of his all-time favorite televangelist, the crybaby, Jimmy Swaggart, and just looked on. It really was amazing. Jones and Bradley were both so full of energy, so full of telegenic beauty, so full of light—they virtually vibrated—giving off the particles and waves of celebrity. They seemed almost destined to be famous, destined to be idolized. After all, could John Lennon or Paul McCartney have not been famous? Could Madonna have been anything but a star? What about Tiger Woods or Beyonce? Jones and Bradley inhabited that same privileged plane of existence. They were different from the rest of us. They were beyond us all. We could applaud their brilliance but never hope to touch them.

"Jack Winthrop?" a woman's voice whispered into Winthrop's ear.

"Yes."

"Danielle Jackson."

"It's a pleasure to meet you, Danielle."

"Abe and I are absolutely delighted that you've joined us."

Apparently they were very delighted, indeed. For Danielle had somehow succeeded in generating an inordinate amount of publicity over the announcement that he had joined the ALJ team. More, it seemed to Winthrop, than he had ever garnered on his own, even for his two Pulitzers. Danielle's press release had not only gotten plenty of play in the New York media, it was also all over the Web, having been picked up by the *HuffPost*, the *Daily Beast*, *Politico* and a host of other sites as well as being liked and retweeted thousands of times.

"I'm absolutely delighted, too, Danielle," Winthrop replied.

"Jack, I know the ending for today's show is just a knock-off for you," Danielle continued, "But I suggested to Abe that it would be fun to have you do it."

"Once again, it's a pleasure.

"We're excited about the parade, too. I know there'll be a wonderful turnout. The African-American community fully supports it. Abe is a great draw, and having Jason on board doesn't hurt either."

As Danielle and Winthrop spoke, the African-American Day Parade was about to begin, awaiting only the arrival of Jones and Bradley. The theme of the parade was "Black and White Together." In the front line at 42nd and Fifth, the site of the New York Public Library, marching ahead of neighborhood groups from across the city were the Reverend Al Sharpton, Alicia Williams of the Urban League, Isaiah Woods of the NAACP, Representative Arthur Lyle from Harlem, Mayor Martinez, Governor Ross and Cardinal Boyle.

The Clintons, perhaps somewhat surprisingly, were no-shows. Bill was on an Asian tour, picking up a fast million or two from some speechmaking in Tokyo, Hiroshima, Hong Kong and Seoul. Meanwhile, Hillary was in Washington. Rumor had it that she was locked behind closed doors with a team of advisers, planning her 2016 run.

As part of today's festivities, there would be some speechmaking at the Grand Army Plaza at 58th and Fifth, with Bradley and Grand Marshal Abraham Lincoln Jones highlighting the program. Then the parade would pick up again and continue marching north toward Harlem and another round of speeches at the site of a showpiece community redevelopment project.

On stage at Radio City, in honor of the parade, Bradley was winding up his critique of race relations in America. "Abe, if there is one thing that history has taught us, it is that the struggle for freedom and equality never ends. Let us never forget . . . the courage of Rosa Parks. Let us never forget the vision and the leadership of Martin Luther King Jr. and let us never forget those who, I fear are now long forgotten—James Byrd Jr. . . . . Amadou Diallo . . . Abner Louima."

"Amen, brother. You have always been with us. One hundred percent. That's why I have always said, that Jason Bradley is the blackest white man I know."

It was then, amid the laughter and applause, that Winthrop saw her for the first time. Live and up close, that is. He had, of course, seen Sheena Bradley many times on television. She was the darling of the talk show circuit. But it was her magazine work that had made her famous. With her natural ash blonde hair, pale blue eyes, and perfect figure, she had become the ultimate American super model. By now, she had appeared on dozens of magazine covers.

Since Jason won reelection to the U.S. Senate, Sheena had chosen her public appearances with the greatest of care so that every one was a special media event. Today, for example, the ALJ Show would be blessed with her presence, but the parade would not.

At the same time, Sheena had stepped up her photo work. In recent months, *Cosmopolitan*, *Vogue* and *Vanity Fair* had all featured Sheena on the cover. What's more, the first week in August, she was the cover story in *People*. *New York* put her on the following week. And this year, she would again grace the cover of the *Sports Illustrated* swimsuit issue.

On the merchandising front Sheena was riding high. Her *Sheena* line of swimsuits and leisure wear, sold exclusively through Macy's, was a cottage industry in itself. There was even a Sheena doll. Last year, it had outsold Barbie 2 to 1. As inspiration for doing today's show, Winthrop had gone out and bought one. Back at Winthrop's apartment, a naked, plastic Sheena was hanging upside down from the nozzle of the shower.

On stage, Bradley was talking about the Sotheby's auction. Just then Sheena breezed by Winthrop and Danielle. "Way to go, Jacko," she said and made her entrance. The laughter died on the spot as the audience sucked in its breath. For a moment there was the silence of revelation. Then came the roar. Unrestrained. Animal. This was it. This was Life. The audience knew it. And, for once, they were there while it was happening.

Sheena glided across the stage bathed in light. The camera panned to Jason, capturing take upon take. Behind his plexiglass desk, ALJ stood transfixed in admiration, unable, it seemed, to breathe. Now, the embrace. Sheena and Jason were together, framed by the camera.

The audience response was immediate, visceral, rising out of the depths of adulation in a British invasion shriek. Winthrop held his breath. The audience had become an adoring mob. There were just seconds left in the show. Winthrop felt a pressure against his left hand. Danielle was squeezing it hard. "Sheena," she said. "She's beautiful."

The camera moved in closer on Sheena and Jason. Ten seconds of airtime remained. Sheena and Jason smiled, waved. Five seconds. "We love you, America," said Sheena, and the credits rolled.

2

Exiting Radio City, Winthrop turned east on 50th and walked the long block from Sixth to Fifth Avenue. At Rockefeller Plaza the flags of the world hung dead from their poles. As Winthrop turned north on Fifth and headed for the Grand Army Plaza, he could see the park shimmering in the airless August heat like some weird urban mirage.

Fifth Avenue was even more jammed with people than usual. Normally, most would be hurrying as if they had somewhere extremely important to go. Today, many of them stood behind police barriers and stared down toward the 40s, waiting for the first glimpse of the parade. It was strange to see so many blacks in the Fifth Avenue 50s. The cops were out too, lining the streets at intervals, looking corrupt and bored.

At St. Thomas's a crowd had gathered around an armless young man with long, luxurious blond hair. He was painting with his feet in imitation high-Renaissance style. The subject of the sidewalk painting was the Holy Family. A few people placed dollar bills or coins in a Gucci shoebox.

The week before, Winthrop had seen a young, undernourished black woman lounging on the steps of the church. She had pulled the top of her dirty smock down to her waist. Her long thin breasts hung low. The oddly disoriented smile on her face suggested that she had done something very clever indeed. How easy it was to beat the heat! She was one up on all the overdressed sweating fools of the city. Some people, probably tourists, did double takes. Most, like Winthrop, glanced peripherally at the woman and moved on.

Today, however, Winthrop stopped. He had plenty of time to get to the plaza and stake out the scene. Plenty of time, too, to take an undercover break. Two fat, middle-aged white guys wearing bad blue suits huddled together in a little pocket of white people a few yards away from Winthrop. Probable cause, Winthrop thought. He raised his invisible antenna and moved closer while continuing to stare downtown.

"What the hell is this shit? Did they finally decide St. Patrick was a fuckin' nigger? No wonder the snakes left Ireland."

"It's August, Herb. The St. Patrick's Day Parade's in March."

"Didn't you hear, Stan? A couple of years ago they figured out Christ was one of them too."

"So the Baby Jesus is one, too, huh? We're in a lot of trouble then, Herb."

"Yeah, haven't you ever seen those fuckin' crosses with the black Jesus? I figure if Christ is one of them, why not the goddamn saints? This has got to be St. Patrick's Day."

"It's the black parade, Herb. Did you you hear who the Grand Marshal is."

"Grand Marshal. What the fuck is a Grand Marshal?"

"C'mon, Herb. It's the guy who leads the fucking parade. Anyway, it's that talk show guy, Abraham Lincoln Jones."

"That fuckin' loudmouth from TV?

"The same."

"Well, Stan, I have just one word to say to Mr. Jones."

"What's that, Herb?"

"Shutthefuckupyoufuckin'nigger."

Having struck gold, Winthrop crossed the street. A woman with a Southern accent was asking directions to Trump Tower. No one admitted knowing it was only two blocks away. Two small black boys begged her for a dollar. "Please, Miss," one said. "It's for the subway. I needs a dollar to get home."

The woman opened her purse. Immediately, two other little boys—both white—appeared. "Me too," they said. "Please, Miss, just a dollar."

Winthrop moved on. Armani, Abercrombie & Fitch, Prada, Tiffany, Louis Vitton. At the corner of 56th Street, a grizzled old man was doing birdcalls. A column of stacked paper cups sat at his feet. Winthrop looked down. The cups were empty.

At Trump Tower the flow of the crowd pushed Winthrop up against the display window where a female mannequin dressed entirely in black leather was performing geometrically precise gyrations. With his nose pressed against the window, Winthrop stared at the animatronic doll.

"How'd you like to get that babe in bed, pal? She'd make mincemeat out of your pecker," a pirate voice shouted in his ear.

By the time Winthrop could turn his head, whoever it was had gone. Fighting his way through the crowd at the window, Winthrop reached the glitzy, golden entrance of Trump Tower. "Welcome," the sign said, "to the most extraordinary shopping experience in the world, Trump Tower."

At 57th street Winthrop could just barely discern the parade approaching. In the distance music played indistinguishably. For all Winthrop knew, it could be the Rosa Parks High School Band performing a John Philip Sousa-like arrangement of "Respect." On the 11 o'clock news on Channel 2 the previous night, Jeff Goode had done a mildly humorous, life-affirming "Goode News Story" on preparations in various high schools for the African-American Day Parade.

Goode was fast becoming a New York institution. Each year he won an Emmy for his human-interest stories. For the last three years he had been named New York Newsperson of the Year. He had also received special humanitarian awards from the Knights of Columbus, B'nai B'rith and the New York Chamber of Commerce. To Winthrop, Goode projected the hyperbolic good cheer of a pedophiliac priest, whose heartwarming homilies were the highlight of Mass each Sunday.

Goode's feature had focused in part on Charles Benchley, the young white principal of Rosa Parks High School in the South Bronx, who stressed the importance of the participating bands performing popular black music in the African-American Day Parade. The interview was conducted on the high school football field. In the background the Rosa Parks band was playing Stevie Wonder's "Place in the Sun." "As the lead band in the parade, we will be paying a special tribute to black music from the 1960s to today," said Benchley. "That means Motown, soul, R&B and hip hop."

Winthrop wondered if Mr. Benchley would ever consider doing a brassy, high-stepping arrangement of 50 Cent's "In My Hood." Meanwhile, the clip had segued to a shot of Goode, dressed in full band regalia, strutting and playing the cymbals. Goode was shouting over a spirited rendition of "Papa's Got a Brand New Bag." "This is Jeff Goode with Goode News from the South Bronx!"

At 57th, Winthrop crossed to the west side of the street. A noisy, shifting crowd, about 50 percent black, filled the plaza area and spilled into the streets. Both 58th Street and Central Park South were closed to traffic. Winthrop circled left by the Plaza Hotel and crossed over to the park side of the Grand Army Plaza, where General Sherman sat on his horse, congratulating himself on the burning of Atlanta. Despite the absence of the hansom cabs, the smell of horse manure and urine hung in the overheated air.

Looking over the heads of the churning crowd, Winthrop brought his binoculars into focus at relatively close range on the wooden stage that had been erected in front of the Pulitzer Fountain. Eight folding chairs lined the rear of the platform. The front of the stage was festooned with traditional red, white, and blue bunting, and at each corner of the platform a limp American flag hung from a pole. In an attempt to provide an authentic ethnic touch someone had placed various examples of African-American sculpture at strategic points about the stage.

A group of Right-to-Life demonstrators had set up along the police barriers at the Central Park South and Grand Army Plaza street signs. Some held signs showing a dismembered fetus lying at the bottom of a garbage pail. At the top of the sign was the word "SHAME" printed in big red capital letters. The rest of the Right-To-Life placards were word signs bearing such messages as Abortion Is Murder, Death To Abortionists, and Baby Killer Bradley. One sign attacked Cardinal Boyle, apparently for marching with Jones and Bradley, or for that matter with Mayor Martinez or Governor Ross, who were also Pro-Choice. Judas Boyle—Betrayer of God's Children—said the sign in blood red lettering that might have been used to advertise the latest Hollywood scary movie.

Throughout the past several weeks, the cardinal had been under intense pressure from Pro-Life groups to refuse to march in the parade. At the same time, the Urban League, the NAACP and other black organizations had gone on record to say that the parade was essentially nonpolitical and that Cardinal Boyle's absence would be interpreted as a racist affront against all African-Americans. The day before the parade the cardinal's office issued a press release that called upon all political and community leaders to support the right to life while expressing the cardinal's strong support for Personhood bills and amendments across the country. It also spoke of the African-American Day Parade as a wonderful opportunity to promote racial harmony and celebrate black pride. So despite the protests of the Right-to-Lifers, Cardinal Boyle was now non-politically marching up Fifth Avenue with Abraham Lincoln Jones, Senator Bradley, Mayor Martinez, Governor Ross, Al Sharpton, et al. Within minutes he would stand on the wooden platform at the Grand Army Plaza and invoke God's blessing on the day's festivities.

In addition to the Right-to-Life protesters, Winthrop observed other small groups of demonstrators as well. Just a few yards from the Sherman monument, the New York LGBT Coalition was pleading for more funding for HIV vaccine research. A handful of people were waving signs that criticized Martinez for failing to provide suitable housing for the homeless. And in front of the stage, several blacks in traditional Zulu tribal dress held signs that condemned America as a land of racism and hate.

Suddenly, Winthrop's attention was caught by a voice bellowing directly behind him. Without lowering his binoculars, Winthrop shifted his view a little to the right. In New York City, it was an unquestioned tenet of the street that you never looked anyone directly in the eye. Consequently, years of living in the city had enabled Winthrop to develop his peripheral vision to an acuteness matched only by the hexagonal lenses of a house fly. Looking out of the corner of his eye, Winthrop saw a burly black man, perhaps thirty-five years old, wearing camouflaged army fatigues and holding a large rectangular piece of brown cardboard covered with words written illegibly with a blue ballpoint pen. The man was hysterical.

"Wake up, black people!" he shouted. "God is dead. Where is God? Who is God? God is the white man, walking the streets. God is the white man burning and pillaging and raping our women. God is that white man over there, looking at you through a glass, spying on your brain. Picking his next victim. Who he gonna shit on next? Who he gonna use? Who he gonna let live and who gonna die? Whoever that is, black people, you know the color of the corpse. The corpse is always black. Because this is the white man's world, black people. Open your eyes. The white man is everything. God is the white man. He white, black people. He white! He white! He white! And, black people—you are fuckin' black!"

No one, black or white, seemed to pay the least attention to the man. Winthrop, the white God, shuffled outside the range of the rant and concentrated on the approaching parade. The music was certainly getting louder. The Rosa Parks Band was banging out "Sweet Soul Music" as the head of the parade passed Trump Tower and crossed 57th Street. Just ahead of the band were the politicians, the activists, the cardinal, Jason Bradley and the Grand Marshal himself, Abraham Lincoln Jones.

As the head of the parade breezed by, loud applause would erupt from both sides of the street. Not just some festive clapping, but real cheers, punctuated by exuberant cries and whistles. As the parade drew closer to the plaza, Winthrop was struck by the degree to which Jones and Bradley stood out from the rest of the parade leaders. As usual, Jones looked like the Second Coming of Jesus Christ. His pure white suit shone like a vision. While everyone else died of the heat, he stayed cool and dry, moving, it seemed in his own transcendental atmosphere, complete with air conditioning and smog control. Bradley, on the other hand, was marching as the hard-working man of the people, with his jacket swung over his right shoulder, his collar loosened, his tie hanging low and his shirtsleeves rolled. The image was a political cliché, but with Bradley, who was obviously so comfortable at the center of a crowd, it somehow worked.

As the parade drew nearer, the cheers grew louder. The Right-to-Lifers were chanting something, too, but it was impossible to hear them above the din. With his binoculars, Winthrop scanned the floors of the Plaza Hotel, the Sherry-Netherland and Bergdorf Goodman. People were gathered at the windows and looking out. The whole plaza area was packed. Suddenly, Winthrop's thoughts were interrupted by a question. "Hey, man, you security?" The voice belonged to a middle-aged man with black shoulder-length hair streaked with gray. He was wearing a tie-dyed shirt, beltless bell-bottom jeans torn at the knees and brown shit-kicking cowboy boots with pointed toes.

Nearly half a century after the Summer of Love, a hippie. Winthrop was ready to call the Museum of Natural History.

"You know, you security guys are cool," the man continued. "You don't talk. You don't smile. You just look cool. But you know something? I don't like your guy, Bradley. He's too smooth for me. And he's too much of a capitalist. But, you know, I voted for him anyway, man, because I really got into his commercials. He was always using Grateful Dead music for the soundtrack. Showing respect for Jerry. "Truckin'," "Uncle John's Band." It was cool, man. Nobody else would do that."

Winthrop knew there were no such commercials.

"Hey, maybe Bradley will run for president. Did you think that someday we could actually have a Dead Head in the White House?"

"When have we ever had anything else?" Winthrop replied.

The man stared blankly for a moment as if he had somehow lost his place. Then, suddenly, he lit up again. "Hey, who'd you vote for anyway, dude?"

"Abraham Lincoln," responded Winthrop, still looking through his binoculars.

"That's cool," said the man as he faded back into the crowd.

The real security people were positioned at strategic points about the plaza and along the parade route. Winthrop knew several of their faces. He also spotted a number of likely candidates standing close to the stage, including some very intimidating black guys who may have been part of ALJ's private security force. Whether black or white, the security people were really not all that difficult to spot. They all seemed to buy their suits from the same retail store. Most wore dark glasses. And they all had that tense look of barely suppressed frustration that came from carrying a concealed weapon that they rarely had the chance to use.

When the parade reached 59th Street, the kids from Rosa Parks shifted to marching in place, while Jones, Bradley and the rest of the front line notables made their way to the plaza. As the group left the rest of the parade behind, they were surrounded by uniformed police and security that held back the cheering crowd. Some people were doing their best to push through anyway, hoping perhaps to touch Jones, Bradley or one of the other notables.

In a crowd such as this there was always the possibility that a celebrity's admirers might trample him. In the early spring of 1968, a prepubescent Winthrop had been part of a frenzied mob that surrounded Bobby Kennedy's open car as it made its way down Northern Boulevard in Queens. Winthrop would never forget how Kennedy hung virtually upside down over the rear of the car while two secret service men held tenaciously to his legs and struggled to pull him back into the rear seat. Meanwhile, the crowd—mindless, oblivious, crazed with love—continued to pull Kennedy out of the car. Winthrop was right in there with the rest of them, straining to touch Bobby.

That day, Winthrop was lucky. A surge of the crowd pushed him toward the rear of the car, and he was within reach of RFK. Just as Winthrop was about to be shoved away, he shot out his right arm over the shoulder of the man in front of him. The man had been spun around and was now staring Winthrop in the face. Stretching as far as he could, Winthrop succeeded in grabbing Kennedy's hand. The contact lasted no more than a second. It was human flesh upon human flesh. Warmth against warmth. Then the mob surged again, and Winthrop was whipped away from the car.

Moments later, the secret service men were able to pull Kennedy back into the car. In the meantime, Winthrop had moved out of the mob and was running ahead several blocks to get beyond the madness and catch a glimpse of Kennedy when his car had cleared the crowd. In a few minutes, Winthrop saw the open car slowly approaching. Bobby was sitting next to Ethel. Formerly coatless, he had pulled a trench coat over his suit like a cape.

As the car passed, Winthrop caught the expression on Bobby's face. It was neither a look of triumph nor a look of fear. It was not even relief at having emerged from the crowd unscathed. Instead it was a look of numbness, the look of a man who had been through long wars and was in a war again. As Kennedy passed and his car drove out of sight, Winthrop thought of the Emily Dickinson poem he had read that day for the first time in his fifth-grade English class. "The nerves sit ceremonious like tombs . . . This is the hour of lead." After Joe, after Jack, thought Winthrop, Bobby had entered "the hour of lead."

A few days later, Winthrop saw Bobby Kennedy again. Kennedy was on television. He was addressing a crowd in an Indianapolis ghetto. Again, he looked numb. Someone had just murdered Martin Luther King Jr. "Martin Luther King Jr. dedicated his life to love and to justice for his fellow man," Kennedy told the crowd, "And he died in making that effort."

Two months later, Bobby Kennedy was dead. A political junkie even then, Winthrop had stayed up late, hoping to hear the results of the hotly contested California Democratic primary. With school the next day, he had been finally forced to retire with the outcome still in doubt.

When Winthrop awoke for school in the morning, he learned that Bobby had been shot in the head. He didn't need to hear anything more. The official word had not yet come, but in that moment Winthrop knew that Bobby was dead. "The nerves sit ceremonious like tombs," he thought. It was then that Winthrop himself entered "the hour of lead." And Winthrop knew that for him the hour would last a lifetime.

As Jones, Bradley and the others reached the stage, a black street musician began playing "Soul Man" on his trumpet. Right on cue, Jones launched into a frenetic dance, transporting himself with skill and rhythmic variety to his seat at the back of the stage. Bradley followed closely behind Jones. He trotted briskly up the steps of the stage, his smile beaming, his right hand waving. With a mocking, jocular flick of the wrist, he saluted the musician, dispensed more smiles and waves to the cheering crowd and took a seat next to Jones. Cardinal Boyle, Governor Ross, Reverend Al Sharpton, Alicia

Williams, Isaiah Woods and Arthur Lyle seated themselves as well, while Mayor Martinez moved directly to the mike.

As far as Winthrop was concerned, Martinez could have been elected mayor only in New York City. He personified the grotesque hyperbole of the city itself. Martinez was loud, egomaniacal, and combative. The word "extroverted" failed to do the man justice. While campaigning for office, he would plunge into a crowd with the enthusiasm of a fat man competing in a belly flop contest. "Qué pasa?" he would shout with a huge grin spread across his face. "Estás!" the crowd would roar in return, and everyone was pleased with himself.

"Hello, everybody!" Martinez bellowed into the mike. "I'm happy to be here today for two reasons. Number one, all of us who are participating in today's African-American Day parade are here to honor all African-Americans. And in honoring African-Americans, we honor America as well. America's the most ethnically diverse nation on earth. It is truly the great Melting Pot, and New York City is the most ethnically diverse city in the world. That is our strength. That is what makes America, America and New York, New York.

"Now the second reason that I'm happy to be here today is that I have the opportunity to march and to share the stage with so many distinguished guests. Our time is short, so let me introduce our first guest, a man who has dedicated his life to serving all people, Cardinal John Patrick Boyle."

Boyle was certainly no hero to the black community, but the cheering and applause were wildly enthusiastic. Winthrop attributed the enthusiasm as much to the crowd's sense of festivity and urge to expend energy as to their desire to welcome the cardinal.

There then ensued some unintentional comedy, at least from Winthrop's point of view, as the pressures of time and the multiplicity of notables prompted the speakers to bob in and out of the spotlight with amazing rapidity. Ignoring the signs of the Right-to-Life demonstrators, Boyle offered a prayer for racial harmony, blessed the parade and sat down. Then Martinez bounced up again and introduced the Reverend Al Sharpton. Reverend Al praised the African-American Day parade as a celebration of activism, exhorted the crowd to engage in activism every day, and then promptly introduced Alicia Williams. Ms. Williams quickly praised the work of the "Crack Down on Crack" youth groups and the "Just Say No Kids" who were marching today, called up Isaiah Woods and sat down. Woods made a quick, commercial-like pitch for ongoing community development in Harlem and the Bronx and called up Representative Lyle as a champion of the same. As a beneficiary of a rhetorical tradition distinguished by the likes of Mohammad Ali, Jesse Jackson, and dozens of hip hop artists from Snoop Dog to Jay Z, Lyle punctuated his brief address with doggerel rhymes such as "unity in the community" and "black and white must join the fight." Then he took great pleasure in introducing Governor Bill Ross and sat down.

With apparently nothing to say regarding African-Americans or the parade, Ross got right down to the task of creating a good usable sound bite for the local evening news. The original plan was for Ross to introduce Abraham Lincoln Jones and for Jones, after a bit of entertaining improvisation, to introduce Jason Bradley. Ross, however, had decided to add some minor theatrics to the mix. "We are honored today," he began, "to have with us as Grand Marshal of our parade one of the most popular and talented men in America. To introduce him to you, I'm going to need a little help. So let's all welcome back Mayor Hector Martinez."

The mayor returned to good-natured, if mild, applause. Yes, thought Winthrop, the two of them do belong together. Ross was fast becoming almost as big a clown as Martinez. Meanwhile the crowd had grown too large to be contained within the Grand Army Plaza. It now filled Fifth Avenue between 58th and 59th Streets and extended to the GM Plaza on the East side of Fifth.

Despite the anticlimactic reappearance of Martinez, Winthrop could feel a shift in the crowd's attention. There was a new concentration, a greater intensity. They were about to commune with a star. To be followed by a bona fide member of a truly elite group—twenty-first century political royalty. But first they would be treated to the vaudevillian antics of Ross and Martinez.

"Well, Mayor, are you ready?"

"You know me, Bill. It's always my pleasure to assist the governor. And this time especially since we'll be introducing a good friend of ours. But, more important, he's a friend to all Americans, black, white, Latino."

"And let's not forget Asians."

"A friend to all Americans whatever their ethnic backgrounds. A champion of equality."

"He's certainly that, Hector."

"And a true people person. But without further ado, Bill, let's introduce him—with apologies to Barry Bream!"

With that, Mayor Martinez and Governor Ross clapped their arms around each other's back, hunched together over the microphone and with huge, self-satisfied grins intoned in unison the famous intro, á la Barry Bream: "Hello, America. From the Grand Army Plaza off New York City's Central Park, it's *The ALJ Show* starring Abraham Lincoln Jones. And now here's the Emancipated Mouth, the Black Hole that swallowed America, the Master Blaster of Talk Show Disaster—Abraham Lincoln Jones!"

The crowd went crazy. The obliging street musician played "Soul Man." And Jones strode majestically toward the mike. Martinez got to him first, and the two men embraced. It was Ross's turn next. Then the three of them locked hands and raised them high over their heads in an attitude favored by victorious boxers, Las Vegas entertainers, and Richard Nixon.

Winthrop, squinting into his binoculars, studied their faces. Ross and Martinez wore identical grins—ecstatic, farcical, mask like; Jones somehow maintained his separateness and dignity even as he postured for the crowd and the cameras. Rather than smile, he exuded a composed self-assurance that said, "I am better than these political hacks. I know it, and you, if you're hip, know it, too. They use me and my blackness, my celebrity, yes, but I use them even more, and I will continue to use them and their phony-ass power connections every chance I get."

Yes, thought Winthrop, Jones was cool. He was in control as much as anyone could be. And he knew what he was about. Definitely.

With Ross and Martinez returned safely to their seats and the crowd noise subsiding, Jones addressed the audience. "Thank you, friends. Thank you, brothers and sisters. I know I'll sound like a white politician when I say this, but I'm going to say it anyway. Today is a great day for African-Americans. It is a great day. Think about it. What do we have here today? We have a big crowd gathered around a black man who's standing on a wooden platform. There was a time in this country when that would have meant one thing and one thing only. A lynching party. Today we're having another kind of party. It's a party to celebrate African-Americans. To celebrate black people. Well, then, let's celebrate!"

Suddenly, Jones began to gyrate. It had become one of his trademarks—breaking into a wild, spontaneous dance. He had done it hundreds of times over the years on *The ALJ Show*, sometimes celebrating a moment of truth, at other times violently interrupting the drone of banal talk. "I feel uptight! Let's get down!" he'd shout into the middle of a guest's self-important sentence, and the audience, which had felt uptight, too, roared its approval. Another guest had gotten the hook!

Then as Jones danced toward the huge pink star that marked his spot at center stage, the band would break into "Dancing in the Streets," and the entire studio audience would get up and dance. And the camera would pan from ALJ to the audience to the band to Barry Bream and back to ALJ, televising the dance, nothing but a crazy dance right on into the commercial break.

When *The ALJ Show* returned, the dance would still be going on, running on its own steam, and so it would continue until Maestro Jones kicked into a climactic, improvisational, ever accelerating movement that put his signature on the dance and, with stage lights flashing, brought the commotion to a close. Then when the cheering and shouting and whoops and hollers had finally died down a bit and Jones had caught his breath, he would characteristically allude to the segment with his now forlorn, dispatched guest. "Whooee!" Jones would shout. "That conversation was Death Valley Days! That was the Reagan administration on blown out tires! That was a genuine, twenty-mule-team bore ass!"

As Jones cavorted on the stage at the Grand Army Plaza accompanied by the lone trumpeter's interpretation of "Dancing in the Streets" and as many people in the crowd enthusiastically joined in with their own free-form choreography, Winthrop knew that ALJ's dance was only partly a celebration of African-Americans. It was a criticism, too, of the speakers who had preceded the Emancipated Mouth. In effect, Jones had just given the hook to Hector Martinez, Bill Ross, Cardinal Boyle, Al Sharpton, Alicia Williams, Isaiah Woods and Arthur Lyle.

Winthrop shifted his binoculars to Jason Bradley. He had almost the same look of composed self-assurance that Winthrop had seen on Jones's face just moments before. As far as Winthrop could see, there was only one difference in Bradley's expression: the most subtle trace of a self-satisfied smile, bearing witness to the fact that Bradley was certainly on Jones's wavelength. He knew that the other speakers had been dismissed, even if they did not know it themselves. They were still there physically, but they were now of no account. Politically and spiritually it was now just Abraham Lincoln Jones and Jason Bradley alone together on the Grand Army Plaza stage.

"Whooee! That felt good!" Jones shouted, his dance now completed. "We got a real party going on here! Yeah! But we got some other business, too. Some serious citizen business. Like introducing my man, Jason Bradley, Mr. J.B., Senator Bradley, our personal advocate in Washington."

Jones and the crowd worked together like a good team. At the mention of the senator, he paused and they came in on cue with cheers and applause. People began chanting Bradley's name, and there was a renewed outbreak of dancing in some quarters. Winthrop again studied Bradley's face. He was smiling broadly now. It was a good-natured smile, very pleased, with that same look of composed self-assurance. It was, Winthrop knew, the smile of a man in power, radiating the warmth and benevolence that came with a liberal's sense of control. My authority is liberating, it seemed to say. Follow me and I'll set you free. At the same time, Jones's face was absolutely beaming for he remained the center of attention. He was the great orchestrator of the crowd's responses. And he luxuriated in that role.

Of course, with Bradley as the main political speaker and Jones as the Grand Marshal, the parade enjoyed an incomparable advantage. It was the electricity of celebrity, the synergy of charisma, with two powerhouse personalities sharing their energies, each lending force to the other. That combined energy was now operating at full power.

"Let me tell you why I support this white dude sitting here," Jones continued, gesturing toward Bradley. "I'm for Jason Bradley, and you all are for Jay Bradley because he's for us. He's on our side. He's for blacks. He's for Latinos. He's for women. He's for gay and lesbian people. He's for transgender people. He's for the poor and the homeless. He's for all of America's minorities. And he knows— like you and I know—that when you add together all us minorities, you get a big majority. You get the real America. The America we honor. The America we love. That's what Jason Bradley stands for. A-M-E-R-I-C-A. America! That's what he's fightin' for now as your senator. And that's what he'll fight for some day when he moves into that big white house on Pennsylvania Avenue. Hey! I sure can sound like a white politician when I want to, can't I?

"Well, enough of this politicking. Let's bring the man himself to the mike. Here he is. My good friend and blood brother. The man who stands for freedom and equality. The man who stands for justice, with the best looking political wife this country's ever seen. Better than Jackie Kennedy! Better than Dolley Madison ice cream! Let's let him know we love him—Senator Jason Bradley!"

As Bradley stood up, the crowd reaction surprised Winthrop. He had expected a big response, but the noise was unbelievable, as if Bradley were a kind of rock star.

Observing the pandemonium, Winthrop wondered, as he often did during such displays, what really was motivating the crowd to behave as they did. Did they seriously believe that Bradley either as legislator or chief executive would ever significantly change their own individual lives for the better? That was rather like believing in a personal God, was it not? Was it also possible they believed that Bradley would make America a better place in which to live? Did he perhaps favor some particular piece of legislation or budgetary allocation that they believed would help resolve a serious social problem? Did they believe that one person could make a difference? Could Bradley, through the force of his personality, inspire Americans to be more tolerant, more understanding, more compassionate? Could he help achieve a new era of freedom and equality for minorities? For blacks and Latinos? For gay, lesbian and transgender people? Could he help create jobs for the poor? Could he provide housing for the homeless? Could he ensure the safety of city streets and subways? Could he deliver homeland security? Could he promise the American people a future of peace and prosperity?

Did such ideas ever cross their minds? Or was Bradley really just another rock star to them? A sexy image? Or was the sports analogy more appropriate? Did Bradley's political success translate into their success as well? Were they fans of the Bradley team? Were they wearing the Bradley uniform? Were they rooting for their team to win it all so they could chant, "We're number one! We're number one!" over and over again?

In fact, even now as Bradley and Jones embraced on the stage, shouts of "ALJ! ALJ!" were mixing with the chant "Bradley's the one!" One young man with a blond crew cut and a thin, wiry build was acting as the main cheerleader for Bradley, bouncing around acrobatically in the comic, frenetic manner of the San Diego Chicken or the Phillie Phanatic. With every passing second, more and more people were taking up the cheer until it seemed that almost half the crowd—indeed nearly all the white people in it— were shouting "Bradley's the one!"

As the crowd noise rose to a deafening level, Winthrop again scanned the plaza area with his binoculars to get an overall pan- oramic sense of the scene. Up and down the crowd he went. Over the Grand Army Plaza. Across Fifth Avenue to the GM Plaza and the huge Apple store façade. Then back beyond 59th Street and up the side of the Sherry-Netherland, where people were gathered at the windows. Visually, Winthrop climbed the floors of the Sherry up near to the top of the tower.

It was then that he saw it. With the distorted vision of first impression, it looked initially like a metal pipe or rod projecting from the hotel window high above Fifth Avenue. But in the next split second, Winthrop knew what he was seeing: the long barrel of a high-powered rifle pointing in the direction of the Grand Army Plaza stage. Then he heard the shots, muffled by the overwhelming din of the crowd, acting as a great, collective human silencer.

But the shots were not coming from the long, dark rod at the top of the Sherry. While the gun in the sights of Winthrop's binoculars maintained a deadly, watchful silence, rifle shots came with mind- less, sickening rapidity from across the plaza, from the area of the Plaza Hotel.

As the last shot sounded, the rifle near the top of the Sherry receded from view. Winthrop wheeled toward the Plaza and scanned the windows of the hotel, but the gunman was already gone. In a flash he whipped around the stunned bystanders who stood in his way and was up the side of the Sherman monument to gain the proper vantage. Then he quickly trained his binoculars on the stage. Abraham Lincoln Jones was lying motionless by the side of the podium. Jason Bradley lay thrashing on top of Jones. And there was blood on their clothes and blood on the stage.

3

IT WAS WELL PAST MIDNIGHT when Jack Winthrop finally arrived at the Tit for Tat. The Tit was Winthrop's second home. Tonight all the other regulars were there along with an assortment of businessmen, blue-collar workers and a few welcome deadbeats. Only a small group of puerile hooters out on a bachelor party binge spoiled the scene. There was also the obligatory psychopath nursing a drink alone at the corner of the bar, waiting patiently until the phone call came from God with directions to the next kill.

At the door Winthrop nodded at the massive Slow Mo then took his usual seat immediately to the right of the bar-top stage. Rita Harvey sat two stools down, reading *The Village Voice* and drinking the Tit's oil slick coffee.

Returning to New York after a summer visit to the Vatican, Fr. Harvey Ritter, S.J., swung through Amsterdam to undergo a surgical procedure that gave the Jesuits the distinction of including among their ranks the first woman Roman Catholic priest. Transgender woman, that is. Fr. Harvey Ritter had become Rita Harvey—Fr. Rita Harvey, that is. As Rita insisted to anyone who would listen, she had been ordained a priest forever. Once a priest, always a priest. That was God's will and the Church's teaching. Rita also made it clear that she had always been a woman, a woman born into a man's body. That had been God's will as well. The surgery had been her choice, but she had always been and would always be a woman—with or without it. As for the "Father" title, she loved it. It was right for her, and she would never give it up.

Within twenty-four hours of her return from Europe, however, Rita was an ex-world culture and contemporary issues teacher at Archbishop Hanratty High, an ex-resident and assistant pastor of Our Lady of Peace parish and an ex-Jesuit in good standing. Months later, Rita was excommunicated from the Catholic Church. The decree marked the final ex-ing out of her institutional Catholic affiliations and identities, except, of course, the most important one of all: in God's eyes, as the saying goes, Rita was still the deity's representative on earth. Rita was still a priest.

Of course, all of the institutional ex-ings raised the question of what to do. Out of desperation, acting on the conviction that she still had a religious vocation, Rita tried becoming a nun. She contacted the Immaculate Heart of Mary, the St. Joseph and the Franciscan orders. But word had gotten around, and she was turned down flatly despite the dearth of vocations in recent years.

With the rejections, however, came the courage to organize. With a few friends, some still on the inside, some out, Rita started GPAC, the Gay Priests Action Committee. Within a month, GPAC had fifty members. Initially, Rita was the only woman in the organization and, by the same token, the only lesbian. Soon, however, GPAC became GRACE, the Gay Religious Action Committee for Equality, as seven lesbian nuns joined the group. By the end of its first year, GRACE was a national organization with more than 1,000 members, including about 500 priests, brothers and nuns and an equal number of lay supporters. Rita was especially proud of the diversity of her lay supporters. They included a host of trans women, trans men, gays, lesbians and gender queer people as well as a healthy sprinkling of straight folks as well. As Rita always said, GRACE was about freedom and quality, and that meant celebrating everybody for who they really were.

While she was busy getting GRACE off the ground, Rita went to work as a counselor for ALFREE, an alcoholics support group. Having been both a counselor and an alcoholic for most of her adult life, Rita felt particularly suited to her role at ALFREE. When two clients in three days swore that they were absolutely committed to remaining alcohol free but still insisted on hanging out at the Tit for Tat, Rita decided to check out the place. The first person she met there was Jack Winthrop, who introduced her to Donna, Sheila, Robin and Bree as well as Slow Mo and Manny Snider, the Tit's owner. She became Donna's sometime lover, babysat for Sheila and held GRACE executive committee meetings in Manny's smoky office. But she would always feel closest to Jack.

For Winthrop, one of the small perfect pleasures of life was to come upon Rita unnoticed. The feat was really not all that difficult to accomplish. Winthrop possessed the noiseless stealth of a cat burglar who stole for the aristocratic art of it. And Rita's consummate absorption while reading anything—but particularly *The Village Voice*—was legendary at the Tit. During the days when she was the Tit's premier dancer, Donna was particularly fond of performing her most obscene and gymnastic solo Kama Sutra routines just beyond the pages of *The Voice*, while Rita read on in primeval innocence. Regulars would place bets on how long it would take Rita to sense Donna's pornographic presence. The all-time record was just over ten minutes. When she finally did emerge from her reverie, Rita would laugh and say, "How much for a rerun?" or "I guess I've been missing something special!" or "You know, Donna, the Lord and I both love that beautiful body of yours, but it's not the center of the universe. While you've been sporting your tender little charms, I've been reading something here in *The Voice* that is truly important. Listen to this, darling . . ."

Now, as Winthrop gazed upon the quiet, unsuspecting Rita, he realized that for the past few moments he had been entertaining the singular image that always came to him whenever he had the good fortune to observe undiscovered and undisturbed a close friend in a private moment. He found himself thinking of a sleeping baby. And no matter how many times he was in this particular situation—looking in undetected upon a solitary friend—he always reacted with the same quiet surprise. Yes, voyeurism did, indeed, have its saintly, meditative rewards. It permitted one to rediscover the essential innocence of the people one loved. And certainly no sensitive, intelligent adult that Winthrop knew was more innocent than Fr. Rita Harvey.

Usually when Winthrop had the opportunity to contemplate Baby Rita's innocence, he experienced the pure pleasure of a mind emptied of distraction. This time, however, other preoccupations tugged at Winthrop's attention. Number one, the events of the afternoon and evening beginning with the shooting of Abraham Lincoln Jones at the Grand Army Plaza. And, number two, the young woman dancing now just inside the periphery of Winthrop's vision. She was apparently Manny's newest employee. She could be eighteen, thought Winthrop, but she was probably younger. Perhaps another Midwestern runaway who had taken refuge with Uncle Manny. A blonde, blue-eyed Minnesotan perhaps, with her pale, ivory skin glowing like neon under the Tit's hot, multicolored stage lights.

Like virtually all of the dancers at the Tit, she had the streamlined muscularity of a spa queen. With her super taut waist and natural oversized breasts (perhaps a 36-D, mused Winthrop), she seemed to float above the bar like Everyman's dream. The male flag was certainly flying at half-mast at a high school somewhere in America. The boys had awakened one day, and suddenly their teenage goddess was gone.

Well, it was axiomatic that one person's loss was usually another's gain, and for the moment at least, Winthrop's spirit was benefiting from the amoral economy of the world. He had watched her for just the few moments that it had taken him to walk silently from the door to his bar-side stool, but he saw immediately that this young woman was special. She had grace. She had poise. She had integrity. She knew she was a biological aristocrat. And she was there to assert her pedigree—all sex and motion right up there on the stage, her hands gliding suggestively along the lithe contours of her teenage body as she danced to Spunk Gism's "Love Surgery." Winthrop noticed too that she was wearing her "D-string" pulled way up high, as high as it would stretch above her hips, so that it slinked down slowly as she danced and you found yourself following it, your mind anticipating the exquisite moment when her long fingers would reach down, find the string and pull it up again with a wicked little snap against the pearl of her body.

The "D" was Donna's improvement on the traditional G-string. It was a G-string pared down to the bare essentials: two thin pieces of elasticized cotton sown together, one piece worn around the middle, the other looping down to be worn, as Donna liked to put it, "bi-cracky." Donna, the consummate entrepreneur, was selling D-strings through her website www.donnadonna.com with additional distribution through exotic boutiques and sex shops around the country, and she had also seen to it that the D was fast replacing the superannuated G-string at topless bars and live sex shows from New York to San Francisco.

As the presence of the teenage dancer and the weight of the day's events pressed upon Winthrop's silent appreciation of Rita's transsexual innocence, Sheila approached smiling from the other end of the bar. She was about to say, "What'll it be, Jack?" when Winthrop put his finger to his lips and nodded in Rita's direction. Sheila knew, of course, what Winthrop was up to, so she stayed at a discreet distance and pretended to clear some glasses from the bar. She was wearing her usual bartending outfit, black patent leather spiked high heels, a cherry-red D-string and transparent pasties with red, white and blue pompons depending from the center.

As usual, Winthrop was struck by the blackness of Sheila's skin. Sheila had the blackest skin, and indeed the most beautiful black skin, that Winthrop had ever seen. Over the years Sheila had succeeded in tracing back her ancestry. She was Zulu. Her great-great-great-great grandmother had come to America as a teenage girl in a slave ship in the mid-1850s. Over the past half-century many of her relatives had been beaten, jailed and murdered by the South African police. Sheila's eight-year-old daughter Karina wore a bracelet with a single handmade charm that said "homeless." Karina loved her favorite babysitter, Aunt Rita. And Rita dearly loved Karina. When the two of them were together, their smiles could melt the world.

The moment seemed right to Winthrop, so with Sheila looking on, he edged off his seat, leaned across the empty stool to his right and kissed Rita softly on the cheek.

"I'd know those lips anywhere," cried Rita before looking up. "It's got to be Jack Winthrop, the notorious spinmeister, himself. You certainly have had some eventful day today, Jack!" Rita declared with a curious smile.

"I take it you've been following it all."

"I've been channel surfing almost nonstop in Manny's office. We've all been following it. Special reports and news updates all day and all night. It's hot stuff. But, you know, we were hoping to see you on the air as either an eyewitness or ALJ's new spokesman."

"Let me get you something, Jack," Sheila interrupted. "How about a real drink, like a double shot of 1800?" As Sheila leaned forward, the tips of one of her patriotic pompons tickled the hairs of Winthrop's right hand.

"Sounds great, and if it's not too much trouble, why don't you freshen up Rita's cup just a bit?"

"Just add some hot coffee, Sheila. Fresh may be asking too much. So, Jack, you never got on the air."

"Well, I'm not his spokesman. I'm the Svengali behind the scenes. As you know, ALJ is the last person who needs a spokesman. He can speak pretty well for himself."

"Who's the sexy black woman?"

"That's Danielle Jackson, Abe's personal assistant."

"I'll bet she doesn't need much help either."

"She does seem to know how to handle herself, but she's pretty shaken by the shooting."

"Well, she was very impressive. In fact, she was all over the tube today—CNN, MSNBC, Fox News, the networks. You name it. She was on it."

"Here we are," said Sheila. "One double shot of 1800. One warmed up coffee."

"Thanks, Sheila," said Winthrop, who immediately banged down the tequila.

Rita smiled, took a sip of her coffee and continued. "We've heard all the TV has to say, Jack. But you were there. You heard the shots. You saw it all happen. You're an eyewitness. And you're the man on the inside. So what's the scoop?"

As Winthrop prepared an answer, he began to notice the growing commotion about him. A group of bachelor party boys was crowding the bar and whooping it up a bit. On the stage, the teenage dancer was leaning back on her hands doing reverse pushups as she rhythmically opened and closed her legs to the beat of Destiny Child's "Bootylicious." Dollar bills were strewn about the stage in the area between her legs, and members of the bachelor party brigade were coaxing their all-but-married friend—a sheepish, halting, plump young man with the joie de vivre of an accountant—to try to slide a five dollar bill behind the thin vertical loop of the D string. Old Abe Lincoln certainly never had it so good, thought Winthrop. But the Great Emancipator would have to wait. As the bachelor party boys stepped up their taunts and bantering, the guest of honor hesitated. Meanwhile, the young dancer continued to writhe, her face detached and composed in the assurance of her power.

At the end of the bar, beyond the shy, salivating accountant and the horizontal, vibrating teenager sat the Tit's resident psycho. In the few moments that passed before Winthrop answered Rita, he absorbed the tableau while recalling in mental shorthand the first time Speck appeared at the bar.

Winthrop saw him as he entered. And he immediately knew who he was: the new Tit for Tat psycho reporting for duty, sir! Winthrop thought of him as Speck. Speck, the loner. Speck, the stalker. Speck, the hunter of human life. Pathology wafted from him like the scent of a cheap cologne. Winthrop could smell it. And he saw it too in the way the man dressed, with a subtly exaggerated fastidiousness, a closet-bred conservatism. His rage was in the starched collar of his white shirt buttoned to the top despite the absence of a tie. It was in the military press of his undertaker pants. And it was in the gold plated cuff links that shone in the lights as the man took his seat at the end of the bar just a few steps from Slow Mo's position at the door. It was also in the stiffness of his posture and the deliberateness of his walk, which said, "Don't get too close. I may be carrying a gun." But most of all the rage was in his silence. It was the silence of a vacuum, of the air sucked out of life. It was silence without peace. The silence that plagues and deadens the timeless moment before an explosion.

Sheila took the man's order that night, so he did speak once. She always remembered everyone's order. And that was something everybody liked. It made a person feel like he belonged, feel that a place had been saved at the table. "You mean the quiet guy at the end of the bar? Sheila asked when Winthrop inquired about what the man had said to her. "Oh, he just ordered his drink, gin on the rocks."

"And later on after that?"

"After that, he didn't say anything. He just nodded or pointed. I knew what he wanted. A refill. The same. Some people don't like to talk, and I ain't about to make them."

Looking at Speck, Winthrop was struck once again by the deeper implications of Sheila's casual wisdom. Often talk was an assault, an affront, an invasion of privacy. Yes, we are all constantly forced to talk, to present ourselves, to identify who we are, to justify the space that we currently occupy. Some people took the affront personally.

"The scoop," Winthrop said to Rita, emerging from his momentary reverie, "is that it's disturbing to have your paranoid fears confirmed."

"That's one of the differences between you and me, Jack. You're paranoid and I'm not."

"Right. I know. And you've always done wonderfully just the same. You've always been able to land on your feet. But I still have to rank paranoia as one of my finest qualities."

"It does give you that sexy suffering artiste look about the eyes, which I absolutely adore, but you were saying?"

"Well, you know my motto."

"That nothing matters?"

"That's one of my mottos."

"Which I don't think for one second you really believe."

"On the contrary, I do. But at any rate I was thinking of another one of my mottos."

"Which is?"

"Things are much worse than we can possibly imagine."

"Upbeat Jack Winthrop. Here you are sitting at the Tit for Tat with a voluptuous naked teenager within arm's reach, and you're still complaining about how horrible life is."

And indeed a crescendo of applause, hoots and hollers had just erupted from the crowd with the bachelor party boys shouting loudest of all. The teenage dancer had just concluded her routine by stripping off her D string, twirling it over her head and dropping it like a gift from heaven into the hands of the stunned accountant, who was still clutching his five dollar bill.

"If that guy has any spunk in him at all," Winthrop exclaimed, "he must be wracking his brain to figure out a way to call off the wedding."

As the accountant's buddies attempted to paw his prize, the teen-age dancer descended the stage and snatched away the bill. As a path cleared spontaneously before her, she strode naked to the small communal dancers dressing room at the rear of the bar, passing Bree, who smiled at her appreciatively as she made her own way to the stage to begin her well-honed twenty-minute routine of gymnastic dance and obscene posing.

"Well, Jack?" exclaimed Rita with a tone of vindication in her voice.

"Well, I suppose I have to admit that God is not a total under-achiever if she or he could at least produce a woman like her. But just bear with me for a minute. I want you to understand my reaction to the shooting."

"By all means continue."

"Well, I mentioned that motto of mine only to give you the context of my reaction."

"Jack, is this supposed to be news? We all know you're paranoid. I asked you for the scoop. The inside, exclusive story."

"This is a scoop. A personal scoop. And that's the most important kind." Just as Winthrop was about to continue, he was momentarily distracted by the fact that a foot was pressing against the crown of his head. It was, Winthrop knew, Bree's foot. Without bothering to look, he knew she was using his head as a perch while she assumed some outrageous, obscene pose. "What is it this time, Rita?" Winthrop asked, ignoring the juvenile laughter of the bachelor boys.

"Just a simple, classic moon, Jack. But nice, very, very, nice. Now, you were saying?"

"I was saying," Winthrop continued, with Bree's foot still pressing against his head. "I'm giving you the personal scoop first before I get to the Jack Webb/Dragnet stuff about the shooting."

"Just the facts, ma'am."

"Right." As a cheer went up from the crowd, Winthrop felt the pressure lift from his head. Now he turned and looked at Bree, who was already into her "Rover's Revenge" routine.

"Thanks, Jackie," Bree said. "I couldn't have mooned the crowd as well without you."

"Any time, Bree. That's why I'm here," Winthrop said with a smile, wondering as he turned back to Rita how Bree could possibly kick her leg up so high doggy style. "Anyway, Rita. The point is this. When terrible things inevitably happen, I find that I'm both disturbed and surprised. As I said, it's disturbing to have your paranoid fears confirmed. It's disturbing to know that your perceptions of the potential for violence are true. True even if you don't want to believe they're true."

"And why are you surprised?"

"I'm surprised, I suppose, because I'm naive."

"You realize 'naive' is the last thing anyone would call you."

"Nevertheless, it's true. The surprise is a result of the fact that a microscopic particle of me still doesn't want to believe the perception of my own mind. So that particle of naiveté sends up a little bubble of surprise. Oh, my God! It says, so people really are that bad. This is the world I live in. It's really as violent and absurd as I thought it was. There's no denying it. I am an eyewitness to the insanity of life. But today there was a difference. "

"Namely?"

"I felt the bubble burst. It was as if I'd finally grown up."

"So, Jack, that means your idea of maturity or adulthood is believing in the truth of your paranoia."

"Right. Knowing and believing that in an insane world, paranoia is the only sanity. So with all due respect to you, Rita, and your blessed freedom from paranoia, as far as I'm concerned, if you're not paranoid, you're just not paying attention."

"Thank you, Jack Winthrop. Only you would find fault with me, a transgender, lesbian priest, for not being crazy enough—and then call it a lack of perception."

"Actually, Rita, you're the exception that proves the rule. And I love you anyway, whether you're paranoid or not. So that's the personal scoop. My tiny little bubble burst."

"And now you're a man."

"Right. Bar mitzvahed by a rifle—hey, your coffee's getting low. How about another refill?"

"Actually, Jack, no. I have to leave in a few minutes. Sheila's baby-sitter has a two o'clock curfew, and I always like to be sure I'm there on time."

"Of course. Karina. I love the relationship the two of you have."

"She's a beautiful child. By the time I get there, she's been asleep for hours, but I spend the night, and we have breakfast together and play games and watch cartoons in the morning, while Sheila gets a little extra sleep. After all, she needs it. She doesn't get home until 5:00."

"You're a saint, Rita."

"No, just a friend. Sheila needs someone she can depend on what with all the horror stories these days about child abuse. A lot of people would be surprised to learn that the person she depends on is a priest. But listen, Jack, please continue with your story. I must hear about the shooting before I go."

Winthrop took a big, cleansing breath and called over to Sheila for another double. For inspiration he cast a glance at Bree, who by now had abandoned posing in favor of maniacally bouncing about the stage to the tune of "Girls Just Want to Have Fun." As Bree danced, she balanced a bottle of Bud between her huge silicone breasts and somehow managed to avoid spilling a drop. What really happens, thought Winthrop, what goes on every minute of every day, is crazier than anything anyone could ever make up.

"You heard what the cable news channels and the networks reported," Winthrop began, taking a small sip of his newly delivered tequila.

"That's all I know."

"Yes, you've heard the TV version. Now I'll tell you what really happened. I was at the Grand Army Plaza to take the measure of the crowd, get a sense of the people in it and their reaction to Jones. By the way, where was GRACE?"

"Unlike God, Jack, we cannot be everywhere. We had a meeting of our own. In fact, we've been meeting all week, discussing tactics for Sunday's demonstration at St. Patrick's. Some of the members are pushing hard that we have to be more confrontational. I think that will just alienate people all the more from our cause. Give the hate mongers an excuse. Bring more LGBT bashers out of the closet, so to speak. But some of our people aren't convinced. Of course, it's a fine line. Hard to say what's too confrontational and what's not confrontational enough. I'm calling my friend, Callie, later tonight to get the final word on some of our more radical members. She's closer than I am to some of them. But at any rate, Jack, please continue."

Winthrop wondered for a moment what tactics existed, whether liberal or radical, peaceful or nonviolent, that could make the pope, Cardinal Boyle, or any of the millions of bigots inside or outside the Catholic Church accept homosexuals and transgender people as normal human beings—this despite the absolutely absurd fact that a huge percentage of Catholic priests were themselves homosexual. Immediately hitting a dead end, he continued with his story. "I was scanning the crowd with my binoculars. When I went up the side of the Sherry-Netherland, I saw the barrel of a rifle sticking out of one of the windows near the top of the tower. As I said, seeing that rifle pointing down toward the plaza stage confirmed my paranoia and my fears—about politics, about race, about the cult of celebrity, about life in general."

"Seeing something like that—it must be like a nightmare materializing in the middle of the day."

"Yes, precisely. And that's the true, underlying message of every nightmare, especially those deep, dark disturbances that our minds erase the moment we awake, screaming in a cold sweat. Our nightmares tell us that one fine, sunny day we'll turn or look up to find a gun pointed at our heads or a knife thrust at our throats."

"But what did you do when you saw the gun?"

"A second or so after I saw the gun, I heard the shots."

"But wait a minute. You're saying you saw a rifle pointing from one of the windows of the Sherry-Netherland. I thought the shots were fired from the Plaza Hotel."

"That's the point. They were. As the shots were fired from the Plaza, the rifle at the Sherry was withdrawn from the window."

"Oh, my God!"

"I immediately climbed the side of the Sherman statue and swung my binoculars over to the Plaza, but I was already too late to see the sniper. He was gone, and Jones and Bradley were down on the stage. Bradley was on top of Jones, and there was blood all over."

"At that point you couldn't have known what exactly had happened."

"No. After the shots were fired, all I could see was that Jones wasn't moving at all, and Bradley was flopping about frantically like a fish out of water."

"Hold on. Let's go back to the two snipers. I'm sure you reported what you saw to the police."

"Of course."

"Then why aren't we hearing anything on TV about a Sherry-Netherland sniper? All I heard were some initial reports saying there was a lot of confusion among eyewitnesses over whether there was one or more snipers."

"And then within an hour or so the media were simply feeding the public the official police statement that there was no physical evidence indicating the presence of more than one sniper and that shots were fired only from the eleventh floor of the Plaza Hotel. Correct?"

"Yes. That's what they said."

"And technically it's true. The shots did come from the Plaza and no place else. And so far no one has found physical evidence of another sniper. The only problem is there was another sniper. My sniper. Perched high up the Sherry tower."

"Why aren't the police doing everything they can to track these people down? Not just the Plaza shooter, but your Sherry gunman as well?"

"Listen, Rita, when those shots were fired, there was panic in the streets. People went crazy. It was easy to get trampled. Dozens of people ended up in the emergency room at Roosevelt Hospital. People were running in every direction. Screaming. Diving for cover. Not knowing where they'd be safe. After the four shots were fired, the crowd was a lot more dangerous than either of the gunmen. They were a mob. And they didn't know what in the hell was happening.

"The upshot of all the chaos is that the police were deluged with eyewitness sightings of phantom assassins. About half the people who spoke to the police swore they saw multiple snipers. And these were all by and large very responsible people, including two TV reporters and a freelance journalist. On the other hand, some people saw a single gunman but didn't locate him at the Plaza. Taken all together, there would have to have been an invasion force of snipers at the Grand Army Plaza for all of the eyewitness accounts to be true. People saw shooters perched on the floors of several buildings in the area. At the Plaza, of course, at Bergdorf Goodman and on the floors of the GM Building."

"And at the Sherry-Netherland."

"That's the curious thing. I was the only eyewitness who claimed to see a sniper at the Sherry."

"How is that?"

"With all the spurious sightings, it's partly coincidence. But you know how tall the Sherry is. The sniper was way up near the top of the tower. I really doubt there was anyone else in the crowd with a pair of binoculars scanning that building at the time. Actually, I didn't see anyone else in the crowd with binoculars. Also, in all likelihood the rifle was at the window for only a few seconds. I probably caught the rifle in my sights just after it appeared and the gunman was taking aim. Then came the shots from the Plaza, and the rifle withdrew from the window. It was all over in seconds."

"But, Jack, you're a well-known writer, a journalist. I'm sure you have extensive police contacts. Certainly your eyewitness report is taken more seriously than the confused sightings of panic-stricken people."

"Yes, it is, Rita. And, actually, as luck would have it, one of my closest contacts was there. I told him everything."

"And?"

"And so far nothing. His search of the apartment at the Sherry turned out exactly the same as the searches at the phantom sniper locations. No physical evidence. No sign whatsoever that a shooter had been present."

"Was the room checked out to anyone?"

"Actually it was one of the full-floor apartments, unoccupied, and up for sale. There were no prints, either. There are security cameras throughout the hotel, of course—in the lobby, on the elevators, on every floor. They should show something. I'm waiting for him to get back to me on that."

"Are you going to write about what you know in the paper?"

"Not yet. I'd like to get more information before I go public with the story. Also, I don't want to do anything to drive the Sherry gunman back into his hole. At this point he may think no one saw him. Maybe he'll do something that will lead us to him. Maybe I can act in the best interests of Jones and get the real story at the same time."

"So there's more to come on the Sherry gunman."

"Quite possibly, Rita. I at least want to give my contact a chance to do his stuff. He's one of the good ones. He and his people will keep at it. Take it beyond the limit. He'll even follow up on his own time. Right now, though, we're nowhere."

"Nowhere as far as the Sherry gunman is concerned. But what about the Plaza sniper who actually fired the shots?"

Winthrop took another hit of tequila, draining the glass, and signaled for a Dos Equis from Sheila. He was suddenly very thirsty. Mojave Desert thirst. As soon as Sheila handed him the beer, he began drinking in big satisfying gulps. Normally given to sipping and savoring alcohol, he continued drinking until he had drained the bottle completely. When he finished, he found himself breathing in air at the end like a still hungry infant sucking on the nipple of an empty bottle. Winthrop realized that he was still a long way from even a mild buzz.

"You look like you need another, Jack," said Sheila.

"You read my mind, honey."

"Not your mind. Your lips, baby. Don't suck so hard. You'll break the bottle." And another Dos Equis was in Winthrop's hand before he could even blink. Meanwhile, the bar was getting noisier. It was rough, aggressive noise with an undercurrent of drunken, juvenile hostility. At the door, a cab driver was talking to Slow Mo, who signaled toward Rita. It was just about time for her to leave.

"Well, Rita, darling," Winthrop continued, looking straight into her eyes. "That's the bitch of it all. The police didn't find a damn thing at the Plaza either. Lots of people saw the sniper at the window, but no one seems to have gotten a good look at his face. Whoever it was got away clean. Again, the room was supposedly unoccupied. There was no sign of a break in and nothing of interest in the room itself. All the police have right now are the four bullets and whatever might be on the hotel security cameras."

"Don't they know at least one thing?"

"What's that?"

"At that range from the Plaza wouldn't the sniper have to be a terrible shot?

"You mean since Jones survived and Bradley wasn't hit."

"Yes."

"In fact, the sniper is very likely a terribly good shot who knows his target and can hit the mark every time. You know, to some minds, Rita, torture is far more amusing than murder. At least it may serve as an indispensable appetizer."

Rita just stared at Winthrop for a moment, looking chilled, looking stunned. "I take it, you went to the hospital, Jack," she continued, changing the subject.

"Yes, I went there. Got the news on the situation. Touched base with Danielle. As I said, she was pretty shaken."

"And then?"

"And then I just walked. One of my little walking tours of Manhattan. Then I stopped here."

"But, Jack, that means you were walking the streets for hours."

"Clears the mind. Circulates the blood to all the right body parts."

"But where did you go?"

"Well, from a little coffee shop a block away from Roosevelt Hospital, where I found Danielle, I took off for the *Times*."

"To touch base?"

"Right. Anyway, I called my contact, found out that the hotels were clean, got an update on the eyewitness reports and picked up the newsroom buzz. Then I took off, swung over to Broadway, headed back up town and just kept going until I was ten or fifteen blocks north of Columbia University. Then I turned around and began to zigzag my way over to the East Side."

"Did you stop anywhere to eat?"

"I stopped at a little tavern in the eighties called Mick's Place, where they had a TV going, caught another news update, had some black coffee. Then I set sail again and headed down Lex. I hung out for awhile at a place in the East Village called The Blue Moon."

"I know that place. It's a pretty friendly gay bar."

"Seemed so. Actually, I blew quite a few chances at getting picked up."

"Jack, you still don't know what's it's like to live."

"That's what my mother always says. But I never knew until now that she was actually trying to get me to embrace my gay inner self."

"You listen to your mother, Jack. She's a smart lady."

"You have my word on that, Rita. No way I try bucking you and Mom at the same time—at any rate, while I was at the Blue Moon fending off some well-intentioned advances, I stole some time to call my police contact again. He reconfirmed that there was still no hard evidence. After that, I had a few Dos Equis and headed to my beloved second home."

"To the Tit."

"To the Tit."

"Well, you are certainly the marathon man. But seriously, Jack, you really believe this gunman is playing with your Mr. Jones."

"I know it, Rita. Some things you just know. I know this psycho is into torture. So the fun has just begun."

"On that reassuring note, Jack, I'll have to leave."

"I know. Your driver's been waiting for you."

Just then a cheer went up from the crowd behind Rita and Winthrop, followed by a muffled thud and the sound of a beer bottle shattering against the bar. Winthrop felt little bits of glass spray the back of his neck. The bachelor boys, who had grown temporarily dormant with the departure of the teenage goddess, were suddenly erupting again.

"That's definitely my cue to go," said Rita as she backed away from her seat. "I'm on my way, Sheila."

"OK, Aunt Rita, give my little baby a kiss. But you'd better go this way," said Sheila as she likewise backed away from the commotion.

"See you, Rita," shouted the tireless, boogying Bree, seemingly oblivious to the disturbance just a few feet from the stage.

Winthrop was likewise unperturbed. The Tit's *deus ex machina*, Slow Mo, would slowly but surely intervene. "Give Karina a kiss for me too, Rita," said Winthrop as Rita kissed him good-bye on the cheek, smiled and went quickly on her way, circling around the far side of the bar. Winthrop always feared for Rita's welfare. But whenever he saw her smiling her own special smile, warm and genuine, he felt a particularly sharp pang of concern for her. She was such an obvious target. He wondered what odd accident of grace, what random play of luck, had spared her thus far. Though he had never been a father, he associated his concern with the constant, sleep-disturbing parental fear that one's child would someday be destroyed by the world. Like a father, Winthrop felt powerless to prevent what he was afraid would be the inevitable crush of disaster.

Rita just doesn't belong in this world. She's too good for it, thought Winthrop, as a beer mug crashed to the floor and the bachelor party boys whooped in approval. In response, Winthrop swiveled around to take advantage of his ringside seat. Yes, indeed. It was now long past midnight, and the mood was right for another Tit for Tat brawl. Slow Mo, you're on, Winthrop mused appreciatively. You're on in your own good time.

4

WHILE WAITING FOR THE ARRIVAL OF SLOW MO, Winthrop wondered if the accountant had ever before found himself in such a position. The bachelor party's guest of honor was on top of one of his friends, perhaps, thought Winthrop, a member of the wedding party, perhaps even the best man, riding piggyback. Clearly, however, this was not a case of good-natured horseplay. The accountant's right hand was wrapped around the throat, while his left hand covered the nose and mouth of his friend. Apparently the accountant was trying simultaneously to strangle and suffocate his bachelor party buddy. Whichever worked first would prove the better method.

Meanwhile, the friend staggered wildly about, knocking over bottles and glasses while elbowing the accountant in the gut and holding at arm's length the teenage dancer's D-string, which was by now soaked with beer. The accountant was screaming over and over again in a hoarse, petulant voice, "It's mine, goddamn it! Give it the fuck back! She gave it to me! It's mine!"

The friend was prevented by his predicament from being as articulate. He was capable of producing only a variety of animal noises, ranging in pitch and timbre from the shriek of a strangled parakeet to the roar of a hibernating bear unable to awaken from an endless, bestial nightmare. Animal sounds likewise emanated from the rest of the bachelor party boys who voiced their appreciation of the proceedings through assorted squeaks, barks, whistles, clucks, oinks, moos and hee-haws that leant a remarkably authentic barnyard ambience to the bar. All in all, thought Winthrop, it was a rather curious human spectacle, rather like a dress rehearsal for *The Jerry Springer Show*.

As the barnyard calls grew increasingly annoying, Winthrop glanced over toward the door. It was clear that, without ever bothering to look in the direction of the barnyard crew, Slow Mo knew all. It was likewise clear, at least to Winthrop, that without lifting a finger, Slow Mo was in complete control of the situation. What's more, he now seemed on the verge of rousing himself. With sad resignation he slowly set aside an oversized plastic container of salad. Apparently Slow Mo had just sat down to enjoy his customary late night repast when the fight broke out.

So far as Winthrop knew, tossed salads were all that Slow Mo ever ate. He even ate salad for breakfast. The salads were all Slow Mo's own special creations, with a wonderful homemade vinaigrette dressing that had just the right combination of extra virgin oil, vinegar, Grey Poupon mustard, salt, ground black pepper and dill weed. Huge and amazingly various, Slow Mo's salads were always of four-star, gourmet quality with an eclecticism unparalleled in the history of salad making. Breaking with hundreds or perhaps even thousands of years of salad-making tradition, Slow Mo would begin by combining an extensive potpourri of lettuces and greens in the same salad. Never iceberg, but watercress, red leaf, radicchio, Boston, romaine, Swiss chard, arugula, escarole and endive might make their way into the same creation along with a generous portion of spinach. As a result, for Winthrop at least, eating a Slow Mo salad was a continuing education in subtle differences in the color, texture and flavor of lettuces and greens.

Slow Mo's approach to the goodies side of salad design was

equally inclusive. He would toss in a veritable cornucopia of vegetables in colorful and witty combinations: red and green peppers, artichoke hearts, mushrooms, broccoli, kale, scallions, carrots, avocados, olives, cauliflower, squash, zucchini, cucumbers, celery, pea pods and radishes. Virtually any green, red, yellow or otherwise colored vegetable might find its way at one time or another into a Slow Mo tossed salad. Eggs, however, were out.

Shortly after Slow Mo first arrived on the Tit for Tat scene, Sheila innocently suggested that a hard-boiled egg or two might enhance the taste and appearance of Slow Mo's salads. Sheila could hardly have anticipated the response. First, Slow Mo frowned horribly. Then he began to shake his head, all the while staring hard in astonishment at Sheila. It was as if Slow Mo were about to reveal some terrible fact of life—something shocking and strange—which he hated to disclose but which Sheila, being a mature and worldly woman, should surely have known already.

"That's gross, woman," Slow Mo exclaimed with a shiver of disgust. "Don't you know where eggs come from? That goddamn egg you eat for breakfast—soft-boiled, scrambled, poached, sunny side up, over easy, whatever—that egg you put hard-boiled on top of your salads, that egg came out of a goddamn chicken! And that egg, if you don't eat it first, that egg will grow up to be another chicken. So don't go asking me about eggs no more. I don't want to talk about them. No way! No ma'am!"

"So I suppose you don't eat chicken then?" Sheila asked somewhat tentatively.

"Chicken!" Slow Mo shouted, practically choking on the word. "Chicken!" he repeated incredulously. "Tell me something, Sheila James. What do people say when they want you to eat a snake?"

Sheila stood there silently, confused at the question. Apparently she had never come across snake-eating people or even imagined that they existed.

"I'll tell you what they say," Slow Mo continued undeterred.

"They say snake tastes like chicken. And what do people say when they want you to eat a frog?" Slow Mo paused dramatically. "They say the frog tastes like a chicken! The same with the down-and-out people in the goddamn streets. I know about them, too. They catch a rat. They cook it up hot and crispy, and they go to eat it. They always say the same thing. They say, 'Try some. It's good. It tastes like chicken.' Now let me ask you something, Sheila. If a rat tastes like a chicken, what's a chicken taste like?"

Winthrop listened in silent admiration. As a writer, he was a devotee of sound logic. He relished the sane precision of well-reasoned arguments. So he stood in quiet respect before Slow Mo's inevitable conclusion.

"Sheila, an egg is just a chicken waiting to be born. You want me to put that in my salad. No way! Ain't no way at all! No thank you, ma'am!"

"I take it then," Winthrop finally interjected, "that you're a vegetarian?"

"Right," Slow Mo responded. "If it grows, I might eat it or I might not. But if it walks on two legs or four or if it hops or crawls or slippy slides or flies in the air, I don't want it on my plate."

"What about fish?" Winthrop asked.

"Fish swim and flip flop around. I don't want to know them either. Listen, Jack. Listen, Sheila. I don't need no animal zoo to keep me alive and healthy. Just give me a salad, a good goddamn salad any time of the night or day. That's all I need to get by."

Winthrop and Sheila were certainly convinced. Salads were all Slow Mo needed. In fact, from the very beginning of Slow Mo's reign as the Tit for Tat gatekeeper and bouncer extraordinaire, the Tit regulars were impressed with Slow Mo's powers of persuasion. Of course, his persuasiveness was the result of more than just effective argumentation. There were also his stature and appearance. Slow Mo was the living embodiment of the worst nightmare that David Duke ever had: a six-foot, eight-inch, two hundred seventy-five pound man with coal black skin and a platinum blonde mohawk.

A few days after he started work at the Tit for Tat, Sheila asked Slow Mo why he wore a platinum blonde mohawk. He gave what she and Winthrop felt was the best answer of all. "It's me," Slow Mo said. "And I don't give a damn about what anybody thinks. I like it. I just like it."

"So do I," said Sheila, who always sort of had a crush on Slow Mo.

Actually, at the time, Slow Mo was known simply as Mo or sometimes Mo Mo. His real name was Maurice Monroe. Manny Snider called him Mo from the beginning, and most of the Tit for Tatters picked it up as well both as a nickname for Maurice and in recognition of his mohawk. Donna and Robin called him Mo Mo. The name Slow Mo was Winthrop's creation. It was an honorific nickname, saluting Mo's unique personal rhythm, which was always very, very slow. More specifically, the name celebrated Mo's handling of the peace-keeping portion of his job.

Basically, Slow Mo had the same approach to breaking up fights as a National Hockey League referee. When a brawl broke out, he always seemed otherwise occupied. Once he finally did bother to look over in the direction of the fight, he would be slow to react at all. Then, moving with what seemed like glacial speed, he would make his way over to the scene of the scuffle, stake out a good vantage point, and observe the action.

Essentially nonviolent himself, Slow Mo seemed to view barroom fights as part of a bar's attraction. The Tit for Tat offered the two basics: sex and violence—along, of course, with unlimited access to alcoholic beverages. The violence, however, always seemed to remain on the level of play. It was really hockey game violence. Usually, no one was actually hurt, and the penalty box was a boot out the door, though Slow Mo was often willing to look the other way if a repentant brawler wanted to return a half hour later.

Tonight's bachelor crew brawl was no exception. By the time Slow Mo had made his first move toward restoring peace, setting aside his salad and rising from his seat just beyond the Tit's front door, the face of the accountant's friend had begun to resemble a dried prune. Nevertheless, he still refused to relinquish possession of the prized, beer-drenched D-string. And despite the extremity of his own condition, he continued to give the accountant the bucking bronco ride of his life. Meanwhile, the other bachelor party boys were cranking up the decibels on their barnyard mimicry.

As Slow Mo made his way to the front of the stage, a path cleared almost magically before him. A few of the revelers more or less bounced off his chest, but overall the effect was rather like Moses parting the Red Sea. Once he arrived at the stage, Slow Mo settled down to observe the barking and squealing and shouting with an intent, quizzical look on his face. When he emerged from his reverie, Slow Mo turned to Winthrop, shook his head slowly and said, "These boys are goddamn fools, Jack. What would their mamas say?"

"They'd all say, 'That son of mine doesn't have the sense he was born with! But he's a good boy, Slow Mo. So don't hurt him. Please, don't hurt him!'"

"I don't hurt nobody, Jack. You know that."

"I sure do," said Winthrop, smiling warmly. In fact, Winthrop had never seen Slow Mo throw a punch. Nor did Slow Mo practice the martial arts of karate, judo, or jiu-jitsu. His technique was simpler and more direct, with its own primitive elegance. When Slow Mo finally decided through some mysterious, never to be explained, sense of synchronicity that it was the right time to intervene in a Tit for Tat tussle, he would simply grab each of the brawlers by the scruff of the neck, lift them a good foot and a half off the ground and then, with their legs kicking and their arms flailing, proceed to shake both of them back and forth until their bodies hung limp in the air.

For Winthrop, observing Slow Mo in the role of peacemaker was a bit like watching a dog subdue its prey, but with less deadly results. Invariably, the vanquished brawlers would experience only a temporary paralysis, which gave Slow Mo enough time to drag them from the scene of the fight and deposit them outside the Tit's front door.

With his laudable safety record, Slow Mo presented no real threat to the accountant and his friend. In fact, he was really there to save them from themselves. But the bachelor party boys were no doubt unaware that Slow Mo was a uniquely benign bouncer. When it became clear that this hulking black man with an outrageous mohawk was about to enter the fray, one of the boys let out an ugly, ear-piercing shriek of horror. It was as if he had awakened in the night to find the space monster from *Alien* rearranging the bedroom furniture. Others in the crowd gasped out, "Oh my God!" or "Shit!" or "Fuck!" or other noises less intelligible as Slow Mo made his move. Stepping forward, Slow Mo pried the accountant off the back of his friend. As the friend fought to take his first breath in some time, Slow Mo lifted him off the ground. With the force of the move, the precious D-string went flying and landed in Bree's hands. With a quick flick of the wrist, Bree flipped the D-string to Winthrop.

"It's all yours, Jack," she said without missing a beat of her dance. "You'll probably appreciate it as much as anyone."

"I'll add it to my private collection," Winthrop said with a smile, thinking that the D-string might serve as a means of introduction to the amazing teenage dancer. Not exactly like returning a lady's handkerchief, thought Winthrop, but gallant nevertheless in its own way.

Meanwhile, both former combatants were still airborne. As Slow Mo held them at arms length, they continued to gyrate, moving their arms and legs in utter futility, each looking like a child's mechanical toy, winding down while being held in midair. Then as he slowly moved his head from side to side in an attitude of sadness and regret, as if he were personally disappointed in their behavior,

Slow Mo began to shake the young men. Back and forth, back and forth, he shook them until their bodies hung limp like victims of a hanging. Then with the much subdued crowd of bachelor boys trailing him in awe, he marched the seemingly lifeless brawlers to the door. Manny was there, tending the gate during Slow Mo's absence. Manny opened the door. Slow Mo took a step or two outside and then dumped the erstwhile rowdies onto the pavement. The bachelor party contingent exited as well to tend to the task of scraping their buddies off the sidewalk. They would one and all have some king-sized hangovers and bruised egos to cope with in the morning. Slow Mo stepped back inside and shut the door behind him. The accountant, thought Winthrop, would always associate headache and nausea with the commencement of marriage.

Inside the bar, order had been restored. Yes, finally, thought Winthrop, it's like home again, comfortable and private, a refuge and a haven from the world. There were still a dozen or so strangers in the bar, but they were quietly observing proper barroom decorum, unobtrusively killing off brain cells while brooding on the day's defeats and inconsequences. For the moment the mood was turning mellow, and Winthrop hoped it would last. Bree was winding down her set to the cool rhythms of a Herbie Hancock instrumental. Soon, Robin would take the stage. She was standing by the door with Slow Mo and Manny, sampling the salad. Winthrop caught her eye, and she smiled and raised her plastic fork in a gesture of sharing, but Winthrop just smiled back and shook his head. He didn't want food now—not even a Slow Mo salad. Instead, he needed to think. So he drained what was left of his beer and ordered a Jack Daniels on the rocks from Sheila to sip while he gathered his concentration.

It sometimes seemed to Winthrop that the world was mindless and that virtually everything in it conspired against thought. A few things helped. Jazz, blues, Jack Daniels, slow moving, naked women and the night—late, late nights at the Tit with the yahoos all gone.

When Sheila brought the Jack, Winthrop took a long, slow pull and closed his eyes. Instantly, he was back again in the plaza. And again he saw the long barrel of the rifle protruding from a window high up the Sherry tower. The rifle looked like death. It looked inhuman, but there was a human being behind it and a human finger on the trigger. Then came the shots; four of them, one right after the other. Four small explosions to the ear. Winthrop flinched as he heard the shots and again felt disoriented at the dislocation of sight and sound—seeing the silent, ugly rifle at the Sherry and hearing the volley of gunshots ring out from the Plaza Hotel. And his stomach dropped as he watched the silent rifle slide from view until it was gone like a dream, leaving behind only a memory as a witness that it was real.

Then Winthrop swung his binoculars over in the direction of the Plaza Hotel. Again, he scanned the floors, but the assassin was gone, escaping down the corridors of the hotel then back into the protective chaos of the Manhattan streets. With the sniper gone, Winthrop was leaning against Sherman's horse and turning his binoculars to the stage. The bodies lay there. The senator flailing like a fish; the talk show host motionless.

"You'd better go home and get some sleep, Jack." It was Robin. She was about to take the stage. Bree was stepping down.

"Jack wasn't asleep, Robin. He was thinking. I've never seen Jack asleep at the bar—or anywhere for that matter," said Bree over her shoulder as she made her way to the dancers' dressing room, where the teenage wonder had earlier disappeared.

"You look exhausted, Jack," said Robin.

A Chick Corea number was just starting up. Robin was sticking with jazz, and Winthrop approved. He smiled at Robin appreciatively, affectionately. "You're beautiful, Robin," he said. He paused and took another hit of Jack Daniels. "Thanks for your concern, but I'm really fine. I just need to chill out a bit, and I can do that better awake than asleep."

Meanwhile Robin had begun dancing, slowly and sinuously. It was immediately clear to Winthrop that she wanted some distance, too. Soon she would be floating, insulating herself from the world by the fluidity of her own movement. Then she could be naked and safe at the same time. Then, though everyone could see her, only special people could approach her.

As Robin floated off on her dance, Winthrop looked around the bar. Speck was still there, sitting at the end of the bar, looking every bit the closeted, conservative psychopath, brooding on God knows what. Just behind Speck, Manny was standing by the door, huddling with Slow Mo and Pat Mahoney, a Tit for Tat regular. Winthrop wanted to talk to Manny about the new teenage dancer, but that could wait until some other time. As for Donna, she was still hiding in her office. The tireless entrepreneur was apparently constructing elaborate Excel spreadsheets and concocting an endless series of pornographic what-ifs long into the night. Winthrop wanted to talk to her, too—but not yet. First, he needed to return to the Grand Army Plaza.

The shots had set off panic in much of the crowd. Most people were getting into each other's way, trying to run for cover. There were bone-crushing collisions. A few clumsy or unlucky people were trampled. On the stage the dignitaries had flattened themselves against the wooden floorboards at the sound of the shots. Now that the shooting had stopped, they leapt to their feet and ran for the wooden steps on the east side of the stage. Cardinal Boyle and Mayor Martinez got to the top of the steps at the same time and collided in Archie Bunker/Meathead style as they both pushed to be the first one off the stage.

With a silent laugh at the cardinal's and the mayor's expense, Winthrop ran down the three or four steps of the Sherman monument, losing sight for the time being of Jones and Bradley. Then he took off toward the stage, darting and dodging through the chaos. As he was crossing Central Park South, Winthrop again saw the angry black man with the illegible cardboard sign. He was standing in the middle of the street, waving the sign above his head and shouting, "The corpse is black. The corpse is always black." There was a small group of people, a collection of rubberneckers and blood voyeurs, standing about the stage. A sick human curiosity had killed their fears of the sniper. Now they were pushing and shoving to get a closer look at the damage.

The stage itself was filled with people, some in uniform, some not. As he jogged across the street and onto the crowded sidewalk, Winthrop took a series of quick visual snapshots of the scene. A few take-charge guys stood about defiantly, looking tough, as if bullets would bounce off their hides, while several no-neck professional wrestling types were shouting and gesturing. Half of the men were armed with assault rifles. It was as if they had plucked the guns out of the air. Others were crouched into positions of readiness, their eyes scanning the plaza, handguns drawn. Still others were leaning over the spot to the left of the podium, where Jones and Bradley had gone down. They had a look of concern and importance as if they had suddenly been thrust into Life itself. As if they were suddenly heroes in an American moment that would surely turn into history.

From years of working in New York City Winthrop had become an expert at snaking his way through a crowd. The secret was not to push. Instead you had to nose out the cracks and crevices in the shifting human mass. Once you understood that, it was simply a matter of Zen and flexible proctoscoping. And there you were at the front of the crowd.

It took Winthrop less than twenty seconds to move through the mob and arrive at the front of the stage. It had been less than thirty seconds since he had dropped from his somewhat precarious perch by the side of Sherman's horse—less than thirty seconds since he had last seen Jones and Bradley lying on the stage.

Since then Winthrop had tried his best to keep his attention fixed on what he could see of the action on the stage. When he got there he felt a rush of almost childish surprise, for Jason Bradley was gone. It was as if in the blink of an eye, some master magician—David Copperfield or Blackstone or the Great Renaldo—had made an elephant disappear from the stage. Because of all the twisting and turning that it had taken for him to move to the front of the crowd, Winthrop had found himself turned away from the stage several times—but only for brief, fleeting seconds. Yet somehow Bradley had gone without Winthrop seeing him leave. Perhaps he had left on his own power, crawling or crouching below Winthrop's plane of vision. Or perhaps he had been swiftly carried or dragged away. Whatever the means, to Winthrop, it was as if Bradley had simply vanished.

Meanwhile, Abraham Lincoln Jones lay on the stage, his bleeding imperfectly staunched by makeshift tourniquets made from ripped white T-shirts. Winthrop stared at him through the legs of the take-charge guys, the no-neck wrestlers and the other would-be American heroes who stood about. There had been four shots. Each of them had found its mark. Good-sized bites had been taken out of Jones's upper arms and thighs. Hot gun surgery, thought Winthrop. Just a little message from a maniac. A warning. It said, "Talk your talk, nigger. Have your crazy love-in with all the goddamn nigger-loving liberals of America. You'll see what you get. A bullet in the brain. And a slab in the morgue."

No doubt Abraham Lincoln Jones had gotten the message—long ago. He of all people did not need reminding. He knew, as Winthrop did, that if millions of Americans had gotten their black love connections for years from groove tubing it with Oprah and Bill Cosby and, yes, the marvelously controversial Abraham Lincoln Jones, still thousands (or was it hundreds of thousands or even millions?) of Americans got their black hate fixes from the same hypnotic and transcendent TV images. As he lay there leaking blood from the gunshot holes in his arms and legs, Jones was rapping out his own bullet-crazed counterpoint to the maniac's message. No one else seemed to be paying attention. It was as if they didn't even hear Jones's rant. But Winthrop felt that he was getting the chance to eavesdrop on the unedited mind tape of the Black Hole that swallowed America.

"I know who did it! I know who did it! I know who did it!" Jones repeated again and again until something in his overcharged brain tripped the track forward and he screamed, "History's motherfucker, motherfucker, motherfucker!" and Jones was stuck again, rasping out the obscenity for perhaps ten seconds until the real revelation inevitably erupted from the pit of his existence. "The white man!" he shouted. "The white man!" he shrieked.

The pause that followed this terrible declaration of fact made Winthrop shiver. Jones lay there, wide-eyed, his face drained of life, as if for a single moment he had stared down deep into the bottom of one global, timeless image of all the violence, all the injustice, all the hatred, all the pure, inexplicable evil that the white man had ever rained down upon the life of black humanity, and died. He lay there with the face of death for what seemed forever. When he finally blinked, his features softening with the pain of conscious existence, he looked directly up into Winthrop's eyes. Winthrop felt his heart stop and start again. He held his breath and returned Jones's stare, steady and true.

All around there was chaos. In the distance a siren roared, while the stage toughs and stage heroes maintained their TV poses, oblivious to the man they thought they were protecting. In the eye of the tumult Abraham Lincoln Jones and Jack Winthrop met. First in silence. Then in words.

"I know the white man," Jones whispered. "You know him, too."

"When you know," asked Winthrop, "What do you do?"

"Everything," Jones answered, "Or nothing."

Then he passed out. The siren became very loud. Then it stopped. And a team of paramedics was on the stage. They ministered to Jones as they had to thousands of others and as they would to thousands more, victims of old age, auto accidents, clogged arteries, domestic disputes, street violence, what not. Winthrop watched them carry Jones away. They slid his body into the back of the flashing ambulance parked on Central Park South, slammed the back door shut and jumped in. Then, with its siren at full blast, the ambulance sped away to the emergency room at Roosevelt Hospital.

5

Winthrop watched the ambulance pull away. Then he turned his attention to the stage once again. The men of action, the men of history, still stood there. But now they looked strangely shrunken—frustrated and diminished by the false call to action. Now they merely looked like a group of city policemen with too much time on their hands. For a moment there had been the hope of an exchange of fire over the body of a victim. Urban guerrilla warfare. The force of law against the madness of terrorism and assassination. For a second there was the possibility that the old primal itch could be satisfied in the most deeply rewarding of all experiences for the deputized man of action—a legal, public kill. Unfortunately, the sniper had not cooperated. He had fired just four shots in quick succession. Then he was gone.

Winthrop knew quite a few New York City policemen. He had gotten to know a number of them quite well during his time in the *New York Times* city room before he became a journalistic aristocrat and turned to writing a column three times a week. Most cops in Winthrop's view were normal people, sometimes peaceful, sometimes violent, sometimes fair, sometimes not. A few were among the best people Winthrop had ever met. They actually were public servants, brave and principled, risking their lives to maintain law and order, protecting people from the horrible commonplace violence of the city's streets and subways. Other cops, however, were thoroughly corrupt. They did whatever they wanted. They were on the take. They sold drugs. Ran guns. Appropriated the spoils of their arrests. Harassed and abused gays and transgender women. Beat up blacks and Latinos. Even murdered people when no one was looking. They did some or all of these things and were rarely caught. Most often they won commendations, had long careers, grew old and lazy on their pensions and spent their golden years improving their beer bellies and building legendary reputations as barroom storytellers.

Notwithstanding their criminality, these cops were sane. Call them bad cops. Call them common crooks. But don't call them crazy. They were tuned right in to what most people call reality. They knew what they were about. They were just good, healthy, meat-and-potatoes guys with a taste for licensed goon-squad crime. The real crazies were a different breed of cop altogether. The psychos were not in it for the money. Instead, blood was their currency. Violence was their psychic pay. The violence was not only gratuitous. It was deranged, devoid of moral content. Indeed, it was fundamentally anti-social, anti-human behavior. It was violence directed against people because they were people, vulnerable people, people without a voice or means to defend themselves. It was violence indulged in for its own sake. The psychos, in Winthrop's view, were neither evil nor crazy in the sense of being psychotic. Instead, they were morally insane. It was as if some vital element of their humanity was missing, as if something as essential to the psyche as the heart or brain was to the body had been left out of their makeup, and yet they had continued to grow and develop anyway. They had gone on living. They looked like normal human beings just as the body snatching pods of science fiction did. But like the body snatchers, they concealed an alien, monstrous nature behind the appearance of normality.

As Winthrop's views on New York City policemen in general and deputized psychopaths in particular flashed through his mind, he realized that Don Germany was among the would-be heroes standing on the Grand Army Plaza stage. Formerly a homicide detective, Germany was now a member of the new elite NYPD special security force. Germany was still staring up at the Plaza Hotel apparently in the hope that the sniper would respond to some absurd death wish and reappear at the window.

Winthrop had known Germany for years. Germany's real name was Felix Quinn, and Winthrop continued to call him Felix for the simple reason that he liked the name. However, Felix had legally changed his name back in the early '90s when he was promoted to detective. Don was Felix's favorite name. Germany was for the country. Felix was a nut about Germany. He was an expert on German history, loved German music, particularly Wagner, and while repudiating Hitler, he heartily embraced the old Teutonic military heritage. As he liked to put it, "Historically, Germans don't fuck around."

Not fucking around was a pretty good summary of Germany's code of living. He was a good cop in the sense that he wasn't on the take and was one hundred percent loyal to his fellow officers to the point of lying, if need be, in their defense and risking his life to back them under fire. He did his job with consummate seriousness, was obsessive about the details of investigations and had an encyclopedic memory of virtually every case he had ever investigated.

Despite his professionalism, Germany was also a legendary barroom brawler and snap-out artist. Germany could go weeks or even months without losing it. Then without warning he would snap. Almost anything could set him off; a physical confrontation certainly. But a word, a look or some vague gesture or body language might just as easily serve as the trigger.

One night Winthrop had the opportunity to observe one of Germany's performances. They were drinking around midnight at the Woodpecker Lounge, a neighborhood bar in what was once known as Hell's Kitchen. Winthrop was working at the time on a series of columns on the emergence of New York City street gangs as formidable crime organizations. He was in the neighborhood to check into what was apparently a gang- and drug-related murder. The victim was a sixteen-year-old boy named Terry McClain, a member of the West Siders and reputedly a major force in expanding the gang's influence into Northern New Jersey and Queens. McClain's naked body had been found in a Popeye's trash dumpster. He had been beaten, sexually tortured and shot in the head execution style. The word "Jams" was written in blood in graffiti script across McClain's chest. The Jams were a Jamaica, Queens, street gang that was apparently sending a message that it would not allow the West Siders to threaten its proprietary right to peddle dope within its own declared territory.

Germany was involved in investigating the murder, and Winthrop had succeeded in drawing him into talking about what he knew of New York City's gangs. Germany knew a lot, and something, perhaps the brutality of the murder itself, had put him in an expansive mood. The conversation had begun in a small coffee shop, and it was Germany who suggested that he and Winthrop continue it at the Woodpecker.

Germany confirmed some of Winthrop's own conclusions about New York's gangs in particular and street gangs in general. They had come a long way since the fairy tale days of *West Side Story*. Gangs were crime organizations. In many ways they were more ruthless than the Mafia. As Germany put it, "It's like these fucking kids were raised in a war zone or something. Like fucking Baghdad or the West Bank. Killing's nothing to them. Less than nothing. Or else it's a fucking turn on."

As Germany talked, Winthrop found himself growing increasingly uneasy. When they entered the Woodpecker, he sensed only the normal hostility that you get when you walk into somebody else's neighborhood bar. You're the outsider invading the home turf.

You'd better drink your beer and go or the local pit bulls will maul you. When he worked as a reporter, Winthrop found himself in unfamiliar, provincial, all-male neighborhood bars on more than a few late nights, and in the proper frame of mind he could actually sit back, relax and enjoy the hostility—at least from an anthropological point of view. The hatred was so pure, so mindless, yet ever so silent and deniable that it impressed Winthrop as quintessentially human. There he was, a fellow human being, a fellow American, a fellow New Yorker, for Christ's sake, sitting down after a hard day's night of work to drink his humble brew and what did he get from his bar mates? Poisonous thoughts. Stifled curses. The wish that he were dead. Yes, it was perfect.

The night with Germany, however, Winthrop felt that with each passing moment there was getting to be a little extra edge to the intimidation. Maybe the Woodpecker crew was perpetually in a rage since their bar, along with everything else on the block, was scheduled for demolition, legally condemned in the name of progress and gentrification courtesy of Mayor Hector Martinez. Perhaps the murder had raised the level of their frustrated hostility a notch or two. Perhaps, thought Winthrop, they were just a handful of hateful bastards. Whatever the reason, Winthrop could feel the hostility of the Woodpecker regulars increase with every word that Germany spoke. It was not what he said. Winthrop doubted that they were even bothering to listen to Germany's words. Instead it was the way he spoke and the way he looked—his words coming out in an intense, hoarse whisper with his lungs working away like a blacksmith's bellows, pumping hot, alien air into the barroom.

"These fucking kids. Christ, these neighborhoods are doomed," Germany whispered with feverish intensity, the bellows working away. "They ought to drop a fucking bomb on them. A little tactical nuking. Start all over. Easier that way. Then Martinez could put up his fucking yuppie boutiques and co-ops. That's what everybody wants anyway." And all the while Germany never once looked at

Winthrop, keeping his eyes fixed instead on the beefy, tattooed bartender with the greased handlebar mustache and shaved head and a little dried up turnip of a man whose every pore exuded alcohol, who Winthrop assumed, for God knows what reason, was the owner, Mr. Woodpecker himself.

As Germany stared and blew out his hoarse whispers of doom and destruction, Winthrop could feel the tension rise in the bar. He could feel the regulars collectively calculating the moment of attack, collaborating through the extrasensory mists of alcohol. At the same time he knew beyond all doubt that Germany was tuned in as well—his antenna, the ultra-sensitive psychic receiver of the flip out artist, enabling him to predict within a nanosecond the precise moment of his opponent's attack and take the offensive with a mad preemptive strike of his own.

As the tension reached its climax, Germany looked at Winthrop for the first time and spewed out the words, "Time to pay the fuck up," his spit catching Winthrop in the right eye. Then he jumped up in a flash, took one quick, connected hop-skip-and-jump for momentum, hurled himself sideways over the top of the bar in the manner of a traditional high jumper, and landed a perfect body block on the bald, tattooed bartender. The force of the block drove both Germany and the bartender into the rows of liquor bottles that lined the wall behind the bar, destroying the better part of the Woodpecker's supply of vodka, whiskey, gin, rum, rye, tequila and other assorted distillations.

Before Winthrop could react, he was grabbed from behind and lifted out of his seat. His first emotion was an indulgence. He felt the absurd and petty searing of hurt pride. Someone had actually gotten the drop on him despite the radar of paranoia, despite the extrasensory warnings—yes, his own psychic Star Wars system had failed him after so many years of existential research and an inestimable expense of mind, heart and soul. In the next instant, however, wounded pride and sentimentality were forgotten as Winthrop felt his arms separating from his shoulders. Just in time, he tensed every muscle in his body, reared forward and flipped his assailant. The man went flying over Winthrop's shoulder, cracked his spine against a bar stool and fell to the floor. With adrenaline pumping through his veins and memories of old movie saloon fights and cowboy heroes flashing through his mind (Alan Ladd! Gary Copper! Duke Wayne!) Winthrop braced himself to meet the charge of another Woodpecker adversary.

Winthrop had always wondered what would happen if he ever really uncorked one and let somebody have it right in the jaw. Would his fist smash through bone, teeth and cartilage, leaving behind enough damage to subsidize an East Hampton summer home for some lucky plastic surgeon? Or would his hand bounce absurdly and impotently off the presented jaw, as in some cartoon-like bad dream from which he would awaken in a sweat to escape his own comic destruction? It seemed for a second that he might finally have the chance to find out. At the last moment, however, his body shifted its tactics and produced a more lethal defense.

As the next attacker moved into the line of fire, Winthrop met him not with a fist but with a foot. Behind the bar the Turnip was riding piggyback on Germany. As Winthrop took two quick punter's steps toward his onrushing assailant, he saw Germany whip the Turnip off his back. In the next moment, the action was perfectly synchronized. As Germany flung the Turnip over the top of the bar and into the stratosphere, Winthrop punted. If the man had been a football, he would have spiraled. Fifty yards with a hang time of over four seconds. Winthrop had caught the man right under the chin. The force of the kick lifted him up and back against a bar stool, where he landed with a look of surprise, stared momentarily at Winthrop, spit out a tooth and slumped to the floor.

There were only two other Woodpecker men left—both of them now frozen in place. For a moment Winthrop thought that their reticence might have been inspired by his prowess as a barroom brawler. But when he glanced again at Germany, he saw that there was a much more persuasive and cogent reason for their caution: Germany had pulled his gun.

"All right, you fucking shit-faced drunks. The party's over," Germany announced. There was a brief pause during which Winthrop could tell that the thought of unloading his weapon on the entire Woodpecker crew came and went in Germany's mind. Then he resumed his announcement. "My friend and I are walking out that fucking door. If any of you fucking lowlifes move, I'll shoot your fucking balls off. Come on, Jack, let's climb out of this fucking pit."

Winthrop did not need a second invitation, although he waited for Germany to make his way slowly around the bar. When Germany reached the table where he and Winthrop had been drinking, he stopped. Without taking his eyes off the room, he reached down, grabbed his mug and drained the rest of his beer even though little more than the foam and spits remained. Then he and Winthrop moved out the door. When they got outside, Germany had a huge smile on his face. With his gun still drawn he turned to Winthrop and said, "Jesus Christ, Jack. That gets your blood going, doesn't it? What do you say we bar hop?"

"Felix," Winthrop called. Germany continued staring up at the Plaza, his gun drawn. A little German flag stuck into the lapel of his sports jacket picked up the gleam of the afternoon sun. "Felix," Winthrop yelled, "Hey, Felix, Mr. Germany, give it up. The guy's half way to Jersey by now."

Germany turned finally to Winthrop and threw back his head with a little laugh of recognition. Then he frowned. "That fucking guy's somewhere, and we'll get him."

Winthrop just stared.

"A fucking guy wants to take pot shots like that, but he doesn't have the balls to stick around for the real fucking party."

"Hey, listen, Felix. Where is it written that a killer doesn't want to live?"

"You say he went to Jersey. You call that living?"

"It beats rotting in a goddamn hole."

"Jersey is a goddamn hole, and you know it."

"OK. I agree. Jersey sucks. Most places do. But forget Jersey. Tell me. What the hell happened to Bradley?"

"He was gone in a flash. His security guys carried him the fuck out. Didn't look like he was hit or anything."

"Look, Felix, I've got to get to Roosevelt Hospital, but I've got something for you. Maybe it'll cheer you up. Maybe it'll piss you off. I don't know."

"So take your shot."

"Your friend at the Plaza isn't the only gunman."

"That's gonna cheer me up?"

"It might. Think about it, Felix. Where would you cops be without criminals? They're your meal ticket."

"I don't know why I like you, Winthrop. You've always hated cops."

"I'm just perceptive."

"So where'd you perceive this other fucking gunman?"

"Near the top of the Sherry tower, thirty-fifth floor—one of the full-floor apartments. He never fired a shot. When the Plaza guy opened up, he pulled back. All I ever saw was the gun. Some kind of high-powered rifle."

Germany smiled and shook his head slowly. His interest was definitely piqued. "What the fuck were you doing anyway, Winthrop, looking up there with those binoculars? Looking for girls in their underwear?"

"What can I say? I'm getting paid to be a voyeur."

"That's what all you news guys are anyway. A bunch of fucking pervs."

"Maybe you haven't heard. I'm still with the *Times*, but I'm also working with Jones."

"Hey, I heard. Who hasn't? You got enough play out of it. But let me tell you something, Winthrop. You don't like cops. I don't like your new boss. He's a loudmouthed fucking loon. I'm surprised somebody didn't shoot the bastard a long time ago."

Winthrop smiled. "Germany, you're such a sentimentalist. Listen, I have to run. Will you see what you can find on this? Not just the Plaza guy but the other gunman, too?"

"Hey, if there's any fucking thing to find, Winthrop, I'll find it."

"Keep me posted, OK?"

"Fuckin' A," said Germany to cap the conversation, and Winthrop was off to Mount Sinai Roosevelt Hospital.

The hospital was at 59th and Tenth—not that far. In this mess, the fastest way might be on foot. Winthrop was slim, trim, walked a lot and generally felt that he was in pretty good shape—until he tried to run. He would feel incredibly light afoot for the first fifteen or twenty strides—visions of a sub-four-minute mile flashing through his head. Then he would begin to fall apart fast. His calves, knees and thighs aching, his throat going sore, his breathing turning heavy, the lungs working hard, heart pounding, head exploding, body alarms going off in muscles and joints, everything signaling SLOW DOWN! Middle-age heart attack just one block away.

At twenty-five or thirty strides his run would turn to a jog, then to a walk-and-jog and private astonishment that even this compromise between the desire for speed and his body's need for emergency relief could not be sustained. Finally he would shift into a fast walk, modified Olympic style, and feel good again, back in his element, middle-aged, yes, but all things considered still in pretty good shape.

Today, however, he would have to push himself. Go beyond his normal limits. So he fought his way back out of the crowd and took off with a weekend athlete's optimism across the plaza and over to Central Park South. Because of the crowd, Winthrop kept to the street until he made it to the Helmsley, a side stitch torturing him at every stride. When he reached the Ritz-Carlton, just a few paces later, he'd had it and shifted into lower gear, promising himself, however, that he would at least sustain the jog until he reached Sixth Avenue. And somehow he did. Standing on the corner, his heart and head pounding out a percussive beat, Winthrop gazed at the flow of traffic. Typical, he thought, feeling a familiar sense of mild disgust. The street's jammed with cabs, and every single one is full. Even the goddamn gypsies.

When the light changed, Winthrop took a deep breath, blew the air out of his sore throat and slogged across the street, thinking, "Yes, it's true. I will be dead some day, and this proves it." His side stitch started up again too, a particularly sharp pain, knifing through him at the absurd thought that he would never get a taxi but would have to schlep the entire way to the hospital. Then he saw it—like a miracle, a gift from God—an unoccupied Yellow Cab headed his way. Thrusting his arm into the air while lunging fearlessly into the taxi's path, he somehow got the cabbie to stop.

"Roosevelt Hospital," he gasped as he climbed in, hoping for a maniac behind the wheel. And the cab took off like a rocket ship toward Columbus Circle for the short ride to the hospital.

Flying through the city in a taxi was one of Winthrop's private pleasures. Broadway was best, of course, providing—especially from the Park down through the 50s—the perfect manic flight path, a magnificent drag strip with rollercoaster rises and falls, glutted with people, jammed with traffic, all of it excessive and driven, and at night exploding with light, glowing in neon. Yes, Broadway was best, but rocketing in a cab down any of Manhattan's main streets, you got to see the city at its true velocity. As the cab picked up speed, everything around you accelerated too, and you realized that, yes, this was really it, this was the true pace and rhythm of Manhattan. You couldn't quite see it if you were walking or jogging or running or riding in a bus or driving a car at reasonable speed through the streets of New York. But in a cab, driven right, driven by a maniac, you could see it. You did see it. You saw the real city in operation—a mad, reckless machine, all but out of control. Unlike the cab, however, the city had no driver—not Mayor Martinez, not the police, not the people themselves. The city was running on its own inexhaustible energy, grooving on its own momentum, going faster all the time, forcing everyone in it to move at the same hyperbolic pace or be crushed, hit-and-run style, under its wheels.

Ironically, Winthrop never felt safer than when he was riding at warp speed in one of these crazy cabs. Then he would truly relax and observe the accelerations of the city, his chronic paranoia temporarily allayed. Now that he was seated in the very eye of the storm, he knew that nothing would get him.

In this state of secure and serene detachment, Winthrop would often speculate silently on the character and background of the cabbie and then engage in some exploratory conversation. Cabbies' backgrounds had become increasingly diverse and exotic in recent years as a result of a tremendous influx of foreign, and especially Third World, nationals into the ranks. Winthrop would often go dozens of cab rides without encountering an American-born driver. And he could not recall the last time that he had been in a Manhattan cab driven by a person who had actually been born and raised in Manhattan. In lieu of locals, he found Indians, Sikhs, Pakistanis, Afghans, Lebanese, Palestinians, Haitians, Cubans, Nicaraguans, Salvadorans, Maltese, Sudanese, Ethiopians, Turks, Iranians, Iraqis, Vietnamese, Laotians, Thais and Koreans in addition to newly-arrived immigrants from Eastern Europe.

As Winthrop rode to the hospital, suspended in the psychic security of taxi mania, he studied his driver's I.D., focusing first on the photo. The picture was worse than a mug shot. It reminded Winthrop of the photos that terrorists released of their hostages. The faces strangely devoid of expression, the eyes staring out across unbridgeable distances of human experience, eyes deadened by the affectless knowledge of doom—for their future held only three possibilities: death, endless captivity, or an ironic release into the lifelong prison cell of the all but unsharable hostage experience.

Winthrop noted the cabby's name, Muhammad Hassan. "Where are you from originally?" he asked as the driver swerved left to pass a lumbering city bus.

"Lebanon," replied the cabbie.

"When did you leave?"

"Oh, very soon, very soon."

"Very soon after what?"

"Oh, Long time, many years, but very soon, very soon after Sabra and Shatila. You know them? You remember? Very sad."

Sabra and Shatila were the Palestinian refugee camps where in 1982 Christian militiamen massacred hundreds of men, women and children. There had been so many massacres, but Sabra and Shatila stood out because of the scope of the brutality, and it had received a lot of coverage in the American press.

"Yes, I do remember. Very well," Winthrop said." Actually Winthrop had been to Lebanon twice. Once in '80 as a young free-lancer, he had gone on a tour of the Middle East and done a series of pieces on the monumental cultural conflicts within the region. Then he had returned in '83 as a newly hired reporter for the *Times* immediately prior to the suicide bombing of the Marines. Both times he had been overwhelmed—not only by the dimensions of the human tragedy, which was terrible, but by the insane and wanton destruction of what had once been one of the most beautiful cities in the world.

"You are not the usual American then," Muhammad said. "Americans remember only the marines."

"No, I remember Sabra and Shatila very well. I also know that Beirut was once a very beautiful city."

"Oh, most beautiful, most beautiful. I miss it. I miss my country very, very much. But no place for wife and babies."

"You have children then?" They were now at 59th and Ninth, just a block away from Roosevelt Hospital. They would arrive momentarily. Winthrop felt the anxiety that he had been harboring for Jones spike as he stared at the street sign.

"Oh, yes," Muhammad answered, "Two boys, men now—Mustafa and Qaddi."

"And your wife?"

"Very beautiful, very good wife. Her name is Farrah."

"And how about you, Muhammad? How are you?" Winthrop asked finally as the cab stopped short by the Emergency entrance to the hospital.

"I am very good, very good. Happy, always try to be happy, but, you know, also always sad."

"Keep the change, Muhammad" Winthrop said as he handed the man a twenty-dollar bill and stepped out of the cab. "I wish the best for you and your family."

"Oh, thank you, sir. You are very kind," he concluded and sped away to his next fare.

Winthrop walked from the cab, passed through the doors of the emergency room and was immediately struck by a double dose of nausea. One dose came from the hospital itself; the other came from a crazed mass of TV and newspaper reporters who had crammed themselves into the waiting room to get the scoop on the ALJ shooting. The combined associations of death and reportorial feeding frenzy made Winthrop literally gag. He had always associated hospitals with mortality rather than healing and avoided all contact with them except when dire circumstances forced him to do otherwise. He hated the sights and sounds of hospitals, and even the very touch of hospital surfaces suggested morgue drawers and toe tags hidden down the hall from the Coke and snack machines. But it was the smell that got to Winthrop most of all. It was a stagnant, captive, institutional smell shared to a greater or lesser extent by schools, police stations, court houses, prisons and churches—a smell that in hospitals was exacerbated by the combined scents of medication, alcohol, stale food and blood.

Hospitals were surely bad enough all by themselves. They told Winthrop in no uncertain terms what he already knew, namely that he was a disease-breeding, injury-prone, double-jointed sperm and egg combo that had accidentally bleeped onto the life screen one fine day or night as a result of a freakishly timed and positioned parental coupling, and he would sail off the screen on an as yet unknown calendar date in a geometrically satisfying flat line as a result of some equally freakish twist of fate. And this would happen to the ultimate discomfiture of no one—not even himself—providing perhaps to a jaded, amnesiac public some minor twitter of survival pleasure at the knowledge that yet another semi-notable name had indeed bitten the dust.

"Did you hear about Jack Winthrop?"

"Who?"

"Jack Winthrop, you know, the writer."

"Oh, oh, yeah, he's out of here, right?"

"Finished."

"I heard it on the news last night. Say, did you see Jeff Goode's report on the new *Golden Girls*?"

"Yeah, they're bringing back Madonna to play Blanche."

"They should have cast her as the mother."

"Right."

That was how Winthrop imagined it. Or some such conversation. Or quite possibly no conversation at all. So, indeed, for Winthrop, hospitals were bad enough. They signified you were toe jam, coffee grinds, squeegee gunk—blue-gray fibers in some self-cleaning cosmic lint trap. But add reporters and it was worse. Much worse.

Despite being a member of the esteemed profession, Winthrop hated reporters. They were by and large unreliable, especially TV reporters. Norman Mailer once wrote that the secret to talking to reporters was never to speak a sentence more complicated than they themselves could write. But Mailer's remark was more a statement of the problem than the identification of a workable solution.

Winthrop had himself been interviewed many times. And he still found it remarkable that he had yet to read a single piece on himself that did not include inaccuracies, misrepresentations or misquotes. Of course, the net effect of all this free-floating misinformation was probably salutary. If, for example, politicians were always accurately quoted, let alone represented in the light that they and their handlers deemed most appropriate, then the public would have no protection whatsoever from what would undoubtedly be a pure and unadulterated stream of self-serving, self-absorbed lies. So the jaded, cynical, shallow, inept and superficial Fourth Estate acted as a critical check and balance in the mix of contemporary American life. Winthrop would defend to the death their First Amendment right to add their own distortions and half-truths to the lies and deceptions of the politicians and celebrities they covered.

With such thoughts flashing through his mind, Winthrop stood in the foyer of the emergency room at Roosevelt Hospital—stood as Dante Alighieri Winthrop, gazing at the anonymous lost souls pressing upon each other in the roiling antechamber of hell. Off to the side of the infernal, madding crowd sat Bill "Jake" Barnes. Barnes was a bottom-feeding sea slug with a nose for news and cocaine. In fact, Barnes had received his literary nickname, courtesy of Jack Winthrop, not from any spiritual or physical resemblance to the unmanned Hemingway hero (of whom he had undoubtedly never heard) but instead from his incredibly annoying habit, while a colleague of Winthrop's at the *Times*, of running to the men's room at least twice every hour to snort yet another line or two of coke.

For Winthrop's money, Barnes was one of the best reporters he had ever seen. He was also one of the most reprehensible human beings on the face of the earth. Jokes abounded concerning Barnes's imperviousness to common human decency as he pursued his lofty journalistic objective of capturing the truth. There was even an apocryphal though nonetheless revealing story that circulated when Barnes's mother died. Supposedly, upon learning of the news, Barnes rushed to the parental homestead, burst through the front door, charged past mourning family and friends and found his father, who was dissolved in grief at the kitchen table. The moment his father looked up, Barnes thrust a microphone in his dad's face and said, "So tell me, Pop. How does it feel to lose your lifelong companion of forty years?"

Over the years Barnes had moved back and forth between local newspapers and TV. Rumor had it that he was about to go in a new direction, leaving his current gig at *The Post* to work as a correspondent for the *National Enquirer*. Winthrop wondered why it had taken him so long. Everyone needed a home, and Barnes would undoubtedly find one at the *Enquirer*, where "Inquiring minds want to know."

Winthrop knew that Barnes was enjoying a leisurely and studied observation of emergency room pandemonium because he had already gotten the word on Jones's condition and phoned it in while the remainder of New York City's elite journalistic corps awaited the official proclamation from a hospital spokesperson.

"Hey, Jackie boy," Barnes called out as Winthrop approached. "What do you have to say about this one? Somebody's playing with your home boy."

"Who'd you talk to Jake, the paramedics?"

"Yeah, I got lucky, Jack, as usual. Turns out my buddy, Fresco, was the lead guy that scraped poor Mister Master Blaster off the stage. I kind of needed a ride to the hospital anyway, so I jumped in with the boys."

"Why didn't I see you when they loaded Jones in?"

"Hey, you were too late. I was already inside."

"So what's the story?"

"Leaked a lot of blood all right. But he'll live. I always say some people got more blood to give than others. Some of it even got on the inside of my goddamn socks."

"Did Jones say anything inside the truck?"

"No, he was out, man. Almost turned white, he lost so much blood."

"No official announcement yet, I suppose."

"No, they're still working on him. Then they'll take him to either ICU or a step-down unit. That's when the poor slobs here will get the announcement. Of course, I got the pictures, too—and that's page one material."

"Fresco let you shoot inside the truck?"

"Come on, Jack, get with it. He never even knew I was shooting. Besides, I know Fresco'll never get fired. He supplies his boss, and he's got shit on half of the motherfucking assholes in EMS."

"Like I've always said, you're a good man, Jake. You get the job done. End of story. By the way, have you by any chance seen a young black woman, tall, good looking? She works for Jones."

"Danny Jackson? Sure, I talked to her too. She's pretty shook up. She may be outside the building, getting some air."

"Thanks, Jake, catch you later."

"You bet, Jack, and listen. You're with Jones now, so you got to be my main second-day source on this one. You know I'd do it for you."

"Right, Jake," Winthrop responded, drifting back through the electronic doors and onto the street in search of Danielle. As he walked over to 59th Street, Winthrop could picture her precisely, sitting over a coffee cup at a local cafe. However strange it might seem, he knew exactly where she would be and how she would look when he found her. So he walked toward 60th, walked another half block, went through the doors of Cafe Solo, and there she was, looking as he had expected her to look, looking younger than her twenty-four or so years, the edge and the certainty all gone, looking like a kid who had just seen her pet collie hit by a septic-tank truck.

She looked up from her booth as Winthrop passed through the door and tried vainly to put on the old face of confidence and self-assurance. Then she bowed her head and dropped a string of tears into an untouched cup of black coffee.

"He's going to be all right, Danny," Winthrop said as he slid into the booth and took her hand.

"Jack," said Danielle.

"We can talk to him tomorrow."

"I won't know what to say."

"Don't worry about it. I have a sneaking suspicion that, as usual, Abe will carry the conversation all by himself."

"But this changes everything, everything we planned."

"What was the plan?"

"You know, the tour, everything that Abe discussed, taking his message to the people. The whole plan, the dream, and they went and shot him before he even got started."

"Danielle, Abe got started on this road a long time ago."

"But he's always controlled everything. That's been the beauty of it."

"Look, Danny, Abe doesn't control shit. No one does. He's gotten this far through sheer luck or grace or good fortune. Call it anything you like. He was beaten up once a long time ago. Fine. That happened. Then nothing happened for years. OK. That's true too. But now someone's shot him four goddamn times, and he's still alive, and that's where we are right now."

"And tomorrow?"

"Tomorrow his brain will be working again, and his mouth will be working again, and we'll see exactly what's changed and what hasn't."

"But now somebody has actually tried to kill him."

"Come on, Danny, think about it for a moment."

"What?"

"Think."

"What?"

"Think about what happened. Just think."

"That he's not dead."

"Right."

"He's alive."

"And?"

"And so whoever shot him wants him alive."

"Why?"

"To get him again."

"Right."

Danielle turned to Winthrop and kissed him then. It was a surprising kiss, a revealing kiss, coming, it might have seemed, out of nowhere. But Winthrop knew that it had come from the heart, and, as he returned the kiss, he knew as well that they were feeling their way together, feeling their way uncertainly to try to find some solid ground.

When the kiss was over, Winthrop looked at Danielle for a long moment. Then he took a deep breath and said, "Listen, Danny, I need to take a walk. Would you like to come along? Later tonight we could meet some of my friends at a local bar."

"You're talking about the Tit for Tat, right?"

"You and Abe certainly seem to know everything about me," he said smiling.

"We don't have a problem, Jack, with the fact that you hang out at a strip joint."

"Well, it's a strip joint, and it's sort of home, too."

Danielle smiled. "Actually, Jack, I'd love to go with you, but not tonight. I love taking walks. And I'm sure your friends at the bar are great. In fact, I have a girl friend who used to dance there. Do you remember Maxi?"

"Sure. Maxi. She left about two years ago to work for CNBC."

"Right. Well, Maxi was my roommate at Columbia. She spoke highly of the bar—and she spoke especially well of you."

"Maxi's a good kid."

"She is. And very smart. But listen, Jack, not tonight. I really need to be alone now. I know it's going to get really crazy for me and for all of us after this, even crazier than it is now. And I need one solid night to chill out my head."

"Well, we'll continue this conversation at a later date to be sure," Winthrop said, giving Danny's hand a parting squeeze.

"To be continued," she responded, kissing him again a little harder this time as he was getting up to leave. And Winthrop knew then that his life had truly taken a turn. He knew, too, that he was bound to follow that turn wherever it might lead.

6

BACK AT THE TIT it was home indeed with Robin still floating freely to the music of Miles Davis and Bree lying on the bar, humming her own improvisational jazz tune, wearing only her Back Door Black D-string, her implants poised like sidewinder missiles, a glass of Cakebread Chardonnay by her side. Now there was only Donna to see, with the clock inching closer to 3:00 a.m. Winthrop rose slowly from his seat, noting that Speck was still sitting by himself at the end of the bar.

"Don't go yet, Jack," Robin begged. "I'm just getting off."

Winthrop tossed back an understanding smile to Robin and held out his hand to Bree for the slap of a lazy, ceremonial, high five as he made his way back to Donna's office, expecting, as always, God knows what, since Donna could at this moment be in any state, in any mood, at any point in her own personal day, having liberated herself by sheer force of a colossal appetite for work and pleasure from all ties to calendar time—day, night, weekday, weekend could not have mattered to her less. If she were hotly pursuing a new entrepreneurial project, as she was now with her vision of providing a subscription service of personal strippers, porn stars and escorts that could be downloaded to your cell phone or iPod, she might start her work day at 1:00 a.m., blow straight through the entire morning, afternoon and night without ever leaving her office and finish work only when she had reached some self-defined breakthrough point in her Napoleonic plan, celebrating her success perhaps with a bar-top dance before catching three or four hours sleep at her Central Park South penthouse apartment and then starting all over again.

As for Winthrop, he felt as if he had been in love with Donna from time immemorial. And he had certainly lusted after her since men first stood erect. But he had long since learned that Donna was always and forever unattainable. That was her beauty and her strength, and Winthrop admired her fierce independent spirit, despairingly yet resignedly, more than he could ever express. After a short signature knock, Winthrop entered Donna's office.

"Jack," she said. "You're here now." Discarded spreadsheets lay scattered across the desk.

"I'm here," Winthrop replied.

Donna leaned back and smiled, her legs spread wide and stretched out on the desk, her skintight black leather skirt hiked by her angled legs a good eighteen inches above the knees. Donna took a long satisfying hit of her Stolichnaya. As a vodka purist, Donna eschewed ice, choosing instead to keep her Stoli in a personally designed D-inscribed marble cooler and connect the deeply chilled alcohol to her mouth by a series of interlinked crazy straws. "You know, Jack," Donna said. "You were the first thing I thought of when I woke up today—or I should say, yesterday."

"What time?"

"It was one of those 1:00 a.m. days. I couldn't sleep anyway. I just knew I was ready to put the whole service together—the talent, the membership, the pricing, the staffing, my cut—Jack, you won't believe the fucking cash that's going to come from this download deal."

"No, I can believe it."

"It's positively overwhelming. So with all that going on in my head I just couldn't sleep, but as I jumped out of bed, already planning my calls and crunching numbers, suddenly there you were."

"Me?"

"Yes, and it's weird because I thought to myself, here I go again. Whenever I get really turned on by my work, I need to fuck."

"And you thought of me."

"Jack, you know I love you and your cock more than just about anything in the world."

"Why do I sense a 'but' coming?"

"Well, because you can see by now I'm totally exhausted. It would be all I could do right now to crawl under these spreadsheets and finger myself to sleep."

"This is my second rejection of the day."

"You do get around, don't you, Jack? But, listen, what about the shooting? I'd like to strangle the lowlife motherfucker who shot Abraham Lincoln Jones. I love that man. He's the one person aside from you who has the balls to tell the truth."

"The good news is he's going to live."

"What about your gig with him?"

"This certainly raises the stakes."

"Meaning?"

"Meaning we were planning a barnstorming, in-your-face tour of the country. Abe is calling it his Emancipation Tour. We were going to talk about the real issues, the human issues. The ones the politicians lie about or ignore."

"Exactly. The more real, the more human, the more important— the bigger the lie. But now what are you going to do?"

"That's Abe's call."

"But, Jack, don't you know what he's going to do?"

"I think so, Donna. You're either in the game or out. And you don't get out when a bullet tells you how real it was all along."

"Just be careful, Jack."

Winthrop looked back at Donna for a long moment. Then he

smiled and said, "Listen, Donna, I promise to be the very first sub-scriber to your download service, but the next time you wake up thinking about my cock, would you please do me a favor and call?"

"I owe you one, Jack."

"Just one?" Winthrop replied.

As he turned to leave, Donna said, "I'm serious, Jack. This psycho is playing around. And I've got a sick feeling he wants to play with you, too."

Winthrop nodded and walked out of Donna's office. Noticing immediately that Speck's seat was vacant, he kept on moving past the bar, past Robin and Bree, on to the door where he gave Slow Mo a friendly tap on the shoulder and exited alone into the street.

*   *   *   *

WINTHROP'S APARTMENT was not a typical bachelor hole. It was perfectly neat, and the neatness was part of a simplification process that was transporting Winthrop with astonishing rapidity to one of two destinations—absolute, unassailable good health or alcoholism. He would find out which one when he got there—unless, of course, it turned out that the two destinations were not mutually exclusive but in his case somehow co-existing, interactive realities, the one refining and distilling the other.

An illegal alien, a young woman from Brazil for whom Winthrop most definitely did not pay FICA, cleaned the apartment once a week, although in recent months there had been precious little to do. As a gesture toward adding purposefulness to her life, Winthrop left his bed unmade on the days of her visits and might also, if it occurred to him, place his much-used Edgar Allen Poe coffee mug in the sink, waiting to be hand-washed and dried. Beyond that, there were only dusting and spot cleaning the kitchen and bathroom, each of which betrayed signs of only the most minimal use.

Typically in the cupboard there were only Maxwell House coffee,

coffee filters and several bottles of vitamin C. In the refrigerator, a bottle of Louis Jadot Pouilly Fuisse or Cakebread Chardonnay and several six packs of Poland Spring water. In the freezer, ice cubes. In the living room, a fully stocked bar of hard liquor, with the inventory skewed heavily in the direction of 1800 and Jack Daniels. Since Winthrop drank coffee for breakfast, skipped lunch, never ate dinner at home and hated snacking, there was no food in the apartment whatsoever.

Winthrop found the less he ate, the clearer he thought, and the clearer he thought, the less he really knew about anything, acquiring in the absence of knowledge an increasingly fine, acupunctural sense of the absurd ambiguity of existence. At no other time in his life had he ever felt that sense as acutely as he did now, approaching the door to his apartment—not even upon the deaths of the Kennedys, Martin Luther King or John Lennon. Not on the day, coincidentally or not, of his twelfth birthday, when he realized that he and his parents would never communicate in any meaningful way despite anything that the three of them might strive to do over the next half century. Not in the instant when he realized Donna was unattainable. Not even in the moment when he realized that he would always remain a stranger to himself, faithful as ever in his own life to the ineffable laws of quantum physics, which dictated that the measurer would always change the measurement and vice versa, with each always a little ahead or a little behind the other until all one had finally was a passport photo of oneself with the wrong name and face.

No, not even then had he felt such an overwhelming sense of absurd ambiguity. No, because this particular moment, this singular epiphany, striking as Winthrop opened the door to his immaculate apartment, both contained and transcended all those previous bulbs of incandescent truth. In fact, the revelation was so strong that it literally stank—of burnt wiring, charred rubber and displaced electrons—stank indeed like a short-circuited dishwasher—so much so that Winthrop had to remind himself that he had not used the infernal machine in months.

Revelation. Winthrop actually thought of the word as the reality opened in his brain, opened with the unashamed vaginal innocence of a Georgia O'Keeffe still life. Yet in this instance the opening was foul, an exposure of another kind, like the opening of a Rafflesia plant that reeked of decomposing meat.

What made the revelation even more powerful was the consciousness that this was the kicker to his conversation this evening with Rita—the business about his naiveté. The acknowledgement, however sincere, had come too easily. It had been glib, superficial. There were depths beyond the apparently ironic admission that Winthrop was naive and depths within those depths, and he was learning again as he moved with this revelation through the surface and into the depths how little he knew of the truth of his own thoughts and ideas or the meaning of his words.

And so the revelation came all in an instant and yet in dimensions and perspectives as well that Winthrop's mind could identify and dissect. There were the lessons: yes, Winthrop, you are still naive. Other bubbles must burst. Your paranoia is true to life. And there was the moral and psychological categorization: yes, Winthrop, this is evil. This is psychotic. This is sick. And there was also the personal threat. Not just to Abraham Lincoln Jones, Winthrop, but to you, yes, you, brother. There is no exemption for you or anyone else. You, too, must suffer. You, too, will die. But, above all, there was the single word, the monosyllable, that contained all these associations and more. It was the word itself that stank, that burned the air and set off psychic alarms as Winthrop entered his home. The word that spoke of misery and tragedy, forever stalking, ever ready to strike. And that word, that revelation, was Speck.

Yes, Speck was the one. He was not a mere projection of Winthrop's malignant mind. He was the one, and Winthrop could feel his presence, almost feel the warmth of his breath even as he could most certainly smell the terminal rot of the man's psychosis. Not that Speck was now in the apartment. No, that would have been too simple. But rather that he had penetrated Winthrop's life, had invaded his senses, had stolen his privacy and his refuge, had usurped his very home.

Slamming the door closed, Winthrop walked rapidly through the living room and into his bedroom. He picked up the phone. A red number 1 showed on the answering machine. Winthrop hit play and heard Rita's animated voice.

"Hey, Jack, it's about two. I knew you wouldn't be home yet, but I just wanted to remind you about the demonstration Sunday at St. Patrick's. I spoke to Callie—you know, Callie, with the gorgeous buns—and she says everyone's in agreement. No violence. No smart bombs or nukes. Just some very assertive nonviolent resistance. As a good ex-Catholic, Jack, this is right up your alley, so please be there if you can. 10:15. It'll be worth it just to see the expression on the good cardinal's face. I'm going to go now. All's quiet here. Karina's a doll, a little sleeping beauty. Hope to see you on Sunday. Bye."

Winthrop hung up the phone and waited. One second, two. The ring was like a primal scream. Winthrop picked up immediately.

Silence. More silence. Then the voice. "Nigger," it said. "Nigger."

"Speck," Winthrop replied.

"Call me anything you like, nigger."

"So you do speak."

"Depends on the subject, nigger. I can be very talkative. But you know the old saying, 'Bullets speak louder than words.'"

"So what's the subject, Speck?"

"The subject? Why, it's you and me, the two of us, and your pathetic African-American friend, Mr. Jones."

"So you want to play, Speck."

"Play, you say? Here's how I play, homey."

"Jesus," Winthrop screamed and threw the portable phone across the room as the one hundred megaton sound blew right through his left eardrum, shot through his brain and exited from the right side of his head. For Speck had most certainly fired a gun directly by the telephone receiver.

"The bastard," Winthrop gasped, his head pounding in the after echo that reverberated in wave upon nauseous wave. Falling onto the king-size mattress and squeezing hard against the sides of his skull in a futile attempt to reduce the pain, Winthrop now knew what it must be like, sound like, feel like, to blow one's brains out—if such an apocalyptic event could be experienced in the nanosecond prior to annihilation. He also knew that he was truly dealing with a radical, psychopathic artist of the absurd.

Of course, Winthrop should have seen this coming. It was evident everywhere in the country, everywhere in the world. From the original Speck who had murdered eight student nurses to Charles "Texas Tower" Whitman to John Wayne Gacy and Juan Corona and the Son of Sam and Ted Bundy and Jeffrey Dahmer and Henry Lee Lucas and BTK and finally all the anonymous, never-to-be-caught psychopathic mass murderers and serial killers who hated women and children—hated all the beautiful, young boys and girls who, because of them, would never have lives—who hated beauty and truth because they themselves were not beautiful or true, who hated goodness and greatness because of the wretched smallness of their own lives. Yes, it had been there, been obvious for ages. And it had become an increasingly intimate part of Winthrop's own life, of his life as a writer and of his life at the Tit for Tat.

For Speck was actually the third generation Tit for Tat psycho. The original Tit for Tat psycho was a biker, and, unlike Speck, the biker did talk, but only on rare occasions and only about guns and motorcycles. Also, he would speak to no one but Pat Mahoney. Pat taught English at Medgar Evers High School and knew absolutely nothing about guns or motorcycles. In fact, he had never held a gun or ridden a motorcycle. Pat's contributions to conversations with the biker were usually limited to frequent demonstrative nods and affirmative remarks such as "Really," "Hmm" and "That's something." The biker never seemed to mind or even notice Pat's minimal participation in these conversations.

Winthrop learned from Pat that the biker, who called himself D, was a founding member of the Chain Gang, a combination motorcycle club and crime organization. According to Winthrop's sources, the Chain Gang was a thriving entrepreneurial concern doing several million dollars a year in drug trafficking, prostitution, protection and contract killing, the latter an activity in which D was reputedly proficient.

Whenever Winthrop found himself observing D, he always experienced a nagging sense of déjà vu. There was something strangely familiar about the man, but Winthrop simply could not place it. After months of observing him once or twice a week at the bar, it finally came to Winthrop in a flash. D was actually Bobby DePietro. Winthrop had not seen DePietro since they were boys. They had been classmates at Our Lady of Lourdes Elementary School. One day DePietro returned home after his sixth-grade classes to find his mother lying dead on the kitchen floor with a bullet through her head. His father was down in the basement. He was dead, too, hanging from a copper pipe. A handgun was lying a few feet away on the washing machine.

DePietro never returned to school, and in fact was never seen in the neighborhood again. The rumor was that he had been sent to live with an aunt in Rockville Centre but had run away immediately and was never located again.

Winthrop was sure that DePietro did not recognize him and decided against approaching him. Winthrop's identification of DePietro was confirmed several weeks later, however, when a third subject was added to Pat Mahoney's conversations, namely D's mail. One night without explanation D asked Pat if he would be willing to receive his mail for him. Pat maintained his own post office box so that he could receive hard-core porn and conduct kinky personal ad correspondence without his wife, Joan, knowing about it. So he gave D his post office box number and let him know that he was welcome to use it.

"Anything addressed to D or Robert DePietro or Bobby DePietro is for me," said D.

Periodically Pat would bring up the subject of D's mail. "You know, about your mail," Pat would say.

"Just save it for me," D would always say in response.

Pat never had the heart to tell D that he had never received any mail for him. Finally Pat did receive a piece of mail for DePietro. It arrived shortly after D was killed when his Harley collided head on with a double tractor-trailer. Pat received news of the fatal accident from his wife. Joan had gotten a call at about midnight one evening while Pat was at the Tit for Tat. There was a man by the name of Stump on the line asking for Pat. Joan indicated that Pat was not at home.

"Then let me ask you one question," said Stump. "Does your husband hang out at a strip joint called the Tit for Tat."

"Yes, I suppose he does. Sometimes," Joan admitted, not sure where the conversation was leading.

"I've been going through the Pat Mahoneys in the phone book," said Stump. "I just thought your husband should be told. So give him this message. Tell him Bobby DePietro got killed today in a head on with a double tractor-trailer." Stump then went on to add a few grizzly details concerning Bobby's injuries, which included the loss of an arm and a leg. "Like I said," Stump concluded, "I thought your husband should be told, you know, by somebody who knew Bobby. Bobby used to talk about him. He said your husband was a good guy."

The letter was addressed to the family of Robert DePietro. It was from the owner of the trucking company. He was looking for somebody to sue. A follow-up letter arrived a month later. But after that there was nothing.

A few months after Bobby DePietro's death, Ray Hallee arrived on the Tit for Tat scene. If DePietro was rather taciturn with the

exception of his conversations with Pat, Ray was positively garru-
lous. He talked constantly to anyone and everyone whether or not
they listened. His conversational range was, however, limited. Ray
had, by Winthrop's count, essentially six topics: the dark side of the
moon; pancakes; the intelligence of dolphins; the music of his supposed second cousin, Bill Haley; his fears of homosexuality; and the
peculiar delectability of cat food.

Ray's opinions were firmly established as well: the dark side of
the moon was inhabited by invisible gremlins; the marvelous variety of pancakes was a blessing of God, and it was most difficult to
determine if chocolate chip or potato pancakes were best; dolphins
had souls and were smarter than human beings; Ray's cousin, Bill
Haley, was the greatest rock star of all time; the fact that one may
have had a homosexual experience did not make one homosexual;
and canned cat food was the perfect hors d'oeuvre.

Over the eighteen months or so that Ray patronized the Tit for
Tat, Winthrop had perhaps fifty extended conversations with him.
No matter what tactic he used to try to lead the conversation in a
new direction, Ray would always find a way to return to the familiar
ground of one of his obsessions. The old standby of talking about
the weather invariably led to gremlins, as did discussions of science or technology. ("Science is poppycock, Winthrop. The gremlins will have their way.") Music inevitably brought up Bill Haley or
dolphins. (Ray owned an album of dolphin sounds.) In fact, references to any product of human intelligence or imagination such as
books, films or art suggested to Ray the genius of dolphins. Women
or sex led to homosexuality, which led to gremlins. ("Gremlins are
gay.") Restaurants and food inspired intense, if one-sided discussions, of pancakes and cat food. And politics elicited speculations on
the structure and dynamics of dolphin society or an update on Ray's
campaign to have the governor name pancakes the official food of
the State of New York.

Winthrop rarely disputed or questioned any of Ray's assertions.

On one occasion he did, however, ask how Bill Haley and he could be related since they spelled their last names differently.

"That was my doing," said Ray. "I changed the spelling of my name to H-A-L-L-E-E so that I wouldn't be accused of trying to capitalize on Bill's success."

"Well, your strategy has certainly worked," said Winthrop.

"Of course," Ray replied.

As a result of their many conversations Winthrop was able to uncover a few basic facts about Ray's personal life. Ray lived in a small Lower East Side apartment with his widowed mother, Ida. They had two pets: Sal the parakeet and Pat the cat. The household subsisted on Ida's social security benefits and Ray's commission-only job selling extended service contracts over the phone for a local appliance dealer who had been a friend of Ray's father. It was no doubt Ray's limited means that prompted him to nurse a single lemon lime seltzer through the entire evening at the Tit for Tat until Winthrop or Rita would spring for another or Sheila would offer him one on the house.

Actually Winthrop was both amused and frightened by Ray. He enjoyed Ray's obsessions and was taken with his talent for wacky non-sequiturs, but he considered him more lost, more troubled and perhaps, in his own way, even more dangerous than Bobby DePietro, whose penchant for crime was more or less conventional. And he saw no way whatsoever of approaching Ray's problems. As usual, thought Winthrop, real problems had no solutions. That's why they were called problems in the first place.

From time to time Winthrop was frightened, too, by Ray's innocuous appearance. He looked like a big, overgrown baby, with thin, sandy hair, a moon face, smooth whiskerless cheeks and a torso covered with rolls of baby fat. Winthrop could imagine Ray chatting amiably about dolphin intelligence with concentration camp inmates as he led them to the delousing showers at Auschwitz. And he could likewise conceive of Ray discussing cat food and gremlins with the Son of Sam, David Berkowitz, as they sat together in their bathrobes and pajamas watching the Flintstones in the rec room at Attica State Prison. As far as Winthrop was concerned, Ray was a time bomb, a ticking time bomb hidden inside a child's roly-poly toy.

On Ray's last night at the Tit for Tat, he had cornered Winthrop and was animatedly debating the comparative merits of chocolate chip and potato pancakes. Winthrop's attention, however, was focused on a celebration. It was Bree's twenty-first birthday. On cue Donna and Rita had begun honking on noisemakers the tune of a rowdy, triumphal march. Meanwhile, Manny Snider was placing a huge birthday cake on the stage. Winthrop noticed an out-of-touch Ray putting on his coat. "Ray, aren't you going to stay for a piece of Bree's birthday cake?" Winthrop asked.

"I've finally decided," said Ray, ignoring Winthrop's question. "Potato pancakes are best." With that, Ray turned and left the bar.

The next afternoon, Winthrop saw the story in the *Times* city room. Normally a candidate for page one because of its sensationalism and follow-up potential, the story was targeted for the New York/Region section because of extensive coverage of a suicide bombing in Baghdad that had killed more than a hundred people, including a dozen U.S. soldiers. According to the report, a thirty-eight-year-old man by the name of Ray Hallee had stabbed his sixty-eight-year-old mother to death with a Boy Scout knife. Winthrop immediately phoned Don Germany, who provided him with some additional details not included in the *Times* report.

The basic facts were as follows: some time between 2:00 and 3:00 a.m., Ray murdered Ida, stabbing her forty-eight times with the Boy Scout knife. Apparently Ray also fed Sal the Parakeet to Pat the Cat. Then he strangled Pat and disemboweled him. At 9:00 a.m. Ray walked into the local SPCA office and confessed to the sacrifice of Sal and the ritual killing of Pat. When an animal abuse caseworker went to Ray's apartment to investigate, she found Ida lying in bed with the Boy Scout knife still in her.

Even though he felt he should, Winthrop could not bring himself to visit Ray in jail. He was simply too shaken by the murder. Although he had often contemplated the possibility that Ray would one day do something terrible, he found himself having an extremely difficult time accepting the fact that Ray had actually done it. Yes, it was deeply disturbing to have one's paranoid fears confirmed.

Finally, one day during the relatively brief trial, Winthrop dragged himself to the courtroom. When Ray spotted Winthrop, he gave him a big smile and a thumbs-up sign and shouted across the courtroom, "Potato pancakes are best."

Winthrop somehow managed to stay until the noon recess, but he did not return for the afternoon session, and he never saw Ray Hallee again. Ray was found not guilty of the murder of his mother by reason of insanity and was sent to Attica State Prison, where he would undoubtedly spend the rest of his life.

So much then for Bobby DePietro and Ray Hallee. But what now, thought Winthrop. Now he was involved in something far more serious. Now it was his own life. Before there was always the guilt ridden, phony distance of the perpetual survivor. Bobby DePietro was the guy with his parents dead and his life ruined. Not Jack Winthrop. Bobby DePietro was the guy who took a header into a double eighteen wheeler, while Jack Winthrop was healthy and happy. And Ray Hallee, he was the one with the genetic misinformation, the one with the DNA curled this way and that, the pathetic little nobody with his life screwed up on a molecular level—this gene combining with that one to produce, God knows what, a freak or geek or mutant human of warthog strain that the self-righteous religionists through pretzel logic called evil—not, no, never Jack Winthrop, Mr. Pulitzer Prize. Mr. Write-the-Shit-Out-of-Experience. Mr. Whoremaster O'Lucky with a draft exemption from life itself. Mr. Black-And-White Races, ye shall come together over me, for miscegenation is my middle name. No, not Jack Winthrop. Not Jacko, the Prince, the Kennedy of his own imagination. Not, he, himself. No. Never. He was not the psycho. He was not the target. He was not the victim. Until now.

And "now," Winthrop realized with crushing certainty, was all that mattered. Everything else was a mind game. But "now" was reality. And now his ears hurt. His goddamn head hurt because some worthless psychopath had just shot off a gun by a telephone line that led directly to his own personal, self-inscribed, mono-grammed eardrum. And now, with his head migraining to the max, he not only felt like the target, he somehow felt personally, indeed conspiratorially, involved with the psycho, involved with Speck. For Winthrop knew down to the bottom of his own miserable existence that the closer you looked into the eyes of another human being, the more you saw yourself.

And so, as he slowly sank from exhaustion into the comforting vales of sleep, Winthrop dared to look into the eyes of all the peo-ple who had made up his life—looked into the eyes of his mother and father, of his childhood friends and teachers, all the priests and nuns; looked deeply into the eyes of Donna, Rita, Slow Mo, Sheila and all the Tit for Tat regulars; looked across the divide of race and experience into the eyes of Danielle and Abe; and finally looked hard through the mask of psychosis and into the eyes of Bobby DePietro, Ray Hallee and Speck. It was all there within the men and women, the whites and blacks, the sick and healthy. In every pair of eyes Winthrop saw something very near and something quite distant, saw something he knew and something he did not know, saw something human and something alien. And in everyone and everything he saw, there was always his face, strange in its familiar-ity, breaking unavoidably and inevitably through the reflecting pool. It was all too much, thought Winthrop, too much to bear. Then exhaustion overcame pain, and he released himself into the free fall of deep, oblivious sleep.

7

VOID. DREAMLESS SLEEP. Suddenly a small group of men and women, dressed in white and wearing surgical masks, begin working assiduously, busy as PBS beavers, implanting some type of metal device between the lobes of Winthrop's brain. Winthrop does not know what the device is, but he wishes they would stop since he is very tired and he would like to go back to sleep.

The workers finish quickly, sewing Winthrop up, and congratulate themselves on the successful operation. Everyone synchronizes watches, and a young black nurse in a white bustier and D-string begins the countdown—ten, nine, eight—and Winthrop knows. They have installed an alarm in his brain loud enough to waken every living being in the entire solar system. Helpless to prevent the inevitable, Winthrop joins absurdly in the countdown—three, two, one, zero! Armageddon and apocalypse as the infernal siren blows the doors off outhouses beyond the rings of Saturn!

Rolling over with a groan, Winthrop picked up the phone and gasped, "Yeah," as a sledgehammer came down on his head, marking the official beginning of the single worst headache of his life. Unable to grasp complete sentences, Winthrop concentrated on key words only.

"Jack . . . Danielle . . . Abe . . . miracle . . . press conference . . . one o'clock."

He managed again to say, "Yeah," say it in fact several times at what he took to be strategic points in the transmission and hung up. It was 8:30. That gave Winthrop more than four hours. He rose slowly to his feet and pointed himself in the general direction of the kitchen. Poland Spring, Maxwell House, Krups coffee maker and filter. Pulling the plug of the coffee maker out of the wall, he grabbed his Poe mug and headed clumsily, hands quite full, for the bathroom. After dumping his awkward cargo on the bathroom counter, he took one of the longest pisses of his life—just a hair over a minute—placed the coffee maker on the toilet seat, plugged it in and set it up with coffee and water for ten cups. Then he stripped off yesterday's clothing, turned on the bath faucet full blast and eased his wretched body into the tub.

The intensive care unit of the Hey Jude Hospital for Impossible Cases was now officially open for business. Jack Winthrop, Hey Jude's Chairman, CEO and sole, chronic patient, leaned back into the warm, bubbling water and began focusing on the naked Sheena Bradley doll hanging precariously from the shower nozzle. Danielle, he thought, as the comforting pig grunts of the Krups reverberated from the toilet, Danielle, our friend, Abe, is one amazing man— one amazing man, indeed.

*   *   *   *

GERMANY WAS WAITING in the main lobby of Roosevelt Hospital when Winthrop arrived a little before one, slipping through the crowd of ALJ fans who had been standing vigil on the street and in the lobby since the shooting. "Hey, Winthrop, you look like shit," Germany called out in greeting.

"This is my new look, Felix."

"No, it's your old fucking look. It's you, my friend."

"I'm glad you got my message."

"No problem. You know who else called me this morning? Your buddy, Barnes."

"Barnes?"

"Yeah. Mentioned the press conference. Wanted to know if I'd picked up any new information on the shooting."

"What'd you say?"

"I told him I got better things to do than find out who shot some loudmouthed black celebrity. Fucking people get shot every day. What's the big deal?"

"Felix, you're definitely one of the good ones."

"Hey, Barnes is a fucking asshole. Why should I tell him anything?"

"You have anything I don't know already?"

"All I have so far is your unimpeachable eyewitness report."

"Well, I've got something else for you, Felix. That's why I wanted to see you. It's about our friend in the Plaza."

"Yeah?"

"I know who he is."

"How the fuck do you know?"

"Trust me. I know. It's a guy I've seen hanging out at the Tit for Tat."

"That strip joint in the 40's off Lexington?"

"Right. I hang out there. And I've been keeping an eye on one particular guy for weeks. The guy never talks to anybody. I always thought of him as a psycho. When I got back to my apartment late last night, it just hit me. Like a goddamn religious experience. I just knew he was the one. Then two minutes later, there he was on the phone."

"He called you?"

"Yeah, on my home phone. I've always kept it listed—it's a reporter thing."

"Smart. So what's the deal with this guy?"

"Like I thought, he's a psycho. A stalker. I don't know his name. But I've always thought of him as Speck."

"After the guy who killed the nurses?"

"Yeah. He hates blacks. Hates Jones. Called me a nigger. Fired his gun off by the phone and almost blew my goddamn brain right out of my skull."

"Well, you know he's a fucking joker. You probably already figured this out, but this Speck character is playing with your guy. Put holes just a little nastier than flesh wounds in both arms and legs. The biggest danger was that Jones would bleed to death."

"That's what I understood from talking to Barnes. He rode with the paramedics."

"That little prick gets his nose in everywhere, doesn't he? So you knew then once they stopped the bleeding, Jones was out of danger."

"And ready for Act II."

"Right."

"I definitely get the feeling we're going to see Speck again."

"You're probably right. What's he look like anyway?"

"Nothing. Looks like a computer programmer. You'd never notice him except that he looks so invisible."

"Did he confess? Did he take credit for shooting Jones?"

"Not exactly."

"What did he say?"

"He kept repeating the word, 'nigger.' Calling me a nigger. I said, 'So you do speak.' He said, 'Depends on the subject, but bullets speak louder than words.' I said, 'What's the subject?' He said, 'it's you and me and your pathetic African-American friend, Jones.'"

"Good stuff, Winthrop. Doesn't prove shit. But it's good stuff. Now I suppose you're going to tell me your two gunmen are off on their own separate psycho trips."

"Exactly. There's no way Speck would ever work with anybody else."

"You going to write about any of this? So far you've been keeping the Sherry business a secret."

"I'm not ready to write about anything yet."

"Good."

"I want evidence. I want proof just as much as you do, Felix, on both gunmen. So let's see what you can find out first. Maybe then I'll have a real story to tell."

"Let's start with a bug on your phone. I'll get a couple of my guys to monitor it. Have a car watch your building."

"OK. When Jones gets out, Felix, make sure security is tight around him too. I know there'll be a security plan, and he'll have his own people involved, but double check the arrangements. And do me a little favor. Jones's assistant, Danielle Jackson. Keep an eye on her, too. Have a car watch her building."

"You got a hard-on for her or something, Winthrop? Why would this guy care about her?"

"Just a hunch."

"OK. You're the man with the big visions. We'll do the girl, too. And listen, don't worry about your drinking buddy, Speck. I'll find him. And I'll try to turn up something on the Sherry guy, too."

"You're the best, Felix. Thanks for everything."

"You got it, Winthrop."

"Later, my man."

"Later."

*   *   *   *

AFTER STOPPING AT INFORMATION, Winthrop took the elevator to the tenth floor. Jones was in a private room, having been moved early in the morning from a step-down unit where he was under observation following his emergency room treatment. At about the third or fourth floor Winthrop's hospital phobia began kicking in once again. Of all the stereotypical fantasies perpetuated by the mainstream pornographic media, the least credible, thought Winthrop, was the one about the erotic, ministering nurse. Who could even think about sex in a hospital?

As the elevator bumped to a halt and the doors opened, Winthrop realized once again how much his own peace of mind and happiness were based on diversion and denial—realized it all the more as he heard in the distance the buzz and tumult of life resurgent and felt in his own veins the pulse of the indomitable Abraham Lincoln Jones. What energy, thought Winthrop! And, really, what courage, what death-defying nerve, despite all the theatrics.

"Places, everybody, places. This is a set," exclaimed a directorial voice, and, yes, it was indeed Barry Bream, with Danielle standing tall and composed by his side, yesterday's uncertainty and doubt apparently all gone.

As Winthrop entered the room, Danny mouthed the word, "Jack," and blew a subtle kiss in his direction, while Jones raised his eyebrows and nodded once or twice in magisterial approval. *The ALJ Show* was ready to roll once again—this time with an audience of about a dozen handpicked reporters and TV news personalities. Winthrop knew them all. There were two or three true journalists, depending on how one categorized the ubiquitous Barnes, along with the usual collection of hacks, pretenders and TV mannequins. In view of the tremendous publicity surrounding ALJ's shooting, the local network affiliates and independents had all sent their anchors. Present were CBS-TV's Katlin Saunders, named in an informal poll among *Tit for Tatters* as the most fuckable woman on New York TV news, and Matt Brophy of the local ABC affiliate, the most fuckable male.

"I know you all have your questions," Bream continued, "But ALJ has a statement to make before the Q&A begins. Abe."

"Thank you, B.B. Thank you all for coming. And most of all, thank you, my people. I know I sound like one of those old-time Catskill Mountain comedians, one of those Henny Youngman,

Friars Club guys. Mr. Saturday Night. But this is the truth. I got a real love thing going with my people, and they got it going with me. Sometimes it may seem like a love/hate thing. But it's really deep down brother-and-sister love. Family love. And that means something.

"Danny here has been monitoring the calls and the emails and all the vigils going on—here in the lobby, outside Radio City, outside dozens of TV stations that carry *The ALJ Show* all around this country. And it's a love vibration that keeps on coming, keeps on going. So I want to say thank you, my people. Thank you, one and all.

"Now that's the first part of my statement. Here's the second part. When I got shot yesterday, when those bullets hit me, everybody got shot. Everybody was hit. When I say 'everybody,' I mean all the people, all my people, everyone who believes in the dream, everyone who holds the vision of harmony and peace among all races, all minorities, all the dispossessed and disenfranchised, all the real flesh and blood people who just want to work hard, love their families, draw a little enjoyment from life and live in peace. They were the targets, right along with me. And this is no ego trip, people. This is not TV. This is not *Entertainment Tonight*. I'm not talking legendary jive. Mythical B.S. I'm just speaking the truth.

"Brother Martin knew this. You could see it in his eyes. See it especially the night before he was murdered when he spoke to the Memphis sanitation workers. He knew the hate mongers go after the leader; they go after the symbol of the dream, but they really want to get everyone. That's why they love the swastika and all that Nazi goose-stepping crap. The skinheads, the neo-Nazis, the Church of Latter Day KKK—all the gun toting, book burning, pure breeding, wife beating, nigger hating, Jew baiting, white supremacist groups. I know them all. I've had them on my show many times, many, many times. And they've got a look in their eyes too. They've got their own dream, their own vision. And that nightmare vision, my friends, is our future Holocaust.

"So I say here today to the man who shot me, the man who is targeting the people: You can't touch me. You can't touch any one of us. You can't really touch anything. And you will not stop us. You will not succeed. We shall overcome. We shall continue as we always have.

"On behalf of all the people, on behalf of everyone who cherishes the dream of equality, I vow that I will carry our message forward. I will carry on the work. I will rise out of this would-be deathbed and take this great message to all the people throughout the land. That is my mission. Touch what this hateful man cannot touch. Do what this assassin cannot do with his guns and his bullets. Talk to the country. Embrace its heart and soul. Bathe our nation in the cleansing waters of freedom and equality. Communicate with the people. Communicate with America.

"That's it. That's the word. That's my statement. Now I'll take your questions. "Barnes, you go first. You look like you're going to die if you don't get a chance to open your mouth and ask a question."

"Thank you, Mr. Jones. Good to see you recovering so quickly. But that raises a serious question. Given the nature of your wounds, don't you think this gunman is playing some kind of game with you? Couldn't he have easily killed you if he wanted?"

"Sure this man's playing. It's a game with him. But like I just said, he's not going to win. He's not going to stop anything. The people shall overcome."

"OK. I heard everything you said," Barnes continued. "But let me just ask this anyway. You seem to believe the shooting was racially motivated. Assuming that's true, why do you think you were the target?"

"Because I am the racial lightning rod. My people love me. But you know something? Sometimes the more you're loved, the more you're hated as well. You know I am not now and never will be a middle-of-the-road Negro. A black Mr. Rogers singing about the beautiful day in the neighborhood. I got my views, and they are strong views. I've been expressing them since I was a cocky kid DJ back in the sixties, expressing them in your face, my brothers and sisters, and I will continue to do that—continue to slam dunk my ideas right down the throats of the real enemies of America at every opportunity. Now, when you do that, there are bound to be some negative repercussions, right?

"You've seen that old Santa Claus movie, *Miracle on Thirty-Fourth Street*? Well, that's how much mail I get every week, and a portion of it's hate mail. We've turned it all over to the police. Haven't we, Danny? Decades of poison and venom. And it will take the police some time to go through all of it, believe me. John?"

It was John Garvey from NBC. "Mr. Jones, initially there were multiple eye witness reports of another gunman. The police have said that these were a result of the confusion of the moment and that there's no physical evidence to suggest there was anyone other than the Plaza sniper. Do you have any additional information on another gunman?"

Winthrop stared straight ahead. In just a few minutes Jones would definitely have additional information. Yes, he would share what he knew with Jones and Danny and Bream. He was on the team. But he'd be damned if he was going to breathe a word to any of his highly esteemed colleagues. Let them get their own leads.

"Hey, John," Jones responded. "Don't look to me for more information. I was just a little bit busy at the time all this was happening—bleeding all over poor Senator Bradley. I didn't see a thing. I just know what the police have said. Katlin?"

"Mr. Jones, you mentioned your hate mail. Perhaps it's unlikely, but do you or your people have any idea who might have done this from the mail you've received or from any other sources? Thus far the police don't seem to have a clue."

"Let me put it this way, Katlin. I know him. I just don't know his name."

"Meaning?" Katlin asked.

"Meaning I know the man's core. I know how he thinks. I know what he believes. The man's core is hatred, see. Pure hatred. When he thinks of me, he thinks "nigger," and he thinks niggers are animals. Now, what does he believe? That's simple. He believes in death. Death is what he wants more than anything else. Death is his only friend."

That was right, thought Winthrop. Death was Speck's only friend. Jones had done it again. Amid the theatrics and hyperbole he had touched the truth. Speck was alone except for death. It was his ally, his confederate. He could always depend on death. On the other hand, without death Speck was nothing, a mere cipher that somehow occupied space without ever really existing. Death shaped and framed his play. It sharpened his master plan of torture, serving as both limit and purpose.

Winthrop half listened as the reporters continued with their questions: What did Jones feel when he was shot? Did he think he was going to die? When did he learn that Senator Bradley had not been hit? What did the senator, governor and mayor have to say on their visits earlier this morning? When would he be leaving the hospital? And so on and so forth. But it was all mere background music as Winthrop ruminated further on Jones's stark perception. Death and Speck. Speck and death.

Suddenly it was all so clear—Speck's character, yes, but more, much more than that. And it all came down to one thing—death. Embrace death as a friend and that was it. There were no bounds, no limits, no restraints. For all that existed had been nothing and would come to nothing in the end. And, however cowardly, however craven, one could become a superhuman actor in that apocalyptic drama through the amplitude of murder and the nullity of suicide. Through serial killing, mass murder, pogrom, holocaust, genocide. Through a personal, biological war against life. Through the choice of evil, for it was unmistakably evil, despite the sickness, despite the psychosis and, yes, despite the absence of meaning. It was the heart of darkness, the silence of the lambs. It was skulls on bamboo poles and trophies in the refrigerator. It was evil. It was Speck.

Hearing again the director's megaphone voice, Winthrop rose from the depths of his meditation.

"Final question, ladies and gentlemen," exclaimed Bream.

"Last call for alcohol!" countered an increasingly buoyant Jones as the reporters clamored to extract one last sound bite. "Morton, we'll give you another shot. After all, you are from *The Times*."

It was Morty Lawlor, Winthrop's colleague from *The Times*. Lawlor somehow blended the hardcore investigative skills of Jake Barnes with the manner and acumen of an Ivy League philosophy professor. It was an odd combination, which Winthrop found by turns annoying or amusing, depending on his mood. Today he could go either way.

"Mr. Jones, we all know of your love for the theatrical. We also know that you've always been a man to speak your mind and that you have a wonderful forum for doing so in your nationally syndicated television program. I sense, however, a difference in you today. In your opening remarks you spoke quite eloquently of the dream of equality and alluded with something of an evangelical fervor to a mission. Exactly what are you proposing to do once you leave this hospital? Are you planning, for example, to run for office? Was this your first campaign speech?"

As he had done so often in the past, Morty Lawlor once again put his finger on the truth. He had divined the real message. It was the mission of greatness, the proposed ascendancy of Jones from celebrated TV slug to national savior, a transfiguration to be accomplished, however, not by any conventional campaign but instead by the crazy alchemy of the Abraham Lincoln Jones Emancipation Tour.

"Morty," Jones answered, "I've been campaigning my whole life.

A good liberal like you should know that. In fact, I know you know that. You got to know that like every other black person, I've had to campaign for a place for myself in this country, a place where I belong, a place where I can live, a place that I can call home. It's a fact. It's not an opinion. It's a fact that I live with and my brothers and sisters live with each and every day. When your ancestors were kidnapped and enslaved and brought here, how can it ever be any other way? Maybe it's impossible, but that's what I'm campaigning for. I'm campaigning to find another way. And not just for black people. What about all of the people who have come here to find another way, but they just don't have the right papers, the right documents? Latinos, yes, but really people from all over the world, people of every color—brown, black, yellow, and white. Yes, white people, too. They and their children—all of them looking for a dream.

"Now I just said people of every color, right? But I did leave one out. I left out one very important color, the color red. Because the red people, the Native American people—they're a special case. They're homeless too, but unlike everybody else, they didn't come here. They were already here, and to this very day—the few that are here, the very few whose ancestors survived the genocide that nobody ever talks about—they are homeless; they are dispossessed. And what's more, they are treated each and every day like they are invisible—like they don't even exist.

"So that's why I said I've always campaigned. Life is a campaign for me and for all of my brothers and sisters of every color. Forget public office. Forget politics. Politics is over. Nobody believes in that any more. The faith is gone, Morty. The faith is gone. But the people are still out there, see. They're out there in the void. And that's where the campaign begins. Address the void. Admit it's there. Then you can fill the void. Throw off the chains. Liberate the body. Liberate the spirit. You say it sounds evangelical. It sounds religious. Well, you're right. It is. It's goddamn religious. We're talking about freeing the soul from its burdens. Freeing the soul of America—that's all Americans, all the colors of the old Jesse Jackson rainbow. Soon as I get out of here on Monday, that's what I'm going to do.

"Go ahead, Jack. You do the honors. Yeah, there he is, everybody. Turn around. Right there by the door, Jack Winthrop. You all know him from the *Times* and the Pulitzer Prizes and *The New York Times* Bestseller List. Earlier this week we announced that Jack was joining us in a new role. And here he is with us today. My friend, my partner, the great orchestrator and executive maestro of the once-in-a-lifetime, transcontinental, all aboard, transcendental, free the slaves, Jesus saves, body and soul, lick the bowl, give me more and shut the door, Abraham Lincoln Jones Eeeh-mancipation Tour!"

For one solid moment, longer than a lifetime, Winthrop stood there stunned. Astonishingly, the reporters had turned to him and were applauding. Somehow, Abraham Lincoln Jones had transformed his hospital room into a talk show. *The ALJ Show*. The reporters had become the audience, and he, Jack Winthrop, was now the guest.

"Well, yes, thank you, Abe," Winthrop responded, as he struggled to recover his composure. "Thank you. That was quite an introduction. Hello, everyone. Good to see all of you again. As Abe just announced, we are planning a U.S. tour. It will include quite a few major cities. We'll release the itinerary as soon as it's set. As Abe just described so eloquently, the whole purpose is to contact America. To communicate. To break through the boundaries of traditional politics and mainstream media. We are going directly to the people with Abe's mission and message."

"So you're taking *The ALJ Show* on the road?"

"Not really, Katlin. It's that, but it's also a great deal more. Again Abe has really said it all already. This is a campaign to reclaim the soul of America. We will let America speak. We will give the country a hearing. We will provide a public forum to open the lines of communication. And while we're at it, we'll make a little noise too. Put on a show. Get a little loose."

"You said it, Jack!" Jones exclaimed. "That's my man, folks. Now you see why I teamed up with Jack. I don't need and I don't want no handler, no media consultant, no architect, no pollster telling me what I got to believe and what I got to say. No Karl Rove, no Dick Morris, no Karen Hughes cooking up lies and seasoning them just right so they go down nice and tasty, not too spicy, not too sweet. No, I don't work with no PR spinmeister, no puppeteer, no master of mass hypnosis, Svengali-ing the country. I only work with an artist. And that artist, people, is Jack Winthrop." Jones gave a barely perceptible nod, and Bream stepped forward once again.

"That's it for now," Bream said. "Abe thanks you all. The entire ALJ family thanks you. We love you."

As the reporters filed from the room, Winthrop shook hands and exchanged good-byes. Barnes was the last one to leave. He sidled over to Winthrop with a knowing look on his face. "I got to hand it to you, Winthrop. You finally wised up."

"How's that?"

"PR. Show biz. This is a whole new career for you. Congratulations."

"As Abe just said, this isn't PR."

"Yeah, right. You're talking to me, Winthrop. Give me a break. If it isn't PR, then what is it?"

"I don't know what it is. That's what I'm looking to find out."

Barnes gave Winthrop an even more jaded look, sniffed and strolled out the door. Winthrop looked across the room toward Jones. For the briefest of moments they shared again that meeting in the plaza, the meeting of two human beings, beyond race, beyond differences. Then the curtain came up and the show went on.

"Jack, my man, way to handle the announcement!" Jones exclaimed.

"Thanks for throwing a fast ball at my head."

"Hey, that was nothing for you. You can handle anything. That's why we're partners. You know where I want to go. You're the mission man. You're the maestro. But, hey, Mister Jack, let me introduce you to my old friend Barry here. Barry Bream. Jack Winthrop."

"Pleasure to meet you, Jack."

"Same here," said Winthrop, shaking Bream's hand. On the show, it had always been so incongruous—Bream, all buttoned up, Ivy League, white bread—the polar opposite of ALJ, but it was even more incongruous, even more puzzling, to consider that that they had been a couple on and off for years. Bream was fiercely protective of his relationship with Jones, and Winthrop would have to tread carefully around that. Then, of course, there was Danny. That was altogether another story. As he looked from Bream to Danny and she looked at him, he thought, you did kiss me yesterday, didn't you? And her look said, yes, kissed you twice, and the next chance I get I'm gonna go and do it again.

"Jack," Jones said, "I understand Danny and you are already the best of friends. No introductions needed. So now the whole goddamn family is here. Let's go over the game plan. Today's Saturday. My doctors are as stubborn as I am. They're keeping me here one more day, so first thing Monday morning, I'm out of here. What you say we have a little celebration at lunch? My apartment. Trump Tower. Give us all a chance to go over the details of the tour.

"You all heard what I said. You all know what I'm going to do. This is it. This is the chance. Jack, you said it, too. We are going to let the American people speak. We're going to listen to them. And they are going to listen to us. Back and forth. Two way. Human intercourse. Intercourse, PA. No limits. No restraint. Just the uncensored soul rocking and rolling, laying out the message, bare-assed on the stage. We'll have the decibels. We'll have the lasers. We'll have the special effects: the fireworks and explosions and the multimedia images and objects, all the techno-wizardry flying through the crowd, but we'll have the silence, too. The listening silence. The silence that enables speech. Jack, you know this. You know this well. You're the writer. You know the silence."

"Yes, I do know, Abe," Winthrop said and could say no more. But he looked at Jones, and Jones looked back, and Winthrop looked at Danny and Bream, and they all looked at each other until finally Jones began to laugh and everyone laughed together.

"Hey," Jones said, "Getting shot can make a man turn serious. Turn a man into a philosopher. Of course, most philosophers should be shot. Don't know the hole of experience. Don't know about bleeding through the hole. Bleeding through the void. Don't know about the special pain. But we gonna tell them, children. Gonna say it out loud, real clear and strong, so even philosophers like old Morton with his NYT Ph.D. can get it right along with the rest of America."

"You got that right, Abe!" Danielle shouted. "We gonna make it happen!"

Winthrop smiled, but he was actually thinking about Bette Davis of all people. Bette Davis in *All About Eve*. "Hold on, everybody," she declared. "It's going to be a bumpy ride." Yes, Danielle, Winthrop thought, all this was going to happen. Yes, Jones was going to say it. Gonna tell it on the mountain, even if the mountain was a pile of bull shit built of talk itself. And, yes, Bette, it was going to be one hell of a bumpy ride. And there he was, little Jackie Winthrop, with his pants pressed, his cowlick flattened, his ticket ready and his P. T. Barnum hat in hand, all ready to hop on board.

"Listen, Abe, Danny, Barry, I've got to tell you all something," Winthrop said. "I know who the gunman is."

"Jesus Christ almighty!" Jones exclaimed. "Who did I hire as my tour maestro, Bruce Wayne, the Batman of Gotham City?"

"No credit for me on this, Abe. Turns out the guy who shot you hangs out at the same bar I do."

"You mean the Tit for Tat, Jack?" Danny asked.

"Right, Danny."

"Isn't that a topless bar?" Bream asked, looking at Winthrop as if there were something fundamentally wrong with him.

"You're not going to believe this, Jack," said Jones, "Especially since he's been working for me for so many years, but good old B.B. here is a goddamn prude."

Winthrop raised his eyebrows. "Yes, Barry," he answered, "It is a topless bar. It's where I hang out."

"May I ask why?"

Now Winthrop looked at Bream as if there were something wrong with him. "Well, Barry, you meet some very interesting genitalia there. Other than that, I don't have a clue. But that's not important now. What's important, Abe, is I know who shot you. I couldn't prove it in a court of law, but I know it's this guy who's been coming to the bar. I've always thought of him as a psycho. Thought of him as Speck, a psychopathic killer. Well, late last night he called me at my apartment. Kind of a terror call. Called me a nigger, mentioned you, Abe, and fired off a gun by the phone. I've let the police know. One of my special contacts is working on it. The point is the guy is very dangerous, and I got to believe he'd try something again. After all, he could have killed you easily if he wanted to, Abe."

Danny and Bream looked disturbed, but Jones was smiling. "I know that already, Jack," he said waving around his bandaged arms and legs. "I know he's dangerous all right. I know he's playing. I surely got that point. But you know what? This doesn't change a goddamn thing. We sure as hell knew it was somebody, right? Knew he got away. Knew he could try anything. Now at least we got some kind of handle on who he is. So this is good news."

"I've got some other news too, Abe." Pause. Pause again as Winthrop took a deep breath. "You know about all the false reports of another gunman. Garvey just asked about it again. Well, there was a second gunman. He was up in the Sherry-Netherland. I had my binoculars on the building. I saw a gun pointing out of a window up the tower at the moment the shots came from the Plaza Hotel. As soon as that happened, the gun in the Sherry window disappeared. And that's all I know about the other gunman. Again, my police contact is working on all of this. The only other thing I can say is that I'm almost certain that the two gunmen are entirely separate and unrelated. There's no way Speck would ever work with anyone else. He's a total loner."

"Jack, I'm shocked by all this," Danielle said. "Why didn't you mention the Sherry gunman yesterday at the coffee shop?"

"I didn't want to get into it then, Danny. It just wasn't the right time. But now we all have the same information. We're a team. If any of us gets additional information, let's share it."

"I certainly hope you don't have any plans to share this with your readers, Jack," Bream said.

"Barry!" Danielle exclaimed.

"Really, Danny, my sole concern is Abe, and for the sake of Abe's safety I feel very strongly that Jack should not disclose any information. Who knows how that might hamper the police investigation. I'm pleased, Jack, but somewhat surprised that you haven't rushed out already to get what you know into the *Times*."

"Listen, Barry. I appreciate your concern, but I know how to balance my commitment to Abe and my responsibilities as a journalist. I'm not about to jeopardize Abe's safety. If I write anything, Abe, I'll talk to you about it first."

"Hey, everybody, chill out here," Jones said. "Barry, Jack's cool. If he wasn't cool, I never would have asked him to join us. So, Jack, you make your own goddamn decisions."

"Thanks, Abe," Winthrop said. "Actually, I don't have much to go to press with. What I saw at the Sherry won't necessarily be any more believable to most people than any of the other eyewitness reports. As far as Speck is concerned, as I said, I don't have any real proof. I just know what I know, so I'm playing it by ear, working with my police contact, seeing where it all leads."

"Fair enough," said Jones. "Now why don't you two kids take off," he added, looking at Winthrop and Danny, "Barry, you and I got some bore-ass details to tend to about my security when I leave here." Jones began to chuckle. "Got to get deep into the security thing now that I've become a victim of urban violence. Two gunmen, huh, Jack?" Jones continued to laugh. "Just remember, guys, at lunch on Monday—it's the plan to take over America."

So they said their good-byes, and Danny took Winthrop's hand, and at that moment he felt the train pull out of the station, moving slowly, almost soundlessly at first, gliding down the track with the force of inevitability. And Danny's hand clutched his, tighter and tighter, her leg rubbing hard against his as they moved down the hospital hallway. Then she pulled him by the hand, and they ducked into—Oh my God, thought Winthrop—an empty bathroom! Empty by chance. Empty by the luck of the Lord.

And nurse Danielle began kissing him right there on the spot—so there you go, wrong again, Winthrop, why not make a career of it, for experience is the great teacher and there is sex in hospitals after all, or at least kissing—and Danielle was speaking to him now in between the kisses. She said, "Dinner at 8:00, Jack. My place. Get yourself ready for some real home cooking." Then she went back to kissing him hard on the mouth as Winthrop's brain played the chorus to REM's "End of the World" over and over again.

8

DANNY ANSWERED THE DOOR WEARING A TOWEL. It was purple and pink, and it said, "Welcome to Margaritaville."

"Jack!" she exclaimed and planted a big, wet kiss smack on his lips. "I've barely had a chance to shower. I've been working so hard on the dinner, thinking about nothing but the tour. Pour yourself some wine. I'm really into vino," she said as she sauntered back to the bathroom. "It's right on the table—Cakebread Chardonnay."

"How'd you know I like it so much?"

"I called the Tit for Tat and spoke to Rita. What a marvelous person! I talked to Donna, too," she shouted and closed the bathroom door, leaving Winthrop to his own considerable devices, the terra incognita of Danielle's apartment stretching out before him. As the water ran in the bathroom, Winthrop poured a glass of the chilled Chardonnay, took in a deep, satisfying breath of the seafood and asparagus in the air, the breath of a voyeur about to gourmandize, and set about on a sweet, leisurely exploration of Danielle's apartment.

The living room was small but simply and comfortably furnished in cool, contemporary decor—two white leather swivel chairs with matching love seat; a small white marble coffee table; complementary end tables; oddly shaped, tubular black metal lamps, a handmade eight-by-ten Persian rug (blues, greens and browns against a pristine white background); original water color abstracts signed by unfamiliar women artists, and books, everywhere books, filling tall, substantial handmade mahogany bookshelves lining the walls.

Winthrop approached the shelves with great anticipation, savoring sips of white wine. Examining a woman's books was almost as good as going through the contents of her underwear drawers. There was so much to learn, and it would all come so quickly, so easily, so intimately.

Like Winthrop, Danny was organized. The books were arranged alphabetically by genre—literature, contemporary affairs, history, philosophy, travel, cooking. Winthrop was impressed with the breadth and eclecticism of the collection. He had pegged Danny as a reader. She was too clear headed and articulate, too committed in her idealism, to be strictly a child of blogs, chat rooms and video games. But the extent of the library was a wonderful surprise. Winthrop had met voracious readers before. Rita was one. His cousin, Lenny, his high school history teacher was another. Of course, he was one himself. But this was something special. This was truly the daughter of Susan Sontag.

Absorbing quickly the concentrations of taste, Winthrop noted a mix of surprises and confirmations. In literature, Victorian novels and romantic poetry predominated over contemporary literature, with collected works represented and well-thumbed, though, judging by the signs of usage, Winthrop gave the nod to Eliot and Dickens as the most favored among the Victorians with Keats and Blake winning the battle of the Romantics.

Among the contemporaries there was a healthy representation of black and women writers, with John Edgar Wideman, Toni Morrison and Sylvia Plath apparently special favorites. In the contemporary affairs section, Winthrop found numerous works on urban culture and race, including his own, as well as books on the power and influence of the media. In the field of history Danny preferred American, with volumes on the revolutionary war, the American Indian, the Civil War and Vietnam turning up with the greatest frequency. In philosophy her taste was toward existentialism. In travel, she favored the Far East. And in cooking, it was French and Italian. A number of disparate, uncategorized titles grouped alphabetically by author at the end of one bookshelf were particularly interesting. There were, for example, gathered together Michael Chekhov's *To the Actor* and Selma H. Fraiberg's *The Magic Years* as well as the *Hite Reports* and *Miss Manners Guide to Excruciatingly Correct Behavior*.

It was a miracle, really, thought Winthrop. He had always viewed his own personal education as something of a miracle given the abysmal, reformatory quality of the Queens Catholic school system in the sixties and early seventies, with its emphasis on rote learning and corporal punishment. At a certain point it was as if he had simply awakened and discovered himself engaged by writers—Poe, Twain, Hemingway—by politics and by rock and roll. No matter how hard he tried, he could never trace his engagement back to its beginning, back to the first moment of revelation, back to the initial spark, back to the creation of his world. He wondered now how it had happened for Danielle. How had she been saved, or how had she saved herself from the epidemic of ignorance and apathy that was infecting America?

Winthrop had no illusions about idealizing Danielle. And he had few illusions about himself. He knew that he continued to labor under a species of seemingly irremediable illiteracy that reflected itself in a million different ways, and he knew his many flaws, lapses, weaknesses and vulnerabilities. He also knew that there were vast expanses of his character and personality that he would never understand. He was sure that Danielle was no different. They were both after all nothing but human, stuck in the swamp of their innate depravity, as the Puritans so aptly phrased it. But somehow they had been saved, blessed by God knows what, blessed perhaps by the force of an irresistible grace transmitted through biochemistry and the accidents of experience, blessed, alas, with intelligence.

As he heard the water shut off in the bathroom and the hair dryer turn on, Winthrop suddenly felt a great urge to strip off his clothes, crawl beneath the covers of Danielle's books and cocoon his life away. Danielle would join him there after retrieving her gourmet dinner from the oven and setting up IVs of Jack Daniels.

"I have my books and my poetry to protect me," so sang Paul Simon, but that was before his hair fell out and his partner left him. That was also before Speck. Long before Speck and the second gunman. Sure, there have been Jack the Rippers from time immemorial, but psychosis had always been something of an elitist pursuit, harrowing the Gothic margins of life. Now America had democratized it, had marketed it, had brought it into the mainstream like everything else. "You too can be a nut," the Home Shopping Network announcer would promise. "Call now for your own do-it-yourself psychosis kit, including a complete guide to ritual murder and trophy preparation, a wide array of spectral voices and a customizable enemies list with automatic death threat capabilities. Just $29.95 plus shipping and handling. Order now and receive absolutely free a copy of *Autopsy, the Pathologist's Handbook*."

That was about it. That was where things stood. Actually, thought Winthrop. It was even worse than that with instructions to making your own IED just a Google search away. So here he was, Jack Winthrop, musing in the midst of Danielle's great Alexandrian Library, sipping Chardonnay, awaiting dinner, conversation and so much more, while outside, chaos raged. The murderers were busy murdering. The robbers were robbing. The rapists raping. And everywhere babies were dying of starvation as a sunburned Icarus plummeted into the ocean and the executioner's horse wiped its ass with a brand new roll of Charmin.

Yes, it had always gone on, and it had always been enough to disturb one's dinner, to ulcerate the soul. But now it had indeed gotten personal. He was feeling that now. It was the same feeling of personal violation that he'd had after Speck fired his gun by the phone. Now he felt it even more acutely—because of today's meeting with Abe, because of the sanctuary of Danielle's apartment, because of all that was at stake and all that loomed ahead just around the bend of the evening.

This afternoon when he returned to his apartment, he had found five messages on his answering machine—all of them dead air. Was that Speck calling again? Or could it be the other gunman? Or perhaps both? Or possibly some other sicko or some mutant ninja teenage prankster who had hit upon his number? Fuck it, thought Winthrop. It doesn't fucking matter. Draining the wine from his glass and hearing the hair dryer expire, he poured himself another glass of wine and raised the crystal high in the air. "This is for you, Speck," he shouted. "This is a big fat hairy fuck you to you and all your psychotic brethren. You and the other filth like you can't change a single page in one of these books. You can't erase a word. You can't stop ideas. You can't stop thought. All you can do is kill people and blow up buildings."

"Are you talking to someone, Jack?" Danny called out as she walked from the bathroom to the bedroom.

"Baying at the moon, my darling. Just baying at the moon."

"Well, quit baying and start relaxing. I'll be out in a sec."

And with that, Winthrop decided to let it all go, at least for the moment. Raising his glass high, he whispered three quiet final fuck you's, one to Speck, one to the Sherry gunman and one to all the other pathetic psychos still waiting to be discovered, and sat down to wait for the revelation of Danny.

*　　*　　*　　*

AND A REVELATION IT WAS. Danny, looking fresh as Eve on the first morning in Eden, entered the room with the warmest smile imaginable, a smile that said to Winthrop, "It's OK, Jack. It's OK for us to get to know each other. It's OK to have fun. Trust me. Trust your feelings. The world is bad, really bad, but for the moment at least, we're safe. For the moment the world exists outside my door."

"You look beautiful," Winthrop said, taking another sip of wine. And indeed Danny's beauty vibrated through the room. She was wearing a black, low-cut, silk-crepe evening dress, a solid gold necklace and matching ankle chain and black high-heeled shoes. It was simple, elegant and stunning. Winthrop found himself privately thanking Donna for her influence on his own wardrobe, for it was now on only the rarest of occasions that he ever really looked like a bum. In fact, his appearance tonight was not half bad: a cotton, navy blue pullover shirt, sans alligator; a light, tan sports jacket; khaki Dockers, black socks and oxford topsiders. Notwithstanding the absence of the alligator, Winthrop was positively preppy.

"Thank you, Jack," Danny replied as she glided Winthrop's way, took both of his hands in hers and kissed him softly on the lips. "You know, you're not looking bad yourself. Try relaxing a little, though. I caught you talking to yourself in here."

"Actually I was addressing my remarks to the psychos of the world."

"Baying at the moon."

"Precisely."

"What you told us today was really frightening, Jack. But I decided to put all that out of my mind. It's called thought stopping. You do the same. Forget the psychos for once. Sit down and take it easy. We have a lot to talk about. Like I said when you arrived, I've been thinking about nothing but the tour all day, and I think I've come up with some pretty hot ideas."

"I have some ideas myself."

"Great. I can't wait to get into it. I'm also looking forward to getting to know you just a little bit. You realize, we don't really know each other," she said, smiling again, that same it's-OK-to-be-a-human-being smile. "But first let me tell you what we're having for dinner. I've been working my ass off preparing it."

Sinking down further into the white leather chair, Winthrop felt comfortable. He knew now how the evening would go, provided there were no untimely interruptions. And the knowledge ironically heightened his expectations, even as it spurred and deepened his feelings for Danny, making her seem almost too thoughtful, almost too warm and kind.

"You've already sampled the vino," Danny continued. "And there's another bottle chilling in the kitchen."

"I see my reputation has preceded me, but you did mention your own affinity for wine."

"Well, I'm no expert."

"But everybody needs a hobby, right?"

"Exactly. And you do seem pleased by the selection. I only hope I've done as well with the rest of the dinner."

"I'm just sorry I won't be able to return the favor. My culinary repertoire is limited to two dishes—instant grits and Lipton chicken noodle soup—but, hey, you were about to reveal the evening's menu."

"Yes, indeed. I've learned from some very reliable sources—"

"Rita?"

"Rita and Donna—they both said that even though you never eat at home you're really quite the gourmet in a restaurant setting."

"They said that?"

"Yes, and tonight's dinner is composed solely of Jack Winthrop favorites."

"Danielle, you're really much too thoughtful. As usual, I don't deserve such treatment."

"Well, whether you do or not, you're getting it, so sit back and enjoy—beginning with the appetizer."

Winthrop took another deep breath of the dinner-laden air. "The best part of the meal," he said.

"I agree," replied Danny, "And I couldn't decide on just one, so I made both of your favorites—escargot in garlic and oil with fresh parsley and grilled calamari soaked in lemon. And let me tell you, it was a real bitch to keep the breading on those guys, so you'd better love every single tentacle."

As Danny glowed with warmth and good humor, Winthrop found that he had to make a special effort once again to keep the world, with all its miscellaneous psychos and calamities, outside. The amoral economy of the universe usually dictated that if life ever became too idyllic—even for a moment—the forces of darkness would conspire in short order to redress the balance with a double dose of disaster. Surely the phone must ring. The hooded messenger must arrive at the door. But, no, thought Winthrop, no, just let the evening take its course; release yourself and the letting go will serve as its own amulet. "You have my word, Danny," Winthrop interjected, filling the momentary pause.

"Every single tentacle, breaded or not, is doomed to disappear quickly in honor of the entree, which is—broiled swordfish steak!"

"Perfect."

"The vegetable du jour: asparagus in a special vinaigrette sauce."

"Better than perfect."

"The dinner served, of course, with plenty of warmed French bread and chilled Poland Spring with a sliver of lime."

"And for dessert—"

"A potpourri of sorbet—raspberry, lemon and kiwi. Topped off with homemade cappuccino brewed on my brand new machine, which I bought today and tested to my own complete and unconditional satisfaction."

"You know how to do the foam then?"

"I've got the knack."

"That's impressive. Everything, Danny, is just overwhelming. Really overwhelming."

And just then, as Winthrop was ready to make an untimely joke about cholesterol and open heart surgery born of his chronic inability to have a good time, the timer went off with an abrasive buzz and Winthrop flashed on this morning's dream—Danielle, the young black nurse in the white bustier and D-string. Winthrop looked across the room to Danny who was now scurrying around the kitchen. She was, of course, still wearing her beautiful black dress, but Winthrop was morally certain that she was naked underneath.

"Time to eat," Danielle sang out.

"Yes, indeed," Winthrop responded, emerging from his reverie. "No better time than now. Let's do it."

*   *   *   *

THROUGHOUT THE DINNER Winthrop was amazed and actually, if he were honest, just a little bit frightened, by how quickly he was getting to know Danielle. It was partly the autobiographical turn of the conversation, for Danny was easy with words, as indeed she seemed easy about everything.

In words, Winthrop learned about Danny growing up in White Plains, suburban, protected, happy—the parents loving, the family close. Her mother, Barbara, a first-grade teacher at the Church Street School. Her father, Charles, a conductor for Metro-North working the Harlem line. Her older brother, Ron, the quiet, studious one, always a project going, always busy, always moving ahead—Boy Scouts, Junior Achievement, the National Honor Society, a Merit Scholar—graduating from Fordham in three years, working now as an account manager at Jefferies. Her younger sister, Clarisse, the spitfire, the funny one, the spirited life of the family, getting ready now to start her junior year as a business major at SUNY Purchase. Danny, herself, by her own admission, always a little different, absorbing both her mother's love of books and her father's practicality, learning from him that if you did things yourself they got done, and if you did them again and again, people would respect you because they knew they could count on you, regardless of color. Learning by her own experience that she had a way with people. They liked her. She knew that. And she could use that. Not in a manipulative way. But she could take advantage of that strength. That was important because there were bigger goals in life than just taking care of business and having a good time. That was where she was different from Ron, different from Clarisse. Bottom line, she was an idealist, a romantic. She wanted to be an agent of change. She wanted to make a difference. And she would make a difference. It was her choice. Her life.

That was what Winthrop learned from Danielle's words, through her own self-assessment—so very knowing, so very conscious and assured of her personal assets and the objectives she was pursuing. But actually it was in all the other ways Danielle communicated that Winthrop absorbed the essence of her character and the beliefs that she carried through life. It was in the very way she presented herself, her poise and bearing. It was in her quick and easy smile, her instantaneous laugh. It was in the brightness of her eyes and the glow of her warm brown skin. It was in the way she listened and the way she talked. It was an attitude, a style of existence. And if Winthrop had to sum it all up in one word, he would call it "confidence." The confidence of an actor who has already won the part. The confidence of an athlete who knows she must win because she always has. That was where Danny lived and breathed—in her confidence, a confidence which had been momentarily shaken by the shooting but which was surging ahead once again, empowered and sustained by the promise of the tour.

It was all so foreign to Winthrop, the easy self-revelation, the idealism, the confidence. Despite all the reading, despite the miracle of her education, Danielle did not know yet that she was nobody. For Winthrop this was basic stuff. He had known that he was nobody for almost as long as he could remember. Had known it ever since he was three years old, playing in the sand at Jones Beach, with his little Mickey Mouse bucket and shovel, and a huge wave came in and picked him up, along with the bucket and shovel, and dumped him unceremoniously on his ass.

Of course, he later learned that the world itself wasn't all it was cracked up to be either, despite its size and force. In fact, the entire universe was doomed to collapse on itself one fine day and somehow end up occupying a space no bigger than Winthrop's left nut, actually unimaginably smaller than that a Planck length—that or else expand forever into one big, never ending God fart. Either way, what was the point? Meanwhile, nothing really worked the way it was supposed to. At one end of the scale, Black Holes sucked up galaxies; at the other end subatomic particles popped whimsically in and out of existence whenever they felt like it. Then Winthrop discovered that 99 percent of the universe was missing anyway. At that point he simply gave up. He still couldn't decide, however, if the missing matter was the problem or if the real issue was why the other 1 percent was here in the first place.

Yes, universal faucets were dripping everywhere, and the plumber wasn't returning calls. Of course, there was nothing you could do about it. So, in response, young master Winthrop turned philosophical. We're here, he thought. It's queer. Get used to it. And in any event, if you can't get used to it, don't worry. You won't be here long anyway. Jones understood all this. Winthrop was sure of it. Jones's late night phone call summoning him to the project had proven that. Nevertheless, Jones had an ego of Napoleonic proportions. That was what was remarkable. Whereas Winthrop saw humility as a sign of intelligence, Jones was wedded to a species of relativist logic. I may be a human insect, the thinking went, but as human insects go I'm one of the best. With the notable exception, however, of his hyperbolic ego, Jones was on the same wavelength as Jack Winthrop. On the other hand, Danielle just didn't get it. Of course, Winthrop could hardly blame her for not being a nihilist. She was young, beautiful, intelligent and ambitious. Why should she think that everything was shit? What really struck Winthrop as he and Danny talked throughout the dinner was the total absence of any sense on Danny's part that she was marked or victimized by being black.

Arthur Ashe had once said that the most difficult burden that he had had to bear in life was not AIDS, but race, the fact that he was born black. That, for Winthrop, was an unbelievably powerful statement of the problem. That was it. That was the truth. And yet here was this wonderfully confident, intelligent, beautiful young black woman whose life experience to date—at least prior to ALJ's shooting—said, I'm not burdened. I'm not marked. I'm not victimized. I'm not personally the object of discrimination. I sit before you at age twenty-four, a black woman, whole and intact in my beauty and idealism.

And that was great. That was what everyone had been working for all along—except that for Winthrop, and certainly for Abraham Lincoln Jones, the fundamental reality was Speck. Speck with a gun. Speck breathing the word "nigger" into the phone. Speck the stalker. Speck the racial terrorist who would not be stopped.

At a number of points during the conversation, Danny would say, "Jack, what is it?" or "Jack, what are you thinking?" or "Jack, is everything all right?" So much, thought Winthrop, for his good intentions of letting the evening flow. He was constitutionally incapable of enjoyment. He realized that once again. And he knew that there was really nothing he could say to Danielle about what troubled him. He didn't know her well enough yet to talk about the universe collapsing. That would almost certainly scare her away. On race who was he to say anything anyway? He was white. She was black. As a white man he had no moral standing, ultimately, on the issue of race, especially on how blacks and other minorities should feel. He had even written that in the foreword to his book, just to be clear. His expertise, if he had any, was on the psychology of the oppressor, the transactions of power and the motivations behind bigotry.

As for talking about himself that was out as well. Whereas Danny was easy to get to know, Winthrop was virtually impossible. Like most journalists, indeed, like most real writers, he hated self-revelation. He was not the story, he would say to himself, he was the reporter or, at most, the interpreter of the story. When it came to his own life, Winthrop didn't know what the story was. The older he got, the less he knew. Indeed, now as he moved through middle age, Winthrop felt that he was teetering on the edge of complete inscrutability about himself. He still had his ideas and thoughts as well as his little comic mottos that he would share with Rita or occasionally Donna, but increasingly he found that he just didn't have a clue. In fact, when he did have a little burst of self-revelation, the insight, for example, that he was actually quite naive about the evil of the world, the effect was to undermine whatever else it was that he thought he knew about himself.

So what to say to Danielle? Fortunately, there was his work: the reporting, the columns, the book. Danielle was so eager to hear about his writing that all the difficult questions about his life—his family, his boyhood in Queens, the schools he attended, the relationships he had or didn't have—conveniently disappeared.

"Jack, I have a confession to make," Danny said.

"What's that, Danny?" Winthrop replied smiling, thinking that almost everything Danny had said throughout the evening was a confession of one kind or another.

"When I first met you back stage at Radio City during Abe's show, I was really nervous."

"I never would have guessed."

"And I have to tell you I've been really nervous all day today about the dinner. You are enjoying it, Jack, aren't you?"

"Danny, it's splendid, really. Please don't take it personally when I seem distracted. It's a kind of congenital defect that I have. My body's always in one place while my mind is in another. The two of them have just never gotten along. So honestly it's not you. I'm really having a wonderful time."

"Well, Jack, I have had this case of nerves about you. In fact, I'm just now beginning to calm down after two glasses of wine."

"Danny, you seem to be one of the most self-assured women I've ever met. It's one of the things that impressed me about you right away."

"Well, that's the thing, Jack. Whenever I'm nervous, I always act more self-assured, more confident. I guess it's my defense against nerves."

"That's some defense."

"It works for me."

"But why be nervous about meeting me?"

"You have no idea, Jack, how much I respect your work."

Danny was right, thought Winthrop. He did have no idea.

"I used to have the same problem with Abe," Danny said. "You know how strange life is. People say everything's connections, but I actually got my job with Abe through a blind ad in *The Times*. I was right out of Columbia, applying for anything and everything, so I followed up on this ad that simply said PR assistant wanted. I sent in my resume to the PO box, and a week later I got a call. It was from Abe's assistant, but she didn't give me any details. I showed up for the interview, not knowing what to expect, and there he was. The Man, himself. I almost fell over. He told me he did all his own interviewing. I don't know how I even got through the interview, but I guess I did all right because I got the job. But for months I felt so nervous around Abe."

"But you've done phenomenally. Look how quickly you've moved up in his organization. What's it been, just two years? And he seems to depend on you for so much. You and Barry are the two people closest to him."

"Well, Abe may have a big ego and justifiably so, but he delegates responsibility quickly when he trusts you. I know he already considers you an equal, Jack. In fact, I've never seen him treat anyone else with the respect he's shown you from day one. But that's just how he feels about you, and that's why he wanted you to join the team. In my own case, I worked really hard to earn Abe's trust, and I know I have it now, so I'm very comfortable working with him. Still, every so often I catch myself just staring at the man and the nerves return for just a few seconds. Abe has just accomplished so much with his life. He influences so many people. And I feel the same way about you, Jack. I mean, all I have to do is think of the courage you've shown in your writing. It's been there from the beginning."

"From the beginning?"

"Yes, I've been reading your columns since junior high."

Winthrop was amazed. He did some quick math in his head. "That would be since maybe 2002?" To Winthrop, 2002 seemed like yesterday.

"Yes, you were doing investigative reports. There was one on a nursing home that I remember in particular."

"Greenwood."

"Yes, Greenwood. And I thought, Wow! This is great. Here's this guy who goes out on his own, finds out the truth, writes about it and changes things. I thought, that's the kind of impact I'd like to have. That's when I went back and read everything you'd written from the beginning."

Winthrop was stunned. You never really know who you're reaching. As for the Greenwood series, it did change things—for the elderly residents of Greenwood and for Winthrop. The state investigated, the families sued, the director and many of the staff were fired, and the outrages ended—the human warehousing, the physical and sexual abuse, the malnutrition, the eighty-year-old Alzheimer's victims wallowing in their own waste—all of that stopped, and a new statewide program of quality nursing home care was initiated.

Winthrop would always cherish the memory of his first visit to Greenwood after the state had filed its report and verified his charges. When he and the governor entered the room where all the residents were gathered, those who could, stood and applauded him. The governor spoke quite briefly then relinquished the spotlight to Winthrop, who somehow managed to talk for about five minutes, although afterwards he could never recall a single word that he had spoken. When the gathering ended, Winthrop shook a few hands then quietly excused himself. He located the men's room, entered a stall, closed the door, sat down and cried.

Greenwood was the turning point for Winthrop in many ways. It liberated him to write whatever he wanted in his columns. He still did an occasional investigative piece, and he even had time to write his book. It was a life that for years had suited him well. "Well, for me, Danny," Winthrop said, "There are just a few things worth doing, and writing has always been one of them."

"I have to tell you, Jack, when Abe told me he was going to ask you to join us, I was ecstatic. But I didn't know how you'd react."

"Well, as you know, Abe can be very persuasive, and I've been looking for something different."

"Like the tour?"

"You mean the Eeeh-mancipation Tour?" Winthrop suddenly shouted in his best ALJ voice. And they both laughed, Danny easily and Winthrop, as always, with the knowledge that he was indeed laughing. But the laughter succeeded in changing his mood. He felt connected again, and he was looking forward to brainstorming with Danny. He knew she'd have some great ideas. It would be a real collaboration, and for Winthrop that would certainly be different.

"My God, Jack, that sounds just like Abe. How did you do that?"

"Eeeah-sy," Winthrop replied. "It's all in the Eeeh! You try it, Danny. Let me hear you say Eeeh-mancipation!"

"Eeeh-mancipation!"

"Once more now. Eeeh-mancipation!"

But Danielle was laughing so hard now she could barely speak. "Oh, that's too much, Jack," Danielle gasped.

If the table wasn't separating them Winthrop would have taken her in his arms right then and there. Winthrop's desire to make love to Danielle was now obliterating all other considerations, even the great issue of the tour.

Finally, Danielle recovered somewhat and said, "Hey, Jack, what do you say we break out the sorbet and cappuccino, move back into the living room and get down to it?"

Winthrop raised his eyebrows and smiled lasciviously. "Now you're talking," he said. He couldn't help himself. The imp of love had gotten the best of him.

"No, Jack, sex can wait," Danny exclaimed. "Let's talk about the tour. Like I said, I've been thinking about nothing else all day."

"Of course, I'd like nothing better," Winthrop replied, smiling his best Jack Nicholson smile, the smile he always gave whenever he was lying through his teeth.

*   *   *   *

THE TOUR. It was an idea that, Winthrop believed, might actually hold the secret to reconnecting America. For decades television had isolated the nation while stealing much of what was left of America's mind—so much so that on many nights the country was little more than a vast farm of couch potatoes waiting to be harvested. Just when Winthrop thought that it couldn't get any worse, along came the Internet. Nevertheless, there were countervailing forces as well. To every action there was an equal and opposite reaction, so said one of the venerable chestnuts of physics. And for Winthrop the old universal law had a strange but compelling application to the forces of popular culture.

Yes, we had become a nation of isolatoes comfortable with life only when it was presented to us as a colorful field of electronic dots. But our very isolation seemed to stir within our souls the urge to gather together. The urge to assemble. The urge to bond with the tribe. Rock concerts, political rallies, religious revival meetings—that was where it was happening. Flesh and blood people coming together in public to rock and roll, to cheer their leader, to praise the Lord. It was true, Winthrop often thought, people want life to be television, but they need to beat the tribal drum as well. Abraham Lincoln Jones understood all of this. And Winthrop knew that Jones was the one, Jones was The Man who could put it all together. Give the people what they want. Give the people what they need. Give them television and the beat of the tribe through the medium of the tour and the magic of talk.

"Abe's been looking to stretch out for years," Danny said. "He's been biding his time, waiting for the right moment."

"And that moment has come because—"

"Because mainstream politics is dead," Danny said.

"Exactly. The Democrats and Republicans are the Rosencrantz and Guildenstern of politics."

"And Rosencrantz and Guildenstern are dead."

"That was quick, Danny. You beat me to it on that one."

"Yes, I did, Jack. But what I want to say, and I'm really sorry to say this, is that despite Barack, people are just plain disgusted. Congress is a disgrace, and honestly he just does not know how to push their buttons to get things done."

"I agree, Danny. As Maureen Dowd says, 'there's no bully in the pulpit.' So the time is right for Abe, but let's be honest. This is a career move for him, and frankly, it's one for me, too."

"We all have our personal motives, Jack, but the key is change."

"Change. I know. I had a rather interesting telephone conversation with Abe on that very subject when he gave me my draft notice. But here's the difficult thing. Change is like magic. Only a master illusionist can change reality. It's more than just pulling a rabbit out of a hat. You have to be able to be in two places at the same time. In the world and out of the world. On the bus with the people and floating free with your own vision like some kind of celestial salesman."

"Are you saying, Jack, that you have to fool people into change?"

"To a certain extent you do. You have to fool yourself, too, because real change is painful. And people don't like pain. I know I don't."

"But people put up with so much pain and disappointment every day of their lives."

"Yes, but it's familiar pain, comfortable pain. It's only when the pain becomes too intense, when it becomes unbearable, that people are ripe for change."

"I think we're there."

"Many people are, and that's Abe's opportunity. He's got to seize that opportunity now."

"Beginning with the tour."

"Right, Danny, he's got to use the tour to connect with the American people. And then he's really got to keep that connection going every single day. There's a tremendous amount of apathy out there. Ignorance, too. A lot of people just don't give a damn. Then, of course, there's a gigantic reservoir of hate out there as well. You saw that yesterday when Abe was shot."

Immediately, Danny's eyes filled with tears. For a moment she was back in the coffee shop. Feeling the pain. Feeling the uncertainty. Feeling that the shooting had changed everything. "You know, Jack," Danny said, smiling bravely as her voice shook with emotion. "We should talk about the marketing side of the tour."

Winthrop smiled encouragingly.

"We've only reached out to a few of Abe's most supportive sponsors. That was his preference." The tears were rolling down her face. Winthrop moved closer, leaned over and kissed both streams while Danny continued talking. "You know, the ones who have been with him for years."

"Yes," Winthrop said as he grasped Danny's hand and gently pulled her out of the love seat and onto her feet.

"But I know that we could line up lots of other major sponsors as well."

Winthrop moved closer still and looked deeply into Danny's eyes. Seeing his own face reflected there, he knew the moment was right and kissed her on the lips with all the empathy and compassion and love that he held inside his godforsaken soul, hoping it was enough to give Danny strength. She seemed to want to hold the kiss forever, and when their lips finally parted, she looked at Winthrop and said, "Jack?" Just Jack. There was no doubt—"Jack" was a question. It was the most frightening question, the most overwhelming question that Winthrop had ever confronted, encompassing not only Speck, the other gunman and everything terrible, everything evil, everything tragic, that could ever happen, especially to Abe, to Danny and to Winthrop himself, but also everything that Winthrop could do to prevent it all from happening. He knew that was very little. Next to nothing really, except to be brave and send a faithless prayer for luck and imagination out into the gaping void.

And so with nothing to say and with less than he wanted to give, Winthrop took Danny's hand and walked her to the bedroom, his heart pounding, his soul aching, his cock throbbing. The brainstorming was over for the moment, though it seemed they had hardly begun. Now it was time to go with the beat of the moment. For there were so few real moments in life, and this was surely one.

As they entered Danny's bedroom, Winthrop stripped off her cool, black, low-cut dress with a single flick of his wrist, and, yes, she was naked underneath just as he had known. As his own preppy attire seemed to evaporate at Danny's touch, he grabbed her by the ass and lifted her onto his cock. Then with an Arthur Murray ballroom move that he had picked up one unforgettable afternoon with Donna, he did a quick foxtrot promenade toward the king size bed with Danny's legs wrapped fast around his waist. Twisting to the left, he propelled himself backwards toward the mattress so that Danny could ride like a cowgirl on top and landed on the creamy satin sheets, his eye catching the title, *The Volcano Lover*, for, yes, Momma Sontag's book was sitting on the bedside table.

Free at last for just the moment, Winthrop fucked Danny and she fucked him, and for once it was love and sex together, sex and love combined, building hard toward one big transcendental cum. Danny let loose first—with a low pitched growl—and second, too, in wave upon wave with Winthrop erupting underneath her, erupting in the wetness as she crested again and again while someone was moaning softly, "Danny, Danny, Danny." The moan was Winthrop's answer, his best and only answer, finally, to the overwhelming question Danny had asked—was it moments before? Asked in echo of that perennial question of the heart, first asked perhaps more than a million years ago. Asked in the first moment when human fear was born.

Germany was on the phone. It was half past six. He was shouting, no, singing, in a terrible Wagnerian voice, "Help me make it through the night."

"Felix," Winthrop gasped. Danny was sleeping peacefully by his side.

"Hey, Winthrop, you should send your little buddy a thank-you note."

"My little buddy?" Winthrop whispered hoarsely.

"Yeah, your psycho friend Speck's not half bad after all."

"What?"

"No calls at your girlfriend's, right?" "See, he cut you some slack last night so you could get a full service lap dance from your baby."

"Listen, Felix, you find the guy and get me his address. Then I'll send both of you thank-you notes."

"That's why I'm calling, Winthrop. You've been getting some interesting calls—hang-ups."

"I know. I had some yesterday afternoon."

"Well, there've been a lot more since then. We were able to trace all of them."

"Hey, good work with the bugs, Felix. Did you turn up anything important?"

"Maybe. How about you meet me at the Continental Diner at 9:30 and we'll talk?"

"Eighty-eighth and Columbus, right?"

"Yeah, I'll buy you a cup of coffee and we'll talk. We've got some interesting footage from the hotel videos—the Plaza and the Sherry."

"Fantastic. So it's the Continental at 9:30," Winthrop replied and hung up. He could touch base with Germany, catch a cab and make it to St. Patrick's for Rita's demonstration at 10:15. Meanwhile, Danny lay sleeping, naked and warm, just inches away. Winthrop moved closer in anticipation, led by the pulse of his hardening cock. For he had done this before. Done it more than once. And, while it required great art, required just the right touch, the prize was so very precious: to arouse her barely to awakening, then ever so delicately join together and sink into the mists of the mythic, the legendary, the all but unattainable Golden Slumbers Fuck.

Winthrop moved closer still to Danny, moved as close as he could without touching and gently kissed each eyelid and comically kissed her nose. Then he kissed each cheek tenderly before licking at her lips and penetrating them deftly with his tongue once, twice, three times until Danny opened her eyes sleepily and smiled and opened her legs as well and Winthrop's cock was there—like an obedient little puppy, its tail wagging agreeably, waiting to be called by its mistress. Winthrop slipped his cock inside her, nice and neat, to rest and throb, throb and rest. Then Danny closed her legs again, smiling, and fell right back to sleep with Winthrop following her quickly in the security of their dreamy fuck.

*   *   *   *

THE SECOND HE AWAKENED he knew he was late. But he did not want to move. The tip of his cock was still inside Danny, and for Winthrop the intimacy of that half-inch could substitute for paradise. He raised his head slowly to look at the alarm clock on the bedside table just beyond Danny's pillow, careful not to lose the half-inch.

9:45. Shit, Winthrop thought. Shit and shit again. This never happens to me. For Winthrop was equipped with an extremely reliable internal clock that enabled him to awaken each morning just minutes before his alarm was set to go off. Honed by Winthrop's hatred of the despicable alarm sound, the psychic clock almost never failed him. He had even trained it to adjust semiannually to the disruptions of daylight savings time. Springing ahead one godforsaken, sleep-deprived hour in March and falling back for the compensatory sixty minutes of blissful repose in November.

Today, he had set no alarm at all, relying only on his trusty internal clock, and it had failed him miserably, its arcane rhythms overwhelmed, no doubt, by the psychic barrage of the past few days—the violence and the sex and the dizzying, vertiginous sense that the ground was crumbling away. Soon he would be in free fall, and he knew that if he survived the crash, everything within him and without him would have changed. Then, if he were honest, he would have to start all over again—with what, he did not know. But for now the half-inch was his connection. To Danny. To another living, breathing human being in free fall herself, though she perhaps did not yet know it. And the hope was that they would land together, take the hit, repair the damage and survive. It would require luck, lots of luck, and connection, some enduring connection, if only a half-inch. But now, what? Now he was not where he was supposed to be. Now he was here, lying in bed, with Germany waiting and Rita counting on him to show.

So Winthrop raised his head again. 9:51 and counting, always counting. Dropping his head back down upon the pillow, he took a final look at Danny sleeping, kissed her on the forehead, breathed in a little extra air for strength and let his cock fall out. Then levitating his body from the bed so as not to awaken Danny, Winthrop got back upon his feet and threw the switch, his own personal emergency switch, which instantaneously transformed him from a malingering love-drugged fuck-up into the world's fastest moving life form.

It took Winthrop just two minutes and fifty-seven seconds to dress, pee, throw some cold water on his face, jot down a tersely worded but sensitive explanatory note for Danny, including a promise to call her by noon, exit the apartment, descend the elevator ten floors to the lobby, blow out of the building and flag down a cab for the Continental thirty blocks away. If everything played out just right with the cabbie, the traffic, the lights, he could still get to the diner by ten, spend a few minutes getting the lowdown from Germany, assuming he was still there, then catch a cab to St. Patrick's and arrive just a little bit late for Rita and the GRACE demonstration. Yes, if everything played out just right, he would escape self-indictment. He would escape being an asshole yet another time in his life.

When Winthrop arrived at the Continental, Germany was leaning back in the corner booth, drinking coffee and reading the *Post*. Dirty breakfast dishes were scattered about the table. Some egg mess, pork grease, a side order of toast crumbs, orange specks on the side of a juice glass. As Germany looked up from the *Post* and saw Winthrop approaching, a big, sarcastic grin spread across his face.

"Winthrop, you look like you just crawled out of a fucking sewer."

Winthrop was still breathing too hard to speak. Some vital organ on his lower right side—his bladder? his liver? his kidney—was twitching up a storm. His left hand was numb, and the lights in the diner seemed to be going up and down, up and down every time he blinked his eyes. Germany leaned his head to the left and gave him the eye.

"You know, Winthrop, you got to be doing something wrong. Every time I see you, you look worse. Forget the fucking doctor. You need a goddamn coroner to examine you."

As soon as the taxi had turned north on Broadway, it became hopelessly stuck in Sunday gridlock. After waiting just two minutes,

Winthrop bolted from the cab at 61st Street and began running for the Continental, propelled by panic and self-recrimination. Somehow he had made it without stopping—one block west and twenty-seven blocks north in fourteen minutes. Now he was ready to die. "St. Patrick's," he gasped at Germany. "Got to . . . get to . . . the church . . . leave . . . five minutes."

"Yeah, St. Patrick's, good idea, Winthrop," Germany replied. "Get your ass to a fucking priest and have your last rites read. Last rites, is that what they call it?"

"Leave . . . five minutes," Winthrop insisted as his heart exploded and blood vessels burst in his brain.

"Forty fucking minutes late and you give me a lousy five minutes. You're going to hurt my feelings, pal, if you don't watch it," Germany responded, slurping down the last of his coffee. "Hey, Claire, fill her up here, will you, sweetie, and pour a little for my friend, too. He's about to die for a cup of coffee."

At that moment, like a gift from heaven, the breath of life returned to Winthrop. His liver quit doing back flips. His hand slowly began to regain feeling, and the diner lights calmed down as well. Claire poured him some coffee, and he took a sip. Finally, he was able to speak an intelligent sentence. "Listen, Felix," he said, "I really owe you one. Thanks for waiting. I want to hear what you have on Speck and the other gunman, the hang-ups, the video. I need to hear it. It's just that I don't have much time. How about ten minutes?"

"Hey, come on, Winthrop. Don't mention it. I'm just pulling your fucking chain. So I was counting on having this romantic little tête-à-tête with Mr. Abraham Lincoln Jones's communications guru, and now everything's been shot to hell! So what! I'm a fucking pro. I roll with the punches. So here's the short version."

"Shoot."

"OK. First the video. We got two suspects. Looks like you might be right. One at the Plaza. One at the Sherry."

"Fantastic! Did we get a good look at both of them?"

"Yes and no. Video couldn't be better. But I don't think it will help much."

"Because?"

"Plaza suspect was dressed as a woman. I know a cross dresser when I see one. This one looked pretty good. Probably just your type, Winthrop. But the hips were wrong. The walk was wrong. Five eleven, one fifty, black wig, sunglasses. Navy Blue Hillary Clinton pants suit. Dressed for business except for one thing."

"What's that?"

"Had on a pair of black running shoes—Nikes. Actually two things. Not what she was wearing but what she was carrying—a black guitar case—Martin."

"Well, the height and weight fit, at least. Fit Speck, I mean."

"You mentioned weight. That's what's funny about your Sherry perp."

"Explain, Felix."

"At the Sherry, we have what appears to be a big, bearded man dressed like he just stepped out of a fucking movie about the 1920s or thirties. What's that fucking Sopranos thing from the twenties on HBO?"

"*Boardwalk Empire*. Nucky Thompson."

"Yeah, Nucky. My kind of guy. Well, our guy looks like he belongs back in those days. Dressed to kill, you might say, but very formal, very old fashioned. Three-piece suit, watch chain, bowler hat."

"OK, but what's the problem with the height and weight."

"He was wearing a fat suit and platform shoes. I could tell by his walk. Not sure how high, but maybe four inches. And one other thing."

"Go on."

"We got another guitar player here. Another Martin guitar case. Like he got it at the same music store as our Plaza friend."

"What else?"

"The Plaza lady entered the room where the shots were fired.

Fancy Dan accessed the apartment where you saw a second gunman."

"So they both broke into locked hotel rooms."

"I wouldn't call it breaking in. They both popped the locks in seconds. It's not hard. I'll show you some time."

"Then what?"

"A few seconds after the shots were fired, the lady came flying out the door and took to the stairs. She exited about 90 seconds later onto 58th right before we sealed that door and headed west where she melted into the crowd. No way around it, Winthrop. She was fast. We were a little slow. As for Mr. Fancy, right after the shots were fired, he sauntered out of his room, walked calmly down the hall and took the elevator to the lobby. He walked out of the Sherry onto Fifth Avenue, then headed north, where he also got lost in the crowd."

"Great job, Felix. Now what about the phone calls? You said you traced them, right?"

"You bet your ass, we did. The dead air the callers left gave us all the time we needed, so we got every fucking call."

"And?"

"You definitely have two callers here. Yesterday afternoon you had five calls. We traced all of them to midtown on the West Side. Last night after you left your apartment to go to your girlfriend's, there were eleven more calls. Six calls from midtown, East Side, and five calls from Brooklyn. Two of the Brooklyn calls were within five minutes of the East Side hang-ups. The last two East Side calls were made just a block away from your apartment."

"Cell phones?"

"Two different cell phones on the midtown calls, and two different phones on the Brooklyn calls. All of them reported stolen shortly before they were used to make the calls."

"So I've got both assholes calling me."

"Could be."

"What's going on here? We pretty much know one of these guys is Speck. If the other calls are from the second gunman, then what is this? Why is he calling me?"

"Hey, it's pretty clear that psychos like you, Winthrop. It's no surprise. You're borderline yourself."

"Look who's talking."

"It's not exactly a secret you're working for Jones. It was in all the papers. Page Six in the *Post*. Your paper did a fucking blurb. Mr. Talk Show Host is obviously a target for crazies, and you get a piece of the action, too."

"Have you turned up anything new on Speck?"

"We interviewed everybody at the Tit for Tat. Hey, that kid dancer's something, huh? What is she, twelve years old?"

"About that."

"Jesus Christ. Talk about jailbait. And that manager, Donna Marone. She's not bad either."

"Anyway."

"Anyway, we didn't get much more than we already had from you. A few details from Sheila, the bartender. It wasn't much. But somehow I got to thinking about a case that came down a year ago."

"Similar?"

"Yes and no. You remember the incident at Shorty's, the little neighborhood bar at 1st and Bowery?"

"Vaguely. Somebody got to Shorty, right?"

"Came in after the bar was closed and took out Shorty and his bartender."

"What are you thinking, Felix?"

"Maybe nothing. Shorty was a fucking mess. He owed a lot of money. He gambled. He was into drugs. Did a little pimping on the side. It was a lot of penny ante shit. Anybody could have done him. Two things, though. Number one, the bartender was a girl. One of Shorty's girls. She was black, and she and Shorty were kind of involved. Number two, a couple of the patrons talked about a new guy who had shown up almost every night at the bar for a few weeks. Never talked to anybody. Just drank by himself. After the shootings, nobody ever saw the guy again, and we never tracked him down for questioning."

"You think that guy did Shorty—and that maybe he's Speck?"

"Descriptions don't match. This guy was sort of a dirty hippie type. Long hair, T-shirt, ripped jeans. Your buddy, Speck, is a computer programmer. But that doesn't mean shit. If my hobby was serial murder, I'd change the way I look from time to time too. Maybe even dress up like a girl."

"Don't scare me, Felix. I've always had the feeling that you missed your real calling, and I'm not sure you'd pass as a girl."

"Hey, what's that old fucking poem from high school, Winthrop? About taking one way and not the other. Come on, you're a literary guy."

"You mean, 'The Road Not Taken.'"

"Yeah, that's it."

Winthrop looked at Germany, shook his head and smiled. Germany was amazing. It was true. He would have made a great serial killer. The kind that never got caught. "I'm glad you're on my side," Winthrop said. "But, listen, I got to get to St. Patrick's, so tell me, what are you going to do about this Shorty connection?"

"That's my business, Winthrop. When it comes to hunches, I've got my own fucking methods. You just worry about results. Leave the sniffing around to me. I'm beginning to get a good feeling about this one. Anyway besides me, we have a fucking Normandy invasion team on the case."

Beginning to get a good feeling, thought Winthrop. He had nothing but bad feelings about Speck and the second gunman. And he was feeling worse all the time. He was worried about Jones. He was worried about Danielle. And he was beginning to worry about himself. "OK, if you say so, Felix," Winthrop replied. "And what about our Sherry friend?"

"I talked to the captain about him. I'm on it, along with a few of my boys. Just keeping quietly on the trail. I'm sure Mr. Fancy was very disappointed if he did indeed show up to take a few shots at your boss, but I really doubt that he has any idea that anyone else knows he was there. He may just want to lie low for a while and then take another shot. See if his luck improves."

"That's what worries me, Felix. Worries me a lot. Sherry and Speck. Both of them or either of them taking another shot. Anyway, I really got to go. Thank you, my man." He had stayed fifteen minutes, not five or ten. It was 10:25. The Mass had already started.

"One more thing," Germany said as Winthrop got up to leave.

"What's that?"

"Why are you going to St. Patrick's? You're not exactly the religious type."

"A friend of mine's the founder of GRACE. You know, the gay religious group. They're demonstrating at Boyle's Mass. My friend asked me to come."

"I thought it was something like that. Better watch your ass, Winthrop. We're expecting trouble, and you could pass for a fruit without even trying."

"What do you mean, you're expecting trouble?"

"The gays have shown up at the cathedral before and caused a little disturbance. This time, though, the cardinal's been getting some threatening calls, too. He's fed up, and he's let us know that. It's fine with him for us to do what we got to do. And we intend to be there in a big way."

Suddenly Germany had a slightly crazy look in his eyes. Visions of nightstick beatings were no doubt dancing in his head. "So you guys are planning to get tough with GRACE," Winthrop said.

"Hey, we got to do what we got to do."

Winthrop had no doubt that the cardinal had given the cops the go-ahead to clean house. He was also sure that the police had infiltrated GRACE. Poor Rita, Winthrop thought. Her precious GRACE shot through with moles and informants. Life was beginning to catch up with Rita just as it finally catches up with all of us. Winthrop had no idea what he could do, but he knew that he was definitely not where he was supposed to be. He needed to get to St. Patrick's—now.

"Thanks for the psycho update, Felix. Give me a call as soon as you have anything more. And thanks for the warning, too." Winthrop turned and rushed toward the door.

"Like I said, Winthrop, watch your ass," Germany shouted at his back.

Winthrop figured Broadway was his best bet, so he ran most of the way there. Miraculously traffic was moving. It was now 10:30. Winthrop immediately flagged down a cab. "St. Patrick's," he said. "There's an extra five bucks if you get me to 50th in five minutes," Winthrop announced as he took his seat in the back of the cab. The cabbie, Abdul Azziz, nodded all but imperceptibly and clicked on the meter. He looked as if he'd been driving for at least twenty-four hours straight.

As the taxi shot forward and Winthrop was driven back into the seat, he knew he was in good hands. With nothing but green lights and fleeing pedestrians spreading out before him, he knew that Allah was definitely smiling upon Azziz. Time slowed down as the taxi rocketed down Broadway. At 10:34 Winthrop and Azziz made the turn at 50th and got more than half way to Sixth Avenue before getting caught in the quagmire of crosstown traffic. Winthrop paid the fare and handed Azziz the extra five.

"That was pure magic, my man," he said as he slammed the door shut and ran toward the Cathedral at 50th and Fifth.

Winthrop had not been in St. Patrick's, or any other church for that matter, for several years. In a church Winthrop always felt peculiarly flat. The experience was remarkably similar to how he had felt on a recent visit to the CIA building in Waverly, Virginia, or on a tour of the Kremlin during his one and only visit to the Soviet Union in 1990. Central Intelligence, Soviet Communism and the

Church had all been hit by the neutron bomb of history. The people were dead, the spirit gone, but the buildings were still standing. So despite all the mystic paraphernalia, despite the darkened pews, stained glass windows, burning votive candles, holy water fonts, confessionals, icons, altars, sacristy and crypt—despite all the religious atmospherics—for Winthrop a church was just another institutional building that had outlived its purpose.

To Winthrop it was all really a rather embarrassing and unfunny joke. He had first gotten the joke way back in the first grade at Our Lady of Lourdes Parochial School. It was clear, at least to little Jackie Winthrop, that the nuns were nuts; the priests were weird; and school was a jail for kids. Of course, few of his classmates liked school, but none of them seemed to realize that they were actually inmates of a penal institution—the crime, having been born a human being. The sentence, twelve years without parole combined with the cruel and inhuman punishment of being catechized daily in the tenets of a medieval religion. As he got older, Winthrop realized that true education—that is, the nurturing of independent thinking and creativity—was never the goal of his school. In fact, everything at Our Lady of Lourdes and later at St. Pius X High School militated against it. Learning did occur on occasion, but almost always by accident and despite the system.

Winthrop had to admit it: he was bitter about it all. Bitter about the twelve-year prison sentence. About the fake education. About the institutionalized hatred of the Roman Catholic Church: the subjection of women, the demonization of sex, the hypocritical condemnation of homosexuality and, worst of all, the enslavement of the human spirit.

How then to explain Rita? Not her gender identity or her sexual orientation. They were perfectly explicable. She was simply born a woman in a man's body. Her attraction to women was inborn as well. Her gender identity and sexual orientation were gifts from God, so to speak. Winthrop also had no difficulty understanding and explaining her personality or her character or her intelligence. For he knew they were self-created, built on a foundation that was also a gift. Nor was Winthrop thinking of her talent. For talent was a rare weed. It was not often seen, but when it did appear, by some absurd dispensation of the void, its seed was hardy and self-nurturing. It could grow in the gutters of an inner-city ghetto, flourish in the bombed out bunkers of a war zone or bloom in the backwoods of a sleepy country town.

Winthrop understood the endurance of talent. Talent was its own defense against the treacherous stupidity of the world. What he did not comprehend and could not explain was the survival of a pure heart. A heart had no defense. Its purity was violated daily. It could go on beating or stop, but it could not remain pure. No, it could not. Except that he had seen that purity with his own eyes. Seen it in his friend, Rita. She had been rejected by the Church because of who she was—a transgender woman—yet she had continued to love the Church. Love the Church in its viciousness, love the Church in its ignorance, love the Church in its triumph over her without ever charging it with viciousness or ignorance and without ever recognizing its triumph, because she had never been defeated. Winthrop knew the term for this. He was good with terms, good with words. He knew that this was unconditional love. Rita loved the Church unconditionally in the purity of her heart. That was the truth. But he did not understand it. And he knew in his own ignorance that all he could do was be her friend and try to make sure that she and her blessed heart were not ground to dust.

As Winthrop approached St. Patrick's, he saw the police cars and paddy wagons parked along Fifth Avenue. They lined 50th Street as well together with a long row of TV trucks parked on the other side of the street. Two trucks from CBS were at the head of the line. On one of the trucks "Goode News" was emblazoned in big red letters. The whole area had been blocked off to traffic, and at least a dozen uniformed police officers stood about the cathedral steps.

Winthrop trotted across Fifth and headed for the entrance. Just as he reached the steps, Jeff Goode emerged from the cathedral followed by a camerawoman and his producer, Jane Moore, who was talking into a cell phone. Goode did not look happy. "Hey, Jeffrey, what's the problem?" Winthrop asked.

"Oh, Winthrop, it's you," Goode remarked rather pointlessly, working his mouth as if he were struggling to rid it of some particularly nasty taste.

"Yeah, it's me. What's up?"

"We were here to shoot some B-roll on the cardinal for a special Goode News Story on the children of the Church."

"The children of the Church?"

"Yes, it's part of a series I'm doing on the return to traditional values among young families in the tri-state area."

"I guess I missed that."

"No, Winthrop. It hasn't aired yet," Goode replied, misunderstanding Winthrop's point. "As I just said, that's why we were here—to shoot the cardinal's special children's sermon and get some shots of the families we're profiling."

"So what's the problem?"

Goode was suddenly livid. "The problem, Winthrop, is that everything is wrong! The families aren't here. There's no children's sermon. The church has been invaded by some crazy gay group that's shouting down the cardinal. The place is crawling with police. This is an outrage! No one from the cardinal's office called me to tell me that everything was off. They obviously canceled because of the demonstration, and nobody told me!"

"A gay demonstration at St. Patrick's. Hecklers shouting down poor Cardinal Boyle. The place swarming with cops. Sounds like a good news story to me, Jeffrey."

"Fuck you, Winthrop."

"Say, I saw another CBS truck here."

"That's Jay Gonzalez."

"Why didn't you get the word from Jay? Don't you guys talk?"

"We're both busy. We never see each other."

Winthrop laughed. "Why don't you pitch in with Jay? Provide double coverage for CBS. You've got a camera here. Your producer is here. Best of all, you're here, Jeffrey. You're all ready to go."

"This is definitely not my kind of story. By the way, what are you doing here anyway? Is this going to be the basis for one of your infuriating columns?"

"My best friend's the founder of GRACE—that's the gay group heckling Boyle. She asked me to be here."

"So you're in league with these crazies, Winthrop. You really are as dangerous as they say."

"They? Who are they, Jeffrey? You know, I've heard it rumored more than once that you're gay. No truth to that, is there?"

Before Winthrop could blink, Goode was on him like an attack dog. Winthrop's legs flew out from under him, and his head cracked against the cathedral steps. He felt the skin break and a lump raise. Blood was flowing down both sides of his head, dripping behind his ears, with the migraine setting in immediately, yet he was glad. Crazy and glad. Glad that he had taken a blow for Rita and GRACE. Crazy because the blow had set him free of sense, set him free of reason. He was raving at Goode. "Is that a yes or a no, Jeffrey? Yes or no? Yes or no? That's another good news story. Good news! The outing of Jeff Goode! Come on out, Jeffrey! Come on out!"

Two cops were struggling to pull Goode off Winthrop, but Goode was crazy as well. He clung to Winthrop's midsection with the strength of a lunatic, driving Winthrop's bleeding head back into the step a second, a third and a fourth time before the police could drag him off. Goode was growling and kicking, with spit spewing from his mouth, and the cops were yelling too.

"It's all right, officers. It's all right," Winthrop found himself saying as a third and a fourth cop helped him to his feet. Winthrop didn't know any of the cops.

"What's going on here?" one of the officers exclaimed.

"It's OK, OK," Winthrop insisted. Goode had stopped struggling, but his whole body was shaking in arrhythmic spasms like an exposed nerve. Another half dozen cops materialized, and suddenly it was a police convention. Cops were everywhere. Winthrop sensed that they were one and all in a foul mood. Rita's troops would not fare well with this group. The thought flashed through Winthrop's mind that he and Goode would both be arrested despite the fact that he was the one who had been attacked. Such was the logic of cops in a funk. Then Winthrop spotted Captain Frank McCarthy, Germany's boss. "Frank," Winthrop called out.

"Hold everything," McCarthy shouted. "I know this guy and the other one, too. They're a couple of reporters."

"That's right," Winthrop replied. "No harm done. I was about to go into St. Patrick's, and Jeff here was about to leave when we happened to bump into each other. This is just a friendly professional dispute." Goode glared back at Winthrop with a look of pure hate.

"You two promise to be good boys, and you can both go," McCarthy said. With that, the cops dispersed. Goode exited with his producer and camerawoman, giving Winthrop one final, unforgiving stare and emptying a quiver of psychic arrows into his heart as he walked away. McCarthy handed Winthrop a blue and red checked handkerchief.

"Thank you, Frank," Winthrop declared as he patted his bloodied head. "Thanks, I didn't need to get bogged down in explanations."

"I guess you're covering this gay thing," McCarthy said.

"More or less."

"Well, you better get in there. It's going to be over fast."

Winthrop gave McCarthy a little raised eyebrow look, jogged up the remaining steps toward the entrance, opened the door and went inside St. Patrick's.

THE CHURCH WAS MOBBED. The usual Sunday worshipers and what were probably several hundred GRACE demonstrators had packed St. Patrick's to the limit—they and dozens of police. Winthrop hadn't seen them yet, but he knew they were there as well, biding their time until someone from GRACE stepped over the line.

As he went through his flexible proctoscoping routine to bore through the crowd, Winthrop heard a variety of exclamations— "Disgusting!" "No respect!" "How offensive!" "House of the Lord!" Some of the exclamations were near at hand; some were produced by the amplified voice of Cardinal Boyle. In addition to the exclamations Winthrop could also hear an ongoing series of echoing shouts rendered unintelligible by the cathedral's huge dimensions. Initially, Winthrop could see nothing, his vision blocked by the crowd and the row of mammoth pillars that lined the long aisle ahead of him. Finally, as he broke through the crush of churchgoers and took up a position by the last stone pillar, the scene came into focus.

Dozens of men and women were standing all about the church— in the pews, in the aisles, along the sides of the church and way up front in the center aisle by the main altar. They were all wearing GRACE T-shirts with the bright green and gold Holy Spirit logo—the divine Pentecostal bird, the Paraclete, in flight and emanating rays of light. Every couple of seconds more and more GRACE members stood up. Some of the demonstrators were shaking their fists in anger. Others were waving crucifixes. Almost all were chanting slogans. Some shouted, "Out the Church, out the Church," while others sang out, "Gay priests forever" or "Transform the church."

The police were out in force as well, even more than Winthrop had expected. They were lining the sides of the church, ready for action. There were plenty of TV cameras, too. At first, Winthrop was surprised that they had gotten in. Then he understood the reason. The cardinal wanted New Yorkers to see for themselves the spectacle of gay activism. No doubt he had calculated that the public would overwhelmingly support both him and the police in their repudiation of the homosexual blasphemers. It was time to teach them all a lesson and put an end once and for all to this unholy invasion of the Cathedral. If it required some measured use of force, so much the better. The homosexuals deserved it, and the people would support it. Boyle knew. Absolutely and without a shred of doubt. He knew.

It was indeed a supremely confident Boyle that Winthrop saw standing tall in the pulpit, an imperial Boyle, looking morally and politically superior in his cardinal's robes. As the demonstrators shouted their slogans and berated him, Boyle called out repeatedly to them in a resounding voice rich with authority and replete with moral indignation. "Cease, cease," he commanded the demonstrators.

Not "stop," not "quiet," but "cease," thought Winthrop.

"This is a disgrace," Boyle continued. "You are guests in the house of the Lord. Cease, cease. This is an abomination."

If Winthrop could have reached Boyle right then and there, he would have smacked him. Right in the face. Smacked him hard. The reason was simple. His Eminence was an ass. An ass and a politician, if that wasn't redundant. Just like Martinez and Ross. The biblical reverberations of "abomination" and "house of the Lord" were phony. So was his use of the word "cease." It was all a bureaucratic power move. Slam the demonstrators with the weight of almost 2,000 years of institutional rhetoric.

Of course, the demonstrators were shouting their own slogans, beating on Boyle and the church with the time-honored jargon of political protest. That was what public discourse, indeed, public life in America, had come down to—an animal house of rhetoric, a total breakdown of communication.

Whenever it really mattered, whenever there was something really at stake, communication stopped—or, to borrow Boyle's word, it "ceased." The people in power spoke the institutional language of power, using language as a mask or a weapon, never giving a straight answer, never letting go of the secrets they took to be the source of their power. Instead, they talked like bureaucrats and beat the crap out of you with the sticks and stones of bureaucratese. The disenfranchised, on the other hand, demonstrated, carried signs and shouted slogans. They had no secrets to conceal. All they had was their status—as victims, as outsiders, as minorities. In most cases neither side listened to the other.

Winthrop certainly empathized with the demonstrators for theirs was an all but impossible position. America had been born in a violent revolution. Our venerable forefathers had engaged in guerrilla warfare and terrorist acts to secure life, liberty and the pursuit of happiness. They had won their freedom and the freedom of generations through an act of high treason and had further secured that freedom by executing a Bill of Rights, which guaranteed Freedom of Speech and the Right of Assembly. Having been blessed by the blood of colonial soldiers, protest had special historic sanction. One might even say that protest was definitively American. Except for one thing—that was not how most Americans perceived it.

In fact, public demonstration in America had always been a self-indicting act. Demonstrate anywhere, anyhow, for whatever reason—as part of a union, a political organization or social activist group—and you were considered a troublemaker. You were subversive, a threat to respectable, law-abiding citizens. Demonstrate in a church, as GRACE was doing, and you were what? Well, that was easy, thought Winthrop, as more and more demonstrators leapt to their feet and shouted at Boyle, who was shaking his head and repeating his words of condemnation and disgust. Demonstrate in a church and you were the walking, talking, fist-waving, head-line-grabbing personification of obscenity—the old Judge Potter Stewart version—no need to define it. As the judge had said, "I know it when I see it."

Well, thought Winthrop, America would know it when it saw Rita's beloved GRACE waving the rainbow flag at St. Patrick's. America would be wrong, but that would not help the gay and transgender men and women who were risking bashed heads and broken dreams by confronting the Church in all the splendor of its hypocrisy.

Not to sell the demonstrators short, but Winthrop wondered if they really knew how much they were risking. He wondered too where Rita was as he felt the tension and emotion rise precipitously moment by moment as each additional demonstrator stood to defy Boyle and the Church. He knew that she was there somewhere, probably among the frontline troops in one of the first pews, but he had not been able to spot her.

As he searched the pews for Rita, his line of sight increasingly blocked by demonstrators, Winthrop began to get a sick, sinking feeling, that same feeling that he had experienced all too many times before when he had seen police and demonstrators confront each other. It was the same feeling he had had the one and only time he witnessed an execution. It was down in Florida, the Henry Mann case. It had all finally come to a head just a few months after Ray Hallee had killed his mother, Ida, along with Sal the parakeet and Pat the cat. Winthrop had been brooding about Ray, trying to make sense of him as a person, trying to understand the phenomenon of the psychopathic killer, the mass murderer, the serial murderer. He wanted to do a column on it, but he didn't want it to be a think piece. It had to focus on a real person, somebody other than Ray. Winthrop couldn't write about Ray—not yet anyway. And then along came Henry Mann.

Mann was an illiterate drifter with an IQ of 68. According to all the psychiatric reports, he had the intellectual maturity of a six year old. He had no family. No friends. No relationships. After repeated attempts he had succeeded in running away from a foster home at the age of twelve and had been on the streets and on the run ever since. He had apparently never held a job, at least not for more than a few days. Nevertheless, he had been able to survive on his own resources for more than sixteen years, living off whatever he could scavenge or steal. He also had one undeniable talent. Henry Mann was an extremely accomplished serial murderer.

Henry sometimes exaggerated, and sometimes he made things up, but in general he was very reliable in his confession to the police, which disclosed more than fifty murders stretching over twelve years and ten states, though the preponderance of the killing was in Florida. As a result of Henry's confession the FBI and the Florida state police recovered the remains of twenty-one victims and closed the books on eighteen additional cases.

Henry's methodology was always the same: abduct a young boy or girl (gender and race didn't matter) between the ages of twelve and sixteen. Rape, sodomize and murder the victim (usually by stabbing). Then behead, dismember and bury the body. Henry accomplished all this without ever once being questioned by police or in any way arousing suspicion. He might have gone on with his career forever if he hadn't been involved in a minor fender bender. During a sudden midafternoon thunderstorm he was hit from behind in downtown Orlando by a wrecker from a nearby gas station. The impact caused the two vehicles to lock, so for Henry, there was no escape. When the driver of the truck came over to talk to Henry, he saw the head of victim number 52 or 53 on the passenger seat. The rest of the body was in the trunk.

Henry's court-appointed lawyer pleaded not guilty, citing both insanity and mental disability as reasons for the plea. The judge found Henry competent to stand trial, and he was convicted of multiple counts of murder in the first degree after a long, messy trial in which the prosecution, the defense, the judge and jury took turns proving themselves to be the ones who were incompetent. The judge sentenced Henry to death. In Florida, when you're sentenced to death, you get to choose between lethal injection and electrocution. Appeals went on for more than six years wasting millions of taxpayer dollars, though there was never any doubt in anyone's mind that Henry had murdered dozens of innocent boys and girls. What's more, if by some perverse and unthinkable miracle he somehow beat the rap in Florida, he had capital cases pending against him in a half-dozen other jurisdictions. It was all an elaborate legal ballet, an intricately choreographed pas de deux, in which both Henry and the system danced, never missing a step. And it all came to a climax on death row at Florida State Prison with Jack Winthrop as witness.

Winthrop was struck then as he was struck now at the obvious fact: here was a true conspiracy in action. Henry and the prison guards going through the final, fatal motions, doing it together, moving slowly and deliberately, as if underwater, with never any doubt of the goal, which was death—in this case by electrocution, for that was inexplicably Henry's choice. And here at St. Patrick's today, it was strikingly similar: the demonstrators exercising their constitutional rights, the cardinal, as warden, presiding over all with an unassailable air of righteousness—and the whole elaborate charade leading inevitably to disaster. Yes, thought Winthrop, the legal system needed people like Henry and Henry needed the system, just as the police, the cardinal and the demonstrators all needed each other. How else could they fulfill their destinies as social antagonists? As heroes and villains?

It was all a show. It was all a sham—except that it was all too real. The victimization, the death and destruction—that was all real. Henry's victims were dead, and Henry was dead; the system had administered its justice and continued to grind on. And here today, what would happen? GRACE and their supporters would demonstrate, publicly charging the Church with bigotry and hypocrisy. After all, what was the percentage of gay priests? Winthrop's over/under on the question always hovered around 90 percent. Thus the closeted Church would reassert its moral teaching against homosexuality and cry foul at having to endure this unholy invasion of the house of the Lord. And the public would condemn the demonstrators. The local talk shows would buzz about the incident for a day or two, and then the spotlight would shift again to some other controversy. Everyone would play out their respective roles. Everyone would stay in character, including the police. Yes, thought Winthrop, the police would simply act like police. What else could they do? And Winthrop knew what that meant. Look first at the show of force. This was a small army of cops. Then consider the air of professionalism, the regimental discipline and, above all, the unmistakable pretense of restraint. Factor in the degree of provocation, the outrage, and it all added up to one thing: somebody was going to get hurt.

Winthrop continued to look for Rita, scanning pew after pew, hoping to find her before the dam broke. At least if he located her, he might be able to do something to help her exit unscathed. Then it happened. A cop was arresting a demonstrator, a woman. Whether there had been some specific provocation or Boyle had given the nod or time had simply run out on GRACE—Winthrop probably would never know since the eyewitness accounts and the official statements would no doubt later prove inconclusive. It hardly mattered anyway. All that mattered was that the arrests had begun. A cop was pulling the demonstrator from the end of a pew over on the far left, the north side of the church. The woman immediately went limp, neither resisting nor facilitating the arrest. Then, in an instant, cops were arresting GRACE members all across the church. One demonstrator after another was seized and dragged, limp and unresisting, out of the building.

Finally, Winthrop spotted Rita. She was right there in the second row on the far left, just a few rows in front of the woman who had just been arrested. Winthrop's view of her had been blocked by a huge, hulking demonstrator who was now being dragged away with great difficulty by two cops. Now he could see her in profile, head bowed, fist raised—in pride and defiance, yes, but also, Winthrop felt, in sadness over the need for confrontation, in sadness too, perhaps, over the turn the confrontation was taking. For Rita must have sensed now, as Winthrop did, that she and her beloved GRACE colleagues were playing on the edge, poised on the brink of disaster.

Just then an extraordinary thing occurred. The crowd of churchgoers, which had remained remarkably silent throughout the demonstration, except for a few random shouts and catcalls, which Winthrop had been largely unable to decipher, suddenly rose to its feet, virtually en masse, as if involved in some weird standing ovation, and began to applaud the police. Within moments almost no one was left seated. Men, women, children—everyone was up on their feet, clapping as hard as they could, pounding their hands together in approval.

Winthrop looked back to the pulpit, and there was Boyle, applauding as well, nodding and smiling magisterially as he applauded with just two fingers against his left hand, adding little light taps of pontifical approval to the thundering applause of the worshipers. The total effect was overwhelming. Winthrop looked at Rita and felt the devastation, wondering how it could have turned out any other way. Then he began to move. His personal riot detector had just gone off. It was blaring in his brain like a smoke alarm, signaling that he had just seconds to get to Rita before everything went crazy. With no time for proctoscoping through the crowd at the back of the church, Winthrop sprinted up the right side aisle. By running, he was making himself a likely target of arrest, but there was no other way. His plan was to charge up the aisle, cut between the first row of pews and the main altar, get to Rita and somehow persuade her to walk slowly and peaceably from the church before they were both arrested.

Indiana Jack and the Temple of Doom, Winthrop thought, as he burst up the aisle. The scene was just that insane. The worshipers and Boyle applauding, the police arresting demonstrators at an amazing clip, while those GRACE members left standing continued to demonstrate, some silently, like Rita, some chanting slogans. Before Winthrop was five strides into his sprint, a demonstrator suddenly broke toward the pulpit, bent apparently on knocking Boyle out of the box, and was tackled by two cops just as he got to the altar. The demonstrator, a frail-looking man in his forties, struggled a bit as he was dragged away, prompting a third cop to approach, whip out his nightstick and deal three quick blows to the man's midsection. The cop then turned and grabbed a GRACE member who happened to be standing close by and began dragging her to the door, beating her with his nightstick as he went. That was it, thought Winthrop. Nightstick time. Now the riot had truly begun. One after another, demonstrators made a dash toward Boyle, were tackled, beaten and dragged away.

As Winthrop got to the first pew of the side aisle and turned the corner, he looked toward Rita. There she was, miraculously still standing like the last sand castle on the beach at nightfall. Maybe if he continued with his Carl Lewis impersonation, he could still reach her and get her out before she was grabbed and beaten.

Just then a demonstrator vaulted out of one of the front pews, dashed by Winthrop, narrowly avoiding a collision, and leapt on top of the altar rail directly in front of Boyle. "Jesus will judge!" he shouted and was immediately buried by four police officers, three men and a woman, all with their nightsticks flailing.

Winthrop was fifteen yards from Rita when their eyes met for the first time and whack! Winthrop went down. It had been at least twenty-five years since he was tackled, and it hurt. As he fell, Winthrop caught a fleeting glimpse of one of NYPD's finest descending on Rita. St. Patrick's had turned into a gay Alamo, and, of course, there he was playing Davy Crockett to Rita's Jim Bowie.

Winthrop knew better than to resist arrest, but he wanted to proclaim his status as a reporter, hoping that might make a difference. The tackle, however, had knocked the wind out of him, and although his lips were forming the words, "I'm a reporter . . . *New York Times,*" nothing was coming out of his mouth. As his attacker got up from behind him, Winthrop knew what was coming but was helpless to prevent it: yes, the moment had arrived, and he would get his nightstick lesson as well. Just as Winthrop twisted his body to try to face his assailant, the nightstick caught him on the flank and the whole left side of his body went numb. Three more quick blows landed unfelt, two against his ribs and one against his shin. Now Winthrop was truly helpless. All he could do was wait for breath and feeling to return and hope that he was lucky enough to have nothing broken.

Now came the dragging. His cop—for he had now caught a glimpse of him—was a husky kid of about twenty-five full of red meat protein and esprit de corps. He dragged Winthrop single-handed by the shirt collar toward the church door. As he was dragged, Winthrop felt the scrapes and abrasions, felt the burn against his right side, back and rear, absorbed it all wherever he still had feeling. And he heard the cries of "fag" and "queer" from some of the churchgoers. Heard the hatred, the superior contempt, in their voices. And he was glad. Glad to be queer. Glad to be a fag, if only in the minds of these bigots. And he would be glad, too, to suck the great universal cock to show how glad he was. Hell, he would be glad to suck anybody's cock to show that he, Jack Winthrop, was glad and proud to support GRACE and gay people everywhere who simply wanted to be themselves and to be accepted and respected for themselves like all the other normal people in this absurd and crazy world.

Outside St. Patrick's the cops were loading the demonstrators into the vans, sometimes administering one last whack of their sticks to punctuate an arrest. Winthrop quickly surveyed the scene and just caught sight of Rita as she was shoved into a wagon. She looked battered and limp, and Winthrop wondered again what she was feeling, what she was thinking. Had some victory been won here amid the apparent disaster? Had GRACE made a statement on behalf of gay and transgender rights, on behalf of human rights, that would endure despite the utter lack of understanding and support among the churchgoers and despite the arrests and the beatings? In fact, had GRACE made a statement because of the arrests and the beatings, or was it too late for Gandhian victories, too late to win justice through sacrifice? Winthrop didn't know. As usual, he could ask the right questions. He just didn't have the answers.

Meanwhile Mr. Meat was dragging Winthrop toward a van already packed with demonstrators. As he was about to be lifted and dumped into the rear of the wagon, Winthrop heard a voice. "Jesus Christ, it's you again, Winthrop!" It was Frank McCarthy.

"Frank," Winthrop said. At least his voice was working now. His wind had come back, and feeling was returning to the left side of his body.

"Jesus Christ," McCarthy repeated. He looked disgusted. Winthrop tried to think of a witty remark, but nothing came. McCarthy looked from Winthrop to Mr. Meat then back to Winthrop. "You know, Winthrop," he said. "I always sort of liked you. But you're getting to be a pain in my fucking ass." He looked again to Mr. Meat. "Throw him in with the rest of the fags," McCarthy said.

And so he did. Glad and proud, thought Winthrop, glad and proud, as the door slammed shut, and he waited for the van to take him to jail.

11

By the time Donna bailed out Rita and Winthrop at a thousand bucks apiece, it was well past 10:00 p.m. Winthrop had placed the call to the Tit at about 2:00 figuring correctly that he would find Donna there working in her office. Donna got to the station right away, but the police were making no attempt to expedite the bail bond process. The intent was clearly to let the homos chill out awhile, and at least half the demonstrators would no doubt spend the night in jail.

There was a brief comic contretemps as the Three Musketeers were about to exit the police station. One of the detectives mistook Donna for a prostitute trying to mosey on out of the station prior to being booked. It was not altogether surprising that the detective would make such a mistake since Donna was wearing a pair of bright red leather hot pants revealing a generous portion of her buns, matching red patent leather shoes with stiletto heels and a skin tight tank top that accurately conveyed every subtle heave and sigh of her 36DD's, nipple rings and all. The detective was disabused of his false assumption rather quickly, however. He had come up on Donna from behind, charging at her and yelling, "Hey, bimbo, where do you think you're going?" as he grabbed her by the arm. Any one else might have been flustered, but not Donna.

"Fuck off, Dick Tracy. You got nothing on me," she responded and shot him her sharpest asshole-of-the-day look as she yanked her arm from his grasp and strutted out the door with Winthrop and Rita.

The incident lifted everyone's spirits somewhat, but it was a pretty quiet ride in Donna's baby blue Jag XFR back to Winthrop's apartment. Rita was battered and depressed. She had a black eye from an officer's flying elbow, which was apparently accidental, and some very sore ribs from a couple of nightstick blows, which decidedly were not. All Winthrop and Donna had been able to get out of her was an explanation of her bruises and a declaration of guilt over having been freed while many of her colleagues were still in jail. Winthrop realized that it would have been impossible to persuade Rita to leave St. Patrick's to avoid arrest. Still, his little sprint had been worth it, despite the arrest. He would do it again a million times over. Of course, that didn't change the fact that he felt like shit. It was more than the physical pain, although that was bad enough. His whole left side from his ribs to his shin was one big purple bruise. He had skin burns and abrasions all over his back and right side from the dragging and finally a lump on his head the size of a horseshoe iron (all cartoon references intended) from his warm-up bout with Jeff Goode. But what bothered Winthrop more, what really disturbed him, was the turn life was taking for him—for him and for everyone and everything he cared about. He still had that feeling in the pit of his stomach, that sick sense of foreboding that had gripped him at St. Patrick's right before everything blew. That's what worried him. He didn't want to have that feeling about Life Itself. Paranoia was one thing; chronic nausea was another. He did not want to feel that he was living perpetually in the midst of impending disaster, nor did he want to believe in the inevitability of impotence as everything fell apart—but he was afraid that was where all life was headed.

It was weird, thought Winthrop, everything was becoming unhinged, but it was all still related somehow—yet at what level? He didn't really know. Meaninglessness perhaps, or power relationships, or bullshit. He couldn't quite nail it down. But there it was: insanity all around, in his life and the lives of everyone he knew. Violence winning out. Tragedy becoming routine. Ignorance spreading like a plague. And for the causes he believed in, there were only moral victories.

Look at the demonstration. Rita and GRACE would surely do it all over again, the St. Patrick's gig or something similar, despite the riot and the arrests and the inevitable public condemnation. But what had they gained? In fact, what had activism ever gained? Everything we have, thought Winthrop. But what was that? Martin Luther King Jr. and Malcolm X and so many other civil rights activists had given everything they had for the cause of freedom and equality. Old, crusty, Vietnam-obsessed LBJ had signed the Civil Rights Act, and what was the result half a century later? Well, the result was that we had almost as many nigger haters per square inch in America as we had during the glory days of the KKK. Or so at least it seemed.

Meanwhile everybody did what they had to do. Isn't that what Germany had said? But when the cops did what they had to do, they put people in jail. When the GRACE gang did what they had to do, they got put in jail. And what about Speck? Wasn't he just doing what he had to do? Shooting, stalking, terrorizing. Move to Speck's center stage, as ALJ had, doing what he had to do, doing his ALJ thing, and you got shot. You became a target, as Winthrop, himself, was now and no doubt Danielle as well. The best you could do was to make yourself a moving target, and ALJ had certainly done that for years, shaking things up in the process. That was what Winthrop admired about him. Of course, Speck knew all about Jones's moves. And he would use that knowledge to nail him. And what about the second gunman, thought Winthrop. What about him? Because, when you got right down to it, there was always another gunman.

Bottom line: Winthrop felt like shit. So it was good to get back to his apartment. Good to see Donna strutting around, looking so sweet and fuckable. Good to be with Rita as well. Good to throw off the miserable goddamn silence and speak. And finally good once again to enjoy the music of voices and try to dispel the poison in the atmosphere—try to blow the malaise out of the soul.

"Here's a little Tennessee mash for you, Jack," Donna said with a smile, handing him a huge tumbler filled with Jack Daniels on the rocks. "And some Maxwell House for you, beautiful," she said, offering Rita a cup.

"I don't feel very beautiful just this minute, Donna," Rita said. "But the coffee sure smells great."

"Thank God you had some Stoli, Jack. Too bad I have to use cubes. I always tell you to keep it in the goddamn freezer," Donna remarked with a sigh, kicking off her heels and letting her body drop into a white leather love seat. Rita was sitting catty-corner in a matching leather swivel chair. Winthrop was stretched out on the floor, feeling like a side of beef.

"Next time I promise, Donna," Winthrop said.

"By the way, Jack, have you checked your answering machine?" Donna asked.

What a knack Donna had! Get right to the point. Hit it over the head with a hammer. The phone. His answering machine. That was the one thing Winthrop most certainly did not want to check. He hadn't been home since the previous afternoon. He was sure that Speck and the other gunman had called, as was their duty. As for making calls, after reaching Donna at the station on his cell, he had sneaked a call to Danny as well, but oddly her phone had just kept ringing. She must be wondering about him, he thought, wondering what had become of him. Of course, he was worried about her, while wondering, too, about Abe. He knew the wheels were turning there, dreaming and scheming, fashioning the dimensions of the Emancipation Tour. Yes, he was anxious to speak with Danielle, anxious to hear her voice, and he was looking forward to tomorrow's meeting on the tour with Abe and Danny and Bream. The jail time had given him a chance to think, and he had some new ideas, partly as a result of the riot at St. Patrick's, but he didn't want to face all of that now. He couldn't face it, especially the stalker calls, the hang-ups. He needed an hour. That was all. An hour of spiritual triage among friends.

And that was what it was—for an hour or so, just small talk and quiet relaxation with a little Miles Davis in the background for atmosphere—Donna's choice. Indeed, it was her show to run from beginning to end, with Winthrop and Rita grateful for the rest and entertainment. Donna led the conversation, filled the drinks, provided the charm and levity, and generally made sure that everything was right. Mellow and right.

"Mind if I take this fucking thing off?" Donna asked about half-way into her third Stoli.

"What a question!" Rita exclaimed.

"Of course, we don't mind," Winthrop replied.

"Just being polite, guys," Donna said with a laugh. "That's how my mother raised me." And with that, she yanked off her tank top and threw it across the room. "Wooh, that's better," she said, taking in a deep breath and blowing out the air. "Tight is great but bare is always better. You know, they passed a law saying women can go around now with their tits out—just like guys. Now if they'd just pass another law banning assholes from the streets, I'd walk around like this all the time."

"There's always a catch," said Winthrop. He was almost feeling good again. It was the same old equation—Jack Daniels, jazz and naked women. It did the trick every time.

"Listen, Jack, Rita, I got some news for you and a business proposition, too," Donna said, sinking down lower in her seat, getting extra comfortable now, getting ready to talk about her favorite subject—business, the sex business, that is. Rita seemed to be relaxing now as well. Yes, thought Winthrop, a sense of equilibrium was finally returning. If only that answering machine weren't waiting for him with some red number—20, 22, 25—glowing like plutonium in the dark. In just a few more minutes, he thought, I'll be ready to face it. Now it was time to listen to Donna.

"So what's the news?" Winthrop asked.

"Good news, I hope," Rita said.

"Well, let me tell you," Donna replied. "Manny's giving up the Tit."

"Manny's giving it up?" Rita asked.

"Yes," Donna said, "And he's selling the bar to me!"

"Oh, that's wonderful news!" Rita exclaimed.

"Hey, that's great, Donna. Congratulations!" Winthrop shouted, banging his tumbler in approval against the hardwood floor.

"I'd jump up and kiss you, Donna, but I don't think I can move right now," Rita said.

"Same here," Winthrop added.

"Hugs and kisses assumed," Donna answered. "Anyway, the story is this. Manny's been around the New York scene for years. He's made his money from several businesses, not just the Tit, and now he's cashing out. Taking off for the Bahamas. We worked out a price for the bar, and I'm buying it from him. We close tomorrow."

"That's just the best news," said Rita.

"I would have said something sooner to both of you, but Manny wanted to keep everything quiet until it was a done deal."

"What's Manny planning to do?"

"He likes Grand Bahama. He's going down there, mostly to take it easy. Maybe go in half with his brother, Bernie, on some classy service."

"You mean escort?" Winthrop asked.

"Yeah, something to keep him active, keep his hand in the game," said Donna.

"Well, we'll all miss Manny, but I'm just delighted for you, Donna," Rita exclaimed.

"Absolutely," Winthrop added. "But what's the business proposition you were talking about?"

"Here it is. I thought it would be cool—and good business—to cut both of you in on the deal. That is, you guys, Mo Mo and Sheila."

"A kind of partnership?" Rita asked.

"Right. I've always been the lone gun type, but when it comes to a bar, a partnership is cool."

"It's an interesting proposition, Donna, but I really don't have much money," Rita insisted.

"Doesn't matter. I'd like you to come on board as assistant manager. We'll build up your equity in the business through salary deductions. That's what I'll be offering Sheila and Mo Mo, too. And there's no reason why you can't keep up your work with GRACE and ALFREE. After all, there are twenty-four hours in a day. How about it, Rita?"

"Count me in, Donna. I needed something new to lift my spirits. This could really be great!"

"What about you, Jack?" Donna asked.

"Yes, come on, Jack. Hop on top of the pile here," Rita exclaimed. "We need you."

"Besides, Jack, you've got some bucks," Donna added.

Winthrop hated to be death obsessed, but there it was. While Donna and Rita were getting psyched about the Tit partnership, he was imagining his obituary in *The New York Times*. "Jack Winthrop, Pulitzer Prize-winning author, former *New York Times* columnist and businessman, died yesterday in his apartment in New York City. He was 69. The cause of death was unknown. In recent years Mr. Winthrop was best known for a string of topless and nude bars that he established across the country with his sometime companion, Donna Marone. He is survived by Ms. Marone and Danielle Jackson, another sometime companion. A memorial service led by Father Rita Harvey, a transgendered Roman Catholic priest, is scheduled for Monday at 9:00 a.m. at the Tit for Tat, the East Side topless bar owned in part by Mr. Winthrop, Ms. Marone and Father Harvey."

"Jack?" Rita said.

"Jack, honey?" Donna said as well. "Are you spacing out on us?"

"No, not at all. Listen. Count me in, too. Why not?" Amid the whoops and cheers from Donna and Rita, Winthrop was still thinking, here I go again. In just one week, I've jumped the tracks three times, first, signing on with ALJ, then getting involved with Danny, and now this—becoming part owner of the Tit for Tat. Actually Winthrop had always had the urge to do something totally unrelated to journalism and politics, like becoming an aerobics instructor. Having an interest in the Tit might be just the thing. And Donna was right. He did have some money set aside. Not to mention the deal with Jones.

"We'll discuss the exact amount later, Donna, but I'm thinking about putting in around a million or so."

"My God, Jack," Rita exclaimed.

"I always knew you were in the money," Donna said. "He's been pulling in the bucks for years, and he never spends a goddamn dime."

"I just have one question, Donna," Winthrop said.

"What's that, Jack?"

"What's my job? Rita's the assistant manager. What do I do? I don't want to be the silent partner. As you said, there are twenty-four hours in a day. Who needs sleep?"

"Of course, you have a job, Jack," Donna said. "You're the consigliere."

"The consigliere!" Winthrop exclaimed. After offering his opinions for years in columns that were persuasive as far as he could tell only to the people who already agreed with him (which unfortunately was the sorry lot of all commentators and columnists), he was suddenly besieged by people who wanted his advice. First, Jones; now, Donna. Of course, they were on his side politically as well, the side somewhere to the left of Che Guevara and Noam Chomsky. But neither was looking for his column opinions. Instead they wanted him to help them blaze a new trail. In turn, his life would change as well. When he thought about it, it was really the only way to go—fake out the future, which life and your own pre-determined decisions have already planned out for you, and go off in another direction, any direction, so long as the path was unknown, before you found yourself retracing your own steps when all the while you believed you were moving forward.

"The consigliere," Winthrop repeated thoughtfully. "I sort of like that."

"I thought you would," said Donna. "I want to make the Tit into something really cool."

"But it is cool," Rita insisted.

"Yes, but it's just not out there enough. For instance, we don't ever get into costumes," Donna said.

"You mean burlesque?" Rita asked.

"No, burlesque is passé. I mean fetish, psychodrama."

"I've got just one thing to say here as the newly appointed consigliere."

"What's that, Jack?" Donna asked.

"Whatever we do, let's be sure to keep it dirty."

"God, yes!" Donna exclaimed. "And we won't have just cisgender women dancing. We'll have transgender women, too. Lots of them. I wonder if we could get some transmen, not to mention mixing in a few cisgender men as well. I know I'll be turning off the macho men in the crowd, but fuck them. There's a way of doing it and keeping it cool for the people who are cool. Mix everything in. Give it a whole Paris runway, androgynous fashion feel."

"Just be sure to keep it dirty," Winthrop repeated. He wanted to be sure the point was clear. "I know it's been said before, but it's true," he continued. "There's no point to sex if it isn't dirty."

"You mean there is no sex if it isn't dirty," said Donna.

"No wonder we get along so well," Winthrop remarked with a laugh, feeling better with every passing second. And indeed the mood of the evening had changed. It was Donna who had done it. She had succeeded in pulling Winthrop and Rita back from the brink. Now, as he and his friends sank back into a comfortable, communal silence, deepened by the late night rhythms of Miles, Winthrop could feel Donna's positive spirit flowing through the room. Yes, Rita was smiling again, regaining her customary optimism and aplomb, and Winthrop no longer felt like shit. He was even ready now to face his phone.

While his cell number had limited distribution, Winthrop had always kept his home number listed. Over the years he had received quite a few unsolicited leaks and leads as a result. He had also gotten a goodly number of crank and obscene phone calls, even the occasional death threat. And it was all just fine with him. It was part of the territory, part of what it meant to be a journalist, to be tapped into the chaotic mix of life on planet Earth, New York City style, at the beginning of the twentieth-first century.

Throughout it all he had never once felt violated, had never once felt that anyone had gotten to him, even when they resorted to threats. For no one had ever penetrated beyond his persona as a journalist. To the dozens of sick and warped terror mongers who had taken time from their busy psychopathic schedules to spew venom in his particular direction, Jack Winthrop was merely the sum total of all he had written. He was a kind of literary hologram, an insubstantial projection of printed words, which they had found offensive. The purpose of the calls was to register how badly those words had offended them and to strike back at the perceived source of that offense. The callers may have thought they were angry at Winthrop himself. They may have even thought that they wanted to kill him. In actuality they were angered by words and ideas, and their supposed target was merely a phantasm with the signature of Jack Winthrop.

But this time it was different. This time it was Speck, and Speck had gotten through. His target was not merely words and ideas, though they were targets as well, but Winthrop himself. Winthrop, the man. Winthrop, the fragile and vulnerable human being with a mortal life to lose. Just as Speck had targeted Abraham Lincoln Jones, a man of flesh and blood with a heart that beat and a mind that lived, and then had played with the man, so had he succeeded in capturing Winthrop in virtually the same way. And now Winthrop was in play, with death the only end—for someone at least. Winthrop knew it just as he knew how it was that Speck had slipped through, how he had entered his real life, evading the defenses of words and ideas. For Speck had seen Winthrop at the bar, had seen him, as it were, at home, beyond the veil of words, as naked and exposed as the dancers on the Tit for Tat stage. For all intents and purposes he had drunk with Winthrop, and so he had been able to capture him.

Yes, that was it—and the fact too that he had publicly aligned himself with Jones. Had spoken of it to his friends. Had established the human bond, the spiritual partnership. And there, Speck had caught him again, had cornered him in an act that was what? That was real. Yes, that was it, real, however exaggerated the hope may have been, ALJ's hope and even Winthrop's hope, for change. The decision to join Jones was a real act, a political act. If you wanted to be philosophical, it was a goddamn existential act that threatened change, like Rita's demonstration at St. Patrick's. And once Winthrop had committed himself to such an act, once he had taken the risk, he was out there in play just as Abraham Lincoln Jones had always been.

Of course, there was the other gunman to contend with as well. Was that a matter of one phantasm pursuing another, Winthrop thought? Or had the other gunman also broken through somehow? Was the Sherry gunman also on the trail of the real flesh and blood Winthrop as Speck now was? Worse. Had he, Jack Winthrop, now become the world's target—again, just like ALJ? Did his name now appear on the Psychotics Anonymous Most Wanted List? That was how it was beginning to seem to Winthrop. Global paranoia was in the wind, and the paranoia, as usual, was all but impossible to shake.

Still, Winthrop felt good now, even with the risk and danger, even with the paranoia—they were now in a strange way all part of the feeling as well. Jones would leave the hospital tomorrow morning. They would have their meeting at lunch, their planning session. They would follow through on ALJ's tour, the Emancipation Tour. They would say fuck you to Speck, the Sherry gunman and the hundreds or thousands (or was it hundreds of thousands?) of people like them. The tour would make its statement. The tour would address change. And Winthrop was ready for that change—whether as a partner in crime with Abraham Lincoln Jones or as Danny Jackson's lover or as the consigliere of the Tit for Tat. Yes, let's do it, Winthrop thought. Let's do it all. The only thing that matters is what actually happens. So let's do it—beginning with that goddamn phone and his goddamn messages.

"You know, Rita," Winthrop said at last, breaking the silence. "You're looking much better now."

"I feel better, Jack. Much better. It's because I have such good friends as you and Donna. You stood with us today, Jack. I'll never forget that. And, Donna, you rescued us both." With that, Rita rose from her chair and sat in Donna's lap.

"My pleasure, baby," Donna said and gave Rita three quick kisses on the lips.

"Hey, I'm feeling left out down here, guys," Winthrop complained.

"Didn't I say a few minutes ago, Jack, to hop on top of the pile?" Rita said.

"You certainly did, Rita," Winthrop answered, catapulting himself from the floor in a single motion and landing in Rita's lap. Then, from his precarious position, atop Rita, atop Donna, Winthrop kissed Rita on the mouth, kissed her open, full and long. It was the first time he had ever kissed her that way, despite the many times they had kissed before in friendship and affection. And the kiss was good. More than good. It was perfect. Then Winthrop kissed Donna on the lips as well and for several seconds it was all wetness and confusion and a complicated tangle of limbs as Winthrop and Donna and Rita played together on the leather love seat. When gravity hit, Winthrop was the first to fall, followed quickly by Rita and Donna, who was now on top, laughing hysterically.

"That's the danger of the ménage à trois!" Donna shouted in between the laughs. "One way or another, you always end up on the floor."

"I think this is the perfect way to end a crazy day like today," said Rita.

"Who says it has to end?" Donna exclaimed.

"I'm exhausted," Rita said.

"Listen," Winthrop said, "Why don't you guys take my bed?"

"Only if you come with us, Jack," Donna said. "It's one for all and all for one."

"I'd love to, Donna, but I can't. You mentioned it before. The goddamn phone. I've got to check it out."

"Come on, Jack," Donna insisted. "That fucking thing can wait until tomorrow."

"I can't let it wait any longer, Donna. You know about Danny Jackson, ALJ's assistant. Rita said you saw her on TV after the shooting, and she called and spoke to you guys yesterday."

"Right."

"Well, we're sort of involved."

"That's no surprise," Rita said with a smile.

"Maybe not," Winthrop said. "Anyway, I told her I'd call her around noon. When I sneaked in a call to her from the police station right after I phoned you, Donna, I didn't reach her, and I didn't want to leave a message about what had happened. I'm also worried that the guy who shot Jones may try to harass her. He called me here early Saturday morning the second I got back from the Tit. Called me a nigger in his best heavy breathing, stalker voice and fired off a gun by the phone just to make sure that he'd gotten my attention."

"My God, Jack!" Rita exclaimed.

"Fucking bastard," said Donna.

"What's more," Winthrop continued, "He's a valued patron of our beloved bar. I'm sure both of you have seen him. You know, the catatonic guy who comes in once or twice a week. Looks so straight it hurts. "

"Yeah, Mr. Straight," said Donna. "That's how I always thought of him. That's the guy that detective was asking me about last night. He didn't explain his interest."

"He talked to me too, Jack," said Rita. " Called himself Germany."

"That's my police contact," said Winthrop. "In any event, Mr. Straight is the guy I mean. I think of him as Speck. He shot Jones. And that was just the beginning of his game. Now he's stalking me, too."

"What about the Sherry gunman, Jack?" Rita asked. "I told you, Donna, Jack saw a gunman at the Sherry-Netherland right at the moment the shots came from the Plaza."

"Speck's shots," Donna said.

"Exactly," said Rita.

"Apparently there are no limits to my popularity—at least with psychos. I've been getting lots of hang-ups at my apartment, and I'm convinced that they're from the two psychos. I got five calls yesterday afternoon. I'm sure they were from Speck. I was at Danielle's last night, and I've been out ever since, but I know from talking to Germany this morning that I've gotten a lot more calls."

"So the cops have a bug on your phone?" Donna asked.

"Yeah, we're trying to see if we can get a bead on Speck, maybe the other gunman, too. So listen, guys, I've got to face the phone calls. I'm sure there's a call from Jones on there as well. He gets out of the hospital tomorrow, and we've got a lunch meeting at his apartment to figure out our next move."

"On the Emancipation Tour?" Rita asked. "You know, we saw bits of yesterday's press conference on the news. You finally got some TV time yourself, Jack."

"Jones sort of put me on the spot. Asked me to make a statement. It was kind of an ad-lib thing."

"You were great," Donna said. "But, Jack, you do what you have to do."

"Sorry to be such a bummer."

"Hey, you're not bumming me out," Donna answered. "I've got this beautiful woman here that needs satisfying, and I'm not letting the shit on your phone stop me. In fact, if you don't mind, Jack, I'm going to pull the damn phone jack out of the bedroom wall. I don't want any interruptions."

"No, go right ahead, Donna," Winthrop said.

"Donna, I told you I'm exhausted," Rita said.

"Love juice is the great elixir, Rita," Donna said, taking Rita's hand.

"We're off, Jackie," Donna said. "You know the way to your own bedroom if you want to join us later."

Then she and Rita disappeared into the bedroom.

12

WINTHROP WAS THINKING HE WAS AN IDIOT. It would have
been interesting, getting into another side of Rita, getting it on
with Donna, too. They'd been missing each other, he and Donna,
for weeks, just a matter of bad sexual timing, and here he was putting some other obligation ahead of his pleasure. But he had to. The
time was now. He had to listen to the calls. And anyway he wanted
to do it alone.

He thought maybe if he went through the psycho calls alone
and listened over and over again, he might pick up something in
the transmission, pick up something in the line noise, the static, the
disturbed, electronic silence. Like listening to Beatles records backwards, straining to catch the secret, psychedelic message—"I buried Paul"—or listening to "Revolution 9" with headphones, playing
it over and over, absorbing the messages radiated by the orchestral
noise, the sounds of war, the non sequiturs, the rippling flames and
the agonizing screams and then as a reward for patience and devo-
tion, hearing so very clearly the woman's voice, speaking as clearly
as your mother spoke when she woke you for school in the morning,
as clearly as when she said, "Time to get up, Jack. Time for school."
Yes, as clear as that, you heard Yoko say, "You become naked."

Perhaps it would be like that. Perhaps he would learn something that would lead him to Speck or even to Mr. Sherry, the Fancy Dan, as Germany had called him. As Winthrop imagined him, Sherry would always present himself as elegantly out of date, always be most comfortable wearing a suit and tie, three-piece, double-breasted, in conservative shades of blue and gray. A white handkerchief ornamenting the jacket, a watch chain depending from his vest pocket. And he would be very fond of hats, bowlers in particular. Yes, he would embrace the anachronism. Delight in it. Just as on special occasions he would be given to carrying a cane as he strolled affectedly along the streets of Manhattan or walked at a leisurely pace about the tree-lined Brooklyn neighborhood where he kept a stately, refurbished brownstone, ruminating as he walked, determining his next move, having been absurdly thwarted in his attempt to make a public statement, hating his redundancy, hating what he must now think of as his secondary status, his status as understudy to the shooter who had fired first, putting four neat, little holes in Abraham Lincoln Jones. Not knowing that in choosing to torment Winthrop, he was again mimicking the successful shooter, the Plaza gunman. Not realizing as well that his failure and frustration were known. Known by Winthrop, the journalist, the adviser, the consigliere, the man he had chosen to harass.

Now Winthrop would confront that harassment. He would face the threat. There were three phones in his apartment. One in the bedroom, now disconnected, one on the wall of his half-kitchen, and a third in the study. Winthrop walked from the living room to the kitchen and pulled the phone jack out of the wall. Now there was only the study phone. There had been no calls for the hour or so since he and Donna and Rita had arrived at the apartment. And Winthrop was grateful for that. Grateful for the luck. Grateful that the psychos were asleep at the wheel. It had given him time to revive himself, and now he was once again a match for whatever insanity might come his way.

As Winthrop walked from the kitchen through the living room

and into the study, his favorite room, his haven within a haven, lined with books and filled with personal mementos and awards that he had won over the years for his work, he wondered again what the little red number on the answering machine would say, the number measuring the extent of the violation. Donna had seen it, but he didn't want to ask her when she brought it up. When he was ready, he would see for himself. And now he opened the door to the study, and there it was: 25.

There had been five calls Saturday afternoon, which he had already heard and which were not included in the twenty-five. Eleven calls had come in Saturday night while he was with Danielle. That's what Germany had said. So another fourteen calls since then had come in through the day. Winthrop thought of all he had done through that long, exhausting day—talking to Germany, having it out with Goode, standing up for Rita and GRACE at St. Patrick's, getting his ass arrested, cooling his heels at the police station— and he thought of all the calls, ringing in, adding to the total on the machine. And it seemed so very odd, portions of his life—crazy, deranged portions of his life—went on merrily without him. He didn't need to be there at all. He wasn't needed so long as he had the goddamn machine. And now here he was checking in with the machine to find out what had happened to him.

Winthrop sat down at his desk and stared at the number 25. Then he hit "play" to begin retrieving the calls, knowing the first eleven were hang-ups. He listened to those first eleven calls intently, meditatively, straining to pick up the slightest sounds, in this case urban sounds—the movement of people and vehicles, the hurried activity, the disturbed air, city air—it was all there like the radio noise you picked up on FM on a frequency without a station, the sound emanating from the ever-expanding edge of the universe, sending out a radioactive message echoing through time from the original Big Bang.

Winthrop hit "rewind" and played the eleven calls again. Then he played back the calls once more before moving on. With each listen he would pick up some subtlety that he hadn't heard before, some hum or buzz or maybe even a breath, the breath of a madman, some movement, too, perhaps a pedestrian or cab or delivery truck or perhaps the movement of Speck's hand or Sherry's arm—the hand or arm that had held, that had supported a gun, the gun that had shot Abraham Lincoln Jones. And the sounds were mood music for the meditation, a dissonant natural jazz that opened Winthrop's mind and deepened his understanding of Speck and Sherry—the psycho twins, separated at birth, the one, the parental favorite, an overachiever, always ahead of the game, always first. The other, born ten minutes later, somewhat neglected, an also-ran, always running to catch up, always bringing up the rear.

Yes, it helped, thought Winthrop, to see them as brothers, for they were part of the same family. Charles Manson had understood that and it had given him power. Father Charlie together with the sisters and brothers of the Manson Family. There were hints of it as well in the Symbionese Liberation Army, with Cinque and the Harrises and Patty Hearst. And, of course, Jim Jones—the Kool-Aid King of Jonestown. Not to mention Dave Koresh, the wacko from Waco. The family as cult, religious or political; it hardly mattered which, the hundreds of groups and clans and secret societies were merely varied and brilliant colorations in the peacock tail of psychosis.

So, yes, thought Winthrop, they were all different, but they were also the same, like so much else in life, applying Yogi Berra logic to the analysis of psychotics and megalomaniacs. Different but the same. Some of them led movements and held power over groups—whether denominations, parties or entire countries; others acted alone, climbing towers or setting up shop in book depositories or hotels, but they all belonged together, and even the loneliest of loners, the stalkers, the single assassins, like Speck and Sherry, were part of a family, part of a fraternity. And all of it, ironically, had come from us. That, of course, was the true conspiracy. Forget the CIA and the KGB and the FBI and organized crime and the entire

Military Industrial Complex. Forget all of that, Mr. Stone. That was all a child's nightmare, a puerile fantasy, a tale of the bogeyman, compared to the real story. The true conspiracy. For the true conspiracy was deeper and more disturbing than all of that.

I have met the conspiracy, and it is us, thought Winthrop. All of us. We produce Speck. We produce Sherry, using the raw material of their mutated genes and twisted chromosomes. Then we abandon them, let them operate on their own plane, fending for themselves, making their own way. And they do. They make their way; they develop; they thrive. They join the brotherhood; they become part of the family, and then they kill. They kill us. And so we come full circle. And the chain is never broken, for, yes, that was it, thought Winthrop—there was always another gunman.

That was the message from the electronic lines. The message from Manhattan and Brooklyn. The message from every corner of America. The insane, conspiratorial message born of static and hum. That was it. Winthrop had heard it, and now he needed to hear a human voice.

Winthrop rolled through three more hang-ups. Speck hang-ups, he thought. Then came call fifteen. It was Danny. "Hello, Jack?" Danny said. Her voice was uncertain. Winthrop could tell she was troubled. "Jack, are you there? Maybe? Somehow? No? Well, it was a long shot. You must be at St. Patrick's. Listen, Jack. I got your note. I woke up about a half hour after you left, and I read your note. And then the phone rang, and it was that man, the man who shot Abe, the man you call Speck. He said horrible things to me, Jack." Danny's voice was shaking now. "It was filth, Jack. Racist, sexist filth. I can't even repeat what he said. I only stayed on the line because I was hoping to learn something that might help. It was all over in seconds. But it was terrible. Just terrible. Please call me, Jack, as soon as you can. But don't worry about me. I'm OK. I feel safe here. Just please call as soon as you can. And, Jack. I love you, Jack. Bye."

Winthrop hit "stop," feeling wracked by guilt and anger. The entire day had passed. While he was out—talking to Germany, getting arrested at St. Patrick's, waiting to get out of jail—Speck was busy doing more damage. It was clear. Speck's real love was torture. Psychological torture with the threat of violence, a threat he was sure to make good on in his own time and in his own way. It killed Winthrop that this slime ball was harassing Danny. And he, Jack Winthrop, had failed to be there when she needed him. What's more, he realized now, he had yet to give Abe or Danny his cell phone number. She had given him her landline when she had invited him for dinner. He had called the number once, just once from his cell, and didn't reach her. It had been his only opportunity to call before he was released. But he felt bad that it was only one call and worse that he had indulged his own need for healing since he left the station with Donna and Rita. Now he knew what the endless ringing meant. Of course. Speck had called Danny again, and in self-defense she had disconnected the phone.

Winthrop quickly dialed Danny's number. Ringing. No answer. Irrationally, he dialed again. Still no answer. Only one thing to do—get to Danny's right away. Winthrop stared down at the infernal phone machine. Ten more calls to go. I have to go through these, he thought. I have to hear it all now. But I'm coming, Danny. I'm coming. Then with a pang of guilt like a knee to the liver, Winthrop hit "play."

"Jack, it's me," Danny said, her voice quivering but sounding strong nevertheless as she drew on her reserves, spiritual reserves that had been nurtured over the years, Winthrop was sure, by a fundamental faith in her own worth. The strength sustained as well by the profound conviction that she would not be daunted by evil.

"Speck called again," she continued after a pause. "This time I slammed down the phone as soon as I heard him. I slammed it down so hard I hurt my hand. He must have felt it, too, Jack. Not like the gun he fired at you. But it was loud enough. I got him back for you, Jack, for you and Abe. But, listen. I can't bear to hear that voice again. I'm pulling the line out of the wall, so don't bother to call. Just come, Jack, please, as soon as you can. I'm all right, but I'd just like you to be here."

Winthrop let the tape roll. Call seventeen was quick. Three words, two seconds.

"The column, Jack."

It was his editor, Peter Gallo. Apparently Gallo had not yet learned of his arrest. He was just calling about the column. He had also left a message on his cell. Winthrop should have sent the column in on Friday. At the latest today. No problem. Winthrop piled up columns the way survivalists hoarded can goods and semiautomatic weapons. He had over a hundred pieces on file. He remembered each and every one of them. And he knew exactly which one he wanted now. It was filed under N, as in NRA, the National Rifle Association.

It was always difficult for Winthrop to determine who was more despicable, the Tobacco Institute or the National Rifle Association. Usually, however, he decided that the distinction went to the NRA. They were the lowest of the low by a small but discernible margin—a margin equal, let us say, to the length of the barrel of a Ruger 9mm pistol.

Winthrop was angry now, his anger burning like a cool, incandescent flame, and the column matched his mood. In it he stated no direct opinions and vented no emotions. Instead he created a collage, juxtaposing brief, heart-breaking accounts of senseless firearm deaths—the deaths of children and adults, of beloved sons and daughters, fathers and mothers, some wanton murders, some accidental—against the bankrupt, self-indulgent statements of the NRA defending the inalienable right of good American citizens to own guns. Yes, that was the column he wanted now, and he would email it to Peter in the morning.

Call eighteen was another quickie. It was from Barnes. "Hey, Winthrop, come on out of the closet and answer the goddamn phone." So, thought Winthrop, Barnes knew about the arrest. "Listen, pal, when you feel like you want to tell your deep, dark secret story, give me a call, will you? I'll understand. Honest to God. I got an uncle who's a homo. Hey, just kidding. Give me a call, though. We'll talk."

Winthrop did his best to move quickly through the remaining calls, but it was like running a gauntlet in which he would evade one blow only to run directly into the path of the next. Calls nineteen and twenty were hang-ups carrying the ambiance of Sherry, the static and buzz, Winthrop imagined, of a busy street corner in Brooklyn Heights. And Winthrop rolled right along. He had heard it before. But call twenty-one was another matter. It was a message from Speck. Yes, he spoke again to Winthrop, spoke now for the second time.

"I called your black cunt, Jackie boy," Speck seethed. "I got your cunt. I fucked her over the phone. Like you fucked her last night. Did it feel good? Did you like it, Jackie? You should thank me for it. I let you fuck her. I let you do it, so we could have this little phone session where I talk and you listen. Now listen to this. I'm watching every move you make. I know what you do. I know where you go. I'm watching your little black bitch, too. But most of all I'm watching your nigger boss, Mr. Jones. I have a little surprise I'm planning for him. You'll find out soon enough what it is. And, oh yes, how could I forget? Your detective friend, Germany. Hello, Mr. Germany. You're probably listening now. How do I know about you, you ask. Oh, I have my ways. I have my own investigative techniques. I know where to find you, too. I'm looking forward to meeting you. You see, Germany, you see, Jackie, I know everything, everything that's happening and everything that's going to happen."

That was it. Winthrop played the message once more, trying to decipher the full meaning of Speck's claims of omniscience, trying to divine exactly what Speck would do. One thing was clear: Speck would attack again. They were all at risk, no one more so than Jones.

"I want to talk to the Batman!" Yes, there he was right on cue. Call twenty-two, Abraham Lincoln Jones. "Mr. Bruce Wayne, the Caped Crusader! I always liked the Batman. Lives in the Bat Mansion. Drives the fucking Batmobile." In the hospital, thought Winthrop, flat on his back, shot to shit, not a drop of alcohol in him, and Jones was still wonderfully, irrepressibly insane.

"Hey, Jackie, my man. Man too busy to answer the phone. Too busy fighting crime. Put down your Bat Boomerang and listen to me. We get through my tour. We free up the soul of America. We launch the Super Website of Emancipation Information. We do all that and we're still alive. We're still in one piece. You get the best goddamn perk the world has ever seen. You get the fuckin' Batmobile: the Mercedes S550. I get one, too. I'm telling you, Winthrop. That is one amazing automobile. That car is the damn Batmobile.

"Hey, one other thing, Jack. One serious business thing. For tomorrow's meeting think satellite feeds, webcasts, blogs. That's how we'll do it. That's how we'll spread ourselves across America. That's it. Think about it. Now you get Alfred the butler to fix you up a nice, warm cup of milk and tuck you in the Bat Bed so you get a good night's sleep. Got to be ready tomorrow. Got to make sure those world-class artiste synapses of yours are crackling and popping. Tomorrow be the day. We gonna plan the plan. We gonna dream the dream."

As usual, Jones was right. Winthrop had hit on the idea too. Satellite feeds and the Web were the way to go. They would give each event on the tour additional range and scope. Complementing the drama and presence of a huge live audience, they would bring in people from around the country, telling their stories, challenging attitudes, creating dialogue, communicating across America. Add to all that the music, the entertainment, the magic and the lights, not to mention the Man himself—Abraham Lincoln Jones, the most charismatic and controversial personality on television—and you had unquestionably the ultimate talk show. That was what they were producing. No doubt about it.

But the Abraham Lincoln Jones Emancipation Tour might well be more than that. Perhaps it would create a new grassroots political movement that could help revive the American spirit. Perhaps it would build new linkages across a divided and disaffected society, polarized by economics and race and the discontinuities of generational experience. Perhaps it would truly be an agent of change, even if that meant shaking up the crazies just a little bit. Yes, maybe the tour really could produce change, liberating the nation to rediscover democracy, to rediscover the meaning of freedom and equality—perhaps it would do all those things. But if it did, it would be because they—the ALJ team—had succeeded somehow in communicating. And the communication would come through the medium of the ultimate talk show, the talk show that had dared for once to go beyond talk, to go beyond TV, in order to arrive at something that was solid and true.

That was the gist of Winthrop's response to Jones's phone call. A response that was immediate and deeply felt, experienced in a moment, not so much in thoughts and words but rather in emotions and a burst of positive, much needed energy, for the call had given Winthrop a lift, such a lift that he felt ready for anything, even another call from Speck as he continued on his journey down the gauntlet of recorded messages to the end when he would finally make his long-deferred contact with Danielle.

And the lift was fortunate indeed, for call twenty-three was again from Speck, but this time it was not a hang-up, nor was there a threatening voice on the line, speaking of hatred and doom. Instead, it was a musical recording, courtesy of program director Speck. For one brief moment, Winthrop was unable to place the piece. Then it hit him. It was "Deutschland Über Alles," the German national anthem. This one's for you, Felix, Winthrop thought. Was the recording the entire joke? Or was the punch line still to come?

Winthrop moved on to the last two calls. "Hello, Jack. It's about 10:30." Danny again. Shit, thought Winthrop. I missed her by about fifteen minutes. "I'm getting kind of worried," Danny said. "I thought you'd be here by now. Something must have happened. I hope everything is OK. If you're listening to this, you must have heard my earlier messages. I know I sounded shook up, but I'm all right now. Really. I've just been working most of the day, and now I'm doing some reading. So, listen, you don't need to come over. I'm going to keep the phone disconnected, but I'll call you again before I go to bed. Hope to talk to you soon, Jack. Bye."

There was just one more call. Winthrop let the machine keep rolling. "Hey, Winthrop." It was Germany. He was laughing. So he had just missed his call as well. "I hear you got your fucking ass thrown in jail today with the rest of the homos. Forgive me if I derive some modicum of amusement from your stupidity. It's been some day for you, huh?" It certainly has, thought Winthrop. "Finally get bailed out of the slammer, get home, and you get a fucking earful on the phone, too. Some day! As you heard, your buddy Speck's pulling my chain, too. Asshole. But we'll talk about the calls the next time we meet. In fact, that's why I'm calling. Stop by my apartment tomorrow night. Like after midnight. I'm going after the Shorty angle, and I've turned up some new shit. If Speck and the guy who did Shorty are one and the same psycho, we may be dealing with a slightly different type of animal from the one you're thinking of, Mr. Journalistic Genius. Anyway, we'll talk tomorrow night. My place. After midnight."

That was interesting, thought Winthrop. He had spoken to Germany more than once about Speck. He had described Speck. He had characterized him. If asked, he could easily run down the list of characteristics that he associated with Speck. His intention had been to create an image and communicate that image to Germany. But it had not really struck Winthrop until now that the Speck Germany carried around in his mind was largely his, that is, Winthrop's, creation. More precisely, it was one step removed from Winthrop's creation, one step removed from the image of Speck that he, Jack Winthrop, carried around in his mind. And those images were independent creations, almost as much as was Winthrop's image of Mr. Sherry, who lived now in Winthrop's mind, and perhaps in reality, as the elegant and conservative gentleman psycho from Brooklyn.

So, thought Winthrop, you had your image and you had the reality, the real person. But the real person was the one you were after and the one who was after you. And maybe that person was different. As Germany had said, maybe they were dealing with a different type of animal from the one Winthrop had been thinking of.

Suddenly Winthrop was lost. Funny how a single remark could knock you off balance. Undermine your confidence in what you knew. Winthrop didn't pretend that he really understood Speck's character. But he thought he had some understanding and that understanding was based on a few fundamental conclusions drawn from the contact that he'd had with Speck. Aside from the violence and the obvious psychosis, there were two basic characteristics that defined Speck in Winthrop's mind—number one: he was the ultimate loner; and number two: he was a racist, with a particular hatred for blacks.

Winthrop thought of Germany's remark—"we may be dealing with a slightly different type of animal"—and he thought of Speck as he understood him—violent, psychotic, a loner, a racist—and he said to himself, no, there's just no way I'm totally wrong about this. Speck is all those things. They make up the real man. But he thought he knew what Germany meant, what he was suggesting—that there might be other dimensions to Speck as well, other dimensions and other identities. After all, the elusive patron of Shorty's was a dirty, long-haired hippie, and Speck, the hippie, might be just one among a host of alternative identities, with each identity disguising the other. Might there not be Speck, the physician; Speck, the executive; Speck, the attorney; Speck, the minister; Speck, the successful, workaday professional, as well as Speck, the crazed, nocturnal underground man?

Just then, the phone rang. Winthrop picked it up at once, despite the depth of his distraction. "Hello," he said.

"My God, Jack. It's you!" Finally, it was Danny live, not on tape. At last, they could actually talk. "What happened?" she asked.

"I got arrested at St. Patrick's along with Rita and most of her organization."

"Jesus. I knew something must have happened. And I knew, of course, that you were going to the demonstration, but it never occurred to me that you might be arrested. I feel like such a jerk. I didn't listen to the news all day. That horrible man—he called."

"I know, Danny, I just got your messages."

"After those terrible phone calls, I disconnected the phone and just worked all day and night until I couldn't work any more. Then I read. I did try to reach you a couple of times, and, of course, you couldn't reach me."

"Don't feel bad, Danny. I'm the guilty one. I did call you from the police station, but I didn't reach you and I'd already called Donna to come and bail out me and Rita. I knew where to find her, and I knew she would come over right away."

"I would have too, Jack."

"Of course, you would have. I know you would have, and I thought of calling you first, but I dialed Donna. It was just one of those things where you need to call someone."

"Please don't apologize for calling Donna. There's no need. I'm just glad she was able to come right away."

"She was, but we still didn't get back out on the street until after ten o'clock."

"Ten o'clock, why so long?"

"Combination of bureaucracy and malice. You know, let the godless fags cool their heels."

"So when did you get back to your apartment?"

"Not until about 10:45. And that's where my guilt comes in. I should have called you right away, but I was totally burnt out. I'd been beaten up a bit, too."

"Jack!"

"It's not worth going into now, but pretty much everyone took their lumps."

"Rita wasn't hurt, was she?"

"She was a little banged up, a little depressed. We were all kind of down. So when we got back, I decided to give myself an hour or so to pull it all back together."

"Jack, that's understandable."

"Donna was a big help to me and Rita. Around midnight they went to bed, and I checked my machine. There were twenty-five calls."

"My God!"

"I decided to play back the messages. As soon as I got your message and learned that Speck had called you, I phoned you, but of course you had pulled the plug. Then I got your next message—to come right over—but I just felt that I had to listen to the rest of the calls first. I knew I'd hear from Speck again. Actually all of the messages prior to yours were hang-ups. I think most of them were from Speck, but there may have been a few from the Sherry gunman."

"He's harassing you, too?"

"Crazy, but what else is new?"

"Has he ever said anything?"

"Not a word. It's silent harassment."

"Then how do you know who's making the calls?"

"My detective friend and I are figuring the calls are from two different people based on location. One set of hang-ups are all from midtown Manhattan; the other set are from Brooklyn. We're pretty sure it's Speck and Sherry."

"But Speck called again later?"

"Yes."

"Did he speak? Did he say anything about calling me?"

"Yes, he bragged about it. Actually, Danny, he spoke of it as if he had raped you."

Danny was silent for a moment or two, collecting herself. When she spoke again, her voice was strong and calm. "I'm not surprised, Jack. That's what it was like when he called me. There was all this sexual aggressiveness in his voice. After he hung up, when I could finally think clearly about it, I realized that that was exactly what he wanted to do."

"Rape you."

"Yes, it was very clear. He wanted to rape me—more than anything. And after he raped me, he'd be disgusted, and then he would kill me."

Danny's voice had begun shaking on the word "disgusted." As she finished speaking, she exploded into tears. It was that forceful, and the force of the explosion frightened Winthrop. But he had barely begun to try to comfort her, saying "Danny, Danny, it's OK. It'll be all right," hating the weakness, the sheer impotence of his words, when she stopped crying altogether and again was completely calm.

"I'm all right, Jack," she said. "When I get really upset, that's what I do. It's like throwing up. It's all over in seconds, and then I feel better."

"Listen, Danny, let me come right over. I can be there in ten minutes."

"Jack, please don't. I know I asked you earlier, but I'm fine. Really. I feel safe here. I've got a doorman and four locks on my door. It's late and I'm just going to bed. You should do the same after all you've been through."

"Do you want me to stop by before the meeting?"

"No, I'll be out of here early tomorrow morning. I've got a meeting at the office at 9:00 to sew up sponsorships for the tour. I'll be working there through the morning. We can just meet at Abe's for the lunch session."

"Be sure to take cabs, Danny. Don't walk around."

"I'll be careful, Jack. You be careful, too. I love you."

"I love you, too, Danny."

"Bye now."

"Bye."

It was the first time that Winthrop had said "I love you" in that particular way, with that particular feeling, in a long time. He loved Donna, and he loved Rita. Now he loved Danny. Each feeling of love was different, and each was special. Winthrop thought of what it would be like to spend a lot of time with Danny, to be with her. He liked the idea but he was frightened by it, too. With love came vulnerability. With love there was no defense against loss. No defense against life. You were just out there naked in the wind, the love marking a bull's eye on your soul.

Winthrop got up from the study desk, disconnected the phone, and walked back into the living room. He grabbed the sound system remote and turned off the power. Good night, Miles, he thought. Then he took a pillow from the love seat and tossed it onto the floor. Kicking off his shoes, he picked up the TV remote, flicked on the tube, pressed mute and lay down on the floor, resting his head against the hard leather pillow. He adjusted the sound so that it was just barely audible—just seven little green vertical lines worth of sound showing on the bottom of the screen—then he took off the mute and began channel surfing.

After midnight on a Sunday, programming was hopeless, but Winthrop had an idea of what he was looking for, and within thirty seconds he was all set. On the one side of the split screen three little cheetah babies were burrowing into the underbrush, hiding from predators, while their mother hunted for food. Meanwhile a lion prowled the neighborhood, surveying the terrain, sniffing the air, stopping and starting methodically, knowing the cheetah babies were somewhere nearby. On the other side of the screen an exceptionally well-dressed, half-starved, brittle-looking woman, who bore a striking resemblance to Nancy Reagan, was talking to a middle-aged woman and an older man. The middle-aged woman had long platinum blonde hair and was dressed up like a saloon madam from the Wild West. She was sort of a cross between Miss Kitty and Tammy Faye Baker. The man had a huge gray pompadour piled on top of his head. He was wearing, rather incongruously, a very expensive navy blue double-breasted suit and a scarlet string tie held together at the top by a bull's head clip. The three of them were sitting in a living room with furnishings that might as well have been stolen from Trump's Taj Mahal.

Winthrop was even more exhausted than he had thought, and he could barely keep his eyes open. As the lion closed in on the cheetah babies, the Nancy look-alike was beaming.

"Praise the Lord!" the saloon madam exclaimed. "Praise the Lord, Judy! You are blessed!"

Suddenly Winthrop recognized the Nancy look-alike. The madam had said "Judy," and, yes, it was Judy Lane, a Broadway musical star and cabaret singer from the sixties. Winthrop had not seen her anywhere or even heard her name mentioned in more than twenty years.

"Three times cured!" the pompadour marveled.

Just then the lion found the cheetah babies and killed them. To reduce the competition for food, the announcer said. The cheetah mother, having returned from her hunt, had looked on helplessly as the lion slaughtered her cubs.

"Thrice cured by the spirit of our Lord Jesus Christ!" the madam sang out as the audience applauded and Judy looked about, embarrassed but happy. "The Lord cured our sister, Judy, of the tumor in her back, cured too the arthritis that had twisted her hands. Then he cured the drug and alcohol addiction that was afflicting her life, plaguing her and preventing her from truly walking in the path of righteousness. Thank you, Lord Jesus. Thank you, dear Savior for healing our sister, Judy."

There was a close-up of the dead cheetah babies, lying in the brush, the mother nuzzling them, nosing about their bodies, looking confused. As Winthrop began to drift off, he thought of the camera crew filming the scene, following the "Do Not Disturb" ethic of nature documentaries, and he heard the pompadour saying "Hallelujah" several times and the audience applauding. Then the madam introduced a song, and the audience applauded again, and the pompadour got up to sing, something about Jesus the carpenter building a boat so the pompadour could cross the water, and Winthrop thought he had fallen asleep, but he hadn't, and the pompadour was still singing, and he watched the man's Adam's apple vibrate up and down with amazing speed as he held a long, high inspirational note. And then finally he blacked out and slept like a dead man through the rest of the night.

13

WHEN WINTHROP AWOKE, the TV was off, and a yellow note was sticking to his chest. Donna and Rita were gone. It was late morning. The note was written by Donna with a P.S. from Rita.

> Dear Jack,
>
> Don't forget! I close on the Tit tomorrow. To celebrate, Rita and I thought we should throw a party for ourselves—the three of us, Sheila and Mo Mo—the new owners of the Tit for Tat! We can also work out the details on how I'll cut you guys in, and you and I can talk more about exactly how much you want to chip in—not to mention your new job as consigliere.
>
> But mostly we'll celebrate! And, Jack, I promise to introduce you to that little teenage goddess who's dancing for us now. Rita says you got your eye on her. Who doesn't?
>
> Anyway, see you tonight at the Tit—the earlier the better!
>
> Love,
> Donna

P.S. Jack, I just want to thank you again for standing with us yesterday. I'll never forget it.

Love,
Rita

After reading the note, Winthrop got up slowly from the floor. He was amazed at how sore he was. Like he'd been in some kind of auto accident. What hurt most of all was the goddamn lump on the crown of his head that he'd gotten from tangling with Jeff Goode, Mr. Eagle Scout.

After emailing the NRA piece to Gallo and turning on the Krups, Winthrop threw his body into the shower for a little hydrotherapy. The water was as hot as he could stand it, and it felt good. In fact, he could actually feel the healing begin. "Hallelujah!" Winthrop said to himself. "Hallelujah!" he repeated several more times, thinking of the madam and the pompadour and poor, forgotten Judy Lane with her maladies and addictions all cured.

Then he thought of Sheena and turned to look at her. There she was hanging upside down and naked from the shower nozzle—right where she'd been since last Monday morning, the morning after Winthrop had accepted Jones's offer to join his team. That was just a week ago. A week, thought Winthrop. It seemed more like a hundred years.

And what about today? Today, he had the lunch meeting at Jones's apartment to plan the whole Emancipation Tour, then the celebration at the Tit, then the late night meeting with Germany. Winthrop nudged the hot water faucet slightly, making the water hotter still, so hot that it began to burn. Then he bowed his head and let the burning water run down his back.

It was going to be another incredibly long, full day. Winthrop had the oppressive sense that he often experienced before such days that everything had already happened or at least that the day's events

were already formed and that they were simply waiting somewhere, congregating like unemployed actors or forlorn day labor-
ers, beyond the range of vision, perhaps even beyond the range of
imagination, waiting to appear in his life, yes, waiting to appear—
but as what? As surprise party revelers? As little children innocently
revealing their hiding places in a carefree game of hide-and-seek?
Or, more likely, as muggers and thieves? As assassins who might
steal away life itself? One's own precious, irreplaceable, good-for-
nothing life?

But, no, thought Winthrop. None of that was true. Because, so
far, nothing had happened. If he was smart enough, if he was good
enough, if he was creative enough—shit, if he was goddamn tricky
enough, he would be the one to make things happen. He would
control his own life. Right? "Right," he answered aloud, balancing
doubt and resolve, as he shut off the shower, threw back the curtain
and stepped out to face his life for yet another unpredictable, incal-
culable day.

*   *   *   *

SECURITY AT TRUMP TOWER WAS TIGHT. Several police officers
at the Fifth Avenue entrance. Two outside the 56th Street doors.
Several in the lobby as well. Winthrop wondered how long it would
last at this level. Just one day? Several days? Longer? He knew that
the actual security plan would be driven at least as much by ongoing
publicity about the shooting and Jones's pull with Mayor Martinez
and Police Commissioner Cobb as it would be by a reasonable
assessment of the risk of another incident.

Today, three days after the shooting, the news was all about
Jones. His release from Roosevelt Hospital was page one in all the
papers. There were also extensive follow-up stories on the police
investigation as well as editorials, op-ed pieces and countless essays
and blogs that used the shooting as yet another occasion to discuss

the pathological violence of American society and press for tougher gun control laws. Winthrop's NRA piece would appear tomorrow, and there would most certainly be extensive stories and commentaries through the week on *The Huffington Post*, *The Daily Beast*, *Politico* and all of the other key Internet news sites.

The other major story of the day was the GRACE demonstration and mass arrests at St. Patrick's. In all four papers, the slant was one hundred percent negative, with the cardinal, the mayor and the police commissioner all condemning the demonstrators and praising the police on their professionalism and restraint. There was also a brief mention without context or explanation in each paper that *New York Times* columnist Jack Winthrop was among those arrested. No doubt the hate mail was already pouring in.

Before leaving his apartment, Winthrop had also quickly checked the television and radio for more ALJ coverage. CNN, MSNBC, Fox News and C-Span had covered Jones's release live. Winthrop caught just the tail end of the feed, now on videotape. Jones, in high energy, looking spectacular, even triumphant, concluded what was apparently a brief statement testifying to his great good fortune and miraculous recovery with some hard-sell promotion of the Emancipation Tour. Then he literally danced and pranced his way from the hospital doors to the waiting white super-stretch limo and took off with Barry Bream for his apartment in Trump Tower. On the radio Jones was the lead story on WINS and WCBS, and a quick survey of the various talk shows, from the local call-in programs to Rush Limbaugh, revealed that Jones was dominating there as well.

One of the major purposes of today's meeting, aside from planning the tour, was to figure out how to keep the media focused on Jones. That would be critical to the success of the tour, and Winthrop knew all too well from his many years as a journalist how quickly media attention could dry up entirely. It was one of the things Winthrop hated most about his profession. Real news was constantly contending with tabloid sensationalism for the media's and the public's gnat-like attention. Especially TV. It no longer mattered how big or how shocking an event was. After a few days or, at the most, weeks, no one cared any more. There was always something bigger or more shocking, or at least shocking and marketable in some unexpected way, to grab headlines and titillate both the press and the public. The ultimate importance of any particular issue or event didn't matter. It was all about ratings. A man's severed penis, a girl missing in Aruba, or a celebrity murder trial could easily bump the latest terrorist attack right out of the headlines only to be displaced the very next day by the latest Washington money scandal or celebrity faux pas.

What bothered Winthrop most was not the total lack of discrimination and responsibility on the part of both the press and the public that gave greater play to the personal tragedy of a single missing person than to the outrage of global terrorism—although that was certainly bad enough. Most disturbing of all, however, was the implication that the terrorists had perhaps all gone on vacation or that the wars in Afghanistan and Syria had been put on hold in deference to America's preoccupation with a missing teenager. Winthrop had seen the same scenario replay itself repeatedly through the years. El Salvador, Nicaragua, Panama, Northern Ireland, Israel, Lebanon, Libya, Syria, Iran, Iraq, Afghanistan, South Africa, Somalia, Nigeria, Bosnia, Russia, Ukraine. You could fill in the blank, for the list went on and on. Each of these flash points, each of these global hot spots, had filled the headlines for days or, in some cases, weeks on end only to disappear for an indefinite period, resurfacing only when the media or U.S. interests elevated the tragic events of what were typically interminable conflicts to the status of Breaking News.

It was a similar story on domestic issues. The deficit, homelessness, AIDS, health care, education, drugs, the disintegration of the family, racism, guns, urban blight, FEMA, Homeland Security. Each took its turn as the cause célèbre of the day. Then each disappeared only to appear again, driven back into the spotlight by the brute force of public tragedy or the sudden, surprised, "I could have had a V8" realization that, yes, we, the American people, were indeed in a crisis, a crisis, that directly touched each and every one of our lives. During the overwhelming majority of the time when any particular issue was not in the news—well, then, it was simply not our problem. It was not anyone's problem because the problem did not exist. New Orleans almost wiped off the face of the earth? Hey, that's old news.

That was what Jones was up against. It was a beast, really. The great American news beast. For his tour to succeed, Jones would have to ride that beast better than anyone ever had before. Winthrop could help him with that. He knew the beast. He was, after all, part of the beast. And Jones was born for fame, born to the media. As a result, he also knew better than anyone else that he did not exist without the media. He did not exist without the beast. At least, he did not exist as Abraham Lincoln Jones. Without the headlines, without the media attention, he was just Abe. He was just another anonymous human being, at this point a very rich human being, but by himself powerless for all that wealth to have any real impact on the world in which he lived.

When the elevator doors opened onto Jones's floor, Winthrop encountered more security—Jones's private security team. There were two hulking, steroidal black guys with semiautomatic weapons standing right at the doors as Winthrop stepped out. Fortunately, he had brought along his photo I.D., the photo taken just last Friday before the show at Radio City, for the name, Jack Winthrop, had failed to elicit any response whatsoever from either of the men. They were initially unresponsive to the I.D. as well, staring at it long and hard, staring with eyes that were cold and dead, unmoved by Winthrop's warm, friendly presence or by the matching photo smiling back from the laminated card. Each of the men had the eyes of the elite enforcer, the elite agent. Winthrop had, of course, seen those eyes before. FBI, CIA, Secret Service, border guards, state police, some city police, private security. They were the eyes of a reptile, the eyes of an attack dog that knew only what it knew. Its pride was that it would accept no other knowledge. The switch was either on or off. The answer was yes or no: there was friend or enemy, authorized or unauthorized. No other possibilities existed.

As the security men stared interminably at his picture, Winthrop felt the way he was supposed to feel—like a criminal. The scrutiny was so effective at producing its intended result because it played with the fundamental fact that no one was innocent, that everyone had something horrible to conceal. So Winthrop stood there, waiting to plead guilty as charged and be sentenced for his crimes, whatever the crimes might be.

Finally, the guard who held the I.D. looked up and said, "Yes, Mr. Winthrop." Then he signaled to two other huge black security guards who were standing down the hall by the door to Jones's apartment. Handing back the I.D., he said, "Thank you, sir. Go right ahead." And Winthrop walked down the hall.

When he got to the door, the guards again took his I.D., despite his having been approved for entry by the team at the elevator. After a few more seconds of scrutiny one of the guards pushed a button on an intercom device and spoke to someone inside the apartment. "Mr. Winthrop has arrived, sir," the guard said. Then he handed back the I.D. The door opened, and Winthrop entered the apartment. Barry Bream had opened the door. "Jack, come in," he said, shaking Winthrop's hand and patting him on the shoulder. "It's good to see you."

"Good to be here, Barry," Winthrop said.

"Listen, Jack," Bream said in a hurried half whisper. "Sorry if I gave you a bit of a hard time at the hospital. I'm all about protecting Abe, and I was just a little on edge."

"No apologies necessary, Barry. We're all on edge," Winthrop said, as he stepped past Bream and walked out of the foyer and into the living room.

"Jack!" Danielle shouted in greeting.

"Hey, it's Jackie, the jailbird!" Jones called out.

"Hey, guys," Winthrop said, looking about the luxuriously spacious living room and choosing to ignore the jailbird joke. He was on time, but, not surprisingly, he was the last to arrive, and it was clear they were waiting for him to get started. "This is some place, Abe."

Jones smiled. "Man's got to be comfortable in his own home, Jack. This is my idea of comfort."

Winthrop had known that Jones was a collector and an antiquarian, but he had not anticipated what Jones's taste would be, nor the marked attention to detail, nor the unmistakable display of wealth that the furnishings reflected. As he looked about the room, he felt that he had been afforded a rather privileged opportunity to discern, through the rich panoply of Jones's private aesthetic choices, previously hidden dimensions of the man's personality and values.

Winthrop was certainly no expert. Nevertheless, to his unschooled but extremely observant eye each piece of furniture appeared to be a highly prized and carefully chosen antique, while every element of the furnishings, from the impressive wall tapestries depicting scenes of Venice, Florence or the Italian *campagna* to the smallest knick knacks and figurines, bespoke a highly cultivated love of well-conceived, finely wrought objects of beauty. The furniture itself Winthrop would describe as Florentine in style, with each rich, dark mahogany piece revealing Jones's deep appreciation of substance and tradition. Clearly, for Jones, home was a place of comfort, as he had just said. And that comfort derived in large part from the sense of continuity and stability communicated by these beloved objects.

The contrast between the paranoid world of surveillance that Winthrop had just encountered in the hallway and the reassuring protectiveness of this beautifully appointed parlor could hardly have been greater. Nor, speaking of incongruities, would anyone have necessarily extrapolated such aesthetic taste and values from the

TV personality who aptly described himself as the "Master Blaster of Talk Show Disaster." Yes, thought Winthrop, Jones was certainly a man capable of containing vast contradictions within himself.

"Well, this is certainly the epitome of comfort, Abe," Winthrop said, shaking Jones's hand and giving Danielle a professional kiss on the cheek, which she accepted with a wink. "But it's so much more than that, isn't it?" he continued. "I mean it really does make quite a personal statement."

"It's what I like, Jack. Simple as that," Jones said, emanating a sense of calm that Winthrop had not previously associated with him.

"This is the most beautiful home I've ever been in," Danny said.

"It's very beautiful," Winthrop agreed. "I have to tell you, though, Abe. Your security guys are something else altogether. They could give the Terminator nightmares."

"That's just part of the game, Jack, and those dudes in the hall are what it takes. But let me tell you something. And I'm goddamn serious. This is one place where I want to feel absolutely secure."

Security at home. Yes, that made a lot of sense, thought Winthrop. Outside, moving through the world, you took your chances, always balancing risk against gain, but at home you wanted, no, you simply needed total security.

"Actually, Jackie," Jones said, "I've made special arrangements with my private security force to make sure you, Danny and Barry are all well taken care of."

"They're excellent, Jack," Bream said. "They're really the best."

"Yes, Jack," Danny said. "With all those crazy phone calls, you should use them. You need protection as much as Abe does."

Winthrop could not imagine being escorted about by some alligator-eyed storm troopers, however good they might be. And at any rate an over concern for security was not exactly his style. When he felt that his paranoid psychic alarm system was in full working order, he liked to walk the streets of New York, or for that matter most any other city, with total disregard to whatever danger there might be any time, day or night, muggers and murderers be damned. On the other hand, now that the matter of his personal safety had been put to him, Winthrop did feel for the first time that he might need to do something at least under certain circumstances to feel, well, just a tad more secure, despite the occasional car that Germany had monitoring his apartment.

Winthrop thought that he might know just the right person who could satisfy all his personal security needs. And that person was none other than Mr. Maurice Monroe—Slow Mo, Winthrop's new business partner and perhaps, if they could come to some equitable agreement on terms and conditions, his personal bodyguard and mobile security blanket as well. Yes, indeed, thought Winthrop, Slow Mo would be just perfect for the job. He would be sure to discuss the matter with him this evening at the Tit.

"Listen, Abe. Listen, everybody," Winthrop said. "I appreciate your thoughtfulness, but I'm sort of in the process of making my own security arrangements, so I'm going to pass right now on using your security guys, Abe. OK?"

"Suit yourself, my man," Jones said. "Just don't go and get your ass shot out from under you. We got some contemporary American history to make here, and we need you to help us do it. I wouldn't have asked you to join up in the first place if I didn't need you."

"Thanks, Abe," Winthrop said, wanting to acknowledge the compliment.

"Hey, you know what you're worth," Jones said. "You just make sure that Speck character or that other nut who still hasn't had a chance to show off his assassination skills doesn't make a point of cutting short your brilliant new career."

"At least not until I figure out what that brilliant new career really is," Winthrop said with a smile.

"I know you like to worry, Jack, but you're wasting your time," Jones said. "We won't know what any of this means until we've gone out and done the goddamn Emancipation Tour. But, hey, why don't you grab some food like the rest of us, and we'll commence with our little summit meeting here. What you said just gave me the perfect segue."

Winthrop went over to a long serving table where lunch had been set out. Not too shabby, he thought. Russian caviar, Salmon Florentine, asparagus tips with prosciutto, a bowl of mixed salad greens that would have done Slow Mo proud, warmed French bread, Key lime pie and coffee.

All of a sudden, it hit Winthrop. He was absolutely famished. He had had nothing whatsoever to eat since dinner at Danielle's on Saturday night. Just coffee at the Continental Sunday morning. Then nothing during the entire time he spent in the slammer, only alcohol back at his apartment last night and just black coffee this morning. Yes, without even trying he was sticking religiously to his liquid diet theory. Of course, if he continued on this ethereal path he would soon resemble Kate Moss's androgynous older brother. So without giving it a second thought, Winthrop proceeded to build a huge proletarian pile of food on his plate, including a generous sampling of absolutely everything on the table. Then he took a seat on the sofa next to Danielle and waited to hear what Abe had to say. Bream sat in a chair by the window, looking west over the city toward the Hudson and New Jersey.

Meanwhile, Abraham Lincoln Jones had begun pacing back and forth across the middle of the room. Thus far, he had been positively subdued, almost mellow. Now, however, Winthrop could see that Jones was getting psyched, revving himself up, virtually racing his motor, sans muffler, as he prepared to kick off the meeting in earnest. Jones paced the floor several more times. Then he whirled about, clapped his hands together in a resounding—crack!—and shouted, "OK!" so loud it made Winthrop and Danny jump. "That's it!" he shouted even louder as a mischievous smile spread across his face. "Goddamn it, guys and doll, this is it. Jack, you just spoke some nonsense about not knowing what your brilliant new career is. And I said you gave me the perfect segue. Well, that is the perfect goddamn segue into our private little summit meeting here on the Abraham Lincoln Jones Eeeh-mancipation Tour! You don't know where you're going, Jack. Well, I don't know where I'm going either. Goddamn it. Danielle, Barry—you don't know either. No, not one of us knows where the Eeeh-mancipation Tour is going to lead. And Zen Master ALJ is here to say when you don't know where you're going, that's when you know—you're on the right track, you're going some place special, you're going somewhere new. Think about Moses. He didn't have no map to take the Israelites to the Promised Land but after forty years he handed the ball off to Joshua, and they got there just fine. Think about Christopher Columbus. He didn't know where he was going either. Thought he'd find a Panama Canal to India. A Long Island Expressway to the East. Now he gets credit for discovering this shit pile we all affectionately call the New World even though the Vikings had already beaten him to it by hundreds of years. And what about that comedy team, what's their name—Lewis and Clark? You know they didn't know their ass from a goddamn Indian graveyard, looking for the Northwest Passage or some such shit. Nobody even knows what it is today, except that it was a big deal then. Well, whatever it was, they never found it, but they still made it all the way to the Pacific Ocean.

"So what's the moral of the story? What's the lesson of history? It's this: go with the vision. Follow the path with heart. Discover the new territory. You'll know what you have once you have it. And that's what we're dealing with here on the tour. We've talked about it. We said we're on a mission. We said we want to communicate with America. But we won't know what that means until we do it. Because nobody has ever done it before. Nobody has ever really communicated with America—as in let's tell it like it is for once. Not FDR with his fireside chats or JFK from his bedroom in Camelot or LBJ barbecuing the truth on his ranch or Tricky Dick lying about the break-ins and the bombings or Jimmy Carter spreading malaise or the Great Communicator, Bonzo Reagan, making up stories and smiling into the TelePrompTer or old George Bush saying 'Read my lips. I'm out of the loop' or Slick Willie Clinton biting his lip, wiping away the tears and talking jive or George Bush Jr. blaming Saddam for 9/11 or our beloved Barack talking about the change no Republican can believe in. No, nobody has done it. Nobody has communicated with America. All they've done is talk. That's not a criticism. That's a goddamn fact.

"The point is, we don't know what we're doing. We don't know where we're going. And that suits me just fine. Now just because we don't know what we're doing doesn't mean we can't be organized when we do it. So today we need to be as clear and precise and exact and detailed as we can planning the tour. The unknown doesn't have to be sloppy.

"Jack, you lead with the high-level concept. You lead with the conceptual side I don't see. You present the dark side of the moon. That's why you're here. That's why I called you. Danny, you give me an overview of the entire production: the financial end, sponsorship, the TV connection, the participation of the syndication network, the guests, the staging, the logistics, the cities. Then get me follow-ups from the various staff managers on each of these areas through the week. Barry, you cover the local angle so wherever we are, we know we're connecting with the right people and issues. All four of us will attack the PR monster—constantly, every single day.

"Now just two more things before I shut my big mouth and listen. Number one—and Jack, I already left you a message about this, so I know you got your ideas—number one is satellite feeds and the Web—we need them to give each event on the tour real-time national scope. Number two: New York City—we kick off the tour here. I don't give a damn about gunmen and assassins."

"Abe, I thought you'd want to start in New York City," Danny said. "So I've been working on that this weekend and earlier today, and I've made a lot of progress."

"Sounds great, Danny," Jones replied, his voice quiet now as he prepared to listen. "I always know I can depend on you. Let's give Jack here a chance to lay out the strategy first. Then we'll get into the work you've done on New York City, along with all the other details of the production."

Danny smiled back at Abe, who was taking his seat directly across from her and Winthrop. Then he leaned forward with a look of intense interest on his face and said, "Now let's really get into it. What are your thoughts, Jack? What do you have to say?"

Winthrop had been looking forward to this moment, the moment when he would truly begin to work in his new role. He was used to being paid for writing rather than speaking. He knew he earned his paycheck because he wrote every word himself, and the record remained of what he had written for others to read and consider. But now he was getting a ton of money primarily to speak his mind—to think and to talk. And he wanted to be sure that he was earning every penny.

Winthrop collected himself for one final tick of the clock. Then he dove in. "First, Abe, Danny, Barry," Winthrop said, "I want to tell you how glad I am to be working with you. This is a new experience for me, and you've made me feel a part of the family here, so thanks." Then thinking, here I go, Winthrop began to talk. He started with the need for honesty—beginning with honesty among themselves—so let's admit the obvious: the shooting would serve as the perfect springboard, the ideal launch pad for establishing Abe as a leading force for change in American life. Ahead of all the conventional politicians, including the president, because they had lost their credibility with much of the American people.

So there was the opportunity. Everyone knew that we were in a mess and that the mess was getting worse, and they were fed up. People wanted to hear the truth about the mess, and they wanted to believe that we could clean up the mess. They wanted some hope that we could work together and get the job done. And no one had really stepped forward. Now Abe could be the man to do that. Of course, there were a lot of distractions too. You had to fight to get people's attention. You couldn't just stand up there and preach.

So Winthrop talked about the need to mix truth and hype, substance and show, information and entertainment. Again, this wasn't cynicism. This was simple honesty. Like talking about the shooting as a launch pad. That was the way it was. So, bottom line, the Abraham Lincoln Jones Emancipation Tour would have to be the ultimate talk show. That was where all this was leading. That was what they would use as their vehicle of truth.

The whole time Winthrop talked his small audience listened intently, and for the most part silently, with Jones breaking in only on occasion to say, "Yes, sir!" or "You got that right, Jack!" and Danny shouting an enthusiastic "Amen!" every once in awhile, so that Winthrop began to feel like an old black Baptist preacher who was carrying the congregation along with him on a mighty wave of truth telling. And it was in that spirit that he continued to speak— about the isolating effects of TV and the compensatory need for tribal gathering and how again the opportunity was there to communicate and how they could be the ones to do it through Abe's charisma and personality and his courage to speak the truth.

And before he knew it, Winthrop had been speaking for more than an hour, and he had not even gotten to everything that he wanted to say. That was another problem with talk—at least the public kind—it was addictive. So Winthrop decided to wrap up fast and give Danny her turn to speak. "Listen," Winthrop said, "I've talked enough. I'm starting to get a rush from hyperventilating."

"Keep on going, Jack," Jones exclaimed. "The more you talk, the more I'm getting my money's worth."

"Jack, don't feel you're monopolizing the time," Danny said. "Everything you've brought up is important, and we really need to air out all these issues on the front end here."

"I agree," Bream said. "This has been good."

"Thank you, everyone," Winthrop said. "But just two quick points, and then we'll move on to Danny. Number one: we need to crank up the PR machine like it's never been cranked up before. Abe, short term, forget about overexposure. There's no such thing in your case, at least right now. You need to be everywhere. You need to get inside everyone's head. Think of the president. He's in the news every day, and no one ever says he's overexposed. If all goes well, over time we'll need to moderate the attention you get, but for now, remember, too much is never enough. Number two: I totally agree, Abe, on your idea about remotes. I've thought about it a lot, and I feel very strongly that at least early in the tour we should use the remotes to focus on inner-city violence. Maybe use three cities. Maybe put gang members on and let them talk. It'll open up a lot of other issues too, like drugs, education, poverty, urban blight."

"We could have live audiences at each remote location," Danny said, "With their own moderators, and we could patch them into the live show so they could all watch."

"And they could go on with their own discussions, too, if they wanted," Bream said, "Even after the show was over. Of course, we'd have to invite some community leaders in addition to the gang members."

"This is all great stuff," Jones exclaimed. "This is what I wanted us to get out of this meeting."

"You know," Winthrop continued, "despite the fact that the whole country has been bombarded by negative images for decades, we all still preserve within our minds a certain image of America. That America may have died out years ago. But we all still want to believe it's there. That's why Reagan was so popular. He told us that America still existed. And we wanted so badly to believe him. So much so that we convinced ourselves for awhile that these terrible problems didn't really exist, or, if they did, they were not our problems—not if we made enough money and bought enough guns and built enough jails to house all the criminals and deadbeats who were threatening the American Dream. That was one of the coded messages of the Reagan years. There were lots of those messages: the homeless were bums; AIDS victims were perverts and drug addicts; blacks and other minorities were the cause of crime; schools failed to educate our children because of liberal curricula and incompetent teachers. The list goes on."

"Goddamn it, Jack," Jones exclaimed. "You know what you're doing? You're just telling the truth! And that's cool because we're all sitting here among ourselves, conspiring to take over the country. But try saying that shit straight out in public the way you just did—the way I do when I really get myself going—and we all know what happens. That's when they start hitting you with the labels. They call you a liberal or a radical or some other kind of anti-American monster. Don't matter what—so long as you're discredited. That's what I've been fighting for years, ever since WSOL in Atlanta."

"Well, Abe," Bream said, "You've done as well as anyone could over the years at telling the truth in public."

Winthrop and Danielle were nodding in agreement. Jones sat silently, considering for several moments. "You know what?" he said finally. "Doing as well as anyone could—that's just not good enough. That don't change anything. And that's what my tour is about. We got to do better. Now let's keep going here. We've got some heavy-duty work to do here today, tomorrow and every other goddamn day until what we're doing is good enough. Danielle?"

Danielle had come to the meeting with more than thirty color charts covering all aspects of the tour production. It was a very impressive presentation, fit for any boardroom in the country. But the work behind it was even more impressive. When Jones had hired Winthrop, there was certainly a sense of urgency surrounding the planning of the Emancipation Tour. In fact, Winthrop was convinced that the urgency Jones himself felt had influenced to a significant extent the decision to ask him to join the team and to position him as a kind of spiritual partner in the enterprise. But it was clear to Winthrop as well that, despite Jones's overriding sense of urgency and despite his desire to launch the tour absolutely as soon as possible, planning would have proceeded more or less methodically had it not been for the shooting. Far from canceling or at least deferring Jones's plans to launch his assault on America, the shooting had confirmed that the tour must begin now.

As soon as she overcame her initial shock and grief over the shooting, Danielle had divined Jones's intentions and sprung into action. Saturday had been a day for resurgence and thoughtful preparation. On Sunday, while Winthrop had busied himself with the GRACE demonstration and its aftermath—a neat ten hours of incarceration—Danielle had been hard at work, calculating the finances, plotting the logistics, working out a host of configurations for the show itself. This morning she had placed dozens of calls— to sponsors, agents, production people, members of the syndication network, Martinez's office, the New York City parks commissioner, both Jason and Sheena Bradley's people, facilities managers and various politicians across the country.

The result was that she had made incredible progress in very little time: all of the ALJ Show sponsors had agreed to support the tour. If Jones so chose, as Danielle supposed he would, the City of New York would move with unprecedented speed to make Central Park available as the initial venue for the tour. There was strong interest at Jones's syndication network to televise the kickoff of what, Danielle suggested, would be a series of weekly events spanning the country—even some talk of televising the entire tour as the latest reality TV series. Meanwhile, Jones would continue to do his regular talk show, although he would tape some shows in advance and increase the frequency of reruns to provide time for the tour.

Danielle also had some strong recommendations for the event itself. ALJ would dominate the live show even more than usual, sharing the stage only with celebrity cameos and musical guests. The staff would put much of its energy into securing the success of the remotes. And, once the tour left New York City, Abe's monologue would have strong local content. She also had a list of twenty-five prospective sites, which would soon be narrowed down to the final twelve or thirteen.

The entire presentation lasted more than two hours. When Danielle finished, Winthrop, Jones and Bream applauded. "That was just great, Danny," Jones said. "Now let's go back to chart number one and crawl through all this one more time."

They spent another hour or more reviewing every chart. Then they addressed the public relations issues, establishing an "A" list of media targets, including the three network TV morning shows and evening news programs, the Sunday morning shows, PBS *NewsHour*, Anderson Cooper, Bill O'Reilly, Chris Matthews, Rachel Maddow, Charlie Rose, *The Huffington Post*, *The Daily Beast*, *Politico*, *Rolling Stone*, *New York*, *The New Yorker*, the four major New York City newspapers plus the *Village Voice*, the *Amsterdam News*, the *Wall Street Journal* and major newspapers and city magazines across the country, especially in the locations the tour would hit. The goal was to land interviews, articles and sound bites—whatever was appropriate—and to keep it up day in and day out both prior to and throughout the tour.

"Beat the drum," Winthrop said. "Beat the drum until we're sick of hearing ourselves talk about the tour and then beat the drum some more—although, Abe, I doubt that you'll ever get to the point where you're tired of talking about the tour."

"Impossible, Jack," Jones said. "Absolutely and positively impossible. I'll never get tired of talking about my Eeeh-mancipation Tour."

"Well, let me put it this way. When all us normal human beings get to the point where we feel we're saturated with talk of the tour, that's when we'll just be at the point of breaking through to the country."

They worked for about another half hour on a variety of fine details and then brought the meeting to a close. Winthrop was impressed—with the work ethic, the professionalism, the dedication, the teamwork. It was a new experience for him, and he found that he was enjoying it.

"I'm heading back to the office with Barry," Danny announced. "We're going to do a little more work on the prospective venues."

"I want to check out what's hot locally across the country," Bream said. "That'll be an important factor in helping us decide which are the best sites for the tour."

"OK, D & B," Jones said. "See you tomorrow morning at the office. We'll pick it up again."

"See you, Barry," Winthrop said. "See you, Danny." She pursed her lips in a quick symbolic kiss, which Winthrop returned. Then she and Bream were gone.

"Well, Jack," Jones said, "Just the two of us nuts left. How about a drink?"

"Sounds good, Abe."

"I'm going to have some Chivas on the rocks. What'll you have, 1800?"

"That'd be perfect."

As Jones retired to the bar to fix the drinks, Winthrop pulled a chair over to the window and sat down. There it was, New York City, Manhattan, the city he loved, stretching out before him. Whenever Winthrop looked at the city from a significant height, tens of stories above the ground, he always felt subtly moved. The combination of frenetic activity and soundlessness was strangely beautiful. As he absorbed the full force of that beauty, he thought about Jones. There was truly no one else like him. He had the biggest ego of anyone Winthrop had ever met. That was certain. And he clearly set himself apart from everyone by his manner and bearing. He was after all a man who had invented himself, and he extended to himself all the privileges of self-invention. But he was also capable of working as a member of a team. Working hard. Amazingly hard. And he listened to other people about as well as anyone could.

There was also his sense of humor, which implicitly acknowledged that the excesses and theatricality and hyperbole of his self-invention were finally comic. Yes, it was true. The more Winthrop got to know Abraham Lincoln Jones, the more he liked him. And the more his affection for him grew, the more he wanted to get to know him better.

"1800, Jack," Jones said, pulling up a chair beside him.

"Thank you, Abe," Winthrop said.

"New York, New York."

"There it is."

"You know, Jack, I do this a lot myself. Just pull up a chair and look out."

Winthrop nodded in response. There were so many things that he could have said to Jones. There were so many things they could have discussed. But the moment was right for silence. So they both sat there, sipping their drinks and looking out across the city—for ten, twenty, thirty minutes. Then Winthrop turned to Jones and said, "Abe, this has been good. It's good to work with you. Good to be here with you."

Jones smiled. "Tomorrow morning, Jack. Tomorrow morning we start all over again."

"Tomorrow morning," Winthrop said. Then he got up from the chair and headed for the Tit for Tat.

14

WINTHROP OPENED THE DOOR OF THE TIT FOR TAT, and there was Slow Mo. He had never felt so happy to see him, and it seemed like a lifetime since he had, although it was only last Friday. Mo had his back to Winthrop. He had just finished conferring with a buoyant Manny Snider, who was melting back into the crowd. The bar was packed, especially for a Monday night, and virtually everyone was a friend of Manny's and/or the new owners—Donna, Rita, Sheila, Slow Mo and, yes, Jack Winthrop.

Winthrop noticed that there were several new dancers, moving about the bar and talking to customers. The dancer on stage was new as well. She was very tall and had rather exotic features, a mix perhaps of Asian and Middle-Eastern characteristics. She had also shaved her head and had what appeared from a distance to be a design tattooed into her scalp. There were some new stage lights as well, and the sound system had been substantially improved. All signs that the reign of Donna Marone had indeed begun.

"Mr. Mo. Mr. Slow Mo!" Winthrop called out, tapping Slow Mo lightly on the shoulder. Slow Mo turned and a big, broad smile spread across his face.

"Jack! My partner in crime!" Slow Mo exclaimed. "Let me shake the hand of the man who owns a piece of this bar."

"Let me shake your hand, partner. Congratulations, you own a piece of this bar, too."

"But we know who really gonna run this place, don't we, Jack? Donna, Donna, the prima donna."

"You got that right, Mo. She'll put her personal stamp on this place fast. In fact, I see we already have some new dancers here."

"Yes, we do, Jack. Thanks to Miss Donna Marone. And all of them fine young women. Specially that tall, high-steppin' woman up there on stage right now."

"You like her then."

"Sure do. I like her just fine. I like what she done with her head."

"You're not a big fan of hair, are you, Mo?"

"Some people look fine with hair. Like you, Jack. I don't think I wanna see you baldheaded. Other people need hair to hide their looks. They don't want nobody to see what they look like. Me, I like to see everything the way it is right out in the open."

"Well, you certainly get that here at the Tit."

Slow Mo nodded approvingly. "You sure do, Jack. You get plenty of that—and then some."

The new dancer seemed to be doing quite well on her first night at the Tit. Slow Mo had called her high-stepping, and she was certainly that, strutting about the stage wearing nothing but an "In the Pink" D-string, matching pink garter belts positioned high on each thigh and pink patent leather spiked high heels. The garters were stuffed with rolls of dollar bills. Another dozen or so bills were crumpled up and strewn about the stage. And there were a lot more on the way as well, with every front-row patron holding up a bill and waiting patiently for the appointed moment when the tribute could be offered.

Clearly, the dancer owned the crowd, and part of her mastery was in the attitude she brought to her performance, an attitude of natural ease and confidence. The music helped, too. It was "Shake That Thing" by Sean Paul, a particular favorite of Winthrop's. And it was obviously a favorite of the dancer's too, for she was lip-synching every word with remarkable poise and precision as she moved about the bar top stage.

"She's a hit," Winthrop said. "Looks like she's having fun, too. What's her name?"

"Name is Z," Slow Mo said."

"And the tattoo on her head? I can't quite make it out."

"Z."

"Makes sense," Winthrop remarked, getting ready to switch gears, anxious to talk to Slow Mo about what was really on his mind. "Listen, Slow Mo, I need to talk to you about something important."

"What that, Jack?"

Just then a huge cheer went up from the crowd. Z had completed her set and was departing the stage. She had stripped off her pink D string and thrown it a remarkable distance, way out into a dark corner of the bar, where several of her admirers were now scrambling for possession of it like young boys wrestling over a home run ball in the bleachers at Yankee Stadium. Winthrop thought of the prize he had been carrying with him since last Friday evening and poked a finger into his pocket for reassurance. Yes, it was still there, safely tucked away. He wondered if the teenage dancer might not be somewhere in the bar at this very second.

"Is that new teenage dancer here tonight, Mo? You know the young woman who was dancing here last Friday night."

"Got those bachelor party guys all shook up! That the important thing you wanna ask me about?"

"Yes. I mean, no. I mean, I was just wondering if she was here tonight."

"She sure is here, Jack."

Another round of hearty applause broke as Bree took to the stage. As she started her dance, she cast a glance toward the door and shot a quick smile at Winthrop and Mo. They both smiled and nodded in return.

"Everybody here tonight, Jack," Slow Mo said. "It's party time. But what you really wanna talk about?"

"Well, my life's been getting kind of complicated lately."

"I heard you did a few hours in jail yesterday, Jack, with Rita and her group."

"Right. I did. But here's the thing. You know how I'm working now for Abraham Lincoln Jones, and you know all about the shooting and what not."

"Sure. Rita said the man who shot Jones was that guy used to sit right over there. Never say a word."

"Exactly."

"Detective was in here askin' questions about him."

"Don Germany."

"That the man."

"I'm seeing him later tonight. But let me tell you. There are actually two separate gunmen."

"Rita said that, too."

"And ever since the shooting I've been getting calls from both of them."

"They on your case, too, not just Jones?"

"Seems like it. I'm pretty sure the one who used to hang around here is following me around sometimes too."

Slow Mo looked thoughtful. "You gotta be careful, Jack. I know how you like roamin' around everywhere in the city. But you gotta stop thinkin' you livin' some kinda lucky charm life."

Winthrop smiled, somewhat embarrassed, for he did have a tendency to nurture the delusion that he was invulnerable, particularly as he walked about the city, protected by some strange journalistic amulet.

"Walkin' around uptown after midnight," Slow Mo said, "Only white man on the streets. People stay away from you, Jack, cos they think you a crazy man."

"You're probably right."

"First time you run into somebody crazier than you or somebody don't give a damn if you crazy or not, that be it. You a dead man."

"How would you like to be my bodyguard, Slow Mo?"

"I pack a gun?"

"No, only on special occasions."

"Good. I don't like guns. But what's your idea, Jack, of a special occasion?"

"I'll leave that up to you."

"You know, Jack, I been thinkin' about gettin' into security. A few of my guys interested, too. We can use them if we need some back up."

"Sounds good," Winthrop said. Then he and Mo quickly worked out the terms of the security arrangement. Winthrop made an offer, and Slow Mo said, yes.

"You a good man, Jack," Slow Mo said. "When do I start?"

"How about tonight after the party here? I've got a meeting with Germany at his apartment. He may have turned up something new. Why don't you get someone else to watch the door and come along with me?"

"Gerard can take the door."

"Who's Gerard?"

Slow Mo gestured toward the end of the bar. A tall, well-built black man, almost as big as Slow Mo, was sitting in between Robin and one of the new dancers, a black woman with emerald green tinted hair. "Donna wanna do things to bring in more business," Slow Mo said. "I tell her that mean more security. She say then do it, and I ask Gerard. Dude got a lotta experience. We need more muscle for you, Jack, Gerard be there."

"Great. Right after midnight OK for the trip to Germany?"

"Ready any time, Jack."

"OK, Mo. Catch you later. I'm going to sit at the bar and talk to Sheila and Rita."

"OK, Jack. See you later."

As Winthrop made his way through the crowd, he found himself feeling a bit apprehensive about the bar, and he was just a little annoyed that he felt that way. Tonight's big crowd was certainly due to the celebration. But Winthrop had no doubt: Donna would take the bar to a new level. Winthrop would contribute as well. He had something of a business sense himself, and he was sure that he would help Donna establish the Tit as the hottest sex spot in town. That was exciting, and Winthrop was all for it, but he had a concern. Success meant that the bar would change. He had to admit he was just a little bit afraid of that—and it bugged him. Here he was, the journalistic rebel and spinmeistering guru of Abraham Lincoln Jones, afraid that a bar might change. But it was true. All good things were delicate and vulnerable in their own way. In the case of the Tit for Tat, at least as far as Winthrop was concerned, it was a matter of innocence. That was the special quality of the place.

Perhaps no one else would understand it just as those who were driven by bigotry would never see Rita for the special human being she was. But Winthrop knew what he knew. And he would stand by his knowledge. The Tit for Tat was a place of innocence because at the Tit, sex was sex—pure and unadulterated. It wasn't merely commerce, although the dancers did it for the money and tribute was offered; it certainly wasn't shameful because there was no morality to produce shame. It wasn't sexist either for those who understood the equation. No, it was just sex and the sex was simply there, like life. It existed without apology or explanation. That itself was a form of innocence, which Winthrop did not want to lose.

So, Winthrop thought, when it comes to change, he was just like everyone else. Change was frightening because it threatened what you had. The trick, he knew, was to continue to embrace change anyway—despite the threat and despite the fear, and, while changing, to do your best to recreate what was good in some other form. That's what you had to do whether the change concerned a bar, your career—or even an entire culture. Nobody liked it, but there it was.

As Winthrop broke through the crowd surrounding the bar, he was smiling once again. There was Rita, sitting next to her friend, Callie, and there was his usual seat waiting for him. "Hey, Rita," Winthrop said, "You saved my seat."

"We all know it's your seat, Jack. No one would think of taking it."

"I guess I'm almost as bad as old Archie Bunker about my seat," Winthrop said as a Jack Daniels on the rocks slid in front of him courtesy of Sheila James. "Thanks, Sheila and congratulations," Winthrop called out as Sheila moved quickly on to another customer, smiling and giving Winthrop a big thumbs up sign as she went.

"You needn't tell us how you feel about your seat. We know, Jack," Rita said. "You've met my friend, Callie Rodriguez."

"Of course, Callie. Good to see you again."

"Good to see you, Jack. I understand you spent some time in jail on Sunday with the rest of us."

"That's right, Callie. I was doing my best to keep New York City's finest busy. But what's your read on the overall reaction to the demonstration? I know the papers were pretty tough on GRACE."

"There's been a very negative reaction from all the straight media," Callie said.

"Everyone's lined up against us, Jack," Rita said. "The newspapers, TV, radio. All the commentators and columnists and bloggers and the radio talk shows—especially the right wing shows that pander to all the bigots."

"I'm not a bit surprised," Callie said.

"All of us were prepared for what the cardinal and the mayor and the police commissioner would say," Rita explained. "And we expected the media coverage to be slanted against us. But I don't think most of our members were entirely ready for the hatred that's trying to pass as responsible commentary. Callie's right. She and a few of our other members predicted it."

"Callie, I assume you were a strong supporter of the demonstration," Winthrop said. "If you anticipated this kind of reaction, why did you think the demonstration was a good idea?"

"I still think it was a good idea," Callie said. "Sure, we're taking a beating from the straight media and the city. But on the positive side, we've been deluged with calls from ex-priests, brothers and nuns as well as other supporters, including some straight people, like you, Jack."

"It looks as if our membership is going to grow substantially as a result of the stand we took," Rita said.

"And our members are more dedicated than ever to winning recognition and fair treatment from the Church," Callie said.

"Well, you can add me to the list of dues-paying members," Winthrop said. "You know, when you consider the number of gay priests and lesbian nuns, the self-righteousness of the Church's position is really an outrage."

A cheer went up from the barroom crowd as if in approbation of Winthrop's point, but in actuality the applause was all for Bree. She was alternating with great dexterity impersonations of a frenetic swimmer and a dazed, nodding automaton. Just behind Winthrop, Pat Mahoney and Gene Green, a Tit for Tat semi-regular, were singing, "She's so fine. There's no tellin' where the money went. She's all mine. There's no other way to go."

"You know, Jack and Rita," Callie said. "I'm not sure I approve of all this. But I am tolerating it."

"Toleration's the key, Callie," Winthrop said.

"Oh, come on, Callie," Rita said. "Loosen up just a little bit. Tonight's a double celebration."

"Double?" Winthrop asked.

"Yes, Jack. Donna and I decided to order two cakes. One for Manny and one for ourselves. We're bringing them out at midnight."

As Rita was talking, Winthrop noticed that Manny Snider was approaching. Apparently he was moving through the crowd, accepting congratulations and saying good-bye to long-time friends. Manny had never looked better. He already had the self-satisfied, I-beat-the-world-at-its-own-game look of the retired entrepreneur, a man who had cheated other cheaters out of their ill-gotten booty and had now won the right to enjoy every penny.

Winthrop had always liked Manny—liked his abrasive personality and high energy—but he never felt that he had ever really connected with him. They were just too different from each other. For Manny, life was making one deal after another whereas for Winthrop it was more like taking one breath after another, and beyond that he didn't know.

"Jackie, boy!" Manny shouted in his Ernest Borgnine/McHale's Navy voice. "Let me shake your hand, my friend. You are the man who paved the way to my retirement one dollar bill at a time."

"Actually, Manny," Winthrop responded, "I'm quite the philanthropist. I've also contributed substantially to the college funds of quite a number of deserving young women."

"The world's a better place because of you, Jackie. Everybody knows that. Just keep your ass out of jail. Now let me give a hug to our other little jailbird—Father Rita." Manny wrapped Rita in a big bear hug. "I was worried about you, kiddo, when I heard the news. You OK?"

"Yes, Manny. I'm just fine. Let me introduce you to my friend, Callie Rodriguez. Callie, this is Manny Snider. He's been the owner of the Tit for Tat for years."

"As long as it's been the Tit," Winthrop chimed in.

"Hi, Manny. It's good to meet you," Callie said.

"So what are your plans, Manny, now that you're retiring?" Rita asked. "Donna said you'd be moving to the Bahamas."

"I'll be staying at Grand Bahama. I've always like Grand Bahama. And I'll be doing a little of this and a little of that."

"Well, I'm sure you'll find things to keep you busy, Manny," Winthrop said. Donna had mentioned that Manny might get involved in an escort service. Actually, it was Winthrop's under-standing that Manny had been a partner for years in a number of very lucrative Bahamian services.

"You know me, Jack," Manny said. "I can't sit still. Nothing too stressful, though. Just some silent partner stuff. But, listen. Let me congratulate you and Rita. I know Donna's including you in the partnership. Lots of luck with the bar. Donna's got a million ideas. I've just been holding her back."

"She's a dynamo," Rita said.

"One of the best business minds around, bar none," Manny said. "She'll make a killing."

She already has, thought Winthrop. It was amazing really when you considered how much money Donna had made in just a few years from her website, her mail-order business and her 900 num-bers. Winthrop was sure that she had outmaneuvered Manny in the negotiations to buy the bar. Even so, she would have had to put up a substantial down payment. The location alone was worth a hefty sum. Then there was her idea of the partnership. It was certainly a tremendous break for Rita, Sheila and Slow Mo, providing them with equity in a growing business. Of course, in return Donna was ensuring the dedication and loyalty of people who would contrib-ute to the business for years to come. In Winthrop she had access not only to advice, which she could have gotten anyway, but also to another substantial source of investment capital while retaining strong majority control of the business. As a result, she was able to do in essence whatever she wanted. No, there was no denying it, Donna was one shrewd operator, and Winthrop could only love and admire her all the more for it.

Meanwhile, Winthrop could see that Manny had the urge to move on and continue working the crowd. His eyes were darting about impatiently, picking out all the people he wanted to speak to next. "Jack, Rita, Callie, not to be abrupt," Manny said, "But I've got to keep circulating. Don't want to miss anybody. Not tonight. Jack,

Rita, lots of luck with the bar. Callie, it was great meeting you. And remember, everybody, stay out of jail!"

They all bid Manny good luck and goodbye. Then Rita took Winthrop's hand. "Jack," she said, "Don't take it personally, but Callie and I are going to mingle a bit as well."

"You're all leaving me," Winthrop exclaimed.

"Leaving you to your thoughts, Jack," Rita said.

"That's dangerous."

"I know," Rita said smiling. "Let the world beware, but I want to be sure to introduce Callie to everybody."

"Just as long as you keep her away from Pat Mahoney. He'll try to convince you, Callie, that you're a lesbian only because you haven't found the right man."

"Well, if he does, I'll tell him the only reason he's straight is that he hasn't found the right man."

"That'll get him, Callie," Rita said.

Winthrop laughed and took a sip of the Jack. "Well, have fun meeting everyone. If you need me, I'll be right here doing my best to defend the values of Western civilization."

As Rita and Callie disappeared into the crowd, Sheila began doing a sexy little runway model strut behind the bar in time to the music, which was George Michael's "Too Funky." In a fast second Bree joined her, and the two women began playing expertly off one another's moves. All the while Sheila was holding a drink in her hand high above her head. Toward the end of the song, Sheila and Bree lip-synched, "Do you want me to seduce you?" and right on cue at least a dozen guys called out "Yeah! Yeah!" just like director George. When the song was over, everybody applauded wildly, with Sheila and Bree each taking a bow. Then Sheila came directly over to Winthrop and gave him a big friendly kiss and said, "Here's another drink, Jack, on the house. Notice, I didn't spill a drop."

Winthrop quickly drained his old glass and took a neat little sip of the new Jack. "That was some dancing, Sheila. You know, you were always my favorite dancer before you decided to become the number one mixologist in the world."

"I'm only good for short spurts now, Jack."

"Feeling good tonight?"

"You bet."

"Congratulations."

"You, too, Jack. It's going to be fun."

And she was off to fix another round of drinks for a group of guys who worked at the pizza place next door. Sheila was one hard worker, thought Winthrop. And the hard work was finally going to pay off for her and little Karina. It didn't often turn out that way, and Winthrop was happy for her.

Meanwhile, up on stage the mood had changed. The song was Madonna's "Justify My Love," and Bree was moving slowly but purposefully about the bar top, wielding a whip with all the authority and bearing of an experienced dominatrix. Maybe it was the images in Madonna's video for the song, but Winthrop found himself immediately thinking of Germany. Yes, he definitely had something new. Winthrop was certain. Germany was somewhere right now. Perhaps he was at his apartment. And he had information about Speck that Winthrop did not have. And the information was important—too important to leave on a telephone answering machine or even to communicate over the phone. The conversation had to take place in person. That way he and Germany could really talk. They could discuss how the information changed their understanding of Speck and figure out where the new information might lead.

In just a few hours it would happen. If all went well, he and Germany would talk, and then he would know. Then he would have the information he needed. But for now he would have to wait, diverting himself through the naked dancers and the music and the drink and the celebration.

Perhaps some would find it hard to understand, but Winthrop was always exceptionally frustrated whenever he was prevented by either distance or time from knowing something he really wanted or needed to know. And at those times he would imagine what it must be like to look down on everything from high above, look down from the perspective of a providential God, beyond time and space, and see, for example, Germany alone in his apartment and Speck in his and Sherry, too. Look down on himself as well through the mysterious power of the divine, as God the Father might look upon God the Son, and instantly know all.

It was absurd really. We all lived alone in our own little cubicles, lived inside our opaque circles turned in upon ourselves, and except for rare instances of vision we could never really see, from our hard-won private spaces, beyond the circles, beyond our isolation, to grasp what another human being might know.

When Bree/Madonna finished with her S&M ringmistressing and stepped down from the stage to wild applause, she was relieved by one of the new dancers—the black woman with the green tinted hair—who immediately did a back flip, which resolved gracefully into a perfect split. A gymnast, Winthrop thought, as the first monster chords of "Money for Nothing" rocked the bar. What a nice surprise! A black chick into British rock. The fulfillment of a dream, thought Winthrop. Then he felt warm, vodka-heavy air blowing against his ear. He looked up, and there was Donna, decked out in a black leather jump suit zipped only to her navel, with the mythical teen goddess standing beside her, wearing nothing but a black pushup bra and a "Back Door Black" D.

"Jack," Donna said, barely controlling her laughter, the teenage goddess laughing too, "You talk about Rita not noticing what's going on around here! Where is your mind? Do you know how long we've been standing here?"

"Sorry, Donna, sorry," Winthrop said. "You caught me. I was lost in thought, chasing the bright, elusive butterfly of love."

"Well, your butterfly is here," Donna said. "Jack, this is Misty. I told Misty how much you wanted to meet her."

"Yes, Donna, that's right. Misty, I don't know how to say this because compliments are always misunderstood, especially from men to women. I don't know why exactly."

"I do," Donna said, "And so do you, Jack, you liar! It's because all men want to do is fuck."

"Well, you've certainly taken every advantage of that, Donna," Winthrop said.

"You bet your ass, Jack," Donna said. "Too bad it isn't more of a challenge."

"Men are slaves," Misty said.

Winthrop smiled and looked at Donna.

"Don't look at me, Jack. Misty was born knowing that. Now let's hear your compliment."

"Actually, you've just suggested it," Winthrop said. "As soon as I saw you, Misty, I thought this is a woman who knows. This is one powerful, self-assured woman."

"I can take care of myself all right," Misty said.

"I'm going to let you two get to know each other better," Donna said. "Jack, we'll talk later."

"See you later, Donna," Misty said, taking the seat next to Winthrop.

Winthrop smiled as Donna walked away. Then he turned to Misty. "So," he said, "Your name is Misty. Misty what?"

"Just Misty."

"Just Misty?"

"You only need one name, Jack," she said, putting her arm around Winthrop and giving him a little squeeze.

Winthrop took another hit of Jack Daniels. "What do you drink, Misty?"

"Cranberry juice and ice."

Winthrop got Sheila's attention. "A cranberry juice on the rocks for Misty, Sheila, and a refill for me."

On stage, the new dancer's "Money for Nothing" routine was

coming to a comic close. Mark Knopfler was singing "Money for nothing/Chicks for free" over and over, with Sting whining in falsetto about his MTV. On "Chicks for free" the dancer would shake her head no, move her index finger back and forth and point first to her pussy and then to the rolls of dollar bills stuck in her garter belt. True, thought Winthrop, as Sheila brought the drinks, nothing was free. One way or another, you always paid for everything. "Where are you from, Misty?" Winthrop asked, thinking Minnesota or Wisconsin.

"Nowhere," she said.

"What do you call nowhere?"

"Eden Prairie."

Ouch, thought Winthrop. Not even Minneapolis. That was nowhere. "Just got up and left one day?" Winthrop asked.

Misty turned and gave him a knowing look, born of experience more than a million years old. "That's how you do it," she said.

"No good-byes?" Winthrop asked.

She just looked back at him again, this time with a kind of X-ray vision, as if she could see everything she needed to know about him. "Do you want to dance?" she asked.

Sting had just stopped whining. There was silence for one eternal moment. And Winthrop felt it coming. Misty's D string was burning a radioactive hole in his pocket. The new dancer—Winthrop had just heard someone call out Angel—was standing still, head and upper body slightly bowed, in anticipation. Then it hit as he knew it would. Strip joint synchronicity. The right offer, the right woman, the right music.

"Hey, hey, mama, love the way you move. Gonna make you sweat. Gonna make you groove." It was "Black Dog"—Winthrop's favorite Zep tune. There was another vocal blast—Plant's primal scream and then Page's demented guitar. Angel erupted. Lights flashed. The bar went crazy.

Winthrop's hand found the D. He offered it to Misty. She took it with a smile and rubbed it against her tits. Then she slowly dragged the string down toward her pussy and rubbed it there as well. She gave it back to Winthrop, and he stuffed it in his pocket.

"It's on Donna," Misty said.

Winthrop gave a nod and pulled out two twenties. "It's on me too," he said.

Misty slipped the twenties in her D-string and sat in Winthrop's lap. She positioned herself carefully, finding just the right spot. Then she danced the dance for Winthrop, doing it wild and right, confiding to him secrets the Eden Prairie boys would never know.

*　　*　　*　　*

AFTER MISTY MOVED ON, Winthrop had his time alone. Despite the crowd and the celebration, the bar was the same as always, a place to stabilize and think. As the night wore on and one dancer followed another, Winthrop found himself thinking again of just one thing—Germany. What does he know that I don't know? Winthrop asked himself again. How would the information change his understanding of Speck? Where would it all lead? Above all, would it enable the police to track down Speck before he struck again?

Winthrop had faith in Germany. Like Winthrop, Germany had a special sense about certain things—crazy, psychotic things. It was part of Germany's own eccentric makeup, and there was really no way of explaining it—like remembering the Shorty case in the first place, pulling it out from among the hundreds of other New York City homicides, thinking there could be a link even though the Shorty suspect in no way resembled Speck. Yes, thought Winthrop, that took a special sense, and Germany had it. If anyone could close in on Speck, he was the one.

Throughout the night, as he steadied his nerves and brooded about Germany, Winthrop observed Donna moving about the bar. He saw clearly that she was establishing herself not merely as the new owner and host, entertaining customers and spreading her energy throughout the room, but really as the glittering pornographic personification of the bar itself. In her new incarnation Donna was the Tit for Tat. She was the dark, fantastic angel of sex, the promise, if not the reality, of a fuck. And she was thriving in that vibrant new role. Loving every minute. She was so busy filling the bar with her presence and personality that she didn't get back to Winthrop until just a few minutes before the scheduled midnight celebration.

"There he is," she said when she finally returned, "The poor abandoned artist in heat."

"I like being abandoned," Winthrop said.

"And you like being in heat, so I'm not going to feel sorry for you. How about a hug and a kiss? We both deserve it."

"You deserve it," Winthrop said, giving Donna his very warmest hug and a crisp smack on the lips as well. "You are the bar. I'm just along for the ride."

Donna was smiling and looking him over. Winthrop could tell she was pleased by his compliment, especially pleased because she knew he was right. "So how much you in for, rider?"

Winthrop told her.

"That's some ride," she said.

"Well, I believe in you, and I believe in the bar."

"You know, Jack, you believe in the strangest things."

"The truth is strange, Donna. It's never what you're taught to expect."

"So are lies, Jack."

"That about sums it up."

Just then drinks appeared as if out of the air. But Sheila had actually brought them—another Jack Daniels for Winthrop, ice-chilled Stoli for Donna. Sheila had a drink as well, a little shot of tequila. And there was Slow Mo, standing by the bar, holding a glass of seltzer, and Rita with her coffee and Callie was there, too. Suddenly it seemed that everyone was blowing on noisemakers or singing. The song was "We Are Family," the old Pointer Sisters tune, and yes, there was Manny, beaming and lifting a drink high in acknowledgement as all the Tit for Tat dancers came streaming out of the dressing room—all of them stone, cold naked, Robin leading the way holding a big white cake high above her head, followed by Z and Misty and Angel and the other new dancers and Bree bringing up the rear carrying another cake, this one with chocolate icing. Donna jumped onto the stage and shouted above all the noise and the music, "We love you, Manny!" Manny blew a kiss to Donna and finished it off with a big, generous wave of his hand to include everybody in the bar. Then Donna shouted, "I love you, Jack, Rita, Sheila and Mo Mo! I love you all! This is the best goddamn bare ass bar on earth!" Then Donna kicked off her heels, stripped off her jumpsuit, threw it into the crowd and started to dance, and all the Tit for Tat dancers climbed on stage and started dancing too, one big naked line dance, with the Pointer Sisters still singing about family. And Winthrop looked around at everyone and smiled, thinking this is it. This is what the shits don't understand.

*   *   *   *

WHEN THE PARTY LEVELED OFF A BIT, Winthrop said his good-byes and slipped outside the bar with Slow Mo. It was like stepping from one world into another. The weather was warm, and the sky was clear, but the streets were just the streets. The weirdest thing was how dangerous it all seemed now that he had protection.

He and Slow Mo walked over to Park Avenue and hailed a cab. After midnight it didn't matter, but Winthrop hated crossing Park Avenue. He always got caught in the middle.

As they rode together in the cab to Germany's apartment, Winthrop wondered what Slow Mo was thinking. He never liked to ask anyone what they were thinking. It was unfair. An invasion of privacy. If you wanted somebody to know what you were thinking, you told them. Otherwise, your thoughts were your own. But right now he really wanted to ask Slow Mo. And he knew why. He needed to escape from his own thoughts—because he couldn't stop thinking about Germany. It was the information. What Germany knew that he didn't know. But he realized now that was a cover.

Sure, he wanted to know the news about Speck, but what he was really thinking wasn't a thought at all. It was an anxiety, a worry. It was fear. The fear had been masked all night by the party, masked by the celebration. But now that was over, and he was riding in the streets on his way to see Germany. And the fear was out there. Winthrop rolled down the window and felt the fear in the wind. The cab blew through an intersection, and he saw it in the yellow light. The cab turned a corner, and he heard it in the tires as they pulled against the gravel in the street.

"Slow Mo," he said, "What are you thinking?"

"I'm thinkin' we're goin' to Germany's apartment, Jack. We're goin' to see Germany."

And the cab continued cutting across town, hitting every light on the way to Germany's. And then Winthrop felt they were getting there too fast. And already they were on Columbus Avenue. Then finally Slow Mo spoke. "You like this guy, Germany, don't you, Jack?"

"Yes, I do, Mo. I like him a lot."

The cab pulled up outside Germany's building. They paid the driver and went inside. At the elevator Winthrop hit the button, and the door opened right away. And still everything was moving too fast. Every light said go. Every door opened.

When they came to the floor, they heard the music. It was Wagner. Something from the Ring Cycle. Winthrop couldn't quite place it. He had always avoided Wagner. People thought the music was boring. But he knew it was just too powerful. It was another world, a primitive world, and that was what Germany loved about it. And the music was playing very loud. The loudest music he had ever heard. And they were knocking, but no one answered. But that was because the music was so loud. And they knocked again and they kept on knocking and Winthrop didn't want to stop. And Slow Mo was saying something he couldn't hear, because the music was so loud. But this time he heard him. "Try the door knob, Jack."

Winthrop tried the knob, and the door opened right up. Now they were walking in Germany's apartment. Winthrop saying, "Felix, Felix," and Slow Mo calling out, "Detective Germany," as they turned from the foyer to the living room and saw him sitting in a rocking chair, wearing headphones, so he couldn't hear a thing, and the back of his head was missing, and there was blood splattered all around.

"He dead, Jack. He dead," Slow Mo said. "The joker must have propped him up."

15

A COP GAVE WINTHROP A RIDE HOME some time after 5:00 a.m., and it was a good thing. He couldn't have found his way otherwise. He couldn't think or feel. All he knew was shock.

He and Slow Mo told the cops everything they knew at the scene and at the station. It seemed to Winthrop that he told the story at least a dozen times from beginning to end for different cops and different reports—how he and Slow Mo had found Germany dead, the reason for the meeting, the nature of Germany's investigation, everything Winthrop knew about Speck and the other gunman and all the phone calls, particularly the one in which Speck mentioned Germany. Frank McCarthy and a few of his people arrived and corroborated everything, although McCarthy was noticeably cool to Winthrop, undoubtedly because of Sunday's arrest. Police Commissioner Cobb showed up too and held a press conference in which he released the basic facts to reporters. Cobb said nothing specifically about Speck or any other suspect, but he did say that the police were pursuing several promising leads and that Winthrop and his bodyguard, Maurice Monroe, were not suspects.

Around 2:30 a cop took Slow Mo home since he really didn't have anything more to say that could help. Then they started playing the tapes of the calls, repeating the Germany call over and over again.

Finally, with all the official thanks and apologies, the cops told Winthrop he could go.

Winthrop looked about his living room, where everything was in its place. He thought again of the scene in Germany's apartment, how undisturbed everything was. Just like the Plaza Hotel room or, for that matter, the apartment at the Sherry Netherland. Nothing had been touched, but everything was changed. Germany was dead. That was his blood. That was his head. That was his brain. Yesterday he existed. Now he did not, and he would never exist again. Except for the few people who worked with him, except for the few who knew him, it was as if Germany had never existed at all. That was what Speck had done. He had robbed Germany of everything. He had taken away life itself, while leaving everything else undisturbed.

Before the police arrived, Winthrop had looked about for any sign of the information that Germany had wanted to discuss. It didn't take him long to find it. Underneath a few papers sitting on Germany's desk was a small yellow stick-um pad. On the top sheet Germany had written the name Shorty and drawn an arrow to the name Tanya Lee. Below it were an address and a phone number. The address was just around the corner from Shorty's Bar.

Winthrop reported the note to the police, and it was taken as evidence, but McCarthy and his men already knew about Germany's re-investigation of the case. They knew he had talked to Tanya Lee, a heroine addict and prostitute who had worked for Shorty and was a friend of Shorty's girlfriend. They had no idea what Germany had intended to discuss with Winthrop. Germany had his own way of doing things. And they had nothing to say to Winthrop about the Tanya Lee interview or any other aspect of the investigation. The whole Shorty angle was Germany's idea. It was a pure hunch, and McCarthy intimated that they would probably stop pursuing that aspect of the case. The man Winthrop called Speck, the man who had made all the threatening phone calls, was certainly the prime suspect in both the Jones shooting and Germany's murder. If the police had any further questions for Winthrop, they would contact him. Meanwhile, they strongly advised him against writing about what he had told them. It was premature. It was speculative. It would only complicate the investigation. If Winthrop had any other questions about the Abraham Lincoln Jones shooting or Germany's murder, he should talk directly to McCarthy. As for the so-called Sherry gunman, there was still no real evidence, and there was certainly nothing to link the Brooklyn hang-ups to anything whatsoever. In the meantime, because of Speck's calls, the police would continue bugging Winthrop's phone and watching his apartment.

So that was it. Germany was dead, and the investigation was nowhere. According to the cops, the Shorty angle was bullshit, and Sherry didn't exist. Speck did exist. He was, as they said, the prime suspect, but the police didn't have a clue as to where he was, this man who seemingly came and went as he pleased, a man who apparently could enter and exit any room he liked without disturbance, without leaving a trace of evidence. A man, finally, who killed with total impunity.

As Winthrop struggled to collect his thoughts, he wondered how Speck had done it. Perhaps he had stolen a key from Germany's super, duplicated it and then replaced the key without the super ever knowing it was gone. Perhaps he had developed some superhuman technique for breaking into rooms, using some high-tech method of springing locks that worked without betraying a hint of its handiwork. Or perhaps Germany had simply left his door opened, convinced that his own highly sophisticated psychic alarm system was fail safe, despite the Wagnerian tumult and despite the headphones, which had surely prevented him from hearing a thing. Perhaps, perhaps, perhaps, thought Winthrop. In the final analysis Speck's methods didn't matter. What mattered was the simple fact that Speck could do as he pleased. He had played with Jones at the Grand Army Plaza because it had suited him to do so. Now he had killed Germany because he wanted to kill him. The fact that Germany was investigating the Jones case was no doubt little more than a secondary consideration. It had merely identified Germany as a potential target. As for the re-investigation of the Shorty case, Speck in all probability knew of it, but Winthrop would bet that it really didn't matter either. In fact, Winthrop doubted that Speck had bothered to make even a cursory check of Germany's papers before leaving the apartment.

No, it was simple. Speck had killed Germany because he had wanted to kill him, which meant that he had not killed Winthrop only because he had not yet decided to do so. He would again attack Jones—or for that matter not attack him—according to the dictates of his own private plan.

So now what? thought Winthrop. Now it was another day just like yesterday except that now Germany was dead. That would be true tomorrow and every day thereafter.

Sitting in his living room, staring at the walls of his apartment, with the day brightening minute by minute, the sun intruding its light, like the stark white bulb of an interrogator's lamp, Winthrop felt beyond exhaustion. But sleep was out of the question. He knew what he had to do. He had to tell his story despite what the police had said. He had to tell everything he knew about the shooting of Jones and the murder of Germany, everything he knew about Speck and the second gunman and get it into the paper. But he couldn't help marveling at the chasm that existed between what Speck did and what he, himself, was about to do. It was laughable, really. Speck blew people away, blew them right out of existence. And bang! Winthrop wrote about it. Speck had his gun. And he had his laptop. Yes, thought Winthrop, the pen might be mightier than the sword, but could a word processor beat the shit out of a semi-automatic weapon?

Winthrop got up wearily, went to the kitchen and put up a pot of coffee. Then he threw his body into the shower and set his psychic timer for ten minutes, figuring that by then all his nerve endings would be fully hydrated. When the timer went off, he turned off the water and stepped out of the tub, dripping wet but otherwise feeling no different and certainly no better than when he'd gotten in. He dressed quickly and grabbed some coffee, which at least provided marginal stimulation and zero caloric nourishment. Then he reconnected his study phone and called Danielle.

It was just past 6:00, but she was already up and dressed. He told her everything that had happened and that he wouldn't be able to get to the office until some time in the afternoon. It was a short call and very painful. He couldn't bear to hear Danielle cry. She was crying for him, crying for Germany, crying, Winthrop thought, for herself as well and for Abe and for everyone else in the world who was vulnerable to terror and violence, which was just about everybody. At the end of the call she made him promise something. "Promise you'll stay with me tonight, Jack. I really mean that for your sake more than for mine."

Winthrop promised. Then he told Danielle that he loved her, saying it again the way he had late Sunday night. Then he hung up the phone and dialed Abraham Lincoln Jones. He wanted to let him know what had happened. Not just that his police contact Germany had been murdered but that he was the one who had found him. That would certainly be part of the story, which would no doubt build in the local media throughout the day. He also wanted to get his agreement on the article. After all, Jones was the one who had been shot. The phone call was an opportunity for Winthrop, the ALJ communications guru, to speak to ALJ about what Winthrop, the dedicated *New York Times* journalist, intended to write. He'd feel better at least discussing it with Jones first. He didn't think there would be any problems, but if there were, they would work them out. For if Winthrop was sure of anything, it was that he had to get the story out.

The phone rang once and Jones picked up. He was already up and working, too. Winthrop had been missing something. Almost never having been up at this hour before, he hadn't realized that while he was busy sleeping off the previous night's victories and defeats, all the other ambitious people in the world were up and ready to roll—decked out in full butt-kicking regalia.

"Jackie boy!" Jones screamed into the phone as soon as he heard Winthrop's voice. He was in his usual state of high energy despite the early hour, but he quickly turned quiet and thoughtful when Winthrop told him what had happened.

"Man's playing his own tape in his head," Jones said.

"That's right, Abe," Winthrop said. "There's no way to predict what he might do."

"We'll take another look at our security plan when you come in this afternoon, Jack, especially for our Central Park gig. But one thing for sure, my man. We got a tape to play, too. We got our plan. We got our mission. He keeps on doing his thing. Fine. We keep on doing ours."

Winthrop already knew that was how it would be. On the article Jones had no objections, just as Winthrop had anticipated. "You're the writer," he said. "Write what you got to write." But he made a point that was troubling, especially since it confirmed a concern that had already occurred to Winthrop. "You know, Jack," Jones said. "Your story's big, page one shit. And that's good for us. Good for the tour. But it's a goddamn mess, too."

"You mean the strip joint stuff?" Winthrop asked.

"Tabloids'll have a field day with that," he said, his voice picking up energy again.

"Especially since I just bought part of the bar."

"Hey, you're a regular surprise package!"

"That's me."

"That's cool, too. But let me tell you, Jack, it's not just the Tit for Tat shit. You got another gunman in your piece after all the other crazy eyewitness stories have turned out to be full of shit. You're the guy who found Germany. You just got your own ass sprung out of jail. The list goes on, my man. Nobody cares if one thing's got nothing to do with the other. It's the perception that matters."

"And the perception will be a mess."

"A fucking mess."

"Right."

"But you know what, Jackie?" Jones paused for effect. "Sometimes I like a fucking mess. I like the challenge. It gives me more to work with."

"Well, Abe, if that's true, you've certainly hired the right communications guy because I'm giving you lots to work with."

"Hey, it's all PUB-LIC-I-TY!" Jones said, banging out each syllable like a demented jazz drummer.

"That's where they'll really get me," Winthrop said. "They'll say I'm exploiting the situation to grab more publicity for you and the tour."

"Will I lose any sleep over that, Jack?"

"I wouldn't think so," Winthrop said, marveling at how irrepressible and resourceful Jones was. He was a man who seemed constitutionally incapable of defeat. No matter what life threw at him he was ready to turn it to his own advantage. Now Winthrop was determined to try to do the same.

After bidding good-bye to Jones, Winthrop had one more call to make. It was to Peter Gallo at the *Times*. Peter was another goddamn workaholic and an early morning exercise addict to boot. He had probably been up since 5:00. "How many miles today, Peter?" Winthrop asked when Gallo picked up.

"Jesus Christ, Jack, are you OK?" Gallo asked.

"I'm fine, Peter."

"First you get arrested. Then you show up at a murder scene."

"It's been a rough couple of days."

"Listen, Jack, there are a couple of things I have to tell you. First, we're getting lots of emails and phone calls about your arrest. You know, that substantial segment of your readership that hates you."

"That's why they read me, Peter."

"Everybody here knows that. Everybody's comfortable with that. Just thought you should know that all they all want you fired."

"Tell the truth, Peter. You love this shit. I take all the heat, and we end up selling more papers."

"Now, number two, your gun control piece comes out today. Great piece, Jack," Gallo said. "I love it. It may even be more controversial with your arrest and Jones's shooting."

"Well, Jones's shooting provided the occasion for it, Peter."

"And now this terrible business about the detective's murder."

"Actually, that's why I called, Peter. I know you're looking for another column, but I have something much bigger. Something you might want to put on page one." Winthrop described the piece.

Gallo got so excited he almost jumped through the phone. "This is explosive stuff, Jack. It makes for a great story. But the police aren't going to like it one bit."

"I know. They already told me they don't want me to write anything."

"Well, you'll be dredging up all this second gunman conspiracy stuff that they've been trying to put to rest."

"I'm saying there's no conspiracy, but there was another gunman. I know. I saw him."

"And on this guy you call Speck, you've got the phone calls, but there's no hard evidence he did anything beyond harass you and the girl."

"And mention Germany in one of the calls. That even got the attention of the cops. Look, Peter, cops are control freaks. We're at best a nuisance to them. They certainly see Speck as the prime suspect in both Germany's murder and Jones's shooting—they've said as much—but they're nowhere with the investigation."

"You kept quiet for Germany then?"

"Right. I had faith in him. He was nosing this thing out, but now that he's dead, I have no confidence at all in the police investigation, not when it comes to somebody like Speck. He's a real serial killer type. You won't catch him going by the book."

"So you want to turn up the heat on the investigation."

"Exactly. That's the real reason the police want me to keep quiet. They don't want any pressure in the press, any public pressure, to crack the case. They want everybody to trust that the investigation is going just fine regardless of the results."

"You'll take some heat yourself on the sex stuff. Why the hell do you hang out in places like that?"

"Actually, I now own part of the bar, Peter."

"Christ, Jack, you are over the top."

"Listen, Peter," Winthrop said, taking the opportunity to ignore Gallo's remark, "I'll have the piece for you later this morning."

"That's great. So you've written most of it already."

"Actually, I haven't started it yet."

"How the hell do you write so fast, Jack?"

"It's like breathing, Peter. I don't think about it. I just do it. But, listen, I got to go."

"Oh, one more thing, Jack, before you do. Some guy keeps calling the paper, trying to get a hold of you."

"What's the guy's name?"

"He won't leave a name or number. He says he'll keep trying to reach you. I spoke to him once myself. He sounds a little strange."

"How so?"

He sounds, I don't know, kind of awkward, maybe a little affected, almost too square."

Sherry, thought Winthrop. Goddamn it. I'll bet it's Sherry. "OK,

Peter. Thanks for letting me know. I'll email the piece to you as soon as it's done."

"All right, Jack. Talk to you later."

Winthrop hung up the phone. He stared at it for a few seconds and decided to keep it hooked up. Then he sat down at his desk to write the article. Winthrop knew it would be a fairly lengthy piece. He wanted to be sure to include everything of import, beginning with his decision to join Jones's team and ending with Germany's murder. It was important that he get it all just right—to let the people know what had really happened, yes, but also to challenge the police to acknowledge the existence of a second gunman and to find and arrest Speck before he decided to strike again.

As soon as Winthrop began working, he realized that he must have been writing it all unconsciously from the beginning, right from the moment of Jones's late night phone call, writing it as he was living it, because it all flowed right out of him, despite his exhaustion. By nine o'clock he was done. He thought he'd lie down for a few minutes just to collect himself. Sleep would be impossible, he thought. But a few minutes of rest would be good. Then he'd review the piece and send it to Gallo.

The second his head hit the pillow, he was startled by the phone. Or so at least it seemed. But when he glanced at the clock, he saw that it was a little past eleven. Still somewhat disoriented, he got to the phone and picked it up before the answering machine kicked in. "Hello," he said.

No answer.

"Hello," he said louder.

Silence and still more silence. Here we go again, thought Winthrop. "Hello," he screamed into the phone.

"You needn't shout," a man's voice said.

"What?" Winthrop said.

"There is no need to shout," the man insisted.

Now Winthrop was silent.

"Am I speaking to Mr. Jack Winthrop?" the man asked.

"Yes, you are. Who are you?"

"Mr. Winthrop, you do not know me. We have never met. However, I am quite familiar with you—through your work, of course."

"What's your name? Who am I talking to?"

Silence. "Have you been calling me and hanging up?" Winthrop asked.

"I have certainly called you quite a few times."

"And hung up."

"I dislike speaking to a machine. I assure you, sir, I had no intention of harassing you. I have also tried to reach you at your newspaper."

"Well, here I am. Now what do you want?"

"I need to speak to you."

"Speak!"

"I need to speak to you in person, sir."

This is one fastidious nut, Winthrop thought. Jittery, too. All the more reason to cut the annoyance. After all, the whole point was to talk to him—not drive him away. "In person is fine," said Winthrop. "When and where do you want to meet?"

"I would like to suggest that we meet today at a restaurant. Perhaps for lunch."

"Fine," Winthrop said. Sherry didn't seem like the fast food type. And Winthrop was in the mood for a good meal anyway. Once again he had gone for a long stretch without eating. Nothing but liquid refreshment since the catered lunch yesterday at Jones's apartment. He tried to think quickly of a place that might appeal to Sherry. "How about the front room at Gramercy Tavern?" he asked.

"Excellent choice, Mr. Winthrop. But they don't accept reservations. Are you certain we'll get a table?"

"Don't worry. They know me. How's 12:30?"

"Yes, I believe I can be there by then."

"OK. 12:30 then."

"Yes, indeed," Sherry said and hung up.

Winthrop called the restaurant immediately, spoke to the manager and secured a table for two at twelve-thirty. Then he went back to the piece. He had lost more than two hours, but he was comfortable with what he had written. In less than a half hour, he finished his review, making only minor alterations, and sent the piece to Gallo, just barely keeping his promise to get it to him in the morning.

Before leaving for Gramercy Tavern, Winthrop had one last call to make. It was to Slow Mo. He wanted to know how he was doing after the ghastly night they'd had. He also wanted to invite Slow Mo to accompany him on another little excursion this evening. The phone rang four times, and there it was. Voice Mail. "Mo, it's Jack," Winthrop said. "I hope you're OK. It was rough last night. I know I'll never be the same. But I need you again tonight, pal. Meet me at my apartment at 8:00. It's Tanya Lee. I got to talk to her myself and find out what Germany wanted to tell me. It might not lead anywhere. But I got to know. Eight o'clock. OK, Mo?"

Winthrop hung up the phone and took off for the restaurant. But when he got to the lobby of his apartment, the doorman stopped him. "Mr. Winthrop," he said, "I was just about to buzz your room. A package just came for you."

"A package?"

The doorman held it up to him and nodded. It was a little box, wrapped in brown paper, tied with twine. Winthrop took the box. The thought occurred to him that the box might explode when he opened it. But, he thought, no, this was a message, and that wasn't it. "Glen, what did the person look like who left this?"

"He was a man in his thirties, about your height, sir, with long, brown hair. He had on a work shirt and jeans. He was kind of sloppy."

"A hippie?"

"You could say that, sir."

"Thank you, Glen."

"You're welcome, sir."

There was a small waiting area in the lobby. Winthrop went over and sat down on the couch. He put the box down on the coffee table and looked at it for a few seconds. There was no identification on it at all. He slipped off the twine and tore off the paper. It was a child's puzzle. Ages six to twelve. A map of Europe. Winthrop dumped the pieces onto the table. He quickly put the puzzle together, snapping each brightly colored piece into place, watching the continent take shape, country by country. When he came to the end, there was just one piece missing. It was Germany.

16

WINTHROP HAD AN EXCELLENT LUNCH AT GRAMERCY TAVERN, but Sherry was a no-show. He waited until after two, nursing one cup of coffee after another. Finally he gave up and walked over to Jones's office in the Radio City Building.

When Winthrop arrived, he was moved by how caring and supportive everyone was. Danielle intercepted him right as he stepped into the office, saying, "I heard something, and I had a feeling it was you, Jack." She embraced him there by the door for what seemed the longest time, saying, "Jack, Jack." Then she slipped a key into his hand and whispered, "You're staying with me tonight." A second later Jones was there to give Winthrop a big, affectionate bear hug, and Bream embraced him, too. Then they took him around to introduce him to all the other staff people that he hadn't met and to show him where his own office was. Then they got down to work.

Danny was busy wrapping up negotiations with the city on the Emancipation Tour kick-off event in Central Park. Meanwhile, Winthrop went into a meeting with Jones, Bream and a half-dozen members of the ALJ security team to review every detail of the tour security plan as well as day-to-day security measures covering the next few weeks until the initial event in Central Park. After the security meeting Winthrop led a PR strategy session that went on for two and a half hours with Danny joining the group for the last hour or so. After the meeting Winthrop went back to his office and put in another hour of media planning. The work was therapeutic for him, taking his mind temporarily off Germany and his own exhaustion. When it was time to meet Slow Mo back at the apartment, he somehow felt refreshed—ready for the interview with Tanya Lee.

When Winthrop arrived at the apartment, Slow Mo was waiting for him in the lobby. Winthrop smiled. "Ready to go, my friend?" Winthrop asked.

"That why I'm here, Jack," Slow Mo said.

They shook hands and walked out of the apartment. Winthrop hailed a cab and directed the driver to go first uptown and then west. When he was sure no one was following them, he gave the cabbie Tanya Lee's address, and they headed back downtown and east. Traffic was moving, and they arrived at the apartment quickly, passing right by Shorty's Bar as they reached the intersection of Houston and Bowery and turned left. Tanya's building was just a half block further down the street. It was a shabby, dilapidated walk-up. Tanya's place was on the second floor. Winthrop knew he was taking a chance just showing up. Tanya might not even be there. But he was prepared to wait if he had to. He really didn't want to call in advance. The phone after all was made for saying no. Better, he thought, to approach her cold. Pay her if he had to and not give her too much time to fabricate a story or decide she was far better off not talking at all.

Winthrop and Mo walked inside the building. A tall, lean black man was sitting on a gray metal folding chair right in front of the stairs, blocking any passage up or down. "Excuse us," Winthrop said as he was about to squeeze by.

"Who you here to see?" the man asked. Winthrop was sure he was packing a gun.

"You the super?" Slow Mo asked. "Or you a goddamn pimp?"

"The man looked at Mo with contempt. "Who you?" he asked. "You a john or you a motherfuckin' cop?"

"We're not the police," Winthrop said.

"Then who you motherfuckers here to see?"

Yes, thought Winthrop, the man was definitely packing. "We're here to see a woman by the name of Tanya Lee."

"Fifty dollars, fifteen minutes," the man said.

Winthrop took out his wallet, pulled out two twenties and a ten and handed them over.

"Fifty dollars, fifteen minutes for both of you."

"We here to talk, not fuck," Slow Mo said.

"Don't matter what you do," the man said. "Fifty dollars, fifteen minutes for him and you."

Winthrop gave the man another fifty dollars.

"Apartment 210," the man said as he moved out of the way.

"Is she in there?" Winthrop asked.

"She there," the man said. "Go on up."

Mo and Winthrop went up the stairs and walked down a dark, dirty hallway. There was the smell of something rotting in the air. They went up to 210 and knocked. A voice said, "Come in," and they stepped inside. It was a single room, half-kitchen, small bath. A used needle was on the kitchen counter. Another one was on the floor by the foldout couch, where Tanya was lying on her side, staring out at nothing, her head propped up by her hand. She was wearing a black lace bra and panties. "Two of you," she said.

As Winthrop walked over to Tanya, followed by Mo, he could see, despite the makeup, that she was sick. Her nose was running, and there were some bad tracks down both arms. She was injecting between her toes too. Winthrop saw that she was once quite attractive, but he was surprised that she was still working out of a room. It wouldn't be long, however. Soon she'd be out on the streets, turning ten-dollar tricks. "We'd just like to talk to you Tanya," Winthrop said. "Your name is Tanya Lee?"

"I'm Tanya Lee. You cops?"

"No, we're not cops," Winthrop said.

"Cop was here the other day."

"We're not cops," Winthrop repeated. My name is Jack Winthrop. I'm a writer for the *New York Times*. But I promise I won't write about you. I just need some background information. This is Maurice Monroe. He works with me."

"Hello, ma'am," Slow Mo said.

"What you wanna know?" Tanya asked.

"We'd like to talk to you about the murder of Shorty and his girlfriend a year or so ago," Winthrop said.

"You mean Shorty and Patty."

"Yes, Shorty and Patty," Winthrop said. He felt bad. He hadn't known Patty's name.

"You wanna know about that, you gotta pay."

"You talked to the cop," Winthrop said.

"He paid." She paused a moment. "Two hundred," she said.

Winthrop took out his wallet again. He counted out ten twenties and gave them to Tanya. Slow Mo gave Winthrop a quizzical look as if to say, "What you doin' with all this cash?" but Winthrop had figured that he might have to pay to get the information he wanted, and he had come prepared.

Tanya got up from the bed. "Wait a minute," she said. She walked over to a corner of the room, where there was an old beaten up red chair. She moved the chair, bent down, pulled up a floorboard and took out a small metal box. She put the bills inside, turned and said, "This so that motherfucker downstairs don't get nothin'." Then she put back the box, replaced the floorboard, moved back the chair and returned to the pullout. "What that cocksucker charge you two?" she asked as she sat down on the edge of the bed.

"One hundred dollars," Slow Mo said, obviously still angry at the pimp on the stairs. Winthrop wondered what Tanya's cut was supposed to be and what at this point her leverage was to get it. He was glad she would keep the two hundred, even if it all went to drugs.

"So," Tanya said, "You wanna know about Shorty and Patty and J.B."

"J.B.?" Winthrop asked.

"Yeah, J.B."

"Did J.B. have long hair and sort of look like a hippie?" Winthrop asked.

"Sure did."

"Did he call himself J.B.?"

"Never called himself nothin'. Didn't want nobody to know who he was. Shorty called him J.B. cos all he drank was Jim Beam."

"How'd you meet him?"

"I was one of Shorty's girls. I'd see J.B. at the bar sometimes. He was one of my customers. He was a customer of a lot of the girls—just so long as they was black."

"They had to be black?" Winthrop asked.

"Had to be. Had to be. Patty was his favorite. J.B.'s always goin' off with Patty." Tanya paused. She seemed to be lost in thought. Then she shook her head. "Poor Patty," she said. "That J.B. was one messed up dude. Like to brag, too."

"Brag about what?" Winthrop asked.

"Called himself an inventor. Said he knew all about computers and such. Like anybody give two shits. Said he was a computer genius. That what he call himself. Lots of times, that be all he talk about."

"But, Tanya, what did you mean when you said he was messed up?" Winthrop asked.

"J.B. like to get rough. Like to talk dirty, too. He get drunk, he like to slap a girl around, specially Patty, even though he like her. Shorty have to step in sometimes. Then it was nigger this, nigger that. Fuck you, nigger. You a motherfuckin' nigger. He mean it, too."

"But he only went with black women," Winthrop said.

"Right."

"Man don't deserve to live," Slow Mo said.

"You're sure J.B. murdered Patty and Shorty?" Winthrop asked.

"I know he did."

"Any idea why?"

"Did it cos he wanna do it. Maybe they had some fight. Maybe he didn't like Shorty steppin' in when he beat on Patty. Maybe he got jealous of Patty goin' home with Shorty. Don't matter what. He did it cos he wanna do it."

"Did you tell any of this to the police when it happened, Tanya?" Winthrop asked.

"Didn't tell them a fuckin' thing. I felt bad for Patty and for Shorty too. But they dead. No way I tell the police nothin'. What they gonna do for me if J.B. come around lookin' to get me?"

"So why are you talking now?" Winthrop asked.

"I need money. You give me money. I talk. Anyway, J.B. cleared out. Ain't nobody seen him. Ain't nobody ever gonna see him around here again."

"No," Winthrop said, "I don't think he ever will come back here, Tanya. Thank you for talking to us. You were very helpful."

"Thank you, ma'am," Slow Mo said, and he and Winthrop left the room. As they walked back down the hall, Winthrop thought about the man he knew as Speck, a man who had shot Abraham Lincoln Jones and murdered Germany, Shorty and Patty, a man who had harassed Danielle, a man by whom he himself had been stalked and harassed, the same man whom Tanya knew as J.B. and who could look like a dirty hippie or a nondescript nerd—an all but invisible computer programmer—and he realized with absolute dead certainty that he would never understand the man at all. All he could know were the crimes he committed, the roles he played, the masks he wore.

When Winthrop and Mo got to the bottom of the stairs, the

pimp got up and moved his chair. "Right on time," he said, his attitude now surprisingly sunny. "Come back again," he said. "Whether you wanna talk or you wanna fuck." The man was laughing and shaking his head.

"You just be sure that girl get her money," Slow Mo said.

The man kept laughing and shaking his head as he sat back down in front of the stairway. "I take care of her," he said.

"Just be sure you do," Slow Mo said, and he and Winthrop left the building. "That girl sure is sick," Slow Mo said.

Winthrop nodded.

"You think this J.B. asshole's the same man who shot Jones?" Mo asked.

"I already knew he was," Winthrop said. Then he told Mo about the hippie leaving the puzzle at his apartment.

Mo looked bemused. "He sure is a joker. I'll say that about the man. He want you to know you gotta play his game. But, Jack, if you already knew they was the same guy, why you still wanna talk to that girl in there?"

"I needed to know what Germany knew."

"Now we know."

"Yes, we do."

"Man hate niggers, but that don't stop him from fuckin' black women."

"Right," Winthrop said, and he and Mo began walking up Houston toward Bowery.

"What you think about this inventor shit, Jack? All this bull shit about him bein' some kind of computer genius?"

"The man's got some other life, Mo. Maybe he's a mad, solitary hacker, working away in his basement, trying to crack security codes and spread computer viruses. On the other hand, maybe he's got a respectable day job. Who knows? He could even be a family man. Gets up every day, puts on a suit, says good-bye to the wife and kids, goes to the office, does his job. Maybe he's even a manager.

The boss. Hell, for all I know, he could be a goddamn executive in a computer company. Anything's possible. Anything at all."

When they got to the corner, they walked over to Shorty's Bar. It was open. The name hadn't changed, but a sign in the window said "Under New Management." They decided against going in, and quickly flagged a cab. As the taxi pulled over, Winthrop was thinking of the days ahead, all the planning and publicity. He was thinking, too, of the kick off of the tour, the big event in Central Park. And he realized there was nothing to do except forge ahead. They couldn't let Speck intimidate them. They couldn't let him stop them. At the same time, it was impossible to pretend. Winthrop didn't feel good about anything—no matter what he did or didn't do.

As their cab pulled away to take them back uptown, Slow Mo turned to Winthrop. "Jack," he said, "I got one more question."

"What's that, Mo?" Winthrop asked as he stared out the window of the cab.

"What you think this guy, Speck, is gonna do?"

Winthrop took a moment to respond. Then he turned to Slow Mo and said, "Whatever he wants to, Mo. Whatever he wants to."

JACK WINTHROP, TABLOID HERO. That's how he thought of himself now. From the moment his article on Jones's shooting hit the front page of the *New York Times*, he and Abraham Lincoln Jones—and indeed the entire ALJ team—had been bombarded by publicity. That was how it seemed to him. It was a bombardment. An explosion. A one-hundred megaton blast of publicity.

The calls started coming immediately. The piece appeared the morning after Winthrop emailed it to Gallo, and at 8:00 a.m. that same morning, Winthrop was awakened by the first call. He recognized the number. It was Jake Barnes. He had reached him at Danielle's apartment.

Winthrop couldn't believe it. Danielle had given him the key the day before, whispering in his ear, "You're staying with me tonight," and he had stayed, spent the remainder of the evening with her following the Tanya Lee interview and slept beside her through the night, holding her closely as she held him. No one had been told. It had after all been the most private of invitations. The woman he loved whispering in his ear. No, he thought, no one could possibly know. And yet there was Barnes calling on behalf of the *Enquirer*.

"How'd you do it, Jake?" Winthrop asked, more than a little annoyed. "How'd you know I was here?"

Barnes laughed dismissively. "Christ, Jack! You're about as tough to track down as Gary Hart hanging out on the 'Monkey Business' with his pants dangling around his ankles."

"So how'd you know?"

"I just took a shot. You know, you never called me back over your homo arrest."

"I know, but I did enjoy your message."

"Hey, Winthrop, come out of the closet! Answer the goddamn phone!"

"Right."

"This time when I got your answering machine, I said, fuck it. I can get this guy's cell, but I'm going to go one better and figure out exactly where he is. Maybe he's in his apartment. Maybe he's not. He could be anywhere—except at the *Times*. I've never found you there even once, Jack, this early in the day. But then it hit me. The girl! Remember, you asked me about her at the hospital right after Jones was shot. And I thought, hey, maybe he's at her place. So I called and you picked up. Easy, huh?"

That was the first and only call to him at Danielle's. But there were dozens of others—on his cell, at home, at the *Times* and at his office at Radio City. Everyone wanted an interview. Everyone wanted a story.

If there was anything Winthrop truly understood, it was how the minds of reporters worked. They were always on the look out for cover-ups, ulterior motives. That was what he always expected to get as well. He knew there would be suspicions about the second gunman, suspicions that he was trying to grab publicity for Jones. And he knew everyone would want to know more about his association with the Tit for Tat and with Speck as well as his relationship with Germany. He also knew that the best course of action was to be as open and accessible as possible regardless of what might then be written or said about him. So he found himself talking to everyone, agreeing to every interview.

His main purpose was to get the story out about the shooting of Abraham Lincoln Jones, to tell the truth as he knew it—about Speck and the second gunman as well as Germany's investigation of the shooting, its possible link to the Shorty's Bar killings, and Germany's subsequent murder. That was why he also filed a follow-up story, which made page one of Thursday's paper, recounting the delivery of the puzzle to his hotel lobby by a longhaired man wearing jeans and a T-shirt. In the two articles, Winthrop never mentioned Tanya Lee. In fact, he was careful not to report anything that might suggest that he had any sources beyond Don Germany and what had already been made public a year earlier about the Shorty case.

By the end of the week Winthrop's story was all anybody was talking about, and the heat was on the police commissioner and the mayor to make headway in the investigation of Jones's shooting. Of course, Martinez didn't like it one bit. He resented Winthrop's suggestion that the investigation might well stall out in the aftermath of Germany's murder. He felt betrayed. He considered himself a great admirer and a close personal friend of Abraham Lincoln Jones. He had been on the stage himself when Jones was shot. He could certainly have been shot himself. Any suggestion that he and Police Commissioner Cobb, and indeed the entire New York City police department, were not doing everything humanly possible to apprehend the person or persons responsible for the shooting was patently absurd. And, of course, as everyone knew, the police department and the mayor's office were absolutely moving heaven and earth to arrest a suspect in the apparently related matter of Detective Germany's murder.

Martinez also let it be known in no uncertain terms that his office and the parks commissioner had been extraordinarily cooperative in working with the entire Jones team to clear the way for the Emancipation Tour kick off in Central Park some time next month. He indicated that such speed and resourcefulness were unprecedented in any city administration across the country and that, despite everyone's best efforts, the event would very likely not take place at all unless this terrible public perception were corrected immediately. All these points were communicated with great theatricality and emotion by the mayor himself in a personal phone call to Abraham Lincoln Jones during which Martinez literally demanded Winthrop's head on a platter.

The remarkable thing from Winthrop's perspective was how cool Jones remained throughout the flap. Here was the mayor of New York City threatening to cancel the kick off of his tour, and he couldn't have been more calm or self-assured. What's more, he loved what Winthrop had written, and he stood by him as staunchly as Gallo, or any other editor, could have. "Jack," he said, "What you wrote was perfect. You got the truth out. You gave the police a kick in the ass, and you got everybody talking about me and the tour."

"What about Martinez?" Winthrop asked.

"Don't worry about Hector. I know the man. He's just worried about one thing—and that's himself. He's a politician, and he doesn't want to look bad."

"So we just need to give him the opportunity to look good."

"You got it, my man. He doesn't want to call off Central Park. It's too goddamn big. We give him a way to look good, and we come out of this thing the winners. The investigation's under a microscope with Martinez and Cobb held personally responsible, and the Eeeh-mancipation Tour is a go."

And that's exactly what Jones did: he gave Martinez the opportunity to look good. The details were worked out in a single meeting, and a press conference was held. Winthrop was able to stand by his story, reiterating the importance of getting out the truth while emphasizing that any concerns he may have had about the investigation had now been allayed. He and Jones both affirmed their confidence in the mayor and the police, and Martinez professed his love and admiration for Abraham Lincoln Jones as well as his enthusiastic support of the tour, adding that a date for the kick-off event would be announced within the next day or two.

Throughout the press conference Martinez came across very much as the man in control. And that was what Jones had understood all along—that Hector Martinez in control was Hector Martinez looking good. Give that to the man, concede to Martinez the public image that he wanted, and whatever you wanted would surely come your way.

One area of friction remained, and it was huge. The police continued to insist that there was no credible evidence of the existence of a second gunman. When asked about the contents of the Sherry video, which Winthrop had described in detail in his story, the police continued to say that they had no comment. They were reviewing all of the available video from hundreds of cameras in the immediate area of the shooting and beyond and were aggressively pursuing all leads. Winthrop, of course, insisted on what he knew to be true, holding back only on his theory, built on a kind of visceral certainty, that the Brooklyn man, the man he thought of as Sherry, the man who had failed to show up at Gramercy Tavern, was indeed the second gunman.

The police, of course, were looking after their own image. Having, in fact, made little progress in apprehending the Plaza shooter, they certainly did not want to be held accountable for tracking down another gunman. They were also doing their best to keep the conspiracy nuts off their backs. But it was impossible. No one could silence the "C" word. Not even Winthrop. He kept insisting that the man he called Speck was certainly working alone and that the other gunman was separate and unrelated. But everyone was skeptical. The tabloid reporters were particularly adamant—two unrelated assassins—that was just too crazy to be credible. If there were two gunmen, there had to be a conspiracy. The only other possibility was that Winthrop was pitching his two gunmen story to generate more publicity for Jones.

Winthrop was ready for the objections. "A lot of things seem crazy or incredible, or maybe they just seem too terrible to be true, so people invent conspiracy theories to explain them. How could a lone gunman kill John F. Kennedy? No, that couldn't be true. That would be pointless and absurd. Just too horrible to believe. So there had to be a conspiracy. What about 9/11? How in God's name could airplanes fly into the World Trade Center and collapse those buildings? It had to be a controlled demolition. Bush had to be behind it. There are even people who claim that the Sandy Hook Elementary School massacre and the Boston Marathon bombings were staged. That's crazy, of course, but sometimes what's even crazier and more terrible is what actually happens—children being murdered by a mentally ill young man, innocent people being killed or maimed by two disaffected and psychopathic brothers. My approach is simple. I'm not here to judge. I'm here to report—to tell the truth. If the truth is incredible, if it's crazy and absurd, so be it. That doesn't make it any less true."

They still didn't buy it, but that was the best Winthrop could do. Thank God, he thought, for sex. Thank God for the Tit for Tat. It was finally the only thing that got the reporters off the conspiracy kick. Just when Winthrop thought the second gunman/conspiracy questions would never end, Matt Brophy asked him why he seemed to spend most of his time hanging out in a strip club. That got a big laugh. Winthrop laughed as well. Before the laughter died down and Winthrop had a chance to respond, however, the mayor jumped in and ended the press conference, which elicited a huge collective groan, but Martinez didn't care. It was clear that he had accomplished everything he wanted from the press conference, and he wasn't about to muck it up with questions about Jack Winthrop's sexual escapades.

"Listen, everyone," he said, "We've fully discussed everything relevant to the investigation. If you have any further questions for Mr. Winthrop, I'm sure he'd be happy to answer them offline."

Winthrop was immediately mobbed by reporters, and it took him another forty-five minutes to extricate himself from the room. Jones was kept busy as well, answering one question after another about the shooting and the tour. While doing his best to answer the questions the reporters were firing at him, Winthrop was again struck by how easy all of this was for Jones. It hardly mattered what the question was or whether the intention was to go after him or treat him fairly. In the end Jones always prevailed. He was the ultimate media surfer, riding every wave of publicity safely into shore.

In that moment in which he was answering questions and observing Jones, Winthrop understood for the first time one of Jones's secrets, one of the secrets to celebrity: it was the rare ability to live at peace amid chaos. More than grace under pressure, it was the ability to assume an almost beatific state of being while insanity reigned all around. Jones had that ability more than anyone else that Winthrop had ever seen.

The day after the press conference Abraham Lincoln Jones and Mayor Hector Martinez issued a joint press release announcing the date of the Emancipation Tour kick-off in Central Park. It was Friday, September 13, at 8:00 p.m.—just four weeks to the day after the shooting at the Grand Army Plaza. The release billed the event as the ultimate talk show and quoted Jones as saying that the object was "to communicate with America. To enable Americans to speak and listen to one another. Not to argue, not to fight, not to use ideas as lethal weapons, but to connect. We want to help reclaim the soul of America. We want to free America from the chains of hatred and distrust. We want to liberate our nation from the bonds of bigotry. That's why we call this series of events, which we are launching in New York City, in Central Park, the Abraham Lincoln Jones Emancipation Tour."

The Central Park kick off would be televised live across the entire ALJ syndicated network. The event would run two hours and would consist of a trademark ALJ performance monologue and remote feeds from a church in Times Square and from community centers in Miami and Los Angeles. At each remote location there would be a moderator and a live audience. Guests at each location would include inner-city gang members and community activists. The live audience would view the remotes on three huge screens spanning the back of the stage. The event would also have an opening and closing fireworks and visual effects display, including a special appearance by Rocket Man, who would fly about the crowd and perform a variety of aerial stunts. In addition to ALJ's studio band there would be two musical guests, Yo Bitch, a female hip hop group, and the heavy metal band, Spunk Gism. Special guests would include Mayor Hector Martinez and, remote from Washington, D.C., Jason and Sheena Bradley.

The kick-off event and the subsequent tour would be sponsored by four long-time ALJ Show advertisers, whose logos would be prominently displayed about the stage. They would recoup a portion of their investment through on-site merchandising and through collateral revenues, which would include the sale and rental of a video of the Central Park event. Admission to the kick off would be twenty dollars, with all proceeds after expenses going to nonprofit organizations supporting inner-city youth, the homeless, AIDS research, prevention and treatment, and minority education.

The press release also announced the entire Emancipation Tour itinerary. The next event would take place in Los Angeles at Dodger Stadium on October 8. There would then be one event per week over the next twelve weeks. The additional Emancipation Tour cities would include San Francisco, Las Vegas, Denver, Dallas, Houston, St. Louis, Chicago, Detroit, Atlanta, Miami, Washington, D.C. and Boston. The Boston event, concluding the tour, would take place at the TD Garden on New Year's Eve.

With the Central Park kick off less than three weeks away, Winthrop began putting in sixteen- to twenty-hour workdays at the Radio City office. Everyone was working round the clock, and Jones himself left the office only to tape his regular show, do an interview or catch a few hours of sleep. On more than a few nights when things were really hot, Winthrop and Danielle ended up sleeping side-by-side on the office floor, awakening perhaps at 6:00 a.m. to take the day's first phone call. There was just so much to do and not enough time to do it. What kept everyone busiest was the relentless, overwhelming media attention—most of it positive, although there was criticism from some politicians and commentators that the tour was really just an elaborate Abraham Lincoln Jones publicity stunt.

As a result of all the attention, they had to hire three additional people just to answer the phones and take messages, and interviewing had to be limited to a mere four hours a day. Otherwise, nothing else would have gotten done. What's more, the Central Park event itself was quickly growing out of all proportion. The city originally believed that the twenty dollar admission charge would limit the size of the crowd to somewhere around 100,000. But it was soon clear that the admission charge was hardly a factor at all. Advance ticket sales boomed, and with each passing day the city's crowd estimate rose until they finally set the number at 200,000 plus and made plans to accommodate thousands more.

Initially the incredible pace and workload seemed to have a salutary effect on Winthrop. He felt a connection to the quotidian—the rock solid, unambiguous workaday world—that he had never really experienced before. He also felt a deepening, day by day, of his relationship with Danielle. But not through romance or sex. There was hardly time or energy for either. In fact, they didn't have sex at all during the weeks leading up to Central Park except for a quickie one night on the floor of the office when they awakened simultaneously at about 4:00 a.m., and an irresistible urge struck them both to do it right there by the HP printer, do it as hard and fast and noisily as possible, with grunts and groans and screams, hoping security didn't hear—the whole thing over in about thirty seconds in a ball of sweat and laughter and Winthrop's head banging against Danielle's desk, one, two, three times as he came.

No, it wasn't sex or candlelight dinners that made Winthrop feel that he and Danielle were getting closer to one another, connecting on some fundamental level of being. Instead it was work. It was doing the job together, depending on each other, building trust in a thousand different ways, with each little act or task seemingly insignificant in itself, but important nevertheless in establishing a foundation for a lasting relationship. The few days that Danielle was out of town, traveling to L.A. and San Francisco to help finalize logistics for the upcoming tour dates, Winthrop found that he missed her badly. To honor the feeling, he continued with the routine they had established just as if Danielle were not away—working through the day and night and then sleeping for a few hours on her office floor.

Meanwhile, Winthrop had heard nothing from Speck or Sherry. Nothing at the office, nothing at the *Times*, nothing at his apartment. There had been no messages, no hang-ups, no signals of any kind. As each day passed and Winthrop immersed himself more and more in work and in his relationship with Danielle, he felt his customary paranoia lift a bit. Speck and Sherry were receding somewhat into the background of his consciousness. They were still very much there, of course, but at something of a remove, like a plague or disaster on the other side of the globe.

Winthrop was getting increasingly annoyed, however, at the police and the mayor. They seemed to believe that the release of information could substitute for progress on their investigation. Almost every day they issued a statement citing how many interviews they had conducted, how many leads they were developing.

There was plenty of activity. That was clear. But, as far as Winthrop could tell, the police were no closer than they ever were to making an arrest.

In an odd way the lack of progress on the case helped to bolster Winthrop's sense of security. Perhaps the investigation as well as all the publicity surrounding the case—even the useless flow of information from the police—might act as a deterrent, persuading Speck and Sherry to stay in their respective holes. That at least was what Winthrop wanted badly to believe. It was a desire that he had never really felt before—a wish, indeed virtually a hope, that the forces of darkness and death might keep a respectable distance from his life. And he was able to sustain that hope through several long days of relentless activity, working side by side with Danielle and the rest of the ALJ team.

But one of the nights Danielle was away, Winthrop awoke in a panic. He was lying on her office floor, drenched in sweat, his heart pounding as if he had drunk ten cups of coffee, his chest heaving with pain. For a second or two he couldn't fathom where he was. Then he remembered. He was there by himself on the office floor. Then the thoughts came in a rush one after another. Danielle was out of town. Germany was dead. The Central Park kick off was just days away. And then it was as if someone had thrown a switch, and he was right back where he had always been. Right back home in Paranoia City with his next-door neighbors, Speck and Sherry. Yes, they were there too, even if they refused to come out and play. Winthrop lay there on the floor the rest of the night, dozing off occasionally but always awakening to the same oppressive reality, knowing the security he had felt was an illusion. That was the trouble with love, he thought, it addled your brain. And work—that was a distraction too. Look at all the workaholics of the world, burrowing away, searching for refuge. But when you woke up by yourself in the middle of the night, whatever you were trying to avoid would be right there, staring you in the face.

After that night Winthrop constantly had the same feeling. It was as if he were actually living in the presence of the two gunmen. Whenever he had occasion to leave the office and walk about the New York City streets, he felt as if he were being watched and followed.

Just two days before the kick off he had a particularly strange experience. It was late in the afternoon. He was a little tired, and he thought it would help if he took a walk. He left the office and headed west with no special destination in mind. Immediately, he had the feeling that someone was following him. He tried to ignore the feeling, but it just kept getting stronger, so when he got to Broadway, he turned north and adopted a leisurely pace, periodically stopping along the way, ostensibly to window shop. In actuality, he was trying to see if anyone stopped as well behind him. Broadway was crowded, of course, but he soon noticed one man in particular. The man was staring into the window of a camera store at the other end of the block. He was about the same height and build as Speck. But Speck had brown hair and was clean-shaven, and this man had red hair and a close-cropped beard.

Over the next five blocks Winthrop stopped three more times. Each time the man stopped, too. When Winthrop crossed the street, the man crossed as well. At Central Park South Winthrop turned east and walked toward Sixth Avenue. About halfway there, he looked over his shoulder, and there was the red-haired man still following him thirty yards behind.

At this point Winthrop was in a state. He whirled about and stood in the middle of the sidewalk, facing the red-haired man, who continued to walk briskly toward him. The man kept coming and would have walked right on by, but Winthrop blocked his path. "Who are you?" Winthrop shouted. "Why the hell are you following me?"

The man looked puzzled and was waving his hands elaborately about.

"Who are you?" Winthrop demanded again, staring hard at the man's face as if he were trying to look through a disguise. "Speak!" he shouted. "Say something."

The man began to look frightened. He reached into his shirt pocket, pulled out a card and gave it to Winthrop. Winthrop looked at it. It said, "I cannot speak or hear. Do you understand sign language?" Winthrop felt as if someone had thrown a bucket of cold water in his face. "No, no, I don't. I'm sorry," Winthrop said, patting the man reassuringly on the shoulder. "Sorry," he said again and stepped aside so the man could walk on.

As Winthrop watched the man walk away, finally disappearing around the corner, he thought to himself, "Who's the crazy one now?" Then he turned around and walked back to the office.

18

THE CROWD BEGAN ARRIVING EARLY AT THE PARK. By the end of the four o'clock sound check there were perhaps 50,000 people lined up at the various entrances to the event area. By Winthrop's estimate it was a pretty good mix—about sixty percent white, forty percent black and other minorities. And, man, were they ready to rock and roll! Each time Jones shouted "Eeeh-mancipation" to test the sound system, the gathering crowd would shout it right back at him—"Eeeh-mancipation"—the sound reverberating through the Park like some weird choral echo. When Jones left the stage, doing his signature dance, the people began chanting, "ALJ, ALJ," and they kept up the chant long after he had gone, prompting him to reappear for an encore performance of the dance, which he concluded by nailing a neat little series of back flips, with the last one ending in a split. "I love you all!" he shouted. "See you tonight!" Then he popped back to his feet and disappeared from the stage.

Jones was elated. "You see that?" he exclaimed to the group back stage, which included Winthrop, Danielle and Bream as well as a half-dozen members of the production crew. "You hear that?" he asked, his hands and feet still moving, his body rocking to the rhythm of his words. "That's my people. That's my congregation. They got their invitations, and they are coming to the party, coming to the ball. Somebody ask those headbangers in Spunk Gism if they know that old Three Dog Night song. You remember Three Dog Night? The blue-eyed soul thing? They did that song, 'Celebrate.' Remember that? 'Celebrate! Celebrate! Dance to the music!' And what was that line I always liked? Oh yeah, 'This is the night we're goin' to the celebrity ball.' Yeah, well this is the goddamn celebrity ball. We are going to the ball to ball! The ball of Eeeh-mancipation! I never felt such a vibe! Hey, Jackie," he shouted to Winthrop over his shoulder as he made his way, along with Bream, out of the event area to a private exit where a limo was waiting to take him back to Trump Tower, "Remember what I called this thing on the phone that night?"

"How could I ever forget, Abe?"

"I had it right. No exaggeration. This is a goddamn heavy metal, foot to the pedal, totally digitized, mezmerizing, interactive referendum on freedom and equality in America! This is the Abraham Lincoln Jones Eeeh-mancipation Tour! This is it. This is the real thing. In the flesh. In the nude!" And with that, he made it to the limo, slammed the door shut and was gone.

Winthrop had known that Jones would be up for the kick off, but he was still amazed at the energy, the intensity, of the man. He had never seen anyone so high before in his entire life. And it had nothing to do with drugs. This was superhuman. This was ALJ living on a plane that only he could ascend to.

When Winthrop was a little kid, just a good little Catholic boy in Queens, with a pair of rosary beads in his sock drawer and a scapular around his neck, going to church every Sunday and doing his time like a man at Our Lady of Lourdes penitentiary and parochial school, he liked to read he liked to read the passage in the gospels where Jesus took some of the apostles with him to a place high up on a mountain, and when he got there, he became filled with light and his face shone like the sun. The word the gospel writers used to describe Jesus in this illuminated state was "transfigured." He had become "tranfigured." And for awhile, as a kid, Winthrop believed it might be possible, if you were cool enough and mystical enough and filled with all kinds of light and grace and electricity, to become transfigured too. And maybe if you could transfigure yourself, you could also go on and beat death just like Jesus. And when you had done everything you could do on earth—heal the sick, raise the dead and make the little girls go out of their heads—you would go up to a mountaintop somewhere or other, although this would be difficult in Queens, and you would ascend into heaven. Body and soul. Just like Jesus.

Winthrop had lost that idea for all these many years, but he remembered it now, and, he thought, that's what Abe has done. He has transfigured himself. He's moving out of his old life and into a new one. And that life is the tour—the Abraham Lincoln Jones Eeeh-mancipation Tour.

That's what people were picking up. Maybe they didn't quite know it. But that's what they were sensing, and that was why they were here in the first place. This show was different. Real different. This was something new. This was truly about change, and ALJ was saying no matter how hard it is—and it is the hardest thing of all—if I can change, you can change too, and if we all change together, then America will change as well. America will beat death. America will transfigure itself. Maybe it takes a generation. Maybe it takes a lifetime. Maybe it takes a millennium. But however long it takes, let's start it up right here.

So there was the spirit of something new in the air. The spirit of expanding possibilities. It was what Winthrop loved about the six-ties. It was what all the cool and hip people loved, and it had been gone for all these years. Looking out over the huge empty space of the event area, looking out beyond the fence to where the crowd was gathering, Winthrop wondered if the power and the energy of one man could bring that spirit back. He wondered if one event or even a series of events could spread that spirit through the country. He knew one thing, though, for sure. The country needed it. The people needed it more than they ever had before. And this crowd was the proof.

The day before, Winthrop had gone out to the Park with Danielle to see the event area and the staging, and he had gotten a little scared. It was a bit like gazing into the depths of the Grand Canyon. "Wow!" Winthrop exclaimed. "I know we're expecting a huge crowd, but how are we going to fill this space?"

"I warned you, didn't I, Jack?" Danielle said.

"You did, Danny, but this space just looks so big and empty." The stage was huge as well, long and deep, and there were gigantic projection screens along the back for the remotes as well as mammoth speaker towers, rising like medieval battlements, on either side of the stage.

"We'll fill it," Danny said. "We'll fill it and then some." And it looked as if she would be right. By five o'clock there had to be more than 100,000 people gathered on the other side of the eight-foot high cyclone fence the city had erected to enclose the event area.

Winthrop had also worried that the security might prove discouraging. He had never seen such tight security at any event, particularly an outdoor event, in his entire life. In addition to building the security fence, the city had set up metal detectors at every entrance, and no one could enter without passing through them. There were also city police and even bomb sniffing dogs at every entrance. In fact, several hundred police had been assigned to the event, and it seemed that they were everywhere. There was a particular concentration of force, however, including police and ALJ's private security team, in the area surrounding the stage, which was sealed off as a further precaution by a formidable concrete barrier. The barrier ensured that no one could come within twenty yards of the stage itself.

Winthrop couldn't help but think that the area looked like a war zone under marshal law, but no one else seemed to mind or even pay it any notice at all. So far as he could tell the security and high police visibility were having no effect whatsoever on the size or the spirit of the crowd. As he scanned the various entrances with his binoculars Winthrop could actually see the crowd grow larger minute by minute. In fact, it was building so quickly that the police decided to open the gates early. They had planned on letting people in at 6:00, which was already quite early, but it was clear that the crowd outside the gate would soon become unmanageably large if the gates remained closed much longer.

One of the production coordinators ran off to ask Rocket Man to begin his rehearsal early and, if possible, to cut it a bit short. Within five minutes there he was, flying over the trees beyond the fence, looking like a miracle or a dream. As Rocket Man cleared the trees and broke into the airspace above the event area, a huge sound erupted out of the crowd. It was a combination gasp, scream and cheer—the pure and spontaneous expression of collective awe. Winthrop gasped as well. There was something deeply satisfying, yet disturbing, at seeing a human being fly through the air without any visible aid, without the aid of even a pair of hang glider wings.

Rocket Man was Anthony Baines. Winthrop and Danielle had met him the day before. After watching him fly around the event area, they walked back with him to his trailer, which was parked in a little clearing about a half mile away. They had some coffee while Anthony told them how he had come to know Abraham Lincoln Jones.

Anthony was a history teacher at West Philadelphia High School. Although he was white, his primary area of expertise was African-American history. A few years back, actually before Danielle had begun working for Jones, Anthony wrote Jones a letter asking him to speak at a school assembly that would be part of a week-long program on African-American culture. He wasn't sure what the response would be or even if he would get a response, but Jones wrote back personally right away accepting the offer and waiving any fee or payment for expenses. Jones showed up at the school without any entourage except for his limo driver, put on a vintage performance that was equal parts show biz hype and hard core history lesson and ended up spending the entire day at the school, sitting in on a number of Anthony's classes and becoming friends in the process.

The two men had a number of things in common. Aside from a love of history, both were Howard University alumni, and both were special effects and fireworks nuts. Anthony got to talking about his Rocket Man hobby, and Jones promised that if the right opportunity ever came along, he would invite Anthony to perform with him. Since fireworks and special effects would open and close each Emancipation Tour show, Jones had given Anthony a call, and here he was.

It was interesting for Winthrop and Danielle to get all these details from Anthony because when Jones had announced that someone who called himself Rocket Man would be part of the show, he didn't bother to explain how he had known about him. All he did was describe the act and say that Rocket Man would be perfect for the special effects segments, and everybody had said "great." Winthrop was excited because he had seen a man fly around Shea Stadium many years before, but he hadn't witnessed anything like it since. The man had something called a jet pack strapped to his back and had flown all around the ballpark.

As it turned out, as a teenager, Anthony had seen the same man perform at Veterans Stadium in Philadelphia. He got to know the man, learned the flight technique and technology and after a number of years improved on both. He had, for example, made significant improvements in the jet pack itself, increasing the power while miniaturizing it so that the entire unit fit easily underneath his caped red and gold iridescent Rocket Man costume. As Winthrop watched Anthony do his run through, he marveled at his speed and mobility, his ability to soar, to dive, to change directions at will while shooting off colorful flares all around the event area.

"You know," Winthrop said to Danielle, "If Abe doesn't watch it, Anthony may just steal the show."

"He'll certainly get everybody pumped up right from the start," she said.

In fact, the crowd didn't want him to leave. As Anthony concluded the rehearsal and flew away, the people went wild, cheering loudly and crying out for more. But their disappointment at Anthony's departure was quickly assuaged by a public address announcement: to relieve the crowded conditions surrounding the event area, the police were opening the gates now. Everyone was cautioned to walk slowly in an orderly fashion. And within seconds the first few people were going through the metal detectors. Danielle gave Winthrop a big hug. "Here they come," she shouted. "Now we're really under way."

*   *   *   *

IT WAS NOW ALMOST 7:30. Danielle was conveying some of Jones's last minute suggestions to the stage manager. Barry Bream was about to go on stage and begin his warm-up, and Winthrop was beginning to get worried. Where were Donna, Rita and Slow Mo? They were supposed to arrive at 7:00, find an ALJ security guard, present their special backstage passes and have the guard escort them to the cordoned-off area to the right of the stage, where they would find Winthrop, Danielle and the rest of the ALJ team. Donna in particular was a nut about punctuality. It was hard to believe she would be late. Besides, everyone was excited about Abe's show, and they were all looking forward to seeing each other and to attending the party that Abe was throwing later that night at the Plaza Hotel to celebrate the Emancipation Tour kick off. In fact, there was some catching up to do. Because of his crushing work schedule,

Winthrop had been to the Tit only once during the past three and a half weeks, only once since the night of the celebration, the same night that he and Slow Mo had left the bar just after midnight to find Don Germany dead in his apartment.

Winthrop scanned the crowd with his binoculars. Nothing. He did it again, slowly, meticulously. But they were nowhere to be found. If they had arrived by 7:00, they still would have been able to make their way, albeit with some difficulty, to the offstage area and would have rendezvoused by now with Winthrop and Danielle. But at this point the crowd was such that Winthrop wondered if it were even possible to get from one end of the event area to the other. In fact, within a few minutes it might be impossible to move around at all. Winthrop checked his cell phone. Still no signal. In fact, he had not had a signal for the last hour or so. As a result, for the time being at least, there was no way to reach his friends and nothing for him to do about it but worry.

Winthrop was perhaps the number one worrier in the world. Indeed, he sometimes felt as if the better part of his career as a journalist was built on and nurtured by an inexhaustible mother lode of worry. Characteristically, as he brooded on the whereabouts of Donna and Rita and Mo, his mind proceeded to create an elaborate matrix of disaster from which every conceivable calamity might spring. Hovering above that universe of tragedy, presiding like some malevolent god over the as yet unknown future, was Speck. And beyond Speck, in the shadows and mists of evil possibilities, inhabiting some barely imaginable future perfect time and place, lurked Sherry. It was for Winthrop the ultimate nightmare image, complete and self-contained, for it perfectly defined a world. Your world, it said quite clearly to Winthrop, speaking in an obscene telephone call voice. Yes, your world, our world, the only world there is or ever could be.

Then with the same instinct for self-preservation that compelled one to awaken from the deepest night terror, Winthrop shut the door on that awful, all-consuming image and turned his full attention to Barry Bream, reminding himself that however vulnerable Rita might be, Donna was forever indomitable and Slow Mo was the strongest, most dependable man he knew. Surely they were all together, he thought. And, if they were together, then surely they were safe.

Surely, he thought again, as Bream walked on stage, and the crowd erupted. Suddenly there was only that sound, the sound every child and heir of the sixties knew, the sound of mass, hysterical worship, first heard half a century ago when the Beatles invaded America. The sound, which seemed to exist in and of itself, apart from the very crowd that produced it, vibrating in a delirium of joy and abandonment. That sound filled and enveloped everything in the world, and in turn everything and everyone gave themselves over to it—to the cheering, the applause, the screams, the rhythmic clapping—the voices shouting, "Barry, Barry." Meanwhile, Bream stood there, a lone figure on the stage, saluting and applauding the crowd, warmly acknowledging the tribute—on his behalf, yes, but more on behalf of the Man, on behalf of Abraham Lincoln Jones, and all he could say was, "Thank you. Thank you, everyone. Thank you. We love you," again and again.

Then at the first opportunity he somehow turned, redirected the tribute into a volley of feel-good clapping that magically made the crowd his instrument. Winthrop was amazed. Bream was a pro at warming up crowds, but it was truly remarkable to witness how quickly and how easily he was able to take hold of the audience. To break it down, as it were, into its human components and connect with the people in it. Adapting his traditional "Where are you from?" warm-up formula, since it would be impossible to decipher the names of the places shouted by the people in the crowd, Bream began calling out a litany of American towns and cities, and the people in the crowd responded with a loud cheer when they heard their hometowns named. Montgomery, South Bend, Lincoln, Little Rock, Columbus, Columbia, El Paso, Provo, Skokie, Lexington, Augusta—Maine or Georgia—Erie, Lansing, Charlotte, Duluth. The litany went on and on, and with every name a cheer went up. Winthrop could feel the warmth of the crowd expand with every cheer, feel it penetrate his body and radiate within. And at a certain point the cheers began to build until everyone in the crowd was cheering the name of every U.S. hometown, culminating in a tremendous crescendo of applause as Bream sang out the names of some of the big ones—Boston, Chicago, L.A., San Francisco, Dallas, New Orleans, Atlanta, D.C., Pittsburgh, Philly—concluding, of course, with New York City.

It was all strangely moving to Winthrop, and, he was sure, to everyone else who was there. He and Abe had talked about communicating with America. Well, this was it. It was actually happening. They were doing it already, doing the impossible, and ALJ hadn't even started the show. We were all so divided, so separate, so isolated. Locked up inside ourselves. Walled in and barricaded like survivalists in their bunkers. Winthrop felt that all the time. Felt it to the depths of his soul. And yet ALJ's messenger/announcer, Barry Bream, had walked out on stage and blown down the walls of Jericho by calling out a simple incantation of American places. American hometowns. And there it was again, the impossible made easy, if you just knew the magic words. For a few moments at least, Winthrop thought, America was America again.

When Bream finally jogged off the stage, waving as he went, the crowd was chanting, "Barry, Barry," again. Then ALJ's band kicked in with "Sweet Soul Music," and everyone began to dance, dance as best they could jammed in together as they were—something in the neighborhood of 200,000 strong. They were just minutes from show time now, the band banging out one number after another at a frenetic pace—"I Feel Good," "Twist and Shout," "Hold on, I'm Comin'," "Knock on Wood," "You Can't Sit Down." The crowd was in such a state one might have thought they were clamoring for an encore, having just witnessed the musical and theatrical event of their lives. And to think, it was all still to come.

Winthrop wondered where they might go emotionally from here. How the crowd could get any higher? He thought about the core of the program—after the opening fireworks and lasers, after the gravity-defying performance of Anthony "Rocket Man" Baines and the no doubt mindboggling, *sui generis* experience of the ALJ monologue. After that everyone would have to settle down to what Jones had called "the silence, the silence that enables speech." They would all have to settle down to listen to America. To listen to inner-city gang members and try to understand their world, understand their thoughts and motivations, and listen as well to people in the community struggling to come up with answers, struggling to survive. Yes, the audience would have to listen and in listening perhaps open up the chance to communicate with America.

There would be the music of Yo Bitch and Spunk Gism to spell the listening silence, but silence was really the heart of the show— the heart of what Winthrop conceived of still as the ultimate talk show—and to have silence at the heart of any entertainment or information medium was to take a great risk. In fact, after learning of the elements of the Emancipation Tour show, a number of commentators had professed doubts about how it would all hang together, not to mention how the discussion of serious issues would hold the attention of the audience. Entertainment, they said, was one thing. Serious talk was quite another. How could it possibly work? But the answer was really quite simple. The answer was Abraham Lincoln Jones. He would make it work. He would hold it all together. After all, this was the kick off to the Abraham Lincoln Jones Emancipation Tour. Tonight's show and indeed the entire tour were a perfect embodiment of the Man. Jones was himself a wild combination of extremes. His entire life was an experiment in risk taking. A single grand performance.

In just a moment all the questions would be answered. The show would begin. Abraham Lincoln Jones would take the stage. And he would perform. He would connect with the crowd—through the power of his singular personality, yes, but also through his unique ability to get to the truth, to capture it live and put it out there on the stage.

The truth. That was the real show. That was what Abraham Lincoln Jones would offer the crowd. And Winthrop knew that when they saw it—saw it perhaps for the very first time—they would be captivated. They would be mesmerized. And they would be unable to turn away.

19

THE BAND WAS DRIVING ITSELF AT SUCH A DEMONIC CLIP that they came in one song short to fill the set. In a surprising shift in style they launched into an unrehearsed two-minute crash-and-burn rendition of "Bang a Gong," the old T. Rex tune. The whole thing ended in an orgy of wonderful improvisational noise. The crowd went crazy. It was now exactly eight o'clock.

Then, suddenly, without warning, all the lights went out—all the stage lights and the temporary lights in the event area. It happened so abruptly that it scared most of the people in the crowd. Thousands let out a frightened scream. Others groaned, thinking it was a power failure. Winthrop knew it was coming and he still jumped. Then in the next instant everyone in the crowd went silent.

With the lights out it seemed dark, though it really wasn't. For a moment with the crowd quiet Winthrop felt like a child standing alone in the night. He felt fear whip through him again. And the thoughts came rushing in. Where were his friends? Where were Donna, Rita and Slow Mo? Where at this moment was Speck? Where was the second gunman? Then he felt a hand touch his shoulder. He turned to see Danielle smiling at him expectantly. He smiled back at her and took her hand.

Then there was an explosion. Light, color and sound filled the air. The crowd roared, while the police and the security guards looked on in detachment. The show had begun. The Abraham Lincoln Jones Emancipation Tour was underway.

The band was playing Sly Stone's "Dance to the Music," and the crowd responded instantly. They had already adapted to dancing within the limited space available and were moving together to the music in a rhythmic frenzy like some monstrous single-celled organism reacting to jolts of electrical current. Tiny missiles detonated in midair, dying in a burst of noise and color, and lasers shot in every direction, marauding about the event area like searchlights gone amuck.

To Winthrop it was a bit like living inside a video game. It was all so stimulating and intense but at the same time strangely unreal. And it was exactly what they had planned—the fireworks and the lights serving as a playful, surreal divertissement from the serious talk. As Jones had said, "We'll serve the goddamn dessert before, during and after the dinner, and we'll put a spoonful of sugar in it too with every single mouthful of spinach."

Winthrop turned away momentarily from the spectacle before him. He looked over to a wooden stairway leading to the wings of the stage. Abraham Lincoln Jones was standing by the stairs, looking radiant, outfitted as always in his classic white tux and tails. He looked peaceful now, even meditative. He was exactly where he wanted to be, about to do exactly what he had said he was going to do. He had changed his life as he told Winthrop he would. He had jumped the tracks and set out on another course, another journey, greater than any he had ever undertaken before. He would pursue that course wherever it might lead, and he would take others along with him as well, beginning here tonight in Central Park.

Transfigured. The idea came again to Winthrop on its own volition. Transfigured. And the bells of revelation rang once more in his head, louder than all the fireworks and special effects explosions filling the air around him. And the bells were carrying a message. Yes, they said to Winthrop, yes, it is not only possible. It is real and true. When you get to the point where you are exactly where you want to be, exactly where you should be, exactly where you have to be, you become untouchable. Just like that man standing by the stairway. Just like Abraham Lincoln Jones.

At that moment, perhaps sensing Winthrop's presence, Jones came out of his own thoughts and turned his head. He looked first at Winthrop. Then he looked to Winthrop's left, looked at Danny. And Winthrop realized that she had been observing Jones as well, perhaps thinking the very same thoughts about him. And he had never felt closer to Jones, nor even to Danny, than he did right then. Inexplicably, he had also never felt the differences more acutely— between himself and Jones, between where Jones was and where he, Jack Winthrop, was at this point in his life. For he knew he was anything but untouchable. Far from transfigured. No, at this moment, he was all vulnerability and worry. If anything threatened him, there would be no defense. If anything happened to him, he would be done. But that was his own concern. That was a private matter. That was to be resolved at some point in his life—or not. This moment was for Abraham Lincoln Jones. This was a silent acknowledgement of the Man.

Winthrop looked at Danny and saw that she was smiling. He squeezed her hand and summoned up the courage to smile as well, smile at her and Abraham Lincoln Jones. Jones gave a little nod and a smile in return and trotted up the steps to stand in the wings, along with Barry Bream and Mayor Hector Martinez.

Then a cry came up from the crowd, that same cry of awe and disbelief that Winthrop had heard earlier that evening. And he knew what it meant. Anthony had appeared. Winthrop picked him up in his binoculars. He had just cleared the trees and was flying into the event area, flying high above the crowd, cutting through the rov- ing lasers, circling within the ring of fireworks explosions, gliding beneath a canopy of bursting colors. He looked, if possible, even more magical and mystical than he had before in rehearsal. They really were just run throughs, thought Winthrop. Now Anthony was moving so much faster and more gracefully, performing midair body loops and pirouettes like a stunt pilot without a plane, accelerating too like a crazy celestial drag racer bent on self-destruction, his body rocketing toward the stage, then pulling up at the last possible second to avert the crash and continue his miraculous orbit of the cheering crowd.

Anthony completed several more daredevil circuits of the event area, shooting up flares of his own, as the band played on and the fireworks and light show continued to bombard the crowd. Then the stage lights went dark; a spotlight appeared and an announcer's voice filled the air. "May we have a big round of applause for Anthony "Rocket Man" Baines? Thank you, Anthony." As the crowd cheered, Anthony saluted in return and flew out of the event area. "Now," the announcer continued, "we are very pleased to introduce the mayor of New York City, the Honorable Hector Martinez."

A loud cheer went up from the crowd. The size of the cheer was a good indication of the mood of the audience. They could hardly have been in better spirits. But, Winthrop thought, it was also an honest recognition that this was the man who had in large part made the evening possible, working with the ALJ team to blow away every conceivable obstacle and stage a huge, complicated outdoor event with less than a month's preparation.

For his part Martinez was absorbing every last ray of light and warmth that the crowd was sending his way, standing there in the spotlight with his arms extended graciously and his head nodding affirmatively in a show of imperial appreciation—the emperor benevolently accepting his due. "Thank you, everybody. Thank you," he repeated over and over again. Then when he sensed that the moment was right, he leaned into the microphone and shouted, "Qué pasa?" and the crowd responded right on cue, "Estás!" The mayor queried the people again, and they answered back. He shouted out the perennial question once more, and again they responded. Then Martinez dissolved in laughter, and the audience laughed, too, with many people applauding as well.

Winthrop took Martinez's laughter as a valid substitute for self-deprecation and decided that he would like the mayor for just this one night. He was a politician, indeed. Politics was his life. It was in his blood. Hell, Winthrop was sure that it was written right into the mayor's DNA. But tonight he was their politician. He was playing on their team, and this was a night to embrace one's own.

"Hello, everybody," Martinez shouted. "I would like to welcome all of you personally to this great event in Central Park, the kick off for a very special show that will tour America. We're all here tonight to have fun, to listen and learn. We're also here to extend our best wishes and support to the great super star who will entertain and educate us this evening. Now here to speak for all of us are two special friends—from our nation's capital, Washington, D.C.—watch them appear now on these big screens at the back of the stage, the Democratic senator from the State of New York, Jason Bradley, and his beautiful wife, supermodel, Sheena Bradley!"

And there they were, Jason and Sheena Bradley, their images filling the screens. It immediately struck Winthrop that this was how they should always appear. As larger-than-life images projected on a screen. They didn't need to burden themselves with real lives. They could simply live as images. Like contemporary angels and saints, they would appear out of nowhere to bestow their blessings on the elect or the needy and then vanish without a trace.

"Thank you, Hector," Jason said as the crowd applauded him and Sheena. "Thank you, everyone. We wish we could be there with you tonight. This is a landmark event and a truly memorable evening. As you all know, just one month ago, I marched in the African-American Day parade, and I stood on that stage at the Grand Army Plaza, stood there side by side with the great performer and humanitarian who is the star of tonight's event. You all know what happened that day. What happened then on that stage is what happens every day on the streets of our cities throughout this country. Senseless violence. Young people are dying for nothing. They're dying because of drugs. They're dying because of ignorance. They're dying because guns are everywhere.

"The man behind tonight's event was shot because he has the courage to speak out against the madness. He has the courage to speak his mind. Someone tried to silence him with bullets, but he is back tonight to say that freedom of speech is more powerful than a gun. A bullet is nothing. A gun is nothing. But freedom lives forever. And tonight we are here to show our support for the man and all he stands for. Sheena?"

Before Sheena could speak, the crowd applauded Jason's remarks. Then it broke into a chant of "Sheena, Sheena," in anticipation of hearing her speak. "Thank you, everybody," she said when the noise had somewhat subsided. "I love you all. Like Jason, I wish I could be there in Central Park with all of you, but I'm happy that we could participate in this way. And I'm honored to read a message of good will from someone very special. Here goes. 'For more than forty years you've entertained and informed us, challenging us always to re-examine how we think and feel about the key issues confronting our nation. I applaud your vision and your courage, and I salute you as you initiate your Emancipation Tour, which will provide a national forum for addressing such life-and-death issues as inner-city violence, drugs and education.

"'You are truly an inspiration to me and to all Americans who want to build a better world for our children and for generations to come. Our best wishes go with you. May God bless you and keep you safe. Sincerely, Barack Obama.' There it is, everybody, a message from our president."

As the crowd applauded warmly, Winthrop turned to Danielle, raised his eyebrows and gave a little look as if to say, "Not bad!"

She returned the look, impressed as well, for the presidential message had been a nice surprise. Abe would probably not say anything about it, but Winthrop and Danielle knew that he would be pleased.

"Now," Sheena continued, "Jason and I would like to bring out a man you all know well. He's a good friend of ours and of Mayor Martinez as well. He is without a doubt the best in the business at what he does. Come on, everybody! Help me out here. Let's all welcome Barry Bream!"

Bream walked across the stage to the biggest applause yet and shook Martinez's hand as he joined him in the spotlight. "Good to see you, Mayor. Thank you, Sheena. Thank you, Senator Bradley," he said, waving at their images on the screens. Then when the applause was at its height, Bream started in, apparently wanting to make the most of the moment. Somehow he managed to project his voice over the crowd. "OK, everybody," he shouted. "Are you ready?"

Huge cry—"Yeah!"

"Do you really mean it?"

Bigger still—"Yeah!"

"Really and truly?"

Eardrums bursting—"Yeah!"

"Well, then," Bream roared, "With a little help from my friends, here we go!" Then in the manner immortalized by Martinez and Ross just one month before at the Grand Army Plaza, the day of the parade, the Bradleys, Martinez and Bream joined together to sing out the magic words that would summon forth the Man. "Hello, America," they announced, "From Central Park in New York City, it's the kick off of the Abraham Lincoln Jones Emancipation Tour. And now here's the Emancipated Mouth, the Black Hole that swallowed America, the Master Blaster of Talk Show Disaster—Abraham Lincoln Jones!"

There was a small explosion accompanied by thick white smoke at center stage. The band kicked into "Soul Man," and the crowd went insane. As the smoke began to clear, the elliptical plexiglass desk came into view, having appeared, it seemed, out of nowhere. Seated behind the desk on a slowly rotating platform was Abraham Lincoln Jones, looking regal and serene in his classic white tux and tails.

Buddha Jones, thought Winthrop. At this moment Jones was clearly occupying his own meditative plane, bringing himself to a point of concentration and awareness that would enable him to sweep up the crowd, to elevate them, to lift them up out of themselves and infuse them with his own special vision. The desk rotated once, twice, three times as the band played and the audience applauded. Then with a quickness that took Winthrop's breath away, Jones leapt to his feet, vaulted onto the desk and catapulted himself into the air. He floated there in the multi-colored stage lights, above the music, above the crowd, for what seemed an incredible expanse of time, as if he were equipped with his own special slow motion device, enabling him to alter time itself, transforming it into an infinite transparent pitcher into which he poured his very being. For one unimaginable, timeless moment Jones remained suspended in air. Then the pitcher burst, and Jones exploded out of the moment and back into life, landing on the stage in the spotlight shared by Bream and Martinez.

Jones shook their hands and waved to Jason and Sheena Bradley. Bream and Martinez exited. Jason and Sheena bid ALJ and the crowd good-bye, and the screens switched to a video mag of Jones. Having cleared the stage and claimed it for himself, Jones turned to the cheering crowd and shouted, "Thank you, everybody. Thank you. Are you ready now for a little eeeh-mancipation? Well, then let's do it!"

Every person in the crowd had expected it. And Jones delivered—the dance. But this time with a difference. The band laid down a rap beat, perhaps in anticipation of Yo Bitch, and Jones took off at a frenetic pace, moving up and down the length of the stage, like some mad, hip-hop Roadrunner. When he found a spot he liked, he'd turn to the audience, smile and then launch into a series of manic gyrations. Meanwhile, the crowd was involved in its own remarkable dance, single-celled, as before, but amazingly diverse and alive.

Winthrop had never before seen anything like it. He turned to Danielle to catch her reaction and was surprised to find that she had slipped away. She was over in the reception area, a kind of open air Green Room, with the members of Yo Bitch and a number of the ALJ staff people, and she and all the others were dancing. Winthrop realized that he was virtually the only person there who was not. But that was fine. He was enjoying this in his own way. Taking pleasure in the pleasure of others, he thought, as he raised his binoculars to his eyes and scanned the crowd once again for his friends.

When the dance ended with Jones frozen in a spotlight at center stage—his face ecstatic, rapt—the sound of the crowd was overwhelming. Jones held his position and expression, letting the applause wash over him. Then when the moment was right, his face broke into a radiant smile, and his arms spread wide in an all-encompassing gesture of triumph and command.

"Eeeh-mancipation!" he shouted. "Emancipation," he fairly whispered. "That's one way to get it," he said in a strong, clear, evangelical voice. "You get it through the dance. You get it through the music. You get it by letting your body go free. But you know what? Some people just don't get it." Jones paused for a moment. The crowd was cheering his every remark. "No matter what I say, no matter how much I explain," he continued, "They don't understand what this tour is about. An Emancipation Tour? What's that? they say. And what's that big mouth Jones think he's gonna do? He's a publicity hound. That's what they say. They want to dis me and dismiss me. And they want to dismiss you too because we don't fit their agenda. You know who I'm talking about. The people who run things in this country. The power people. People in Congress. The ones who keep obstructing. Getting in the way of change. Almost all of them white. Let's be honest. Almost all of them Republicans. Let's be honest about that too.

"Like Congressman Adams, Charlie Adams, from North Carolina. You ever hear of Congressman Adams? I never did either 'til this past weekend. I saw him on C-SPAN, talking in Congress, giving a big, impressive speech, and nobody was there. You ever see that? Yeah, it's on C-SPAN all the time. A big, important Congressman, talking away, and nobody's in the goddamn room. Well, last Saturday, good Congressman Adams was doing this crazy gig, talking to nobody except the C-SPAN camera and the good old *Congressional Record*. And what was he talking about? He was talking about me. Abraham Lincoln Jones. Putting me down. Calling me a disgrace. Calling me a travesty. That through my tour I am giving a public forum to criminals. Giving gang members a national stage. Said I should be showcasing the Boy Scouts—Yeah! The no way we going gay but now the gay are here to stay Boy Scouts— or the Girl Scouts or Junior Achievement or the Merit Scholars and such. Well, Congressman Adams, we did try to invite the sons and daughters of the tobacco lobbyists and the gun lobbyists, but they all had previous engagements with their stock brokers."

Jones paused again as the laughter rippled through the crowd. "Now," he said, "You may be thinking, what's ALJ care about a congressman? What's he care that somebody's dissin' him? There's always somebody criticizing. There's always somebody naysaying. Who gives a damn? I say, that's right. I don't care. Not one little bit. But I'm starting out with Congressman Adams because he's representative not just of the people in his district or his state or his part of the country. He's representative of all the people who don't get it. All the people who come up with fake issues to use against you and me and discredit you and me. They want to perpetuate this vague general impression that I'm a black rabble-rouser. I'm a troublemaker, and I'm on the side of the people who are making trouble.

"Why do they do that? Simple. I'm about putting the truth on stage, and they're about telling lies. I'm about attacking problems at the root, and they're about pointing fingers, creating villains. I'm about movement. I'm about action. I'm about change. They're about getting elected and staying in power. That's the problem with power. Power's against change. Power's against anything but power. The power people are afraid of change. Afraid change'll mean they lose power. Their power.

"They'll talk about problems, all right, talk about them all day and all night. But the way they tell it, we're the problem. All the blacks and the other minorities. Hispanic people. Asians. Native Americans. LGBT. Women. All the people. The real people. We're the problem. Talk about crime. We're the problem. Talk about drugs. We're the problem. Talk about education. We're the problem. Talk about the homeless and AIDS and welfare and health care and every other issue under the sun. And guess what? We're the problem! We, the people, are the problem. Well, tonight on the kick off of my Eeeh-mancipation Tour, I am here to tell you that we are not the problem. We are the solution!"

There was huge applause as Jones paused again. Winthrop took the opportunity to survey the crowd. Everyone was cheering. Everyone was with Abraham Lincoln Jones one hundred percent. And Winthrop was amazed once again at the power of the human voice. In an age of electronic images and techno babble, it was still possible to move a crowd, to give them hope and to change how they thought and felt about life through public speech. Possible, at least if you were Abraham Lincoln Jones.

"So tonight," Jones said with particular emphasis as he resumed his monologue, "Are we giving gang members in three different cities a national forum to tell their stories and say what they think? You're goddamn right we are! Why are we doing that? Well, Mr. Adams, we are doing that to get to the truth. If you ain't interested in the truth, Mr. Adams, if you're more interested, for example, in leading congressional fact-finding tours to the beaches of Puerto Rico or participating in charity events in Palm Springs sponsored by Guns R Us, then don't watch. I won't hold it against you. I'll just know the truth is not for you. The truth is not on Congressman Adams' agenda."

There was another loud cheer. Then the crowd began spontaneously chanting, "Truth, truth, truth, truth." The chant went on at a deafening level for the better part of a minute, with Jones making no attempt whatsoever to break in or cut it short. When the chant finally began to subside somewhat, he looked out over the crowd and smiled broadly. "Sounds like you want the truth!" he shouted. "Sounds like the truth is on your agenda! Well, let me speak a truth here that all the crime bustin', three-strikes-you're-out politicians want to deny. All the phony, simpleminded, grandstandin', hop-on-the-bandwagon politicians. They want everybody to believe the answer to crime and drugs is building more prisons. Lock 'em up and throw away the key. That and dealing out the death penalty every chance they get.

"Well, we can do that. That's easy. Let's fill up the Mojave Desert with prisons. Let's line up every goddamn killer in the country and execute 'em. Let's juice up all the electric chairs. Gas up all the gas chambers. Load up all the lethal injection needles and kill them all. Kill all the killers in one big Detroit assembly line. Do it today. Do it right now. Yeah! Let's do it! Cos that's easy, friends. That's easy, brothers and sisters.

"But there's just one catch. And here's where we get to the truth. The truth the politicians want to deny. The truth all those liars say is a lie. We do all that. Fill up the prisons. Kill all the killers. You know what? It won't make a goddamn difference. Nothing will change. Nowhere. Not a thing. And you know why? It's simple. You remember that old Jay Leno potato chip commercial? Jay says eat all you want. Don't worry. We'll make more. Well, it's the same thing here when it comes to violence and crime. Lock up all the criminals. Throw away the key. Kill all the killers. Kill every one. Don't worry. It won't matter. We'll make more. That's right. America will make more. Forget the trade deficit. America is still the world's leading manufacturer of violent criminals. Because we are a criminal society. Every one of our cities is a manufacturing plant for criminals.

"If you want to make a difference by getting tough on crime, Mr. Incumbent, Mr. Politician, then you better lock up society. You better execute society. Because it's our criminal society that's at the root of violence and crime in America. That's the truth we gonna tell tonight. That's the truth you all are gonna see and hear. See it in the faces and hear it in the stories of the teenage gang members—the fine, world-class, made-in-the U.S.A. criminal products—who are joining us tonight."

This time when Jones paused the audience was quiet. Absolutely quiet. He had already succeeded, thought Winthrop. He had already brought the crowd to the listening silence. By now, Danielle had rejoined Winthrop. She gave him a hug right then as he was thinking, "listening silence," and she said, "He's doing it, Jack. He's really doing it."

Then Abraham Lincoln Jones continued talking. Talking very quietly now with some sadness filtering through his voice. So it took silence to hear him. And he was saying, sure, the young boys they were all going to see and hear tonight had committed crimes. In many instances they were violent crimes. And in every single instance they were responsible. For we are all responsible for what we do regardless of how brutal our lives have been. Some people might be confused about that. Some juries might be confused. But Abraham Lincoln Jones was not confused. So responsibility was not at issue here. What was at issue was the violence itself, the root cause. And to get to that root we all had to understand a simple truth. We had to understand that these boys were people too. They were human beings. Just like the rest of us. And that was another truth the politicians wanted to deny. They wanted everybody to think that violent criminals were some other species or subspecies, especially if they were black. They wanted everybody to think they were animals or less than animals. They wanted everybody to think they were disposable.

The truth, though, was that they were human. And they were living and reacting just like human beings—human beings who wake up one day at age six or seven and discover they're living in a jungle and they need to find a way to survive. They're living in a war zone. They're living under attack, under siege, without proper food, clothing and shelter, without the chance to learn, with all the odds stacked against them and, yes, they need to find a way to survive. So they turn to gangs, and they turn to the streets, and they turn to crime. They do it to survive. Yes, they do it because for them that is reality. That is life. And there seem to be no real alternatives. And that, Jones said in conclusion, is the truth everyone would witness tonight as they learned about the lives of the gang members from the streets of New York, Miami and L.A.

Then after a pause that let the truth settle in further, settle in and ensconce itself in the minds and hearts of all the people in the crowd, Jones threw a switch—simple as that—he threw some internal switch that propelled him out of one voice and into another, out of evangelical, sociopolitical, truth tellin' and into his old WSOL DJ jive.

"Now," Jones growled playfully at the audience, as if it were late night on the radio, after midnight on a party night and everyone ready for something special. "Now, I got three hard, tough, freedom-lovin' women comin' up here on stage (audience screams and applause). You know who they are (more audience screams and applause). I gotta feelin' we're all stoked up and primed right now for some very choice, some very powerful, some very soulful eeeh-mancipation (audience goes insane). So please everybody join with me now in welcoming them. Performing two tracks from their number one, double platinum CD, *No Mo' Chains*, here is Yo Bitch!"

Jones exited, and Yo Bitch and their backup musicians took over the stage with the force of an invading army as lights flashed, lasers shot in every direction and the crowd screamed and danced. Afreaka, Yo Bitch's lead rapper, moved to center stage and addressed the crowd over the intro to the group's anthem, "African-American Women." "Hello, everybody," she rapped in a rhythmic take-no-prisoners voice. "We happy to be here tonight. And we come with a message for all the men in the audience. Hey, listen up, boys. This is for you." And with that Afreaka launched into the song that had dominated the airwaves for the past eight weeks. It had a hard, repetitive beat that embedded itself in your brain, where it would start up spontaneously at odd hours of the day and night, playing over and over again until you found yourself begging for mercy. Winthrop particularly liked the first verse:

> *You want a little of this.*
> *You want a little of that.*
> *You want a piece of my heart*
> *as a matter of fact.*
> *But what you want*
> *ain't what you get.*
> *You get nothin' there*
> *'til you give me respect.*
> *You get nothin' there*
> *'til you give me respect.*
> *You get nothin' down there*
> *'til you give me respect.*

None of the men in the audience seemed to mind the message of the song. In fact, by the time Yo Bitch got to their "not" verse, which led into the chorus of the song, the men were all rapping along with the group every bit as enthusiastically as the women in the audience. Again, Winthrop found himself admiring what he thought of as the song's Donna Marone lyrics. Yes, he thought, setting aside the obvious difference in race, Donna could certainly have written the words to this song, particularly the "not" verse and chorus:

> *We are not crazy bitches.*
> *We are not your personal ho's.*
> *We are not the wicked witches.*
> *We don't take that shit no mo'.*
> *We are African-American women,*
> *proud of our sex, proud of our race.*
> *We are African-American women.*
> *'Til you give us respect*
> *get it out of our face.*
> *'Til you give us respect*
> *get it out of our face.*
> *Now get that thing*
> *right out of our face.*

Yo Bitch followed up "African-American Women" with their new single "Goin' Down for My Love" in which the double entendre was definitely intended. At the conclusion of the performance the audience went wild. The entire scene had the surreal look of a controlled riot. Amazingly, however, after ALJ thanked Yo Bitch and retook the stage to segue into the remote, gang member discussion segment, everyone settled down immediately, and the park was quiet again. Winthrop was thinking that Anthony would have certainly loved to have Abraham Lincoln Jones on an every-day basis at West Philly High. For Jones was proving once again, despite the incomprehension of his critics, that entertainment and education can be so inextricably bound up with one another that it becomes impossible—not to say unnecessary—to tell them apart.

As the remote feeds appeared on the big screens at the back of the stage—Miami on the left, New York City in the center and L.A. on the right—Danielle tapped Winthrop on the shoulder. He turned to look at her. "It's great, huh?" she said encouragingly.

Winthrop smiled and nodded. "Sure is," he said.

"Still no sign of your friends."

"No."

"You must be getting worried, Jack."

"It's really not like them to be late, Danielle, especially for something this important."

Danielle clearly did not know what to say, so she moved closer to Winthrop and put her arm around his shoulder.

For Winthrop, the career worrier, the situation was becoming increasingly uncomfortable with every passing minute. He checked his cell again. No it was hopeless—zero bars, no signal at all, no way to make or receive a call. For Winthrop it was really the classic paranoid situation—he didn't know what had happened, but he knew it was bad, and there was nothing he could do about it. The fear was that he would wake up one day to discover that every aspect of his life had become like that.

On stage Abraham Lincoln Jones was introducing the participants in the discussion of gang life and urban violence—the moderators, the gang members and the community leaders. There was also a small live audience at each location. They had been watching the show on TV monitors. Jones, Winthrop, Danielle and Bream had spent a lot of time discussing the best way to handle the first remote segment with the gang members. In the end everybody agreed: let them tell their own story. Then during the second half of the opening segment, ALJ could begin to probe—asking questions, hazarding comments, testing the young men's thoughts and emotions.

As Jones moved from one location to the other, giving the gang members the opportunity to speak, it was remarkable how similar their stories and their attitudes really were. They were, of course, from cities spread across the country, and they also represented by design diverse ethnic backgrounds, including La Vida, a Hispanic gang from Miami; Winthrop's old pals, the Jams and the West Siders, respectively an African-American gang from Jamaica, Queens, and a white gang from the Clinton section of Manhattan; and the Bloods, also an African-American gang from South Central L.A. But to Winthrop they all somehow looked and sounded very much the same, as if they'd all gone through the same program of basic training and were now all fighting in the same civil war. And they all had that same curious double look. Their faces reminded Winthrop of one of those magical children's rings—look at it from one angle and you saw a handsome prince. Look at it from another angle and you saw instead a fierce, fire-breathing dragon. Winthrop's first impression as he looked at each of the gang members was that they were all still teenage boys—hardly more than children. But if he blinked or shifted his glance slightly as he looked at each of the young men, he immediately saw the convicted felon, the emerging career criminal, the psychopathic killer who would take a life for any reason or for no reason at all, take a life as easily and as thoughtlessly as a child might squash an insect. With the double look came a double attitude as well—on the one hand, the unmistakable awkwardness and defensiveness of the adolescent and, on the other hand, the intimidating macho and overconfidence of a member of an organized crime family, of a gangster with backing.

Above all else, however, what each gang member shared was a philosophy, a view of life and the world, never spoken of, as such, but communicated nevertheless not only in everything they said but also in every move they made, in every gesture and facial expression. The philosophy said there is no past or future. There is only the present moment. And in any moment I may live or I may die. I may kill or be killed. All I have is my own strength and the strength of my brothers.

Winthrop let the desolation of it all wash over him. He could understand how these young men felt because he had felt that way at times too. Not the urge to kill, but certainly the anger and the outrage. And he knew those feelings could take over one's life.

As Winthrop had expected, the crowd was riveted by the gang members. It was their energy, their style. They were frighteningly real, and they were articulate as well. All of them, Winthrop knew, were high school dropouts. They could barely read or write. But like so many street kids, they had an innate intelligence that had been sharpened by their experiences. Their voices cut through bullshit, and always for Winthrop at least, there was the music of their philosophy playing through the voices. As Abraham Lincoln Jones gave the young men space to tell their stories, a number of remarks were particularly striking to Winthrop.

EZ Ace of the Jams: "My mama always say. Don't hang on the streets. Stay outta the gang. You end up dead. Now I'm in the gang. I'm runnin' the fuckin' thing. And I never did fuckin' join. The gang was always there. Only thing that was there. I didn't join the fuckin' gang. The gang joined me. Day I was born I was in the fuckin' gang."

Mikey of the West Siders: "Killin' ain't nothin'. Somebody got somethin' you need. They in the way. You kill the motherfucker. You don't think about it one way or another. It's nothin'. And the motherfucker'd do the same fuckin' thing to you if he had to. Like I said, it's nothin'."

K9 of the Bloods: "This is a fuckin' white society, motherfucker. I'm in it and I'm a fuckin' black man. What I do? The minute I'm born I'm dog shit. You know what I mean? So what I'm doin', I'm lookin' for respect. Just like everybody else. You know how you get respect? Just one fuckin' way. You get it with a gun. A fuckin' gun. That's all."

Rico of La Vida: "Gang's a fuckin' business, man. You got General Motors. You got Apple. We got La Vida. Same fuckin' thing. You stay outta our fuckin' business. We stay outta yours. You only get hurt you fuck with our business."

Killer D of the Jams: "Only thing I think about's what the fuck I'm doin' now. When you live in the fuckin' streets, when you in the fuckin' ghetto, that's it. It's what you doin' now. Talkin' to you. Doin' some fuckin' business. Gettin' what I need to fuckin' get. That's what I think about."

Every so often, as the gang members talked, Winthrop would scan the crowd, looking for Donna, Rita and Slow Mo. The more he looked and didn't find them, the more he began to panic. After a few minutes, he found himself going to the binoculars repeatedly until finally that was all he did—scan the crowd and at the same time continue listening to the voices of the gang members.

Finally, miraculously, he spotted Rita. She was standing just inside one of the entrances carrying a big rainbow colored parasol emblazoned with the letters GRACE. She looked distressed, extremely distressed. In a heartbeat, Winthrop knew what he had to do. "Danielle," he said, "I just found Rita."

"Just Rita?"

"Yes, she's by herself. I'm going to get her. There's no way she'd make it here through the crowd."

"But how are you going to do it, Jack?"

"I've got my technique," he said. Then he told one of the guards that he'd be back after retrieving a friend and plunged into the crowd. Actually, Winthrop was hoping that Rita didn't make much progress, because, if she did, there was an excellent chance that he would lose sight of her. Fortunately, there was the big rainbow colored GRACE parasol, which enabled Winthrop to distinguish her amid the crush of the crowd. Even so, to make sure he didn't lose Rita, every few steps Winthrop would stop, stand as high as he could on his toes, fix Rita in the lenses of his binoculars and then resume his journey, adjusting his route accordingly. As a result, progress was painstakingly slow. Winthrop also found that he was unable to follow the discussion on stage as he concentrated on keeping track of Rita and maneuvering through the quiet, attentive but tightly packed crowd.

Finally, after what seemed an inordinate amount of time, Winthrop worked his way to within ten feet of Rita. It was then that she saw him for the first time. "Jack!" she shouted in obvious relief. She had been able to advance only a short distance into the crowd. Winthrop waved and smiled bravely, but it was clear that Rita was distraught. As Winthrop traversed the last few feet of his journey, every psychic alarm in his system was ringing at full volume. Something terrible had happened. He knew it.

When he reached Rita, they embraced. "Oh, Jack," she said tearfully. "I can't believe you found me. I'm so sorry." She was shaking her head back and forth, trying to collect her thoughts, trying to regain her voice.

"Rita, what happened?" Winthrop asked. Where are Donna and Mo?"

"Jack, they're OK," she said, "But someone tried to burn down the bar."

"What?" Winthrop replied, feeling as if the ground underneath him were crumbling.

"Someone tried to burn down the Tit. It was about 6:30, and we were all getting ready to leave when Mo said he smelled smoke. Then we all smelled it, too. It seemed to be coming from the basement. When Mo opened the door, the smoke came pouring out. He started down the stairs anyway and was overcome by the smoke. Luckily the fire department and the emergency truck arrived almost immediately, or we would have lost Mo."

"He's OK then?"

"Yes, it took four men to get him back up the stairs. It was frightening. But they were able to revive him. I rode with him in the ambulance to New York Hospital. He's going to spend the night, but he's fine now."

"Was anyone else hurt?"

"No."

"What about the bar?"

"They were still putting out the fire when I left with Mo. I called from the hospital, and there was no answer, so once Mo was settled, I took a cab back to the bar. Jack, I was so happy to find Donna and Sheila back inside and everything still standing. I just began crying hysterically."

"How bad was it?"

"The fire was contained in the basement. That's pretty much burnt out, but it never got upstairs. The whole place smells of smoke, though. Donna had to put up a big fight before the fire chief would let her in to look over the damage and begin cleaning up. That's what she and Sheila and Robin and Bree and the other girls were doing when I left to come here."

"The fire department's sure it was set."

"They're sure. There'll be an investigation, of course, but they found a timer and some wires, and they talked about detecting some kind of chemical or something."

"Speck," Winthrop said.

"I knew you'd say that," Rita replied.

"Goddamn it," he said. Winthrop had never felt so bad in his entire life. Suddenly he felt as if Speck were everywhere. More particularly, he felt as if the entire Central Park event were now invested with his spirit. He shivered as a wave of nausea passed over him. Now everything was wrong. "Let's go," he said to Rita, taking her by the hand, and he began retracing his steps through the crowd. He didn't know what to think, but he knew that he needed to get back to the stage area as quickly as possible.

When Winthrop and Rita had gotten about halfway through the crowd, the gang member segment ended, and everyone in the crowd applauded. It was rich, full, appreciative applause, and it was all a tribute to Abraham Lincoln Jones. Meanwhile, Winthrop and Rita kept on moving. "Sorry to drag you along like this," Winthrop shouted over his shoulder. "But once everyone starts dancing and jumping around, we may have a hell of a time getting through."

"I'm OK, Jack. Let's keep going," Rita cried out bravely.

On stage, Jones was in high spirits. "Come on, all you head-bangers!" he shouted. "Join me in welcoming our next musical guests. Their debut album, *STD*, was number one for six weeks. Their new album, *Genital Triage*, debuted at number one a month ago. It's already gone platinum, and it includes the current number one single, "Love Surgery." Here they are now, doing that song for you. Let's hear it for Spunk Gism!"

Instantaneously, Winthrop and Rita found themselves enmeshed in a jungle of crazy, body tossing, heavy metal dancers. And coming from the stage was the sound of the sun and planets exploding on the final Day of Judgment. Winthrop was ready to lose it. This was not what he needed right now. His only defense was to keep moving ahead with Rita toward the stage area despite the madness and confusion.

The going was slow once again, but they persevered, driven particularly by Winthrop's feeling of panic, his feeling that they had to get back to the stage area. When they finally got to within about thirty feet of their destination, Spunk Gism finished playing "Love Surgery," and, after the screaming and applause died down a bit, the lead singer, Cato, announced that the group would now perform a special request of Abraham Lincoln Jones. He invited *The ALJ Show* studio band and Jones, himself, to join the group on stage for the performance. As Jones and the band made their way back on stage to the enthusiastic cheers of the crowd, Cato also announced that he and the group had made a special request as well, and, as a result, Rocket Man would be returning for a surprise appearance in honor of the performance.

Winthrop turned and looked through his binoculars toward the sky above the trees just beyond the event area, and, sure enough, there was Anthony. He was just clearing the trees, and he seemed to be moving at a tremendous speed. As he entered the airspace above the event area, the PA announcer introduced him once again; the crowd cheered and Spunk Gism and the studio band began playing "Celebrate," while Jones, himself, danced about the stage.

When Winthrop and Rita arrived at the stage area, Danielle greeted them with hugs and kisses, and Rita broke into tears as she told Danielle about the fire at the bar. Meanwhile, Winthrop couldn't shake his horrible feeling. He knew something was terribly wrong. He panned the stage with his binoculars and then came to an abrupt stop. The studio band pianist was slumped over the keyboard, though apparently as yet no one else had noticed.

Winthrop whirled about to find Rocket Man. He had already made one complete circuit of the event area. Winthrop picked him up in his binoculars just as he was beginning his second approach to the stage. And he saw it immediately. Although it was mostly hidden by the cape, it was unmistakable—a metal rod, a semi-automatic weapon. Rocket Man was firing it at the people on the stage as he flew toward them at an ever-increasing speed.

Winthrop was stunned. Somehow Speck had taken out Anthony and his security guards and then taken his place. Somehow he had duplicated the costume and the technique. And now he was an absurd living nightmare, a psychopathic avenging angel of doom.

Winthrop whirled again to face the stage. His first impulse was to rush up and try to save Abraham Lincoln Jones. But by now the police and the security guards were firing away at the crazy figure in the sky, while two guards were climbing the stage, rushing to alert Jones and the musicians, who continued to dance and play oblivious to the danger. Winthrop looked back through his binoculars at Speck as he accelerated toward the stage through the volley of bullets. In an instant he knew the end game.

A bullet hit Speck in the stomach. Then another struck him in the arm, and the gun went flying. A moment later, a shot blew off his head. But Winthrop knew that none of it mattered. It didn't matter because he knew Speck was wired, and the timer had no doubt been set. Yes, Speck had turned himself into a flying human bomb, a literal rocket man, and in seconds it would all be over.

As the headless Speck flew through the air on an inevitable collision course with the stage, Winthrop took one last fleeting glance at Abraham Lincoln Jones. The guard had just reached him, and Jones, who had his back to the crowd, was looking over his shoulder and staring out at the sky. It was the same look that Winthrop had seen on Jones's face one month ago as he lay bleeding on the Grand Army Plaza stage and he and Jones exchanged a few private words. But now there was a difference. It was all over in an instant, but Winthrop was certain that he saw in Jones's face, the final, unshakable conviction that having confronted the choice of doing everything or nothing, he had indeed done everything humanly possible, done everything he could, to make a difference. He saw too just the barest hint of surprise—not that it was ending this way but that it was actually ending now and not some other time.

As the instant passed, Winthrop turned and grabbed Rita and Danielle. He took a few quick running steps, and then he flung them both to the ground and threw his body on top of them. In the next moment the world erupted in heat and light and the loudest explosion that Winthrop had ever heard. After that, more familiar sounds took over—the shouts and screams of abject human suffering—along with that larger silence that contains all cries and questions.

20

ABRAHAM LINCOLN JONES was killed instantly by the explosion. All of the musicians on stage, except for the studio band drummer and Spunk Gism's bassist, were dead as well. The two surviving musicians suffered multiple serious injuries as a result of flying debris but were expected to live. All told, seven policemen and security guards were also killed, and five more were critically injured.

Miraculously, Winthrop, Danielle and Rita sustained no serious injuries, although Winthrop had a nasty gash in the middle of his forehead along with a badly bruised right shoulder. Barry Bream, who had been standing in the wings, and a number of the production people had to be pulled out from beneath a mountain of staging materials and miscellaneous debris. Barry and the others had a variety of serious injuries, including concussions and broken bones, but they were all expected to recover. The mayor and the members of Yo Bitch had all been in the Green Room area at the time of the explosion and were unhurt.

Fortunately, the crowd had been protected by the concrete barrier and by its sheer distance from the stage. As a result, no one in the audience of more than 200,000 people was killed, although dozens were injured by flying debris, and a number of people were hurt as the surging crowd attempted to exit the event area.

About a half hour into the clean up, word came back that the bodies of Anthony Baines and two security guards had been found by the Rocket Man trailer. They had all been shot from behind.

Winthrop, Danielle and Rita stayed in the park for more than an hour after the explosion. They spoke to police and reporters and did whatever they could to help. Mostly they hugged each other and cried or stared numbly at the scene of carnage and destruction.

When it seemed that there was no longer any point in staying, they walked out of the park and caught a cab to take them to the Tit for Tat. When they arrived, the door was locked, so they had to knock. Sheila came and let them in.

The bar smelled horribly of smoke. There also appeared to be some water damage. Otherwise, the bar looked the same as always. Rita mentioned again that the basement was a different matter altogether. It had been completely gutted by the fire.

When they arrived, Donna was bustling about the bar in high energy. Apparently, she had already recovered from the shock of the fire. She's already planning the grand reopening, Winthrop thought. When Winthrop told Donna what had happened, however, she immediately became hysterical. It took awhile before they were able to calm her down again.

When they finally did, it suddenly occurred to Winthrop that tonight was the first time that Danielle had met his friends. She had spoken once on the phone to Rita and Donna. But she had met Rita for the first time in the park just moments before the explosion, and she was meeting Donna and Sheila now for the first time. Winthrop made note of the fact and handled all the formal introductions. Then Sheila suggested that they have a round of drinks, and everyone sat together at the bar—Winthrop and Sheila drinking Jack Daniels, Donna drinking her Stoli, Danielle drinking white wine and Rita sipping coffee.

About a half hour later there was a knock at the door. Rita got up and answered. It was Robin and Bree. They had left the Tit once the crisis of the fire had passed and had gone home. Bree had turned on the television just a little while ago and learned of what had happened in the park. Coincidentally, she had caught a brief clip of Winthrop talking to a reporter, so she knew he was all right. She called Robin, and they both came over immediately.

It was Robin's idea to put on some music. She chose Chick Corea, and Winthrop was pleased. Then before he knew it, both Robin and Bree had stripped off their clothes and were dancing on the bar top stage.

A few more minutes passed, and there was another knock at the door. Rita again got up to answer, and Winthrop was wondering who this could be. She stood in the doorway talking to someone for thirty or forty seconds. Then she returned to the bar.

"Who was that?" Winthrop asked.

"It was a man," Rita said. "He was at the park tonight, and he said he just wanted to stop by to extend his condolences."

"Extend his condolences—to whom?" Winthrop asked.

"To you, Jack. He said he hesitated for a while, but he finally decided to come by, taking a chance you'd be here. I guess since that article of yours, Jack, everybody knows you hang out here. Anyway, he decided not to come in. He just said to tell you he's very sorry about what happened, and he's sorry too that he didn't make it to Gramercy Tavern."

"What?"

"He said he's sorry he didn't make it to Gramercy Tavern. But not to worry because there'd be plenty of opportunities in the future. He said you'd know what he meant."

"What did he look like?"

"He was a big guy with a beard. Kind of a dandy, actually. He was all dressed up in a three-piece suit. He had a hat on too, a bowler, I think, and he was carrying a cane."

Winthrop bolted from his seat and ran out of the bar. He looked up and down the street, but there was no sign of Sherry. Then he ran up to Lexington and looked some more, but there was nothing there as well. Sherry was gone.

Winthrop stood on the corner for a few more seconds. Then he walked back slowly toward the bar. When he got to the door, he gave one last futile look up and down the street. Then he turned away and went back inside the Tit.

A NOTE ABOUT THE AUTHOR

JOE WENKE is a writer, social critic and LGBTQ rights activist. He is the founder and publisher of Trans Über, a publishing company with a focus on promoting LGBTQ rights, free thought and equality for all people. In addition to THE TALK SHOW, a novel, Wenke is the author of FREE AIR, Poems; PAPAL BULL: An Ex-Catholic Calls Out the Catholic Church; YOU GOT TO BE KIDDING! A Radical Satire of The Bible; MAILER'S AMERICA; LOOKING FOR POTHOLES, Poems (January 2015); and THE HUMAN AGENDA: Conversations About Sexual Orientation and Gender Identity (January 2015). Wenke received a B.A. in English from the University of Notre Dame, an M.A. in English from Penn State and a Ph.D. in English from the University of Connecticut.

Author's photo by Gisele Xtravaganza

"A radically funny book."   *Christopher Rudolph, The Advocate*

"Gisele, the notable transgender fashion model, graces the cover. And that image alone challenges the Bible. A transgender woman in a religious pose. . . . Get [*You Got to be Kidding!*] on your Kindle or take it on a trip, the time will fly by—boring this is not!"

Transgenderzone

"A riotously funny read, I recommend it to anyone who's ever questioned organised religion, especially that of the Bible-bashing, homophobic kind."   *Anna, Look!*

"This is hilarious! Joe Wenke gives a nod to Mark Twain as he looks at the Bible with fresh eyes and with the pen of a thinking comic."
Bill Baker

"This is without a doubt the funniest book I've ever read. I sat with my parents and read aloud some of the passages and we all laughed a lot!"
Emma Charlton, Bookswithemma

"Very tongue-in-cheek, sarcastic and pointed, dedicated to Christopher Hitchens and Thomas Paine, both of whom would, I believe, really enjoy this book!"
Sarah Hulcey

"The cover of the book itself is a slap in the face of transphobia. . . . If this book accomplishes one thing, I hope it pushes prejudiced people toward acceptance of LGBT people just as they are."
Isaac James Baker, Reading, Writing & Wine

"Brave, brilliant and funny. Page after page, biblical chapter after biblical chapter, absurdity after absurdity, this book delivers laugh after laugh. Joe Wenke has crafted the answer to the fundamentalist literal reading of the Bible with the perfect recipe of rationality, candor and humor."
Max Gelt

"Brilliant . . . for once a funny look at ALL the Bible's insanity."
Jo Bryant

"Would make a really wicked Christmas present for your Christian friends who have a sense of humor and a sense of the ridiculous."
Ed Buckner, American Atheists

"Oh my! This is very funny . . . Joe turns everything on its head and makes it a really interesting read."
Stephen Ormsby

"Whether you are an atheist or a Christian who can see the absurdity of some of the anecdotes narrated in Holy Scripture, Joe Wenke's humor won't be wasted on you."   *Mina's Bookshelf*

"Great book! Funny and easy to read."   *Violets and Tulips*

"Funny and to the point read. Takes a look at the Bible and points out all sorts of inaccuracies, illogical stories and questions. Strongly recommend."   *Hertzey*

"Witty and wise. Joe Wenke takes a critical, provocative look at The Bible and he does so with regular hilarity."   *Dana Hislop*

"A must-read for anyone who still thinks the Bible is the inviolable word of God—sense of humor mandatory."   *K. Sozaeva*

"Such a funny read, my son & I actually read it together! Laughter abounds!"   *Rael*

"Deliciously witty!"   *Jack Scott*

"Irreverent and hilarious. I am no Bible scholar, but I feel like I have been given the funniest crib notes on this most widely read and probably as widely misunderstood book of all time. I laughed out loud at Wenke's common sense observations and interpretations of this tome."   *Lorna Lee*

"Will keep any freethinking reader laughing the whole way through."   *George Lichman*

"[*You Got to Be Kidding!* is] entertaining and enlightening."
          Patti Bray

"I could not put this book down."   *Jackie Hepton*

"You will be laughing yourself silly while reading this book! In fact, you may find yourself bookmarking a bunch of pages to discuss with your pastor and friends later!"   *S. Henke*

"This author allows the reader to explore and learn about the Bible with a tongue-in-cheek attitude that keeps you laughing and turning the pages."   *Tricia Schneider*

"Some of it made me feel like I might wind up in hell for reading it, but if you keep an open mind and a light heart, you'll have a blast."   *Jon Yost*

"Don't read the Bible! Read this!"   *Dr. Dan*

"I may burn in hell for even having read this book."   *John C. Wood*

"If you enjoyed Wenke's take on the Bible, *You Got to Be Kidding!* read his exegesis of the Catholic Church's past two thousand years. . . . Mordantly funny, scrupulously researched."

E. B. Boatner, Lavender Magazine

"If you wonder why a 'merciful' God created a no-exit-ever hell or if you entertain thoughts of how boring the traditional religious notion of heaven might be, you will meet a savagely witty ally in Wenke's book."   *Joe Meyers, CTPost*

"I absolutely LOVED this book. . . . I highly recommend it to any Catholic who is considering recovering from his condition."

Philip G. Harding

"Joe Wenke is an extraordinary writer. . . . This book is an enlightening journey (for both the author and the reader) that was tenderly written by an exceptional person who is not afraid to let others know about what occurs in so many families, causing a great deal of pain and uncertainty. It is something that should be read by anyone and everyone, regardless of their religion or how they were raised/ told by others to believe. There are no words to express the depth of my gratitude to Mr. Wenke and I will be anxiously awaiting any other material that he wishes to write, because I am a lifelong fan."

Jules

"Ex-Catholics will love this book. It is an amazing satire of the Catholic Church. Every bit as funny as *You Got To Be Kidding!* I highly recommend."

Holly Michele

"A must read. Excellent!"

Carole

"I love this book! It is not only informative but funny as hell."

Rick Martin

"Whew! I feel like I've been to confession with the universe, (not God, that's a bad fairytale) and I've been absolved of . . . something. Thank you, Dr. Wenke, for putting into words . . . what I've been thinking about religion, especially Catholicism for a long time. . . . The one thought that kept repeating for me throughout the book, was that I need to buy about 2 dozen copies of this and hand them out to my family members, and at least try to spark a conversation." *Deborah*

"Papal Bull is brilliant and funny, well-researched and informative. . . . [Dr. Wenke] writes with humor that is at once scathing, insightful and absurd. His recounting of stories from Catholic grade school made me laugh out loud."   *Lori Giampa*

"Funny, clever and spot on."   *V. Kennedy*

"A cutting, satirical look at Catholic beliefs regarding saints, Mary, birth control, the treatment of women, and of course the huge scandalous cover-up of molestation."   *Tiffany A. Harkleroad*

"Impeccably researched and sharply written. . . . [Dr. Wenke's] wit and incisive perspective consistently deliver humor and important points to anyone willing to open their minds. . . . A work in which you can think, laugh, and ask the important questions is a must-read."   *David Nor*

"For some reason, I kept falling into a George Carlin voice as I read the book."   *Joseph Spuckler*

"I love the cover and I love the term 'recovering Catholic' of which I believe I am one. I think any one who went to Catholic School in the fifties and sixties . . . probably had many of the same experiences that the author describes from his school years."   *Diane Scholl*

A great and sometimes funny book all 'recovering Catholics' should read. In fact it should be required reading for anybody who considers themselves Holy. Brilliant insight & questions every Catholic should ask themselves."   *Robert Kennemer*

"It is necessary to call the church out on their horrendous errors and this book is much needed in society. . . . Papal Bull is timely and makes for some very interesting reading. Enjoy!"   *Lynda Smock*

"Solid, honest, passionate outstanding book."   *Anthony*

"This satirical book mocks the church by using actual historical facts. It is a critical and at times humorous analysis of the church's history from a modern perspective."   *Katarina Nolte*

"I not only laughed a great deal, but [the book] also gave me a lot to think about."   *Michele Barbrow*

"This was a wild ride. I found parts to be rather upsetting but I think the author really did his homework."   *Sher Brown*

"An incredibly clever and humorous take on the Catholic Church."

ChristophFischerBooks

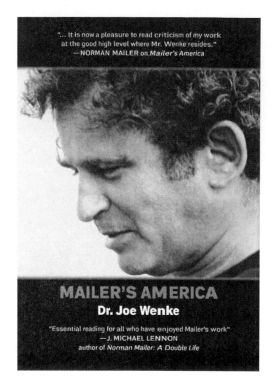

The reissue of Joseph Wenke's thoughtful study, *Mailer's America*, provides renewed hope for a deeper understanding of Mailer's work. No other commentator has focused so relentlessly on the deepest purpose of Mailer's hugely varied oeuvre, namely to "clarify a nation's vision of itself." Wenke's examination inhabits, patrols and maps the territory between the millennial promise of America and its often dispiriting actuality. His study contains probing, nuanced and careful examinations of all Mailer's work though the mid-1980s, including one of the first major examinations of Mailer's most demanding novel, *Ancient Evenings*. Wenke's book deserves a wide audience, and is essential reading for all who have enjoyed Mailer's work. —*J. Michael Lennon, author of the authorized biography, Norman Mailer: A Double Life*